ANGRY PASSION

"What do you mean you're going to Abilene!" she said furiously, whirling on him.

"For God's sake, keep your voice down," Nat said. "Who knows what can be heard through these walls."

Ardeth lowered her voice, but her anger was still very much apparent. "You can't go off and leave me here by myself. You promised you'd stand behind me all the way. I'll never be able to—"

He stopped her words with his lips, grasping her shoulders and pulling her to him with a passion as intense as her rage. She was so surprised that she forgot her fury as the sensation of his mouth on hers sent her mind reeling. His hands tightened on her shoulders, then slid up, caressing her neck, until they found her face. When he finally drew back, his hands still framing her face, her knees had grown so weak she could hardly stand.

"I've been wanting to do that all night," he whispered, then sought her lips once more. Ardeth felt herself swept along on a rising warmth she had never experienced before. Only dimly did she recall that this was not what she wanted from Nat Varien right now. . . .

PASSIONATE NIGHTS FROM ZEBRA BOOKS

ANGEL'S CARESS   (2675, $4.50)
by Deanna James

Ellie Crain was a young, inexperienced and beautiful Southern belle. Cash Gillard was the battle-weary Yankee corporal who turned her into a woman filled with hungry passion. He planned to love and leave her; she vowed to keep him forever with her *Angel's Caress*.

COMMANCHE BRIDE   (2549, $3.95)
by Emma Merritt

Beautiful Dr. Zoe Randolph headed to Mexico to halt a cholera epidemic. She never dreamed her caravan would be attacked by a band of savages. Later, she refused to believe that she could love and desire her captor, the handsome half-breed Matt Chandler. Captor and slave find unending love and tender passion in the rugged Commanche hills.

CAPTIVE ANGEL   (2524, $4.50)
by Deanna James

When handsome Hunter Gillard left the routine existence of his South Carolina plantation for endless adventures on the high seas, beautiful and indulged Caroline Gillard learned to manage her home and business affairs in her husband's sudden absence. Caroline resolved not to crumble and vowed to make Hunter beg to be taken back. He was determined to make her once again his unquestioning and forgiving wife.

SWEET, WILD LOVE   (2834, $3.95)
by Emma Merritt

Chicago lawyer Eleanor Hunt was determined to earn the respect of the Kansas cowboys who openly leered at her as she was working to try a cattle-rustling case. The worse offender was Bradley Smith—even though he worked for Eleanor's father! She was determined not to mistake passion for love; he was determined to break through her icy exterior and possess the passion woman who lurked beneath her.

Available wherever paperbacks are sold, or order direct from the Publisher. Send cover price plus 50¢ per copy for mailing and handling to Zebra Books, Dept. 3234, 475 Park Avenue South, New York, N.Y. 10016. Residents of New York, New Jersey and Pennsylvania must include sales tax. DO NOT SEND CASH.

PASSION'S TENDER SONG

ASHLEY SNOW

ZEBRA BOOKS
KENSINGTON PUBLISHING CORP.

ZEBRA BOOKS

are published by

Kensington Publishing Corp.
475 Park Avenue South
New York, NY 10016

First printing: December, 1990

Printed in the United States of America

Chapter One

"Ardeth, Pa says come. It's time to go."

She leaned down to grasp the handle of her faded cloth bag, then stood to look around the room one last time.

"Ardeth!" Her sister, Phoebe, came dashing from the outer room to poke her head around the door frame, her eyes flashing with excitement even though she was not going anywhere. It was almost as though Ardeth's departure gave reassurance to her younger sister that there really was a world out there beyond the flat plains surrounding their home.

"Pa says hurry," Phoebe cried, pushing her lank hair away from her forehead.

With one last glance Ardeth walked from the room to lay her arm briefly around the younger girl's thin shoulders. "I'm coming. Tell him I'm coming."

Phoebe danced through the front door as Ardeth followed her into the main room of the sod house which had been her only home for all of her nineteen years. Had she felt the least sadness in leaving, it still would not be enough to soften the room's utilitarian ugliness. The only real sadness, she realized, was that she had no warm memories of family closeness to bring sentimental tears to her eyes. Everything in the room represented all her home had ever meant; hard unceasing work and drab loneliness. The heavy pots, their bottoms blackened with use, the dirt floor pounded as solid as wood by the soles of many feet, the angular bed in the corner—given over to her parents' use so the children could all sleep in the only other room—the cradle standing beside it, never empty except when one of the infants died unexpectedly. Though the door stood open and there was one framed window cut through the sod bricks, the room never managed more than a twilight glow. The huge, ugly stove sat like a ponderous matriarch in one corner, a tribute to the stubbornness of her mother, who had insisted it be ferried here from Minnesota Territory when she came with her new husband to homestead in Nebraska. It had a long round pipe that reared up through the roof to the sod above. How many times had the smoke from that pipe, seeming to rise out of the earth itself, guided her home across the prairie. There was one fine, old rocking chair, the other tribute of civilized living that her mother had brought with her from Minnesota, but all the other furniture looked stiff and angular from having been knocked together by her father, who made no claims to carpentry. She walked over to lay her hand on the long heavy table that sat in the middle of the room. More than anything it had been the center around which her family life revolved. Of the nine children who survived of twelve born to Frances and Josiah

6

Royce, she was the first.

She moved to the door and, in one last gesture of farewell, touched the wall, the rough matted grass that had hardened over the years but still managed to be home to a host of insects. No, she would not miss this house.

Outside the sun was brilliant, and Ardeth had to shield her eyes against it. She saw that her father had the wagon hitched and ready near the barn. Their old mare, Granny, switched her tail as she bent her neck around to peer at Ardeth, as though protesting this interruption of her customary routine. Beyond the barn, the plains stretched away like a flat lake surrounding the house, broken on by the distant cluster of stunted cottonwoods along the tiny creek that flowed nearly a hundred feet from the house. The nearby fields had been newly turned and rippled like undulating brown waves. Beyond them the prairie grasses waved in the wind, sprinkled with patches of brightly colored wild flowers. Her young brothers, Arat and Piscah, were fussing around the wagon, as anxious as Phoebe to be part of the leave-taking. In the distance the small dark figures of the eldest boys, Sinai and the twins, Ebal and Elbe, were at work plowing and planting the lower acres. It still amused Ardeth how her father had insisted the boys be named after mountains in the Bible. Her mother had agreed as long as she could name the girls. Only once had she compromised, calling the last baby Olive. The child now sat near the door, watched over by three-year-old Naomi. Ardeth bent to kiss them both on the tops of their dark heads, wondering if they would miss her at all. They were both so ab-

7

sorbed in an old corn-husk doll, they hardly noticed.

Ardeth was halfway across the yard when she saw her mother coming up from the creek with a basket of washing. The older woman stopped before reaching the wagon, and Ardeth, realizing she was unwilling to say goodby near the others, put down her bag and went to meet her. Her mother's lined, severe face, usually so impassive, for once showed traces of strain. The two women stood without touching, silent.

"Well, so it's time," Frances Royce finally said. Ardeth studied her mother's face, seeing her in a way she had not for a long time. Like most farm women, Frances pulled her hair straight back from her head into a tight knot at the back of her skull. Yet the severity of her hair, the weariness from hard work and the toll of childbearing could not completely obliterate the beauty of her features. Though Ardeth was not aware of it, it was this same beauty that she had inherited from her mother, along with her raven-black hair and contrasting pale skin. The strongest difference between the two was in the color of their eyes. Frances's irises were a pale washed green while her daughter's were a vivid blue, a gift from her grandmother.

There were other traits both women shared, as Ardeth knew well: the ambition to want more from life than the drab confines of this Nebraska homestead; the awareness of a cultured world out there with music, light and gaiety; the learning that went beyond simple figures and countrified speech. All these had been nurtured by her mother. Because she was the eldest, she had received a heavy dose of that nurture, but she knew that by the time Phoebe and Olive and Naomi came of age, Frances Royce would be too tired and too resigned with this life to work with them as she had with her eldest. The boys were all like her pa—taciturn, withdrawn, too obsessed with work to ask anything more from life. Phoebe might have the enthusiasm in her to do more than dream, but Ardeth saw little hope for the others. Once again she was swept with a grateful excitement to be leaving this place.

Her mother, never demonstrative, even now seemed loathe to touch her daughter. She crossed her thin arms across her waist and looked over Ardeth's head to where the pigs snuffled around the barn door.

"So, you're on your way then, I suppose."

"Yes, Ma. I'll write to you, I promise. And I'll send money as soon as I get any extra."

"You'll tell your cousin Emma I remember her, even though it's been years. Back in Minnesota Territory it was. Afore ever your pa and I were married."

"I'll be sure and tell her, Ma."

Hesitantly Frances reached out and straightened the starched white ruffle above the high collar of Ardeth's jacket. That ruffle was the only decorative touch on the plain, brown merino skirt and jacket, and Frances had fashioned it herself from a strip of old petticoat she had saved from her wedding finery. "You be careful in that town. Find honest work, keep yourself proper. Watch out for mashers and scallywags. I brought you up to be a good girl. You keep that, now."

"I will, Ma. I promise."

Her brother, Piscah, called from the wagon: "Ardeth, Pa says come right now if'n you're comin' a'tall. Else he'll get back to the plowin'."

"I'm coming," she replied and turned back to her mother.

Frances reached out quickly and pressed a small handkerchief in her daughter's hand, closing her fingers over it. "I been savin' this a little bit at a time, ever since we took up here. It'll help see you through til you find work."

Ardeth gripped the handkerchief, feeling the hard coins within it. "But Pa already gave me enough for the trip."

"It'll take more. You don't want to burden Cousin Emma. I'll feel that much better knowing you have it. Use it sparingly, Ardeth. Make it last. There isn't any more."

"Oh, Ma. I hate to leave you with nothing."

"Oh, I saved a little back. In case Phoebe wants to follow some day. Take it now and use it well."

Ardeth gripped her mother's hands. "Thank you, Ma. I will use it well. And I'll come back as soon as ever I can."

"Ardeth!" Her father's voice this time, near the end of his patience.

Ardeth threw her arms around her mother's bony frame and hugged her tightly. "Goodby, Ma."

There were no tears in Frances Royce's eyes as she laid her hand against her daughter's face. Though she said nothing, Ardeth could almost hear the words conveyed by her mother's gesture. "Don't worry about coming back. Just go and find all the good things that are out there waiting for you." She was leaving this cage to try her wings in the world, and she knew her mother's spirit was with her all the way. Impulsively she took her mother's hand and quickly kissed her palm. Then she hurried back to grab up her bag and run toward the wagon. Her brother helped her up onto the seat where her father sat with the reins in his hand.

"About time," he muttered into his thick beard as he snapped the leather strap across the mare's broad back. The wagon rattled across the yard toward the creek, and Ardeth grabbed the seat as she swayed with its motion. At the bottom of the hollow she looked back to see her mother still standing in the bare yard, shielding her eyes with her hand as she watched the wagon disappear into the distance.

Nat Varien had never herded cattle in his life, but he sat a horse with the easy grace of a cowpoke — horse and rider melded into one efficient machine. Unfortunately there were only a few townspeople about to admire the sight of his sleek roan moving almost rhythmically along Front Street shortly after dawn. An old man with his chair tipped back against the raw wood wall of the hardware store followed his progress curiously. A woman in a drab calico dress and poke bonnet, a basket over her arm, paused as she started up the three low steps to the walkway in front of Callahan's General Store. A young man in shirt sleeves and knickers, sweeping the walk, stopped to lean on his broom. And a drunk, shuffling along toward the saloon to revive himself after a few hours of drugged insensibility, glanced at horse and rider absently. Their eyes fastened on the horse's arched neck, the fancy hat pulled down to shade the eyes of its rider, the elegant, tooled-leather saddle, and the expensive Spanish boots.

Nat did not glance around at them, though he knew they were watching. His whole attention was focused on the stretch of buildings ahead where he could already make out the lettering on the sign over the porch: JOHN BARTLE, SHERIFF.

Pulling up his mount before the porch, he slipped easily out of the saddle and tied the reins to a hitching post. The jinglebobs and heel chains on his spurs made an almost musical accompaniment as he walked up the steps to push open the door, then entered a drab, dark room. To his right, behind a massive oak desk scratched from years of use, a man sat with his chair tipped against the wall and his boots perched on the desk, his hat pulled down over his face as though he was asleep.

"You Sheriff Bartle?" Nat asked.

A voice beneath the hat mumbled, "That's right."

Nat fished in his shirt pocket to pull out a folded paper. Behind the desk, the man's hat slid back to reveal a square chin under a thick brush of moustache. The eyes peering from below the brim of the hat appeared anything but sleepy. Nat walked to the desk, unfolded the paper and spread it out.

"I'm Nat Varien. And I'm looking for this man."

Bartle eyed his visitor for a long minute, then casually reached out to pick up one edge of the paper and glance at it. "Saw you ridin' in. Kind of early, ain't it."

"Do you know this man?" Nat said, refusing to be

sidetracked.

The sheriff righted his chair to take the paper in both hands. "Where you from?"

"Valverde, New Mexico Territory." He made an effort to control his impatience. Bartle was not to be rushed so early in the morning.

"Long way from home, ain't you? TURNBULL. Mmmm. I heared of him. Must have done somethin' pretty fierce to have a price of five hundred dollars on his head."

Nat sat on one corner of the desk and pushed his hat back on his thick, sandy-colored hair. "Terrence Turnbull. Better known as the 'Toad.' Thief, murderer, train robber—a bad lot through and through. I've been trailing him all the way from Utah. Lost him for a while, then sniffed him out near Ft. Morgan. He's in this area now, and I need some men to catch him. I thought you might help."

The narrow eyes looked up from the paper. "You a bounty hunter?"

"No. I don't care about the reward. It's the Toad himself I want. You help me catch him and hang him to the first tree I can find and you can split the five hundred dollars among the posse."

"I judge you got some kind of a grudge against this Toad Turnbull."

"You could say that." When Nat didn't volunteer any further information, Sheriff Bartle folded the paper up and handed it back to him. Nat waited while the sheriff appeared to be thinking the matter over. He suspected that Bartle was much more alert than his slow, laconic movements suggested. He had a reputation as both a fair lawman and a shrewd gunman, and those qualities were not lightly earned in these parts. He watched as Bartle removed his hat and leaned over to spit into a brass spittoon on the floor near his chair.

"Well, I tell you now," the sheriff began as he carefully replaced the hat on his thinning, gray hair. "I don't have too many men available to help run down outlaws, even with such a price on their heads. What makes you think he's in this part of Colorado anyway?"

"Toad Turnbull will steal anything that's handy, but his favorite target is the railroad. I got wind that he plans to hit the Union Pacific spur between Denver and Cheyenne. I spoke to the railroad agent in Cheyenne and learned that the easiest place to corral a train is near the South Platte. I plan to be there when he makes his move."

"Now, I'd like to know how you determine just when that'll be. That train comes through twice a week."

"Yes, but this week it will be carrying a payload from the Wells Fargo in Cheyenne headed for the bank in Denver. That sounds just a little too tempting for the Toad to pass up."

Sheriff Bartle looked at Nat with slightly increased respect. "Now, how did you learn that? That shipment is supposed to be a big secret."

Nat smiled. "I have my sources. And nothing out here stays secret for long, especially when there's money involved. You should know that, Sheriff. If I can hear about it, then you can bet your boots the Toad has too."

Bartle pushed his chair back and stood up to walk

around the desk. He stopped absently beside several faded posters pinned to the wall, looking them over without really seeing them. Nat brushed at the dust on his pants, knowing the sheriff was trying to figure out what to do with him.

"I'll tell you what," Bartle finally said. "I already have a posse ready to guard that train since we figured it might be hit. I can split it up and give you four men to watch the northern side of the river. I think the southern side makes a better target, and I plan to be there. If he comes your way, then it's your game. I figure if you're determined enough to catch this Toad fellow to come all the way from New Mexico, then we can share the trouble. Fair enough?"

Nat smiled grimly, satisfied. "When do we leave?"

"That's the problem. We don't know exactly when that shipment is going to be moved. We've been covering the railroad these past two weeks, but there's been no trouble. There's two more trains though, one tomorrow and one Friday. But we can't go on watching them forever."

Nat carefully refolded the handbill and put it back in his shirt pocket. "Don't worry, Sheriff. It will be tomorrow. I'll stake my life on it. Now, where can a man get a drink and a bed in this town?"

Bartle eyed Nat again, noting that for a man who had been out on the trail for a long time he looked remarkably neat and fresh.

"Mrs. Gordon's Rooms to Let. Across the street. The saloon's two doors down. How can you be so certain it'll be tomorrow?"

Nat stood up and stretched, then straightened his hat. There was a satisfied twinkle in the soft green of

15

his eyes. "Because tomorrow there's going to be someone on that train who's every bit as important as the shipment of money."

There were four other people besides Ardeth in the coach. A young woman clutching a tiny baby hunched in the opposite corner while across from Ardeth an older woman in a drab black dress stared sullenly out the window. Between them a tall, gaunt man in a round felt hat coughed frequently into his handkerchief. Ardeth considered herself fortunate that she shared her seat with only one other person, a short heavy gentleman with a cheery face and an aptitude for nonstop conversation. The jolting of the coach often threw her against her companion, try as she might to steady herself. She felt certain that the gaunt fellow opposite her bore the pasty cast of desperate sickness on his face, and she was thankful not to be jostled against him.

"My dear fellow," her companion said after a particularly violent bump brought on a severe fit of coughing in the gentleman across the way. "You really ought to take something for that, you know. Have you tried a little elecampane and gum myrrh boiled in rain water and mixed with a little wine? I've found it very efficacious in treating congestion of the lungs. I often mix it myself and recommend it to my patients, with quite passable results."

The man wiped the flecks of saliva off his lips with his handkerchief. "I thought you said you were a dentist," he mumbled.

"Oh, I am. But you can see that in many towns in

this unsettled area there is often no doctor within forty miles. And in that case I am happy to offer what help I can for the many illnesses that are brought before me. Indeed, relieving toothache and supplying new sets of teeth are the very least of my talents. That is why I moved on. In my last town . . ."

His voice droned on. Ardeth settled in her corner and stared through the open window. The dust churning up from the road made it difficult to see the hills and stunted trees as they flew past, yet she was reluctant to pull up the curtain and add to the closeness of the coach. Because the dentist was so garrulous, she already knew more about her fellow passengers than she cared to. The young woman cradling the baby against the dust and scrunching away from the man beside her was on her way to join her husband. He was employed at one of the silver mines outside Cheyenne and had filled her head with so many horror stories of Indian attacks that she was afraid to look out the window for fear of seeing a horde of braves bearing down on them. The older woman sitting opposite Ardeth was a spinster schoolteacher from the East on her way to start a school at Fort Laramie. When the dentist as much as accused her of coming west to find a husband, she retired to her corner in a huff and had not spoken a word since. Ardeth herself had volunteered brief and unsatisfactory answers to the dentist's probing questions, so it was left to the gaunt gentleman with the handkerchief so often pressed to his lips to assist the conversation.

She was surprised that coaches were so jolting.

Though she had never been in a boat, she imagined they could not be much worse than this undulating, never ceasing roll. And when the wheels hit a hole or a rock in the road, as they often did, she found herself gripping the window frame to keep from being thrown in the spinster's lap. The brief sickness she had suffered at the beginning had quickly subsided, and by now she was growing accustomed to the rhythmic jolting without thinking too longingly of the next rest stop where the horses would be changed and she could walk around for a while.

"I fancy Cheyenne is not overflowing with gentlemen of my profession?" she heard her companion ask.

"Oh, you won't get much custom there," the gaunt man replied. "You'd do better and head for some of the smaller places. One of the cow towns of Kansas for example. Not much to do there but pull cowboys' teeth, but there ought to be enough of that to keep you busy."

The cheery dentist folded his hands across his paunch. "As a matter of fact, I'm just leaving such a place. I thought to try my luck in a larger town. Denver, perhaps."

The gaunt man gave a hollow chuckle, half laugh and half strangle. "The smaller ones are better. You'll get hard times from the doctors in the bigger places once they see you mixing your own medicines and treating something besides teeth. They can be pretty jealous, you know."

"Might I not find the same from doctors in small towns?"

"It's different. Usually there's only one, if you're

18

lucky, and he might prove to be accommodating. Dentists don't last too long there. Your best bet is to find a spot where the dentist was either run out of town or shot up in some local fracas. They'll be glad to see you then."

This silenced the cheery gentleman for almost a whole minute. "And this happens often?" he finally asked.

"More often that you'd think."

While the dentist appeared to be thinking over this interesting bit of information, Ardeth's thoughts drifted back to the long wagon trip with her father that brought her to the stagecoach station. Never a talkative man, Josiah Royce had been unusually quiet throughout the slow, plodding journey. While Ardeth worked at keeping her excitement and anticipation from bouncing her about on the seat, her father hunched into his beard and studied the trail, occasionally breaking the silence to "gehaw" at the mare.

It was only when the station leanto was a dark smudge on the horizon that he finally spoke.

"A lot of nonsense this! I said it afore and I still say it."

Ardeth chose her words carefully knowing the wrong thing might set him to turn the wagon around even now and head for home.

"It was good of you to agree to let me go, Pa. I'm grateful. I'll try to make you proud of me."

"Humph. Should'a been married these four year, wi' two childr'n by now. Goin' off to some wild town to be carried off by some worthless cowpoke. Shouldn't be surprised to hear you been murdered,

19

or somethin' worse. Makes no sense!"

"I'll be careful. And Cousin Emma will take care of me."

"Cousin Em! That's all I heared for the last month. Don't even know her. She could be runnin' a bawdy house in that town for all I know."

Ardeth spoke very quietly. "She's Ma's cousin." Now, with liberation in sight, she almost wished her pa had not chosen to reopen the old arguments.

"I'm only allowin' this 'cause we can use the money you send back. But I said it afore and I'll say it again. You should'a married Johnny Hickman, or even his brother, Will. Ought to have your own house by now—"

That was too much. "And at least two children," she added testily. "For heaven's sake, Pa, I hardly knew John Hickman and little liked what I did know. He's ignorant and slow witted and poor, and that's what I'd get to be if I married him."

"His pa would have staked him. You ought not to be so choosy!"

"He was our only neighbor within seven miles. How could I be choosy with nothing to choose from?"

"Your ma filled your head with grand notions. I told her over and over she was bargainin' for trouble. Makes no sense!"

A violent fit of coughing brought her back to the lumbering coach. They had evidently hit a boulder in the road, and the driver was slowing to a stop in order to assess the damage. The gaunt gentleman, gradually recovering from his strangulating gyrations, sank back against the cushion with his eyes

20

closed. His face was the color of bread dough.

"Are you all right, my good man?" the dentist asked, leaning forward sympathetically. "I wish I had my chest with me to offer you something, but it's tied on the roof."

The other man waved his hand. "No matter," he said when he could speak. "I've got some Hostetter's Stomach Bitters with me. I take them often."

"My dear fellow! They're fifty proof! You might as well drink raw whiskey."

The gaunt man smiled grimly. "Fifty proof. Always wondered why I liked them so much."

A sudden scream from the woman with the baby shattered the cab. Clutching her child to her, she pointed through the window, her face twisted with fear. All the passengers peered around to see what had caused her outburst and found that three tattered Indians, swathed in loose, dirty blankets, had approached the coach curiously.

"Savages!" the woman screamed. "My baby! Oh, Lord, help us!"

The dentist patted her arm. "My good woman, you have nothing to fear from those poor creatures. They appear to be half-starved and are no doubt only interested in procuring a hand-out from the people on this coach. They mean us no harm."

"But there might be more over those hills. They could swarm down on us any minute while we're standing here helpless."

The gaunt gentleman spoke up as he gently set her back into her corner. "Your husband has misled you, madam. The Indian wars have been over for some time now. Most of the unfortunate creatures are forced onto reservations where they will not raid innocent travelers. Really, you ought to calm yourself."

"I don't believe you. Look at them. They're savage and primitive and lusting for the blood of the white man! Oh, help—"

The schoolteacher had had enough. "Stop that blubbering, woman," she snapped in her most authoritarian voice. "Sit down and be quiet. Both these gentlemen have told you we have nothing to fear. Use your faculties, for goodness sake. There are three miserable creatures standing out there while we have a fellow with a good Winchester rifle sitting with the driver. They have more to fear from us than we from them."

The coach rolled ahead again, gradually picking up speed and leaving the Indians forlornly by the road. The young woman hunched back in her corner, sniffing quietly while the four other passengers fell into a quiet repose. Ardeth noticed how the grasses on the prairie were longer and taller here than those near her home. She recognized clumps of wild sunflowers and riotous sweeps of morning glories among them, and her spirits lifted once again.

It had been right to leave; she was certain of it. Life as Mrs. Hickman would have been too similar to the way her parents lived: four miles to the nearest neighbor, seven to the nearest schoolhouse, twenty to the nearest settlement. Water to be carried two hundred feet back and forth, twenty times a day. And the insects! It was bad enough they lived in the walls of the house, but she could still remember how only four years ago such a plague of grasshoppers had descended from the sky as to make a living hell of their

22

farm. One couldn't walk without crunching them underfoot. They had turned the sky black with their hordes, getting in everyone's eyes, hair, clothes, food. . . .

She hadn't realized she was shuddering until she felt a kindly hand on her shoulder. "You weren't frightened of those poor creatures too, were you, my dear?" the dentist asked.

"No, no. It was not that. I was just remembering something. I'm quite all right, really."

"We should be nearing the rest station soon. I suggest you walk about a bit. We're beginning to move into the hill country now, and I'm told there are some quite fantastic mountains to see."

"Buttes," the gaunt gentleman said. "Sandstone, whose structures are sculptured by the wind into fantastic shapes. Very interesting."

Ardeth's eyes took on an excited glitter. She had never seen real hills, much less mountains. Once again her anticipation began to grow. Still to come were the trains, the towns, new people and new adventures. Pa's doubts and harsh comments were behind her now. What mattered was that there was so much still ahead. And she was going to enjoy it to the hilt!

The cabin was there just as he had said it would be.

"Gawda'mighty!" Carlson exclaimed behind him. "Who'd of built a cabin way up here?"

Terrence Whitmore Turnbull shifted his weight in the saddle to lean forward and spit a stream of amber-colored tobacco juice on the ground. "Who cares. It's here and we're gonna use it. Tyrell, ride back and check to make sure we weren't followed. Sanchez, you look over the inside of this place."

"We wasn't followed, Toad," Tyrell grumbled. He was looking forward to getting out of the saddle and stretching his legs for a while. The flask of brandy in his hip pocket beckoned like a flame. "Just because Carlson here thinks he sees Nat Varien behind every tree don't mean he's really there."

"I did see Nat Varien! I seen his horse anyway, and if his horse is there, he's somewhere close by. He's on our trail right enough. I'd recognize that roan horse and that fancy Spanish saddle anywhere."

"Granny Carlson sees lawmen behind every tree," Tyrell intoned mockingly.

Carlson's horse danced as he jerked the reins. "Goddamn you, Tyrell, I'll—"

A whip cracked between them, snaking like a flash through the air. Both men veered away, deadly quiet. With one hand Toad Turnbull steadied his horse while flipping the long leather thong of the whip over his other arm.

"Jesus, boss," Carlson intoned. "Be careful with that thing."

"If I wasn't afraid gunfire would carry, I'd shoot you both in the balls. Now cut out that jawing and do what you're told. Carlson, you get in there with Sanchez and rustle up some food. We're spending the night here."

Sanchez was already poking at the door of the cabin. Reluctantly Tyrell wheeled his mount and galloped back into the brush while Carlson lumbered out of his saddle. After tying the reins to a tree, he pulled off his saddlebags and ambled after Sanchez. The interior of the windowless cabin was dark after the glare of the daylight, and from the dirt and disorder it looked as though it hadn't been used for months. Carlson threw his saddlebags on the ground and began poking around a blackened hearth.

"Toad Turnbull!" he muttered under his breath. "Looks like a toad. Acts like a toad."

Sanchez leaned against the wall and began to roll a cigarette. "No frog was ever that mean, I think," he said, smiling.

"That's the God's truth."

Outside Terrence Turnbull guided his horse away from the other three members of his gang and slid from the saddle. He could not remember when the name "Toad" had first been applied to him, for it had been so many years ago. His facial features made the nickname almost inevitable: full jowls, protruding, huge eyes like two boiled eggs on his face, and a thick, gravelly voice. He wasn't a tall man; in fact, his upper torso was so thick and muscular in comparison to his short legs that it appeared almost grotesque. That only served to reinforce his similarity to a frog. But the meanness and coldness were well earned. He had been working at them for so long now that they were second nature to him.

He turned to look back over the scrub through which they had ridden. Down the ridge, he could see past the sweep of yellow hills to the valley below. He could not see the train tracks from here, but he knew they were there well enough. Tomorrow! He was looking forward to it, except for one thing. It would be better if they were only after the money—much simpler all around.

Releasing the cinch, he pulled the saddle from his horse and started back up to the cabin. The colonel had been right. This place would suit their purposes very well.

Chapter Two

Though the train ride was almost as jolting as the trip in the stagecoach, Ardeth barely noticed it. She sat on the straight-back, uncomfortable seat filled with an excitement that now and then bubbled over and sent her bouncing about even more. She watched the countryside flying past at the unbelievable speed of twenty-five miles an hour, drinking in the beauty of the high plains with mountains, like dark clouds, on the far horizon. Great swelling grasslands gave way periodically to cultivated fields of hay and barley which waved happily in the bright sunshine.

She was relieved that the car was almost empty. At the station in Cheyenne there had been so many people milling about that she had feared she would not find a seat. Then the marvelous machine that was the Union Pacific had come chugging along drawing so many cars behind it that the passengers were able to spread out quite comfortably. She had had plenty of time by now to look over her fellow travelers. They were all strangers since none of the people who had been' on the coach with her had boarded the train. There were several men, most of them elderly, and only one other woman. Though she could only see her from behind, Ardeth found this lady almost as captivating as the scenery outside her window. She was dressed in a beautiful jacket of burgundy silk with rich brown fur around the cuffs and forming a soft collar. Her hat was large and frilly, decorated with exquisite artificial flowers and a gracefully curving feathered plume. When she turned her face, Ardeth caught a glimpse of a beautiful profile heightened by rouged cheeks and lips. Once, she raised her hand to straighten her hat, displaying a bracelet of bright jewels, almost blinding as they caught the light from the window. Ardeth stared, thinking she had never seen anyone so beautiful or so rich.

"Excuse me, miss. May I join you?"

Startled from her reverie, Ardeth looked up to see one of the gentlemen from the rear of the coach standing in the aisle. He was a plump, older man with long gray sideburns framing a cheerful, round face. With her father's warning of mashers and rakes ringing in her ears, she nevertheless found she could not be rude and so invited the man to sit down.

"Are you going far?" he asked, settling himself beside her, a little too close for comfort. She inched nearer the window.

"I'm on my way to Fireweed, Kansas, to join my cousin," she said, just to let him know someone was waiting for her.

"Fireweed. Not much of a town for a sweet young girl like you, I should think. A cattle town. Quite

28

wild and lawless."

Her heart sank a little. "You've been there?"

"Oh, yes. Several times. Thompson K. Thompson is my name. Run a small law office in Denver. Don't recall seeing you on this train before."

"That's because this is my first time. My home is in Nebraska. I've never been this far away from it before."

Thompson edged closer, crowding her on the seat. "First time away from home. My goodness, I thought you looked an innocent when I saw you climb aboard. 'Now, there's a sweet young thing,' I says to myself, 'and who knows but that she might need someone to keep an eye out for her.' You are traveling alone, I presume."

"Well, yes, I am. But my cousin is meeting me in Fireweed. I was told I could get another train in Denver that will take me directly there."

"That's true, though often as not you're forced to lie over and wait."

"Wait!" She looked at him, her large eyes growing dark with dismay.

Thompson edged closer. "Now, don't you worry, my dear. I may have to go to Fireweed myself. I often do, on business, don't you know. I'll see you safely there."

She was pressed against the side of the train so closely that his large body loomed over her. Ardeth was beginning to be concerned. "Oh, I couldn't cause you so much trouble. I can manage quite well, I assure you."

Thompson reached out and laid his hand on her knee, squeezing it through the thick coarse fabric of her skirt. "It's no trouble at all, my dear."

Ardeth pushed his hand off her knee and abruptly shifted to the opposite seat. She wanted very much to tell this unpleasant man to let her alone, but she was not certain about the rules of hospitality in the great world. Could one be rude to protect oneself? She would have liked to move to another seat, but he was blocking her way.

"So you've never been to Fireweed," he said, not a bit put off by her move. "I can help you there. I know most of the best people, what few there are of them. But you'd do better to see something of Denver first. It's a fast-growing town with all kinds of interesting places for a young woman. There are some fine little shops and even an opera house."

"Oh, I couldn't. My cousin is expecting me," she lied.

"Yes, yes. Your cousin. Who is this cousin of yours? Perhaps I have met her . . . or him?"

Ardeth hesitated, wondering if she should mention Cousin Emma's name. Perhaps if she did, it might put this too eager stranger off for a while. "Cousin Emma Hardwick. She's my mother's cousin, from Minnesota."

Thompson stroked his sideburns. "No . . . but wait a moment. Did your cousin by any chance run a boardinghouse?"

"Yes, I believe she does. She is putting me up there."

"Em's Rooms to Let. I do know of her. In fact, I stayed there myself once before I found the Silver Palace a more accommodating hotel."

It was of some small reassurance to Ardeth to hear

that Cousin Emma was a real person with a real boardinghouse. All at once she felt certain she had been right to come, even without a specific invitation and over the strenuous objections of her pa.

"But, my dear woman, don't you know?" Thompson went on.

"Know what?"

"Why, Em's Rooms to Let was closed down several months ago. The old lady died—I think it was last January or so. Surely your mother was notified."

Ardeth stared in disbelief. "Died? No, no. You must be confusing her with someone else."

"I assure you I am not. From Minnesota, you say. I recall she was from one of the northern states. A tall lady, very thin with white, white hair."

Ma had said her cousin was several years older. Ardeth's heart began to pound. As her own face mirrored her growing dismay, her companion's settled into a satisfied delight. Quickly he moved to sit beside her on the opposite seat. She was too distressed to try to move away, and before she knew it he had one arm sympathetically around her shoulder.

"You poor little girl. All alone with no one to look after you. Well, don't worry your pretty little head one minute. I'll take Cousin Emma's place most gladly. You'll be in good hands."

"Please . . ." Ardeth inched away into the wall. Her mind was a jumble. If Emma really was dead, what would she do when she reached Fireweed? Should she stay on the train at Denver and return to Cheyenne and home? That would be the sensible thing to do, but how could she bear it? All her dreams and longings and hopes would be buried forever, and the rest of her life would be nothing but a dreamless existence in a shabby soddy on the Nebraska prairie. It would break her heart to settle for that just when she thought she was flying free.

But how was she going to be able to manage alone when she couldn't even escape from this idiotic masher on the train!

All at once the sharp point of an umbrella was thrust into Thompson K. Thompson's chest, sending him reeling back against the seat. Ardeth looked up to see the beautiful woman in the fancy hat standing in the aisle.

"I have a notion to sit with this young lady, sir, and I'll thank you to move at once." The command was issued in a low, rich voice that invited no argument.

"Well, really," Thompson blustered. "There are plenty of other seats. This young lady and I were having a conversation."

"I heard your conversation, and I know exactly where you expected it to lead. I suggest you go warm one of those 'other' seats yourself. At once, my good man!"

There was something in the lady's flashing black eyes that told Thompson K. Thompson he was no longer dealing with an innocent. Angrily he pulled down the tabs of his vest and rose, tipping his hat to Ardeth.

"My invitation still stands, young lady. You would love Denver—"

"That's enough, sir. Be off."

Grumbling, Thompson shuffled back to the rear of the coach while the lady in rustling burgundy silk took her place opposite Ardeth. "Wretched man," she mumbled. "Thinking to take advantage of the first innocent young woman he meets. I know his type only too well."

Ardeth smiled with relief. "Thank you. I didn't know how to discourage him."

"I could see that. It's not really very wise for a pretty young girl like you to be traveling around this country alone. Don't you realize how many heartless rakes are lying around just waiting to take advantage of a morsel like you?"

"Yes, but I had no choice. It was either come alone or stay home in Nebraska. Almost anything was better than that."

The woman's sympathetic smile softened the harsh lines of her face. "I thought so," she said softly. "That's why I came to your defense. I remember feeling that way myself once."

"I'm Ardeth Royce," Ardeth said, extending her hand. It was touched lightly by the lady's soft kid glove.

"Medora Melindez. Ah, I see that means nothing to you."

"Should I know you?"

"Probably not. I have some fame throughout the West as a singer of songs. But no doubt word of my accomplishments has not reached the wide Nebraska prairies. Still, I had hoped perhaps it had."

"I'm sorry," Ardeth said. She had not realized this lovely woman might belong to the despised theatrical profession, but somehow she was not surprised to learn it. The gorgeous silk dress, the gaudy, flamboyant hat, the rouged cheeks and lips — it all made perfect sense. Her pa would be horrified to think she was even talking to such a person, but she did not care. This lady had been kind enough to rescue her from a threatening pest, and for that alone she would have been more than polite. Besides, with her expensive clothes and jewels, Medora Melindez was the very picture of all she herself hoped to be some day.

Now that she could see Medora so closely, she realized the woman was older than she had appeared from a distance. There were tiny lines around her eyes and mouth. But her hair was thick and lustrous and arranged in sweeping rolls beneath her hat. Her figure was stunning. She had the smallest waist Ardeth had ever seen on a woman, yet her breasts swelled above it and her hips below, like the hourglass figures she used to admire in magazine illustrations. She wore a large cameo pin at her throat almost as beautiful as the wide diamond bracelet at her wrist, and the ivory handle on the umbrella she wielded as a cane was luminous in the light from the window. Ardeth was almost tongue-tied to be so near such a gorgeous creature.

Medora soon put her at ease, however. She gently drew from Ardeth the details of her life at home and her reasons for leaving, and since she herself had left home years before for almost identical concerns, there soon was a growing sympathy between them.

"But what will you do without your cousin's help? That is, if it really is true that she has died."

"I don't know. I only know I am determined to go to Fireweed as I had planned. To go back home now would be intolerable."

"I'll tell you what," Medora said, her black eyes taking on a mischievous twinkle. "I am on my way to Fireweed myself for a brief engagement. In fact, my trunks have already been sent ahead to be there when I arrive. I shall accompany you and see that you are put up in a decent place."

"Oh, but I would not want to cause you any trouble."

"Nonsense. It is no trouble, and it will give me a delicious delight to rob the saloons and brothels of a new recruit—though I'm not so certain what kind of respectable work you will be able to find in such a town. But we shall see. You are a sweet, pretty child, and you remind me of myself when I was starting out. It was only a few years ago, you understand, and is still very vivid in my mind."

Ardeth sighed with relief. For so long she had focused on the small town of Fireweed as her gateway to opportunity that even without her cousin Emma there, she was reluctant to go anywhere else.

"I'm very grateful to you, Miss Melindez—" she stared to say, but Medora cut her off.

"It is Medora, my dear. And since we have this long, uncomfortable trip ahead of us, I shall use it to educate you in the kind of life you will find in Fireweed. I can tell you know very little about what to expect."

"That is true. We saw so few people on my parents' farm, and my mother had only a few books and magazines she brought from Minnesota. There is so much I want to learn and so much I want to see."

Medora reached out and patted her hand. "There is much about these small western towns that you should not learn and certainly not see. They are not gentle places, these cattle towns of the West."

"Oh, but I want to experience everything! I want to wear beautiful clothes and have expensive jewelry like yours. I want to live in a real house with plaster on the walls and brocade curtains on the windows. I want to go to plays and entertainments—oh, dear. I'm running on, aren't I. My ma was always getting after me for that."

"Your ambitions are very normal for a young girl. What you must guard against is allowing them to be compromised by unscrupulous persons who would draw you into a life worse than the one you left. Here is your first lesson, my young Ardeth." She held up her wrist. "Do you like my bracelet?"

"It is the most beautiful thing I ever saw. It's made of diamonds, isn't it? It must be worth a lot of money."

"It is paste. Quite worthless. Oh, indeed, I have diamonds aplenty, but I would never wear them to journey on a train. You must learn never to accept anything at face value, my dear. Give every offer a good second appraisal, whether it be a job, a piece of jewelry, or a person's character. That is your first lesson."

Ardeth studied the bracelet, stunned. Worthless or not, it glimmered in the light like twinkling stars and was still the most beautiful thing she had ever seen.

Medora chuckled at the look on Ardeth's face. She was quite pleased that her initial effort at sparing this child from an elderly masher had turned out so satisfactorily. It was going to be a pleasant diversion for her to spend the hours of the trip educating this

36

girl. She was indeed very beautiful and very innocent, but she was also ambitious and, Medora suspected, intelligent. Her traveling time could hardly be put to better use than to teach her new pupil a few good principles for dealing with the rowdy, rough life she would be exposed to in a town like Fireweed.

The train slowed to a stop, and the conductor appeared to stride down the coach announcing a short dinner stop. The two women stepped from the train to find themselves surrounded by a cluster of wooden shacks, unpainted and rustic. The building nearest the tracks had the name "Silver City" painted in large letters across one side. Yellow sandstone hills stood behind the low buildings like a backdrop in a theater.

"It doesn't look like a city to me," Ardeth whispered to Medora.

"No, it's just another crossroad depot trying to be more than it is. But let's hurry. I know these dinner stops. We'll barely begin our food before they'll be hustling us back on board."

They moved quickly up the low steps to an open door where Thompson K. Thompson stood, tipping his hat to Ardeth and glaring at Medora. They both ignored him to sit at a long U-shaped counter where refreshments were thrust at them as they took out their money. Ardeth concentrated on consuming her coffee and steak and eggs quickly, but still she was only halfway through when, as Medora had predicted, the call came to get back on the train. Once they were in their seats, the locomotive began chugging along the track again while Medora entertained Ardeth with her descriptions of first-class trains that had sleeping quarters on board as well as their own compartments for dining.

The country through which the railroad traveled grew more rugged as the morning wore on. Ardeth was torn between listening to Medora's vivid descriptions of what she should expect in Fireweed and her desire to gaze out the window at the increasingly high ground over which they were passing. She was captivated by the great bounding, grayish-brown tumbleweeds skimming along in the wind, seemingly in motion with the train. Coming around a bend, she saw a trellised wooden bridge ahead and wondered for a second if it would support the weight of this iron monster. Then she laughed at her fears, remembering that the locomotive must have come this way many times before. The train slowed to a crawl as it inched out over the bridge, and Ardeth looked down in fascination at the river below. Though she knew it was foolish, all the same she was very relieved when they chugged over the end of the bridge and were back on solid ground again.

Picking up speed, the train forged ahead, climbing a steeper grade than any they had crossed before. When it suddenly began slowing to a crawl, Ardeth thought perhaps it lacked the proper strength to get up this hill. Shortly after that it stopped completely.

Ardeth looked questioningly at Medora.

"I can't imagine what it is," the older woman said as she rose to peer through the window. "The grade looks easy enough—" Her hand went to her throat, and she gave a strangled gasp.

"What is it?" Ardeth cried, leaning toward the window. "Who are those men?"

Medora quickly sat back on the seat. "Oh, my God," she gasped. "Outlaws. We're going to be robbed!" Hurriedly she began unfastening the cameo at her throat. "Your money, Ardeth. Hide it. Under the seat. Quickly!"

Even as she spoke, the door to the coach was slammed open, and a man with a kerchief covering the lower half of his face stepped inside, brandishing a long, wicked-looking six-shooter in his hand.

"Everybody outside!" he roared. Confusion erupted in the coach as two of the gentlemen ran for the far door, protesting loudly. The gun went off with a loud blast, shattering glass and stopping everyone in their tracks.

"I said outside!" the robber shouted. The occupants of the coach hastened by him to step down the low steps and stand beside the train. Ardeth could see the other passengers lined up alongside the train, and far ahead, a pile of debris that lay on the tracks, blocking the way. There appeared to be five or six masked men running along the row of passengers, picking pockets and purses. Near their coach one outlaw sat his horse, watching the whole procedure, the other horses grouped around him. He had a gun in each hand and appeared to be looking for any reason to shoot. The train conductor and the engineer were close enough to her that she could see the fury and frustration on their faces. She heard the sudden blast of a muffled gun, then saw one of the outlaws jump from a coach near the engine, carrying a large leather pouch.

"You! Step over here," a hard voice demanded.

Looking up she saw that the man on the horse had

walked over to their coach and was gazing down at Medora. By this time, the other outlaw running along the row of passengers had reached her. Without a word he yanked at the purse she had not had the presence of mind to hide and dropped it in his saddlebag.

"But that's all the money I have!" Ardeth exclaimed, watching her dreams and hopes disappear.

He did not bother to answer but moved on to ransack the pockets of Thompson K. Thompson.

"I'll take that bracelet," the mounted outlaw said to Medora. Without answering, she unclipped it and threw it on the ground.

Toad Turnbull glared at her from his horse, debating whether to frighten her a little with his horsehide whip. But he had his orders. By now Sanchez had finished with his section of the coach. "Bring the extra horse," Toad snapped. "And hurry up there!" he roared to the others.

They were nearly done and in record time. He was beginning to feel quite satisfied when he caught the distant sound of horses' hooves. At the same time the cry from Carlson, who was standing lookout, rang through the air.

"Posse!"

The outlaws scrambled for their horses. Sanchez had just brought forward a wide-backed black mare. "Throw her on it," Toad ordered, and before she realized what was happening, Medora was grabbed up and thrown into the saddle, her skirts tangled. Toad's glance came back to Ardeth. "And that one too!" he shouted.

"Boss! We gotta ride!" Sanchez yelled.

"Do what I say!" Toad roared and stayed his horse long enough to see Sanchez grab Ardeth and throw her over the front of his saddle. Then, leading Medora's mount by its reins, they roared off. Medora grabbed for the pommel of the saddle with one hand and clutched at the horse's mane with the other, still too stunned to realize what was happening. Ardeth, in an even greater state of shock, felt herself righted with an arm around her waist as strong as an iron rock. She bumped up and down on the horse's back and clutched at the man, holding on for dear life as the animal raced over the rocky trail, around rock-faced walls, through deep washes and back up along short grassy plateaus. When at last they rounded a bend to stop for a moment's rest, she struggled to get free.

"Stay still or I drop you down there," a cold voice said in her ear.

Ardeth glanced down at the steep incline that sloped away from the pony's feet to a rocky gorge below. She could still not believe this was happening, but she made a quick decision that it would be the better part of valor to go along with it. She could glimpse Medora still sitting the horse behind them and took some comfort from the fact that at least she was not alone with these brutal men.

The stocky man who was obviously the leader of the gang was studying her. She squirmed uncomfortably, still locked in her kidnapper's tight grip and unable to find an easy way to share the saddle with him. She did not like the looks of the outlaw gazing at her. His eyes protruded so far that it made him appear almost deformed, and the way he looked her

41

up and down made her uncomfortable without really knowing why. When he turned and galloped away, it was almost a relief.

They seemed to travel for hours, but she knew it had not been that long. They climbed ever upward, pausing now and then to look back over the valley for signs of pursuers. Once Ardeth thought she caught a glimpse of dust on the road below and the distant sound of horses' hooves, but the outlaws never stopped long enough to make sure. When, at length, they entered a plateau dotted with jagged rocks and clusters of firs and pine, she gave up any hope that they might be found by the men who were following.

The ramshackle cabin buried in a clump of trees looked almost inviting after the hard, miserable ride. Sanchez pulled up near the door and shifted in the saddle, plopping her on the ground. Ardeth looked around long enough to see that the men were engrossed in dismounting, then scrambled to her feet and took off, running away from the cabin as fast as her legs could move. There was a loud whoop behind her and the clatter of a horse running, and she was scooped up like a sack of flour, caught in the vise of one huge, strong arm, then carried back to the cabin and dumped on the ground again. She looked up to see that it was the bug-eyed gang leader who had retrieved her. It appeared to amuse him greatly. His laughter only made him look more grotesque.

"They're gainin' on us, boss," one of the men said. "We can't afford to stop."

"I know that," Toad replied. "Carlson, lock these two women in that cabin and keep watch. I don't want them to get away from here, understand. If they do, you'll be the one that pays for it. The rest of us will try to throw off the posse. Sanchez, you and Tyrell and Jackie take the south pass. The rest of us will take the east. We'll meet back here at nightfall."

Sanchez glared. "You got the money, Toad. That ain't fair."

"You think we got time now to divide it!" Toad roared. "We gotta get rid of this posse first. I told you we'll meet here later, and I mean it. Now get going."

Toad circled his restive mount as Sanchez sat debating whether or not to believe him. Then the Mexican spat on the ground and wheeled away, the other two men following.

Toad Turnbull gave the women a quick glance. "Keep them here, Carlson. And don't touch either one of them. I'll decide who gets that when I get back."

Carlson stood beside his horse. "I'll be too busy watchin' to bother with them," he mumbled as he watched the last three men ride off. "Get in there," he ordered, shoving Medora and Ardeth toward the cabin. He pushed them inside and slammed the door, then propped a tree limb against it to keep it locked. It was dark inside, but Medora immediately found a niche in the warped boards where she could see a little of what Carlson was doing.

"I was hoping he'd leave his horse," she muttered to Ardeth, "but he's taking it with him."

"Where's he going?"

"To those rocks we passed just before we reached the trees around this cabin. There must be some kind

43

of an overhang there. He's lying down with his gun, watching the road."

"Could we get to his horse before he saw us?"

"No. It's too close to him. We'd have to try to run."

As her eyes began to adjust to the gloom, Ardeth examined the cabin, walking around the walls to test their strength. There were no windows and only the one door. A chimney on the far wall still bore the blackened remains of last night's fire, and the room smelled of acrid smoke and rancid bacon. There was a rickety cot against one wall and a small table on the other. The dirt floor was dusty and cluttered with the debris left from the gang's previous night's sleep; cigar butts, wadded paper, rags used to clean their guns, and two empty whisky bottles.

"These walls seem awfully strong for such an old place," Ardeth commented.

"What about the chimney?" Medora asked.

She stopped to peer up into the black hole. "It looks like it narrows too sharply. We'd never squeeze through."

Medora began to examine the room, using what little light entered through the cracks in the walls, as Ardeth sat on the cot. "What are we going to do, Medora? How can we escape? What do they want us for anyway? They took all my money."

Medora decided not to answer that last question. If they were unable to escape before those men returned, Ardeth would find out soon enough why they brought her along. There was no need to distress her yet.

"Perhaps we won't need to escape," she said,

brightening. "That posse may well come across us before it catches up with those outlaws. They'll rescue us; I'm sure of it."

"But suppose they don't. Shouldn't we try to get away?"

Medora sat down next to Ardeth on the cot. "Look, we're safe enough for the moment. I think we should wait here, keep an eye on that fellow who's standing guard out there, and wait for the posse to come. If they don't arrive pretty soon, then we'll just have to think of a way to trick that man and take his horse."

Ardeth thought of the long rifle Carlson kept cradled in his arm. She had very little hope of outwitting him before he could use it on them. Their best hope was the posse, and perhaps Medora was right in waiting for it. But it promised to be a long, worrisome time ahead.

The time dragged by. The two women spent the long moments taking turns walking around the tiny cabin, examining the walls, trying the door, peering through the small spaces between the logs that offered them a limited view of the outside. When one would finish to plop discouraged on the cot, the other would take up the wandering. In the beginning they were certain that between the two of them some escape route would present itself. As the long afternoon dragged on, they began to think they had been too optimistic.

Only once did Carlson come inside to glare at them. They could see he was extremely nervous, the rifle half-cocked in his arm. It was obvious he wished to be away from the cabin even more than they did. He barked a warning at them, saying that at the first sign of an attempt to run he'd take pleasure in shooting them down; then he stalked back outside, pausing only long enough to fasten the door even more securely.

"Do you think he means it," Ardeth asked tentatively.

"I'm certain he does. He's probably worried about his friends leaving him here to face a posse while they're off distributing the goods. He'd take it out on us the first chance he got."

Ardeth abruptly rose from the cot to tramp back and forth across the room. "Then, what are we going to do? There has to be some way out."

Medora settled back against the wall, frowning. "Give me a little time to think. We're safe enough for the present, and if the posse finds us before those outlaws return, we'll have nothing to fear. Try to find something to amuse yourself, my dear. Sing a little song. Tell a story—"

"You're the singer of songs," Ardeth replied testily. I don't feel like singing right now. Of course . . ."

"What?"

She came to sit beside Medora on the cot. "If it's true that for the moment we're really safe, then why don't you use this time to tell me about all the places you've been and some of the things you've done? Your life must have been full of all sorts of interesting events. Tell me about them."

Medora shrugged. "Not so interesting. Oh, I suppose I've seen some fancy opera houses in my time, but they were all back East. Nothing much out here. And once I met the governor of Missouri, but he

46

wasn't so much. Short, dumpy . . . he looked more like a shopkeeper than an important political figure."

"What cities have you seen?" Ardeth asked, warming to her subject.

"Well, St. Louis was a pretty big place. I remember it fondly, but that was mostly because of the gentleman who took me around there. I was very . . . very fond of him."

"Was he your husband?"

Medora gave a brittle laugh. "No. He had a wife. I was his mistress. But it was me he loved, always. As I did him."

"It sounds so romantic." Ardeth sighed. "I've never met a man I loved. In fact, I've hardly ever met a man at all. Only John Hickman. He wanted to marry me, but I couldn't abide him!"

"What was wrong with him?"

"He had pimples and a huge Adam's apple that wiggled up and down when he talked. Which he seldom did. He never had anything much to say except about raising crops and tending animals. And that was little enough. Any woman who married him would be burying herself alive."

Medora reached out and stroked a wave of Ardeth's raven hair away from her white forehead. "And you think you are better off now?"

"Well, perhaps not at this moment, but I will be when I get to Fireweed. Do you suppose those outlaws knew your bracelet wasn't real diamonds?"

"No, I don't think so. They did not take the time to look closely. They'll find out when they try to sell it."

"Tell me about your real diamonds. Do you wear

47

them when you sing? Do you have other jewels besides diamonds?"

"You are so full of questions, child. I have a diamond bracelet — a true one — several rings, a tiara and a necklace of diamonds and rubies. My lover gave me that one. Many times I have thought I would have to sell it, but I never have. Now I hope I never will have to."

"And your dresses? Tell me all about them. The colors, the fabrics, the styles. I used to dream of wearing beautiful dresses made of soft, glistening colors. . . ."

Medora tucked her legs under her and leaned back against the wall. "I have a few rather gaudy dresses for the stage and a few more very tasteful and beautiful ones for private parties. But most of my clothes are practical and simple."

"Practical and simple!" Ardeth cried, reaching out to stroke a ruffle of burgundy silk on Medora's skirt that fell across the cot. "Is that what you call this? Why, I think it is the most beautiful dress I have ever seen."

"I suppose if I had only worn brown serge or calico all my life, I might be impressed with this outfit as well, but believe me, it is not nearly so grand as those you will see any afternoon in the park in St. Louis. It is only a traveling suit."

Ardeth sighed. "Perhaps to you. But I should think I had died and gone to heaven to have such a beautiful dress to wear."

Reaching up, Medora unpinned her hat, removed it and stroked the feather. "Here, try this on. Let's see how it looks on you."

48

Ardeth's eyes lit up. "May I? Oh, I would love to try it."

"Let me pin it for you. Like so. . . ." She set the hat on Ardeth's head, trying it several ways to get it just right. Then she worked the long hatpin through her thick hair. "I had forgotten that hatpin," she commented, studying the younger girl. "It might make a useful weapon if necessary. Yes, that looks quite beautiful on you, child. You will cause quite a sensation in these western towns once you know how to dress properly."

"If I can ever afford to," Ardeth added, preening around the room. "Oh, I wish I had a mirror. Does it really look nice?"

"Very nice." All at once Medora's indulgent smile changed to something more somber and calculating. She moved to the wall to look through the peephole. "Our guard is still engrossed in watching the approaches to our prison," she commented lightly, "and we, it seems, have time to kill. I have an idea. How would you like to try on this dress you find so beautiful?"

Ardeth's eyes grew round. "Could I? Would you really let me?"

"It would give me great pleasure. We are nearly of the same size. I can wear your traveling suit long enough for you to see how it feels to wear something more beautiful."

"But mine is so plain and coarse. I don't know . . ."

"Nonsense. It will only be for a few moments and it will help us pass the time in an amusing way. It has been a long time since I met anyone who took such pleasure in small things. Come now. Don't tell me you don't want to wear this silk dress?"

"Oh, I would love it beyond anything. But, suppose those men come back. Shouldn't we keep ready just in case?"

"I do not think they will be back for some time yet. See how quiet it is out there. This could be most diverting."

Ardeth eyed the way the light shimmered on the silky cloth. "If you're really sure. . . ."

"I'm sure." Medora was already beginning to unbutton her jacket.

Chapter Three

Once Medora's jacket was removed, revealing a soft, high-necked, white crepe blouse underneath, the two women began to throw themselves into changing clothes with great fervor. Medora would have none of simply giving Ardeth her traveling jacket and skirt. As each layer was revealed to Ardeth's growing admiration, Medora determined that the girl must try everything. And when she learned that Ardeth had never worn a corset, that too had to be part of the switch.

"We would have to put it on you anyway," she said, as Ardeth worked at the laces, "because the jacket will never fit you otherwise. I could not wear it myself if I was not laced up."

"But aren't you uncomfortable all tied up like this?"

"A little, but one soon becomes accustomed to it. My child, a lady must never go out in public without her stays. They cinch the waist, lift the bosom, and accentuate the hips. The corset is your most significant item of apparel. It must be the first thing you buy when you reach town."

"This is so beautifully made," Ardeth said, fingering the lace edges of the corset.

"It is of the finest sateen and whalebone. I had my dressmaker fashion it specially to my specifications. Now, turn around and I will tie you up."

In her chemise and bloomers, Ardeth took a deep breath to pull in her waist as Medora pulled the ties. For a moment she felt as though she would never breathe again, but gradually she grew accustomed to the pain.

"What a small waist you have, child. It is because you are so young. Now, the petticoats."

Medora draped the several lacy petticoats over Ardeth's hips and fastened the tapes around her waist. Then she slipped the crepe blouse over her shoulders and began fastening the tiny buttons.

"It could not fit you better if it had been made for you."

Ardeth pirouetted around to set the petticoats twirling. "It's so soft, so smooth. I love it!"

"You are not even finished yet. Now, stand very still while I put the skirt over your head. There. And now, the jacket. Be still, child. How can I do up these tiny buttons with you jumping around."

"Oh, I wish I could see!"

"Isn't it nice just to know you are wearing this finery? *Madre mia,* but you are a vision," she said, standing back to look at the girl. "Walk over there around the room back and forth. No, no, you gallop like a young colt. I will show you how to move like a lady."

After slipping Ardeth's drab merino skirt over her head and half fastening the jacket, she stood in the center of the room, directing Ardeth back and forth, lifting her chin, straightening her back, correcting her steps to conform to the mincing, graceful glide elegant

52

young women affected.

"That is better. But here, your hat has slipped. Keep the head still, like so."

"It is the hatpin. It keeps coming out."

"That is because your hair is not correctly puffed and curled. Let me fasten it again. There. Now, walk across again."

Throwing herself into the part, Ardeth ambled back and forth across the room, twirling her skirt, luxuriating in the feel of it and imagining how gorgeous she must look. When she heard a sudden noise outside, it took an instant for her to remember she was playacting in the middle of a desperate situation. She stopped dead in the center of the room.

"What was that? Did you hear it?"

Medora's face had turned toward the silent door. "I think it was a gunshot."

Ardeth's hand went to her throat. "Oh, dear. Are they coming back?"

Medora was already at the peephole, straining to see outside. "It looks the same. The guard is still watching the hill. No wait. He's gotten up. He's coming this way."

Ardeth began fumbling with the buttons on Medora's jacket. "Hurry. You'd better have your clothes back."

"There's no time for that now. Don't worry about it."

They could hear Carlson's boots crunching on the graveled soil as he hurriedly approached the cabin. Both women shrank back against the back wall as the bar was loosened and the door flung open. Carlson came in quickly, closed the door and put the bar in place on the inside.

"What's the matter?" Medora asked. "We heard gunshots."

Carlson glared at them without answering and took out his jackknife to begin digging at the mortar between the logs, forcing a hole large enough to place the end of his rifle and allow room for sighting a target. "Sit down and keep quiet," he snarled at them, "or I'll use this gun on the both of you." Ardeth sat on the cot and clasped her hands in her lap, all too conscious that this was no cool, nerveless gunman they were dealing with. If anything, he appeared more anxious and closer to panic than she and Medora.

The far-off reverberations of horses' hooves were becoming clearer by the minute. She glanced at Medora, knowing they were both wondering if this was help on the way or merely the outlaws returning to hole up for the night. They took some comfort in the fact that Carlson had been unsure enough of who was coming to barricade himself in the cabin. The horses were very close now, and they could hear men's voices calling over the sound of pounding hooves. Medora reached out and clasped Ardeth's hand. Then quite clearly they heard one of the voices yelling toward the cabin:

"We know you're in there, Toad. Throw down your guns and come out or we'll blast you out."

There was a zinging whine as Carlson fired his rifle in reply. Both women ducked automatically.

"Toad's not here," Carlson yelled. "You got the wrong man."

Ardeth looked frantically around the cabin, wondering where she could hide if these men began shooting at each other. The chimney was the only place impervious to bullets, but on second thought, she decided the floor might do better. Beside her Medora was already slipping down from the cot.

"We know you robbed the train. Come on out or be shot. You got a choice" came the voice again from the distance.

Carlson looked back at them, his eyes crazy with fear. Ardeth felt certain that at this point it was a toss-up as to whom they should fear the most, this unstable outlaw or the posse outside.

"Why not give yourself up," Medora suggested gently. "You don't have any of the money from the train, and there's no way they can link you to the robbery without it."

"And rot in jail until they decide to string me up? Never!" Swiveling his rifle in search of the slightest movement in the underbrush, he fired again as both women cringed against the floor. "Besides, I got you two, don't I. That's kidnapping. It's all the excuse they need to hang me!"

"This is your last chance," the voice called.

Huddling together, Ardeth and Medora scrunched close to the cot, prone on the floor as a roaring nightmare of gunfire erupted around them. Some of the bullets came zinging through the thin walls, clipping the bricks of the hearth and digging into the logs. Ardeth's fancy hat came unpinned and rolled away, loosening her hair with it. She clamped both hands over her ears and prayed until the noise stopped.

Timidly raising her head, she saw Carlson still kneeling by the wall, his rifle primed.

"You're bound to run out of ammunition," Medora said quietly. "Save your life . . . and ours."

55

"Shut up!" Carlson roared and unleashed a round of gunfire that was answered by another screaming barrage. Once again she pressed her body against the floor, expecting any moment to feel the sharp pain of a hit. Then the guns stopped and all was quiet again. "Isn't there any way out?" she whispered to Medora.

"No. There never was. And they probably don't even know we're here inside."

"Maybe if we screamed at them. . . ."

Medora nodded at Carlson. "He'd shoot us before we made the first sound."

Over her shoulder Ardeth could see the outlaw squirming down against the wall, making his way to the opposite side of the door, where he began digging at the mortar in the walls again in search of a new firing spot. Fear like none she had ever known rose in her throat, choking off her breath. As she watched Carlson, that fear was absorbed by anger, at fate and at herself. How frustrating, how horribly frustrating that her first excursion into the wide world should end like this — as the victim of a gunfight in a shabby cabin in the hills. All her dreams of the bright city and a good life ahead were going to be lost in a barrage of rifle shots, and before she even had a chance to taste anything of life. It was too awful to accept.

She felt Medora's hand on her shoulder. "Maybe we'd be safer on the other side once they realize he's on this side of the door," she whispered, bending close to Ardeth's ear.

"I'm afraid to move," Ardeth whispered back. Somehow the cot seemed to offer a modicum of shelter, poor as it was.

The distant voice outside roared again in the silence:

"Give it up and come out! This is your last chance."

Carlson jammed his rifle in the newly formed hole and sent a zinging shot in the direction of the voice. Ardeth scrunched down under the cot, her hands over her ears as gunfire roared around them, bullets pounding into the wood of the walls, deflecting off the bricks of the chimney. It seemed to go on forever. In the middle of the firing, she saw Medora start squirming across the floor toward the other side of the cabin.

"Don't!" she yelled, grabbing at Medora's skirt — the drab merino she herself had worn only a few short moments before.

But Medora's studied calm had at last given way to a full panic. "I can't stand this!" she yelled. Dragging the skirt from Ardeth's hands, she scrambled across the floor, at first keeping low and then, in her panic, getting to her feet to run crouching. Halfway across she lurched suddenly to her full height, then went careening into the far wall. Ardeth watched in horror as she slid down the wall, clutching her side, to lie with her face in the dirt floor, a crumpled heap against the wall.

"Medora!" Ardeth screamed. She began squirming toward the other woman, but a new round of gunfire forced her back underneath the cot as far as she could go. When it finally let up, she lifted her head to look around the room. Carlson was still hunched low against the wall. The movement of his rifle told her he was still functioning, though there was blood seeping through the cloth of his shirt on his shoulder. Medora lay facedown, deathly still.

"Medora," Ardeth cried, and began working her way across the room as the guns remained silent. She crouched near the still figure, turning her over to cradle the woman's head in her arms. Her face was pasty white, her mouth open, her eyes staring lifelessly at the ceiling of the cabin. Her left side was thick with clotting blood. Ardeth stared dumbly at her own hands which were scarlet with Medora's blood.

Suddenly her arm was jerked away, and she was dragged to her feet. Carlson, limping from a shot in the leg, had pulled her in front of him, his arm tight around her waist. Yanking her over to the door, he yelled in the silence:

"I got a woman here! I'm comin' out. I'll kill her if you shoot."

"What woman?" The voice came from outside.

"From the train. I want my horse. Bring it up and I'll take her out."

There was an ominous silence from the woods outside. Ardeth could imagine how the posse must be debating whether one woman's life was worth allowing this villain to go free. Still in shock from Medora's sudden death, she felt her own chances now were less than nothing. If this outlaw did not kill her, the posse would.

"Which is it?" Carlson yelled impatiently. "Kill me and she'll die too."

Ardeth struggled in the viselike grip of Carlson's arms. He clutched her painfully tight with one arm, his other arm cradling his rifle. He had been hit at least twice and was now so desperate, she figured, that he had nothing to lose. "I won't go with you," she muttered, struggling.

He didn't even bother to answer, only tightened his grip around her waist. Then the distant voice finally came: "All right. Come out. But she'd better be safe."

Somehow Carlson managed to lift the bar using the butt of his rifle and his one free hand. He kicked the door open, still not showing himself.

"My horse?" he yelled.

"We got it here."

"Bring it up. I want to see it."

Ardeth could barely see in the bright sunshine after her long time in the cabin. Gradually she made out the distant ring of pines beyond the cabin and the azure blue of the sky above the sand hills. Then a figure emerged from the trees leading a horse. He did not come very close but stood only a short distance from the trees, waiting.

"Bring it up!" Carlson yelled again.

"Not till you show us the woman is alive" came the answer.

Carlson cursed under his breath, then shoved Ardeth ahead of him through the door. With his limping gait, he half pushed, half dragged her outside into the clearing before the cabin. "Bring my horse and no tricks!" Carlson yelled.

Ardeth could still make out no figures except the one leading the horse, but she knew they were there, hidden in the trees, watching, weighing the possibilities. At least, so far they appeared to feel her life was valuable enough not to shoot them both down.

"Release the woman," the voice from the trees ordered. "Then we'll let you go."

"I ain't that stupid!" Carlson roared. "You got one minute. Send my horse up or I'll kill her right here in front of you."

"Please," Ardeth muttered. "All this has nothing to do with me —"

"Shut up!" Carlson snapped, tightening his grip on her waist to cut off her breath. "You're my ticket out of here, and you ain't goin' nowhere except with me."

She looked frantically out toward the trees, praying the men there would come up with some way of saving her. If she was forced to go with this outlaw, her life might as well end here.

After a long silence, the figure standing beside the horse gave it a slap on the rump, sending it cantering up toward the man and the woman in front of the cabin. Carlson whistled shrilly, and the animal obediently stopped a few feet away. Ardeth's mind was working frantically. Somehow this horrible man whose blood was smearing her clothes was going to have to get himself and her up on that horse. It was probably the only chance she would have to get free of him.

Dragging her along, Carlson limped toward his mount, jamming the rifle loosely in the saddle holster. He grabbed the reins with his free hand, still gripping Ardeth. "Get up," he snapped and shoved her toward the saddle.

"I can't ride," she cried, squirming. "I'm terrified of horses!"

"Get up!" he roared.

Cautiously she lifted her skirts high enough to try to put one foot in the stirrup. As she leaned toward the animal's body, her weight pressed against Carlson's wounded shoulder. The pain was enough to make him loosen his tight grip on her waist. She was still between him and the men in the woods, but she had just enough momentum to turn and shove. The outlaw staggered back, and she ran wildly, blindly, not knowing or caring where. Behind her she heard a wild outbreak of gunfire, twice as loud now that she was out in the open. Diving for the dirt, she scrambled on all fours toward the trees. There was a scream, the high-pitched, agonized scream of a horse. A storm of dust flew around her, obscuring her sight. At any moment she expected the painful thud of a bullet to pierce her body, and in panic she threw herself down to roll away from the fracas, finally coming to rest in a shallow gully, where she crouched with her hands over her head, gasping with dry sobs.

The silence was ominous after the explosion of the guns. Ardeth felt strong hands on her shoulders, lifting her. She looked up into the lined face of an older man, shadowed by his large hat.

"Are you all right, ma'am?" he asked kindly. "It's over. You're safe now."

She couldn't answer. Glancing back toward the cabin, she saw sprawled on the ground before the door a crumpled, bloody, lifeless heap that had been the outlaw, and beside him, the huge, inert form of his horse. Both had died in the fusillade of the rifle fire that had erupted as she ran.

"Is he. . . ?"

"He's dead. And good riddance, too. Come along now, miss."

He got her to her feet, but she was shaking so violently she could not stand. With the man's help, she got out of the gully to watch as the clearing filled with more men. In appearance there was little to separate them from the outlaw, and it was difficult for her to believe that they were not there to hurt her. They swarmed over the clearing, one of them dragging the saddlebags off the dead horse to throw open and examine, two or three cautiously making their way into the cabin, others standing over the bloody mess that had been Carlson.

"He was alone," one man called, emerging from the cabin, "but there's another woman in there."

Ardeth looked up quickly. "My friend . . . she's been hurt . . ." she muttered.

"There were two hostages from the train," one of the men said, and Ardeth recognized the voice that had called from the woods. "Damn. One of them must have been hit in the crossfire."

"Please, can't you help her," Ardeth cried, still trembling and supported by the older man with his arm around her waist.

"It's no good," the man who had emerged from the cabin said. "She's dead."

"Oh . . ." Ardeth cried and sank in the older man's arms. He helped her across to the trees where a rotting limb on the ground made a makeshift seat. Setting her down, he moved off to his horse and soon returned carrying the top of a flask filled with whisky. "Here, ma'am. Drink this," he said. "It'll help."

With unshed tears choking her throat, Ardeth put the small cup to her lips and drank the searing liquid. It was the first time she had ever tasted liquor, and she half choked on it. But it did warm her going down, and she hoped it would ease the pain that filled her chest. Poor Medora! How useless, how unnecessary a death. And how easily it might have been her lying lifeless on the dirt floor of that cabin. It seemed so unjust she could barely be grateful she was still alive.

Dimly she heard the clatter of more horses arriving.

The man who had given her the whisky started up as he saw the new arrivals. "You stay here, miss. You're safe now. I'll be back in a moment."

She barely noticed him walk away. Looking down at her dress, she realized for the first time that the beautiful burgundy silk dress was now yellow with layers of dirt and dust. Then she noticed the darker splotches on it where she had cradled Medora's bloody body against her. Or were they from the outlaw's wounds? She shivered and tucked at her hair, half of which had long ago come unpinned and was straggling down her back. Her face, she knew, must be streaked with dirt, perhaps even blood, for her hands had been covered with it after she reached Medora.

Medora! A pain shot through her again. What a terrible waste! That wretched outlaw deserved to die. But Medora. . . .

A group of men were walking toward her. Ardeth looked up blankly at them. She had not seen them before and judged they must be the new arrivals. One of them appeared to be the man in charge—a tall person with long, sandy hair that framed his face. His guns were slung low on his hips, and he walked with the natural swagger of a leader even though he appeared younger than most of the others.

To her surprise he knelt beside her, looking closely into her face.

"Miss Melindez. I can't tell you how sorry I am that you had to go through such an ordeal."

She looked into his eyes so close to her own. They were a soft green, like the early grasses of spring. His mouth was wide and lightly sculptured in classic lines. His chin was firm and slightly indentured. Blankly she stared at him, seeing the tan skin, the tiny pores, the arched, heavy eyebrows, and the strong, straight nose. What had he called her?

"We'll see that you are well cared for now," he went on. "This unfortunate incident won't be allowed to ruin your tour, I promise you."

"No . . . no," Ardeth mumbled. The whisky was making it hard for her to think straight. "You're not . . . you're not making. . . ."

His strong arms reached out to raise her to her feet. "The moment I heard how they had taken you from the train, I made up my mind they would never get away with it. You're going to be all right now. We've already made arrangements for you to travel on another train to Denver."

"No!" Ardeth cried, clutching at his sleeve. "I don't want to get back on another train, ever. I can't."

"Now, don't upset yourself. We'll see that you have an escort all the way. I've already made the arrangements."

"But you don't understand. . . ."

They emerged from the woods into a crowd of men and horses milling around in front of the cabin. Carlson's dead horse was already being dragged across the dirt away from the house while the outlaw's body was draped unceremoniously across the empty saddle of another horse. On the opposite side of the cabin, two men were digging at a large hole in the earth.

"We need your help, Miss Melindez," the young man went on. "We do not know who that unfortunate woman was who lost her life in there. Did you by any chance learn her name while you were being held hostage in that cabin?"

His words broke the dam on her tears, and closing her hands over her face, Ardeth sobbed through her fingers, her shoulders heaving. It was the first time she had been able to really cry since the firing had started, and once begun, she could not seem to stop.

"Can't you see you're upsetting her," one of the men snapped. "Let it wait until we've got the woman buried."

"We don't have time to wait. Turnbull has still got to be run to earth. I want this woman away from here and safely on her way to Denver. We can't afford any more hostages."

"Hasn't she been through enough, Nat? I think we ought to get her out of here as soon as possible."

"Just a few more minutes," Nat Varien answered through clenched teeth. "Go see what you can do about getting her a horse and a couple of escorts. She'll be all right sitting quietly here for a few moments."

"I'm so sorry," Ardeth tried to say through her sobs. "It was just so . . . so awful! I'll be all right in a minute."

"I'm sure you will." Nat watched the other man make his way back to the clearing where the others milled about. When the two of them were alone, he sat down on a log and pulled her down beside him, taking Ardeth's hands in his own. Then he spoke, very softly, leaning close to her tear-stained face.

"It's too bad this had to happen, Medora, but you don't need to worry now. I'm here and I'll see you get safely to Fireweed. Everything is there, waiting for you."

"Everything?"

"All seven of your trunks. I can't imagine why you brought so much unless you were trying to make it look as if your purpose in coming really was the tour. At any rate, all your clothes are safely there waiting for you." He paused a moment, looking toward the clearing as though to make certain they were quite alone. "Have you got it with you?" he said, almost in a whisper. "Did you manage to keep it safe?"

Ardeth stared at him through the pounding in her head. "What?"

"I know we can't really talk now, but I couldn't imagine that you'd send it with your luggage. That would be taking too great a risk. Medora, are you all right?"

Ardeth rubbed at her eyes, trying to sort out what this attractive man was talking about, aware that she was not really handling the situation and conscious that she was part of some strange conspiracy she knew nothing about. And he persisted in calling her Medora. She opened her mouth to tell him Medora was lying back there dead but was cut off by a voice calling from the clearing:

"Nat, we're ready to roll. The woman's buried."

Nat Varien rose from where he had been crouching next to Ardeth. "Make sure she's well covered. We don't want the wolves digging up the body."

Ardeth gasped and jumped to her feet, clutching at his arm. "We can't leave her here like this! It isn't right!"

Taking both her hands in his own, Nat spoke gently, as if he were addressing a child. "Look, we don't even know who she was. I have to go now, but we'll talk again, in Fireweed, as soon as I can get there. I have the money waiting there for you."

"The money . . ."

66

"Yes, as we agreed. Come on now. There's a horse here you can ride back to the train, and I'll assign two men to ride with you in case there is any more trouble. But there won't be. Turnbull's gang is too busy trying to get away from this area to bother with any more trains any time soon."

"I don't want to go. I won't go!"

He gripped her hands tighter. "Medora, you must. Don't let all this throw you. If it's your friend there you're worried about, I promise you after the Toad is captured we'll come back to return the body to the nearest town where she'll have a decent burial. Maybe by then we'll know who she is."

"But you don't understand. . . ."

"Nat!" one of the men called. Varien, only too conscious that precious time was slipping away, took her by the shoulders and gently pushed her away. "Stay here and compose yourself while I get your horse," he said. "Everything's going to be all right."

He walked off, leaving Ardeth to lean against the nearest tree for support. Her mind was beginning to clear a little from the whisky, and with it came the appalling realization that she had not told him who she really was. For some reason he had assumed she was Medora Melindez, and she had not forced him to hear the truth—that Medora actually lay dead in that newly filled grave.

Why? Why hadn't she confessed at once to the mistake? She must do so at once, before they went any further with this terrible mistake.

She turned and leaned her face against the tree trunk. She had to think. Everything had happened so suddenly and had turned her expectations completely topsy-turvy. She had no money to buy her ticket to Fireweed. Turnbull had taken every cent when he stole her purse. She had no baggage unless somehow she could trace it on the train that had been stopped. There was no Cousin Emma waiting to offer her solace and a home in Fireweed. There was no friend, Medora, taking her under her wing until she was able to get established. She was alone and penniless and surrounded by gunfighters. There was no way she could go forward and no way to go back, even if she had wanted one. The truth was she was in a bad way.

On the other hand . . .

Trunks filled with clothes . . . money . . . people waiting for her . . . an escort to see her safely to Denver and a ticket on to Fireweed — all that was meant for Medora, by some strange miracle was being dropped in her lap. It was not as though she was taking anything from her friend, for her friend was dead. Who would it hurt if she used this opportunity to make her way to the town safely? Once there she could confess everything to this nice cowboy and ask him to forgive her, and that would be the end of it. It wouldn't be right, but anything was better than going back to spend the rest of her life in her parents' Nebraska soddy.

Nat came walking up, his boots crunching on the dried leaves. "We have to leave," he said, taking her arm to lead her to the clearing.

"Is she going to be able to ride?" one of the mounted men asked softly as Ardeth stood unsteadily near the horse's flank.

"She'll be all right. She's just upset. Go easy on your way back to the depot."

Ardeth laid a hand on the saddle, and Nat gave her a

lift up where she sat leaning forward over the pommel, gripping the horn. Jumping easily onto his own mount, Nat reached out and put the reins in her hands.

"Are you sure you can't remember that woman mentioning her name?"

She looked up at him. Over his shoulder she could make out the mound of raw earth with a crude cross fashioned from two skinny sticks tied together and stuck in the ground at its head. What to do?

"I do remember something," she heard herself saying. "Royce. Yes, that was it. Ardeth Royce."

Chapter Four

Ardeth had plenty of time to reflect on what she had done. The long trek by horseback back to the depot was spent mostly in silence. The two men escorting her were sympathetic and did not press her to talk. She was grateful for their silence because she was very busy, carrying on a furious feud with her own conscience. Even if she had wanted to talk with them, she was too afraid of revealing her duplicity to attempt a conversation.

At the depot her escort gave her Medora's purse, which they had found at the cabin. Nat Varien had added funds to help her make the rest of the journey. The two men, who by now were deeply regretting they had lost the opportunity to chase off after Turnbull's gang, nevertheless remained solicitous of her. They bought her tickets to Denver and on to Fireweed, sat near her in the coach, saw her to a comfortable hotel near the depot in Denver, and arranged for her burgundy dress to be cleaned and pressed for the trip the following day that would complete her journey. By the time they took their leave, Ardeth was beginning to become accustomed to being called Miss Melindez and even, now and then, reveling in having someone to take care of these little comforts. If, on occasion, she murmured a little prayer of apology to Medora, she was very careful to not let anyone else hear it.

As the train drew closer to Fireweed two days later, she sat staring out of the window, not seeing the low yellow hills or green undulating prairie at all, her mind endlessly reviewing the events of the past two days, her emotions alternating between guilt and satisfaction. So far she could not help but believe that her small deception had hurt no one while it had reaped her enormous benefits. In her purse she had carefully kept a list of every penny spent since the robbery, and she intended to repay it all once she had an income. The handsome cowboy who had given her the money to travel looked kind enough, and she concluded that once he recovered from any shock or anger over her little "trick" he would allow her time to repay what she owed.

It might be more difficult to explain to the theater manager or whoever it was in Fireweed who had arranged for Medora's visit. But surely that could also be handled. After all, it had been the cowboy, Nat Varien, who had first assumed that she was Miss Melindez. Perhaps once she explained her reasons for going along with his mistake, they would be forgiving. She could only hope so.

"Next stop, Fireweed," the conductor's voice called from the door of the coach. Startled, Ardeth felt a shiver go through her body. All her internal agonizing had been difficult enough, but now she was about to face the real test. Somehow two days of being Miss Melindez with all the attention and solicitation it brought had made it increasingly harder to believe she was going to have to confess to her deception. Now that the town was in sight, she trembled to think of doing it. Yet, it must be done. To allow it to go any farther would be morally wrong and would make it ever harder to give it up. She smoothed her skirts, straightened her hat and steeled her spine. She would go directly from the depot to the theater and confess all. Then with a clear conscience she could set about looking for a place to live and some kind of respectable work. It was even possible that the rumor of Cousin Emma's death was not true at all. If so, half her troubles would be solved.

The train slowed in a cloud of cinders. Through the window Ardeth saw a tiny, one-room clapboard building standing forlornly on a drab, rubble-strewn plateau. Before it stretched a wooden platform. Far in the distance she could just make out a shadowy broken line that indicated the roofs of the town. Without it, she would have supposed the train ended in the middle of the plains.

Yet there were people on the platform. As the coach lumbered toward the depot, she could make out several men attired in coats and hats waiting, no doubt, to board. Ardeth carefully hung the strap to her purse over her arm, brushed some of the yellow dust from her burgundy skirt, made certain her hat-pin was still firmly in place then made her way down the aisle, past the potbellied stove to the exit door.

The conductor touched his cap as he took her hand to help her down.

"So nice having you ride with us, Miss Melindez," he said politely.

She was going to miss all this kindness and consideration she had received simply from being Miss Melindez. She was even going to miss being called by that name. But so be it. She was here now, at the end of her long journey, and she must make the best of it. She gave him her warmest smile.

"You've made my trip so pleasant. Thank you," she said and stepped out on the platform.

The sun was blinding after the dim light of the coach. Ardeth shielded her eyes against it, pausing on the platform to find the steps that would take her down to the street. All at once she was assailed with such a calamitous noise as to cause her to step backward. A screeching, wheezing, thumping bellow swept over her, bringing her hands involuntarily over her ears. Her eyes began to adjust to the light, and she saw that the horrific noise was issuing from a group of men standing on the wooden platform, each of them blowing or thumping on some kind of instrument. A town band! She had read of such things but had never seen or heard one. If this was what they sounded like, she wondered why they were so popular in the more civilized places of the world. But the band was not the worst of it. Even as she watched, a swarm of men surged forward to crowd around the base of the steps. Ardeth recoiled in horror, and only the presence of the conductor behind her prevented her from making a hasty retreat back inside the coach. The men were all talking at once, and she could make no sense of what they were saying over the wheezing of the band. Her worst suspicions were confirmed though when she looked over their heads to see a long narrow strip of cloth that had been tacked to the roof of the depot. Written on it in crude red letters were the words "Fireweed Welcomes Medora!"

"Dear Lord in Heaven!" Ardeth muttered as one of the men climbed up the train steps and shoved a large bouquet of Kansas wild flowers in her hand. He was a round gentleman dressed in a plaid waistcoat, buff trousers, a spotted black coat and a felt bowler hat. His round face was framed with white sideburns while his mouth was obscured by the largest handlebar moustache Ardeth had ever seen. He smiled broadly, puffing out his copious cheeks which were so red they might have been rouged.

"Quiet! Quiet!" he roared at the crowd which quickly lowered its talking to a simmer. Taking her hand, he led her away from the train. Ardeth, her knees beginning to go wobbly, clutched at the wild flowers thrust in her arms and tried to control the stupification that she knew must be written all over her face.

"Allow me to welcome you to Fireweed, Miss Melindez," the round gentleman with the huge moustache said, bowing before her. "The next great city of

74

Kansas. I am Jasper P. Corchran, your sponsor, and the proprietor of the Diamond Ring, the greatest, most frequented, most renowned saloon this side of Sante Fe."

A roar of assent punctuated with scattered applause swept through the crowd at these glowing descriptions of local glory. Turning his pink cheeks back and forth to bask in his friends' approbation, Corchran waved a hand and gave Ardeth another low bow. "As you see, our entire population has been waiting with heightened anticipation for the arrival of the lady from St. Louis, the nightingale of the West, the jewel of the Western world, the enchantress . . ."

"Oh, for God's sake, Jasper. Shut up and let the little lady talk!" came a raucous voice from the crowd. Undeterred, Corchran went on for several more minutes extolling Medora's beauty, voice, femininity and fame while Ardeth stood wishing the ground would open up and swallow her whole. "Come on, Jasper, introduce some of the rest of us," a thin, bewhiskered gentleman standing behind Jasper Corchran said as he elbowed his way between them. He had Ardeth's hand in his and was raising it to his lips as Corchran intoned, "Baskin Sawyer, ma'am, our esteemed barber and undertaker."

Before Ardeth could yank her hand away, it was claimed by another gentleman who pushed Sawyer out of the way. "Lucius Clay, Miss Melindez. I own the bank. Welcome to Fireweed. We've long needed a little culture in our town."

Clay was shoved aside by a stocky man with a

heavily tanned face. "Kyle Meeker, Miss Melindez, the local sheriff. Pleased to meet you."

Ardeth bowed and nodded as the crowd pressed around her, clamoring for her hand and calling out their names and occupations. "I'll never be able to remember . . ." she murmured, but Corchran, hearing her, assured her she'd come to know them all in good time. Then, perceiving her extreme discomfort and chalking it up to the press of the crowd, he began flaying them back with one powerful arm.

"Make room, here, gentlemen, make room! It won't do to suffocate this fair treasure afore she ever gets a chance to warble a note. Stand back, here now, I insist on it."

Corchran apparently had clout with the crowd for they obediently fell back, allowing Ardeth room to catch her breath. Noticing she held one white hand on her throat, Jasper P. began to realize that she might actually faint.

"Lean on my arm, Miss Melindez, please do," he said, bending toward her. "Are you quite all right?"

"Well, I am a little fatigued. The long trip, you know. . . ."

"Of course," he answered, all concern. "And all the trouble you had on your way here. Why, we didn't think. A parcel of oafs and boors we are! Stand back there now and give the lady air."

"Say something, Medora," a voice called from the crowd.

"Sing! Sing something" came several answering ones.

Ardeth gripped Corchran's arm for support. If she

was forced to sing out here in this crowd, it would be her undoing for certain. From all she had heard of cow towns like Fireweed, it would not surprise her if someone ran for a rope.

"Please . . . I really do feel a trifle ill. . . ."

Corchran patted her hand. "Just say a few words of welcome, Medora, and that ought to satisfy them. The rest will have to wait for your first performance tomorrow night."

Ardeth gulped and felt the blood drain from her face. "Tomorrow night?"

"Unless you'd like to wade right in and put on a show tonight. The Ring is ready anytime you are."

"No, no! I . . . I'll say a few words."

Corchran shouted down the crowd which, once they knew she intended to speak, grew very still. "My friends," Ardeth began shakily, her voice sounding to her own ears like the mewing of a kitten. "My friends, I thank you for your very kind welcome. I'm sure . . . that is, I think in time we shall all be great . . . great friends. Now, I'm a little tired from my trip . . . I'm sure you'll understand since we are all such . . . will be such good . . . friends."

A scattered applause went round the crowd as she fell silent, and gradually a growing shout of approval drowned it out. To Ardeth's relief, the men close around her stepped back, and she saw a black leather shay fastened to a sleek bay horse waiting at the edge of the platform. She had already decided if she had to walk to the town in the distance, she would never make it. With great aplomb Corchran handed her up onto the seat, then crawled up beside her and took the reins. Leading the procession, he guided the horse and buggy across the scrubby grass as the others took up their places behind him, some walking, most riding their own mounts, all of them followed by the band which had once again started up its thumping and wheezing. Grateful just to sit down, Ardeth clutched her flowers with one hand and the seat of the buggy with the other while the shay bumped and wobbled across the prairie toward the jagged rooftops on the horizon. The procession gathered steam as it went, the mounted men surging ahead and whooping as they rode, the shay taking its cue from them to come at a brisk clip behind. When one of the men started shooting his pistol into the air the others took up the chorus. By the time they reached Front Street, the one and only street of the town, the shay was thumping and flying, and Ardeth was clutching frantically at the seat, her hat and her mutilated flowers. The dust stirred up by the horses choked her lungs, and the noise of the guns blasted her ears. When at last they pulled to a stop, her hat had slipped down over one eye and she had half slid into the barrel-shaped bottom of the shay. Corchran had to help her back on the seat before he could dismount himself.

Coming round to her side, he took her hand and half pulled her from the buggy. She gripped the rough bark of a hitching post to regain her footing and looked around her.

It was not an encouraging sight. A long row of storefronts lined either side of a wide dirt road that was churned to a foot-high fog of dust with the traffic. She could only glimpse a few of the names painted above the doors and windows of the narrow buildings: The Liberty Barbershop, A. Fradin's General Store, Kenneth's Dry Goods, Jason's Lumber. By far the most imposing was the one facing directly front, The Diamond Ring. Its tall facade standing nearly eight feet above its roof had a large painted ring with spokes of light radiating outward in splendor above the word "Saloon." Underneath, in small black letters was painted, "Jasper P. Corchran, Proprietor."

"Now you come right along, Miss Medora," Jasper said solicitously, leading her with a strong hand on her elbow. "This here is where you'll be performin' and a better stage you couldn't find this side of Abilene. Why, we've even got a backdrop that moves! We can make waves, clouds, even thunder, should you want a little atmosphere. I'm proud to say the Diamond Ring is the best little old saloon in town."

Without stopping for a breath, Jasper led her up the low steps to a wide walkway and pushed aside the swinging doors of his establishment. Ardeth stepped cautiously inside, glad to leave the dust of the road behind yet uneasy at walking so boldly into one of those dens of iniquity called saloons. It was dark inside, and it took her eyes a moment to adjust. She stood in the doorway, seeing a long narrow room with a bar along one side and round tables scattered the length of the hall. At the far end was a raised platform with a valance above painted to look like heavy damask drapes. On either side of this stage a crude box had been built five feet off the ground. In front of the box on the left a narrow flight of stairs led off into the darkness above.

Gingerly Ardeth took a few steps into the long hall. It was then that she saw over the bar a ten-foot-long painting of a reclining woman, absolutely nude. She looked quickly away, hoping her burning cheeks were not too apparent.

"It's . . . it's very nice," she mumbled. Jasper Corchran, his fingers still tight on her arm, nodded his head enthusiastically. "Well, it probably pales next to those fancy places in St. Louis," he said modestly, "but I bet you wasn't in any grander one since coming west."

"No," Ardeth answered. "I never was, that is for certain."

The rest of the throng had begun to pour through the doors, crowding around her. "Stand back, there!" Corchran roared. "Give the lady room. Can't you see she's nearly tuckered out."

Sawyer, the barber, leaned into Ardeth's face. "Go on, Miss Medora. Try out the stage."

"Yeah, give us a song," another voice cried from the crowd, and the chant was taken up by the others. Kyle Meeker, the sheriff, drawing on the strength of his authority, began elbowing the crowd away from Ardeth, and none too gently.

"Stand away here, you clumsy louts! Give the lady room to breathe."

Ardeth's knees began to give way, and she found herself clinging to Jasper Corchran simply to remain standing. "I . . . really don't feel very well, Mr. Corchran. Do you suppose I could lie down?"

"Of course, ma'am. It's that trip that's done you in. Move back, Silas, and give Miss Melindez some air."

Sheriff Meeker's booming voice all at once silenced the crowd with its ringing tones. "Now listen, you fellows. This little lady has just come though a long trip and a pretty awful one. Anybody that has to deal face to face with that skunk, Toad Turnbull, is going to have to need some time to get over it. Now, you all go on home and let this little lady rest awhile. That's an order!"

"Hay, Jasper," a voice rang from the back. "How about opening up the bar while the lady rests."

Corchran glared at the crowd. "It'll open at the usual time. Now, you rowdies get going while I escort the lady to her room."

A howl of jeers went up from the crowd which did nothing to calm Ardeth's anxiety about this whole outlandish situation. "Come along, Miss Medora," Corchran said, gripping her hand and leading her toward the flight of stairs.

She pulled back. "But . . . surely . . . you don't mean I'm to stay in a saloon?"

"Why, miss, we have the finest rooms in town right above the store, so to speak. And I've had one made ready especially for you. You're gonna love it."

"But really. . . ." Glancing aside she caught Sheriff Meeker looking quizzically at her, not really suspicious, more like surprised. "I'm sure I'll be very impressed," Ardeth said quickly and followed behind Jasper Corchran. Whatever was waiting for her upstairs, if it would get her away from this crowd long enough to get her bearings, it would be worth the shame of living in a saloon.

The dark, narrow stairwell emerged into a hall on the second floor. It was about half the length of the lower room and had six doors at intervals, three on each side, all closed. All sorts of trepidations jumbled in her mind as she followed Corchran along the hall to the end where he opened one of the doors for her and stepped back, waving her inside.

Ardeth stood in the entrance, dumbfounded. The room was full of light from the two broad windows along one side which were draped in soft, ruffled muslin curtains. There was a woven carpet on the floor, a design of pale cream flowers against a burgundy background. A fourposter bed with crocheted hangings and a brightly flowered quilt stood against one wall, flanked on the left by a massive chest of drawers and on the right by the entrance to the hall. To one side of the doorway sat a painted stand with a blue and white washbowl and pitcher. On the other side was a brightly decorated, paneled screen half-hiding a large oak armoire. In one corner a rocking chair filled with several tufted pillows sat beside a small table just large enough to hold a mass of flowers arranged in a bowl.

"It's beautiful!" Ardeth exclaimed.

Corchran beamed with pleasure. "I saw to it myself. Only the best for the Great Medora, I says and sets about getting it. Now, here's Mrs. Higley who's going to see to you. Anything you need, just ask her."

A thin, bony woman scuttled around Corchran in

the doorway and bobbed a curtsey in front of Ardeth. With her straight sandy hair pulled back from her thin face and knotted on the top of her head, she looked like nothing so much as one of the countrywomen of Nebraska. She smiled, revealing a missing tooth in front, and twisted her hands nervously in her long, calico apron.

"Martha Higley, Miss Medora," she said, extending one hand then snatching it back as she thought perhaps it was not the right thing to do. "Mr. Corchran here asked me special to tend to you as it's been my pleasure to do. You look all tuckered out, if I do say so. Why don't you come inside here and have a little rest."

"An admirable idea, Martha," Jasper added. "I think that is just what Miss Medora is wanting now." With a flourish he reached for Ardeth's hand and bowed over it. "Shall we talk later, madam? After you've had an opportunity to settle in a bit?"

Ardeth tried to smile. "It would be very pleasant to get out of these dusty clothes and sit quietly a few moments. Are you certain you don't mind?"

"Your wish is my command," Jasper intoned, bowing again over her hand. "Until later, then."

He swept from the room, barely through the door before Ardeth closed it firmly behind him. She turned, leaning against the wood, terror choking off her breath. What had she done! Why hadn't she told the truth right away and got herself out of this intolerable situation. Every moment she stayed with this deception made it more complicated. Change her clothes! To what? And what was going to happen tomorrow when they expected her to sing for them? They would run her out of town if she didn't straighten this thing out and soon!

Martha Higley went bustling around the room, ending up at the high bed where she bent over the bright covers. "Oh, dear, I suppose I'd better remove all these," she said, clucking with her tongue. "I laid them out for you to shake out the wrinkles. And I confess, because I wanted to see them myself. Such gorgeous gowns! I don't suppose nothing like them has ever been seen in Fireweed before."

Ardeth took a few steps toward the bed where she began to see that what she had thought was a brilliantly colored quilt was not that at all. It was, in fact, a profusion of dresses thrown one over the other. Scarlet brocade, emerald taffeta, sapphire silk showered in ruches of blond lace. Goggle-eyed she stared at them, reaching out to run her hand along their silky surfaces. There must be ten at least, each one more elaborate and beautiful than the last.

"But how. . . ?" she managed to murmur.

"Oh, your boxes were sent ahead. Didn't Jasper tell you? They been here since yesterday. Which was good because it gave me a chance to put most things away." A horrible thought suddenly brought Martha Higley's hand to her lips. "Oh, dear . . . unless you didn't want anyone handling your things. . . ?"

"No, no. That's all right," Ardeth said quickly. "I don't have my maid you see, so it's perfectly all right."

"Well now, that's a relief. It was a pleasure for me, Miss Medora, I'll tell you. I been in this town nigh

84

on fifteen years, and I never seen such pretty things. But here now, let me move them to the press so you can stretch out for a spell."

"In a moment," Ardeth said, looking around the room. "If you would be so good as to just tell me where—"

"Nothing simpler," Martha cried, running to the chest of drawers. "In this one's your unmentionables, and soft and pretty they are, too. Why, there's more lace here than I ever wore in my whole life. But then, that's no concern of yours, is it. And here are your petticoats. And here's shawls and furbelows as I guess come in handy when the weather goes cool. Over there on a shelf is your hats—so many of them, I declare, and each fancier than the last. And let's see, sunshades also in the press, shoes and slippers over there, nightrobes—"

"That's fine, Mrs. Higley," Ardeth broke in. "I'll just have a good look around once I'm rested."

"Now, this here box is the only thing I didn't bother," she said, pointing to a square, wooden coffer sitting on the chest of drawers. "It's locked, you see, and I fancied you wouldn't want anyone but yourself opening it."

Ardeth eyed the box, wondering what it contained. A horrible suspicion began to grow in her mind. "Thank you kindly, Mrs. Higley."

"Oh, call me Martha, please, since I'll be serving you while you're here. Can I help you out of those things, Miss Medora?"

"No, thank you. I can manage. I would appreciate some quiet time. I'm sure you understand. . . ."

"Indeed I do. There now, the bed is cleared and all ready, so I'll just bob along. When would you like me to come back?"

"Come back?"

"To help you dress? For dinner?"

"Oh. Well, in about an hour. No, in two hours. That should give me time for a good rest."

Martha Higley's thick brows knitted in a frown. "That's pushing it a little close. But whatever you say, Miss Medora. I'll come knocking on your door in two hours."

She had her hand on the knob when Ardeth remembered. "Martha," she called. "Did you say you've lived in Fireweed fifteen years?"

"Oh, yes, ma'am. Came here when it was no more than one little store on the prairie and saw it grow into this great crowded, noisy place it is today."

Very casually Ardeth began removing her hat. "Did you by chance know a lady called Emma Hardwick? I think she ran a hotel here."

Martha gave a brittle laugh. "Old Emma! Sure, I knew her. Only I wouldn't call that run-down, flea-bag rooming house of hers a hotel. Emma was a tartar, she was. Tougher than nails. She run off a parcel of Indian braves once single-handed, using nothing but a broom handle! Emma was a character in these parts."

"Is she—does she still live here?"

"I reckon she would if the typhoid last winter hadn't of got her. She was carried off along with fourteen others in this town, most of them young but two or three old, like Emma. But don't tell me a

86

lady like yourself ever knew Emma Hardwick."

"No. Just a friend of a friend. She asked me to inquire about her when I got to Fireweed."

"Well, too bad you missed her, but none of us know when that summon's comin', do we now. I'll see you in a while, Miss Medora."

The door closed behind her. Ardeth plopped on the high feather mattress to catch her breath and sort her churning thoughts. So Cousin Emma really was dead, and there was no one and nothing for her in this town. Except for all this . . .

Very slowly she got up and began to circle the room, taking the time to look over everything of Medora's that was laid out there. She turned the gleaming kid leather shoes over in her hand, held the silken skirts up to her waist, tried on one of the feathered and flowered hats, and swung one of the Spanish shawls around her shoulders. They were all so beautiful, so rich, so feminine! It was going to be very difficult to confess her deception and give them all up.

Rummaging in Medora's purse, she found a small key hidden in one of the tiny compartments. Very carefully she tried it in the wooden chest and found that it fit. There was a click as the lock sprang back and Ardeth opened the lid.

Trays and trays of jewels! She had no way of knowing whether or not they were actually real, but they were gorgeous anyway. And surely some of the stones had to be genuine. Coming to the last tray she gasped as she found several stacks of bills amounting to close to two hundred dollars. A fortune!

Quickly Ardeth replaced the drawers, closed the lid and locked it. Then she went to sit on the bed, clasping her hands in her lap.

She had to think.

Chapter Five

Sheriff Bartle pulled his mount to a halt, rested his hands on the pommel of his saddle and looked out over the valley spread below. He was covered with dust, sticky with sweat, thirsty as a hog in a desert and aching in every muscle. All he wanted now was to head down that yellow road below and go home. He glanced over at the man beside him, just as sticky, dusty, thirsty and tired as he, no doubt, but still stiff in the saddle with a subdued, stubborn concentration on his duty.

"They're gone, Nat," the sheriff said, wiping at his brow with his sleeve. "Give it up for now. We ain't gone to catch 'em."

A muscle jumped in Nat Varien's square jaw. "Bastard!" he mumbled. "Outfoxed me again. We ought to of had all of them strung up by now."

Bartle shifted in his saddle. "They had the advantage of knowing these hills. There's a hundred places they could be hiding, supposing they ain't left the territory altogether. The horses are worn out and the men are starting to grumble. We'll just have to go back and telegraph word up and down the line and hope somebody recognizes them."

Nat looked out over the valley, fighting an internal battle between his will and his weary flesh. Finally, the thought of his tired horse tipped the scales. "I know you're right, but damn, I hate it! This was one time I was sure I was going to catch Toad Turnbull. The crafty bastard!"

"Well, he got away with a lot of money. He can't get rid of it so easily without someone becoming suspicious. There'll be other times. He's so cocky, he's sure to slip up one of these days."

"Yes, but will I be there when he does?"

Kicking at his horse's side, Nat started riding down the sloping scrub toward the road below. Sheriff Bartle followed with the posse somewhat behind, all of them stirring up a cloud of new yellow grime. Once at a level spot, they turned to follow a less steep path down the hill, the sheriff walking his mount sedately beside Nat and his roan. Both their horses had better staying power than those behind them and soon they were out in front of the posse by twenty feet or more.

"What is it you've got against the Toad, anyhow?" Bartle asked, his voice low enough not to carry to the others. Once again he saw the tightening of Nat's hard jaw. "I mean, you've come pretty far and rode hard these last days just to hang one shiftless outlaw. I can't believe it's only because you believe in law and justice. Did he do you some hurt back in New Mexico? Steal your money? Rape your wife? What drives you to all this?"

"Kind of nosey, aren't you, Sheriff?" Nat said bitterly.

"Yeah, I guess I am. But it's not just curiosity. I often wonder what drives men out here in this territory. I think about it a lot. Most of them, it's pretty obvious. They're the ones with greed in their eyes, just lookin' for that next big stake. There's the shifty ones you know are running from something back East, probably the law. There's the farmers and sheepherders, the clerks and storekeepers, most of them just looking for a spot to start over. There's the loose women—"

"And the card sharks, and the gunslingers, and the lawmen using their badges as an excuse to shoot off their guns."

An angry flush darkened the tan of Bartle's face. "Well now, that's a little close to home."

Nat grinned at him, a mischievous smile that made it difficult to be angry with him. "Oh, I didn't mean you necessarily. But I've known a few marshals and sheriffs who fit that description only too well. I'm as familiar with the usual types out here as you are. Turnbull fits a type too—the mean, gunhappy killer who'd as soon shoot a man as look at him. As for me, let's just say that he's one of the worst and I think the territory will be better off without him."

Bartle shrugged. It wasn't the answer, he knew, but it was as much as he was going to get. A man with the single-minded purpose Varien had shown toward Toad Turnbull had to have been given a good reason.

It would come out eventually.

They were approaching a place where the road forked, both sides stretching off into the tangle of scrub and gravel that appeared to lead nowhere. Bartle pulled up his horse.

"Well, this is where I head back to Sterling. You coming with us? You can get a bath and a meal there before pushing on."

Nat stopped and rubbed at his chin covered with a two days' stubble of growth. "It's tempting, but, no, I don't think so. I'm anxious to get to Fireweed."

"If that's how you feel, so long, then," Bartle said, extending his hand. "I'll see that the wire goes out on Turnbull as soon as I hit town. We ought to see some results from that."

"You do that, Sheriff," Nat answered. Touching his hat brim, he turned his horse and started down the opposite road, riding on alone. Sheriff Bartle was too optimistic, he thought absently as his weary stallion made its sure-footed way down the slope. The Toad was certain to be far away from these parts by now. Nat was familiar enough with his way of working to know that if he hadn't been caught on the day of the robbery, by the next day he would be well out of the area—either south into Colorado, or east into Kansas or north into Wyoming. Of course, he could go west and hole up in the rockies until the heat was off him, but that wasn't Turnbull's style. The maze of mountains might afford him the best chance of hiding, but he would be too impatient to sit and wait. No, he would be off where he could spend some of that money he had stolen.

Damn Turnbull, anyway! With his string of successful robberies, he must have such a horde by now that he wouldn't need anymore. A killer like the Toad couldn't plan on a quiet retirement living off his loot. He'd be shot or hanged long before that was possible. He stole, at least in part, for the sheer pleasure of it, not to mention the opportunity it gave him to kill a few innocent people.

Because it was getting on toward dusk and his horse was tired, Nat made the decision to stop for the night at an isolated spot he had found. It was sheltered by overhanging rocks on one side and facing a level patch of grass on the other. He cleared his gear off his mount and hobbled the stallion to graze on the grass while he built a crude camp near the rocks. Soon he had a small fire going which served to cook his coffee and bacon and beans as well as provide warmth against the night when temperatures could drop dramatically after darkness fell.

The night came quickly in this part of Colorado. Nat lay with his head on the saddle, nursing a cup of strong, bitter coffee, and watched the brilliant display of stars popping out like firecrackers in the velvet black bowl above him.

Why hadn't he answered Sheriff Bartle's question? Nosey or not, it had been asked before, always inviting the same silence on his part. This obsession with finding and killing Toad Turnbull was bound to make other men curious. And yet he could never bring himself to talk about it. He could never explain the bloody events of three years ago when Turnbull had methodically and without a qualm destroyed six years worth of work. Six years of struggle, of back-breaking toil, of failures followed by undreamed of success, all wiped out in five minutes of violence and bloodshed that Toad Turnbull probably did not even remember. He didn't figure that the Toad had taken merely twenty thousand dollars of his hard-earned money, he had also taken six years of Nat's life.

Even at that, Nat had come out of it better than his two friends and co-workers, both of whom had been gunned down in cold blood by Turnbull, almost as an after-thought. The memory of their two bullet-ridden bodies, which he had had to identify, raised, as always, a surging sickness in his stomach. With an angry gesture he threw the rest of his coffee on the ground, added a few more sticks to the low fire and wrapped his blanket around him. Then turning on his side, his pistol near at hand, he pulled his hat down over his face to sleep.

Far off he heard the faint, mournful howl of a coyote followed by a nervous snuffling of his horse. Remembering the origins of his dogged search for Toad Turnbull did little to help him sleep. Rather it got the old juices stirring, the hatred, the anger, the disappointment that once again he had been cheated of the chance to avenge his friends' lives and his own lost wealth. For three years now he had been following Turnbull's trail, sometimes getting so close that he could almost smell victory, but mostly just trying to fan life into old leads and vague rumors. Always he arrived at the scene too late, after the gang had struck and gotten away with their spoils. This one time he had expected to be there before them, ready to pounce when the villains did. And again, the quarry had slipped away.

Impatiently he turned onto his back, trying to get comfortable on the hard, rock ground. Tomorrow he would reach Greeley and take the train from there to Denver. With luck he would be in Fireweed in two days, there to pick up the strings of his other, more hopeful enterprise. And if all went as planned, who knows, but this one might prove the means to finishing off Toad Turnbull once and for all.

"Oh, Mr. Varien, I'm so sorry, but you see, you just *cannot* visit Miss Medora right now!"

Martha Higley twisted her red, bony hands in her long apron and looked anywhere but directly into Nat's eyes. "You see, she's very ill. She's been ill ever since she arrived. It's a terrible thing; but it happens sometimes, and we've got orders from Mr. Corchran himself that she can't see anybody at all. Only the doctor. He's the only one she's seen these four days."

Nat struggled to control the temper that made him want to take this homely woman by her scrawny neck and shake her like a chicken. He was dusty and tired from a very uncomfortable two-day train ride. He had arrived in Fireweed hoping to accomplish his business there and leave at once, only to be told that he couldn't see the one person he had come so far to find.

"Now, look here, Miss . . . whatever your name is—"

"Mrs. Higley. Martha Higley."

"Now, look here, Mrs. Higley. I've come a long way to see Miss Melindez. I have very important business with her, business that can't wait. It won't take very long, and then I'll be on my way. She can't be so sick that she's unable to speak to me for a few moments."

"Oh, but Mr. Varien, she can't speak at all! Her voice is gone completely. All she can do is whisper, and that so soft you can barely hear. The doctor says she mustn't strain even that much or she'll ruin that fine singing voice."

"What does she have? A cold?"

"A quinsy of the throat, Doc Peale says. A quinsy of the throat."

Nat's face darkened with rage. "Well, quinsy or not, she isn't going to die from spending a few minutes with me." He pushed past the anxious woman, who was trying to block his way on the narrow stairwell.

"But I can't allow that—"

Nat stopped and carefully clasped Miss Higley's shoulders, lifting her up and setting her down behind him. Then he went up the stairs of the Diamond Ring, two at a time with Martha hot on his heels.

At the top of the stairs he paused. "Which one is her room?"

96

Martha's mouth drew into a thin stubborn line. "I won't tell you."

"Then, I'll open them all." He went for the nearest one, about to jerk open the handle when Martha pulled at his arm.

"No, don't do that. Mr. Corchran won't like it! It's the last one down the hall. On the right."

Nat, who had a pretty good idea of what went on behind these doors and why Mr. Corchran might object to having interlopers burst in on his clientele, gave Martha a grim smile of triumph and headed for the last door. Almost in tears she followed behind.

"What am I going to say," she wailed. "I was supposed to keep everything quiet for her. You're the only one to act so bold, even with all the others so disappointed that she couldn't perform."

Nat paused by Ardeth's door and said more gently, "Don't worry about it, Mrs. Higley. I'll take all the blame."

"At least let me tell her you're coming in."

He thought that over. "All right. But no tricks now."

Glaring at him, Martha knocked quietly on the door and pushed it open. Nat followed her as she stepped inside and over to the bed, a big, ornate thing draped with a brightly patterned, quilted counterpane. Martha spoke quietly to the woman lying there, shrouded in the covers and shadowed by the crocheted hanging. He could almost feel the anxiety his presence produced in the invalid and for a moment wondered if perhaps Medora was not more ill than he had thought and he should have been more patient.

After what seemed an awfully long time merely for his presence to be explained, Martha finally turned and beckoned him forward. He stepped closer, nudging Martha aside, and peered down at the bed. His breath caught in his throat, and there was a strange leap in his chest, all of it completely unexpected and catching him by surprise.

A cloud of dark hair lay on the lacy pillow, framing a white face that might have been sculptured of alabaster. The cheeks had shrunk since that terrible afternoon in the hills, making her wide sapphire eyes appear even larger than they were. They stared up at him now, luminous with what, under other circumstances, he might have thought to be fear. Her beautiful, shapely lips were slightly parted and pale against her white skin. A single bright pink orb burned on either cheek, the result, no doubt, of her illness.

"Medora?" he said gently.

She nodded.

"It's Nat Varien, from the cabin, remember?"

Ardeth nodded again and mouthed a silent "yes."

"I'm sorry . . . I didn't realize you were so ill. . . ." He looked around at Martha, who made a smirk at his words.

"I tried to tell you," she whispered back.

Nat looked back at the woman he believed to be Medora Melindez lying on the bed. It burst upon his consciousness that she was absolutely the most beautiful creature he had ever seen. Nothing that afternoon after the robbery had led him to expect such loveliness or to dream that she would affect him so. It left him at a loss for words.

"I really hate to bother you," he mumbled. "Look, Mrs. Higley, could you leave us alone for a few minutes?"

"Well, I really don't think that would be wise."

"I won't stay long. I can see that Miss Melindez is very sick. Just give me a minute or two."

Martha bent to smooth the covers over Ardeth's still body. "What do you say, Miss Medora? Are you up to having this man talk at you?"

Ardeth closed her eyes and shook her head. "Go away," she mouthed, and gestured weakly at the door. "Later."

Nat moved uneasily from one foot to the other. His discomfort only reinforced Martha's conviction that she had been right in discouraging him in the first place.

"Really, Mr. Varien," she said brusquely. "This is too much for her. I tried to tell you it would be."

Nat rubbed at his chin. "All right. I suppose I could wait a little longer. Maybe she'll be better tomorrow."

Ardeth threw him a glance full of gratitude, then turned on her side with her back to both of them, pulling the covers up around her head. Her misery could almost be felt by her two visitors.

Setting his hat on his head, Nat smoothed the brim with his hand and took one last look at the unhappy figure on the bed. As he left the room he heard Martha, still bending over the patient, speaking in her low, motherly voice.

"I've brought you some good beef broth, Miss Medora. Come along now and take some. You need your strength if you're ever going to get well." When Ardeth did not respond, she turned to Nat, who was still standing by the door. "Won't touch a thing," she said in real distress. "She'll never get better if she won't eat. I declare, I don't know what to do!"

Nat shook his head in what he hoped appeared to be sympathy and stepped outside, closing the door behind him. He was gone only a moment when Ardeth turned back to Martha.

"Has he gone," she whispered in a raspy whisper.

"Mr. Varien? Oh, yes. He's gone. Now please, Miss Medora, won't you take a little of this broth?"

Ardeth shook her head. "No. Don't want any."

"Well, at least take your medicine. You must have it, Doc Peale says. He assured me it's very soothing to the throat."

Ardeth made a face but allowed Martha to raise her up enough to take a spoonful of dark green liquid in her mouth. Grimacing, she fell back on her pillows and turned her face toward the wall again.

"There, that's better," Martha said, appeased that her patient had at least downed the medicine. She fussed over the bed, smoothing the covers and patting the edges of the pillows. "Now, you just get a little sleep, Miss Medora. That will help you more than anything. I'll just leave your broth right here by the bed, and when you wake up, perhaps you'll feel like having a little."

Ardeth nodded lethargically and scrunched farther down under the covers. Her eyes were closed, but she could plainly hear Martha tiptoeing from the room and quietly closing the door behind her. She lay without moving for nearly five minutes longer, very still and quiet, just to make certain she was absolutely alone.

Had Martha been peeking through the keyhole, which she wasn't, she would have been shocked to see her weak, ailing patient suddenly sit up in the bed, throw off the covers and grab for the bowl of broth which she began wolfing down in a most unrefined manner. After taking as much of it as she could with the spoon, Ardeth tipped the bowl and drank the remainder down in great gulps, oblivious to the dribbles on her nightdress. In fact, she was so absorbed in consuming the last of the broth that at first she did not hear the scratching noises behind the curtains that were pulled across her windows. When it finally dawned on her that someone was working at the sash, it was too late. She dumped the bowl on the table and grabbed at the covers, pulling them up around her even as a long, booted leg was thrown over the sill. Drawing in her breath, she watched in horror as the rest of Nat Varien followed his boot, pushed aside the drapes and stepped inside her room. At the last moment she remembered not to cry out. Instead she lay back with the covers up over the lower half of her face and her eyes large as saucers as she stared at the man facing her across the room. He stood with his hands on his hips, his head cocked slightly to one side, and a frown dark as midnight on his face.

Without a word he walked over to the bed, his spurs jingling quietly. As he looked down at her, Ardeth slunk even farther under the covers, until all that was visible were her huge, dark eyes framed by a white, bloodless brow and a mass of black hair.

"All right. Who are you?"

When she did not move or answer, he reached down and yanked the covers back from her face. "Who are you?" he repeated. "And where is Medora?"

"I told you," Ardeth whispered in her raspy voice. But Nat was having none of that. He went on, keeping his voice low but horribly intense.

"Don't give me any of that crap about being halfway to death's door. You're not sick; you're scared shitless. I've been around frightened people long enough to know one when I see one. Now, what's going on here?"

Ardeth cringed away from him, but he reached out and grabbed her wrist, pulling her painfully back. "What have you done with Medora! Who's behind this? Tell me or I swear I'll—"

It was too much. All the pent up frustration and fear of the past four days roared to life like an ocean and swept her before it. Yanking away her wrist, she covered her face with her hands and burst into tears, her body wracked with deep, tearing sobs. Still conscious of the need for silence, she buried her face in the bed where the covers could muffle her cries.

Nat's anger was all at once transformed to guilt. He hadn't meant to be quite this terrifying; he only wanted to get at the truth. He sat on the bed, gingerly touching the cloud of raven hair that spilled over the white linens.

"Now, don't do that," he said quietly. "I'm not going to shoot you. I just want to know where Medora is and why you're pretending to be her."

"You'll tell the others," Ardeth cried through her sobs. "They're going to be so angry. . . ."

"Well, yes. I suppose they will be. Why have you let this go on so long anyway? You should have told them in the beginning."

Ardeth wiped at her cheeks with the sheet. "I know. I meant to, truly I did. It's just that it all kept getting so much bigger and so much worse. Every day I swore I'd confess, but somehow, they just wouldn't let me."

"You mean you just didn't want to."

She looked up at him with brimming eyes. His look was formidable, and yet there was a kindness there too, she suspected. The hand he laid on her shoulder was warm and firm, not abusive. But she knew that at last she was going to have to tell the truth—that he would see right through any lies she might concoct. It was somewhat of a relief.

"Here," Nat said more gently. "Sit up here and tell me everything. He reached for the bowl of broth to help her feel better and saw that it was licked clean.

"I see you felt more like eating once we both left," he commented dryly.

"I'm starving. I've had nothing but broth and crackers for three days. Pretending to be sick has been the worst part of all this."

He laughed. "Well, that's that much more reason to get it straightened out. Now, suppose you start at the beginning."

Ardeth wiped at her face with the edge of the coverlet and settled back, resigned to finally confessing the truth to someone. She had noticed by now that Nat was still speaking very quietly, and she kept her voice low as well. Might as well not bring Martha in on all this before she had to.

"Medora is dead," she said simply, noting Nat's start of surprise. "She died back there at that cabin, shot by your trigger-happy posse."

"So that's who the other woman was," Nat breathed. "But . . ."

"How did I get into her clothes? We were just playing around. I'd never seen such beautiful things, and when I admired them, she insisted I try them on. We were nearly the same size, so they fit me rather well. I was about to give them back when all the fighting broke out. After that there was never time. And then when Medora was hit, well, at first I was in such a state of shock that I didn't know what to say. Then when I realized that I had nothing—no money, no clothes, no tickets, no choice except to go back to Nebraska—and that everyone was so anxious to help her to go on to Fireweed, well . . ."

"You decided to take advantage of it."

"Honestly, I never would have thought of such a thing except that everyone seemed to think I *was* Medora Melindez. Even you."

"I know. Wearing her clothes, what else would anyone think." He frowned as an image of the woman in the bloody merino skirt and jacket forced itself into his mind. He barely remembered what she looked like except that she was far too shabbily dressed to be anyone important. Had he known she was Medora. . . .

The tears began to trickle down Ardeth's cheeks once more. "I never meant for it to go this far. I was going to tell Mr. Corchran the minute we got back here to the saloon, but there was never time. And when I realized they had made all these elaborate preparations for me to sing for them, I was never so terrified in my life. The only way out seemed to be to lose my voice."

"And you've been hiding in your room ever since." He shook his head. "Good God!"

"I know!" she wailed. "It was a monstrous deception! I wish I had never started it."

Impulsively Nat reached out and pulled her against him, his arm around her shoulder. Her raven hair spilled over his sleeve, and he was conscious of how fragile she felt next to him. He stroked her hair gently and let her cry it out. "How did you ever get the doctor to go along with this scheme? Bribery?"

"No," she said, wiping at her eyes. "He isn't a real doctor; he's only an apothecary. And he had drunk so much whisky he would have agreed with anything I suggested."

"Lucky for you. Well, I don't suppose you've really done anything so wrong when you come right down to it. You haven't spent Medora's money. You haven't even worn her clothes unless this flimsy thing is hers."

Ardeth nodded and pulled the soft cambric nightdress close around her throat. "I didn't have mine, so I had to use hers. But that's all. Nothing else."

The crying had eased. Nat suspected it had been more the climax of four days of fretting and fear than anything else. He was beginning to enjoy the comfortable feeling of her head nestling in the hollow of his shoulder and the softness of her hair beneath his hand. "It must have been mighty tempting all these elegant things just waiting for Medora, and her dead back there in Colorado."

"I'm ashamed to say that it was," Ardeth admitted, sitting back and wiping at her cheeks with her sleeve. "Where I come from no one has anything like these beautiful clothes and all this jewelry. Not to mention all that money."

"How much money?" Nat said absently.

"Nearly two hundred dollars. A fortune!"

He laughed. "It may seem like a fortune to you, but believe me, it would not seem so to many people. All the same, the first lesson you should learn from this, young lady, is never to attempt to pull off a fraud unless you have the audacity to see it through."

Ardeth pulled away from him and sat back against

106

the pillows, drawing the covers back up around her chest. "I suppose you're right, but I never really thought through what I was doing. It all just sort of fell in place around me, so I went along. Then it got so deep I just didn't know how to extract myself."

Nat got up from the bed and walked across the room to the armoire, where he fingered some of the dresses hanging there. Ardeth, more calm now, watched him, wondering when he was going to go to the door and summon Corchran and the others to tell them of her deceit. It was not a happy thought.

"Did you know Medora?" she asked. "Is that how you recognized I wasn't her?"

"I never met her in my life. We did . . . correspond. And I knew something about her. That she had a reputation as a performer, that she was coming west to entertain in the yokel cow towns like this one, and that she was known to be no better than she ought to be. But that's not how I knew that you weren't her. Back there at the cabin, it never crossed my mind. I was preoccupied with trying to move on to catch Toad Turnbull, and all I wanted was to clear up and get out of there. It wasn't until I walked into this room and saw you lying on that bed. . ." he hesitated. "You were too young. Medora had to have a lot more years on her than you have." No need to say that the youthful beauty that had taken his breath away simply did not fit a woman with a past like Medora Melindez's. "And you were too frightened. I knew something wasn't right, but I couldn't figure it out. When I left I scouted the outside of this building and saw that I could get back in through that window and maybe get some answers. So, I did it."

"And now you know," Ardeth said, her voice weary with discouragement. "I suppose the next thing is for you to call in Mr. Corchran and let me confess all. I hope he doesn't insist on sending me to jail!"

Nat walked around the room, taking in the jars and colognes on the table near the washstand, looking through the shelves of the wardrobe, rummaging lightly among the stacks of shoes and hats, and pulling out some of the drawers in the chest. When he reached the side of the bed again, he pulled up a chair and straddled it, resting his arms on the back and appraising Ardeth quizzically.

"What's the matter?" she asked, uncomfortable under his intense scrutiny.

Nat rubbed his fingers along his chin. "Nothing. I was just thinking . . . you know, when you come right down to it, it wasn't such a harebrained idea for you to take Medora's place, knowing she was dead. In fact, it was rather clever of you."

Ardeth's eyes widened. "You really think so? But it was wrong."

"Well, it could have been had you left town suddenly with all her belongings. But you didn't, and now, here you are in a very interesting situation."

"That may be what you call it," she exclaimed. "I call it desperate!"

"Yes, but it has possibilities. And some of them are kind of intriguing."

She eyed him with a sudden new suspicion. "What are you getting at? And why should you care?" Out of the blue she suddenly recalled something he had said to her back at the cabin. "What was your interest in Medora anyway?"

"I told you. We corresponded." When he saw that her sudden distrust was only deepening, he grinned at her, a disarming grin that had an unsettling effect on Ardeth's efforts to remain objective. "The truth is Medora and I had a business arrangement. She wrote me that she had something of value that I might be interested in purchasing. I wrote her back that indeed I was interested. We agreed that when she came to Fireweed she would bring it with her and I would take possession, after relieving myself of a very large sum of money."

"So that's what you meant by your strange questions that afternoon at the cabin. I didn't know what you were talking about."

"That was obvious, but I credited it to the shock of everything you had been through."

"And what was it she was bringing you? She never said anything to me about it."

"It's a map. An old, antique map. I'm interested in antiques, you see."

Ardeth regarded him coolly. "I find that hard to believe."

"Well, for now that's explanation enough. I don't suppose you came across such a map when you were rummaging through Medora's things?" he asked hopefully.

"No. Nor nothing like it. But I haven't 'rummaged,' as you so politely put it. I've hardly gone through anything that's here. In fact, I could barely bring myself to touch anything that belonged to her, I felt so sick over the way things turned out." Her eyes widened. "Wait. Now I understand. You haven't called Mr. Corchran yet because you want time to go through everything in this room. That's it, isn't it?"

Nat shrugged and abandoned the chair to roam around the room again. "I admit it's a tempting thought. Especially since I can't really be certain Medora didn't tell other people about the map too. It would not be beyond what I know of her character. She liked money, you see."

"Well, having had very little of it in my lifetime, I can understand that. But she was kind to me, Mr. Varien, on the train and while we waited in that cabin. No one could have been kinder."

"I never said she wasn't kind. Just that she liked money."

All at once he turned and moved back to the bed, sitting casually on the corner and speaking softly. "Look here, Miss — what is your real name, anyway?"

"Ardeth. Ardeth Royce."

"Well, Miss Royce, I think that before we call in Mr. Corchran and turn all this right side up we should consider some alternatives. I need time to look through Medora's belongings for that map. It is very, very important that I find it before it falls into anyone else's hands. You, on the other hand, obviously began all this by wanting to live for a little

110

while as Medora lived. You wanted to share in all the good things she had. And it's not that you're taking them from her. She has no use for them anymore."

"That's how I reasoned four days ago, and look where it got me."

"Yes, but you were alone then. I hardly know you, but it's obvious to me that you would never be able to carry this off by yourself. However, with my help. . . ."

"Oh, now wait a minute," Ardeth cried, throwing off the covers and leaping off the opposite side of the bed so that its high mattress was between them. "You can't seriously believe I can go on with this. The guilt alone has made me ill."

"I know," Nat said soothingly. "That's because you are obviously a good, decent girl who means no one any harm. But wouldn't you prefer a little guilt to going back to—where was it, Nebraska? Or maybe to jail? Look at all this, Ardeth. For a little while you can be Medora, wearing her beautiful clothes and jewels, buying any trinkets you might desire. Living in luxury and comfort—"

"And what about singing! I know two or three lullabies. How can I perform in front of all these people? It's a crazy idea."

Very carefully Nat walked around the bed, took her hands and gently sat her down next to him. "That would be the hardest part. But we can go on pretending you've lost your voice at least until I can come up with something. Meanwhile, I'll have a chance to search for that map."

111

"And when you've found it? What happens then? You disappear, leaving me to face the wrath of half the town of Fireweed."

He squeezed her fingers. "No, I promise you I won't do that. I'll help you leave Fireweed as Medora, and when you're out of sight, you can give it all up and become yourself again. Medora Melindez will have vanished from the face of the earth. And Ardeth Royce will go on her way, having earned, say, four hundred dollars to finance her future."

"Four hundred. . . ! Where will you get that kind of money?"

"I told you I came prepared to buy that map from Medora. That's what it would have cost me. I'll gladly give it to you instead once I have the map in my hand."

Ardeth tried to pull her hands away, but they were clasped firmly in his. "I don't know. It just doesn't seem right."

Nat moved closer, his body warming to the delectable sight of the shadowed cleavage that disappeared below the lace edge of her gown. She had the whitest skin of any girl he had ever seen. And the softest . . .

He got a grip on himself. This was business, and it would be foolish to ruin it now with feelings that did not belong here. "It does you credit, Miss Royce, to worry so much about right and wrong. But there really isn't any wrong being done here. We're only trying to gain a little time by not telling everyone that Medora is dead."

Ardeth broke away from him and paced the floor near the bed. "But how can I do it, Mr. Varien? I can't go down there and pretend I'm Medora, even without my voice. I'll give myself away in a thousand gestures. I would have already except that they thought I was so ill. I don't think I can do it."

"I think you can, with my help. We'll work on it up here, and when you're ready, I'll be with you every step of the way. All you have to do is believe in yourself, relax and have fun."

"Fun! I feel as though I'll be treading over Medora's grave every minute."

"Forget Medora—at least, in that way. From what I know of her, she seemed to be the kind of woman who would have reveled in something like this."

"But she was an actress. A singer. I was brought up to think they were the loosest of women."

Nat laughed. "They often are." He caught Ardeth as she passed him and pulled her back down on the bed, laying one arm comfortably around her shoulder. "The truth is, you are a beautiful woman, Miss Royce. All you have to do is stand on that stage and look like yourself. If you croak on a few songs, no one will care. If the crowd gets rowdy, just show them an ankle. It'll be easy."

Ardeth barely heard what he was saying. No one had ever called her beautiful before, and she was lost in the pleasure of it. Then she felt Nat gripping her shoulder and looked back into his lean, square face.

"Will you do it?"

"You'll really be there beside me, all the way?"

113

"All the way. We'll say I'm your, let's see, your manager. That will give me reason enough to hang around all the time. You won't make a move without me."

"Well . . . all right. For four hundred dollars I suppose I could pretend to be the queen of England!"

"That's my girl!" Impulsively he leaned forward and kissed her lightly on the lips. Then he sat back and deliberately let go of her. "Now that everything is arranged, let's get to work."

Ardeth realized her fingers were lightly touching her mouth, relishing the sweetness of his lips against hers. Shaking herself, she brought her attention back to the moment. "Work? What do you mean?"

"You get back under those covers and set yourself to remembering everything you can about how Medora spoke, talked, moved, and acted. The closer you can come to looking and sounding like her, the better."

Ardeth climbed back on the bed. "And what are you going to be doing?"

Nat had already thrown back the doors to the wardrobe. "Me? I'm going to start looking for that map!"

Chapter Six

As it turned out, Nat was so worried that Martha might return suddenly and find him in Ardeth's room that he only made a cursory search before leaving through the window again. Ardeth lay on the bed long after he had departed, thinking through his amazing proposal. It was an exciting prospect and one that she felt offered no hurt to anyone, provided she could carry it off. And with his help she began to be more certain that she could.

Nat returned later that afternoon, this time arriving by the door with Martha hard on his heels. Barging into her room, he proceeded to take charge.

"This woman is ill because she's had nothing but baby's food for four days. Bring her a decent meal and quickly."

Martha looked desperately at Ardeth, wringing her hands. "You'll kill her, Mr. Varien. Doc Peale said—"

"I don't care what Doc Peale said. I say she needs

food. How is she going to get well starving to death?"

"Do you want something to eat, my dear?" Martha asked Ardeth, bending over her on the bed. Ardeth nodded weakly. "All right, but if she dies, Nat Varien, her blood will be on your hands!"

She hurried from the room, leaving Nat and Ardeth to smile at each other like two conspirators. He sat on the bed and spoke quietly. "I've already ordered supper for you. A small beefsteak, oyster soup, lemon pudding and a glass of beer."

"It sounds heavenly, except for the beer."

"It'll thicken your blood. Now, were you able to recall anything about Medora that will help?"

"Yes, I gave it a lot of thought. Her voice and her gestures were a little theatrical, exaggerated. Not much, but more than the average person's."

"That was because of her profession."

"But she also had a dignity about her that I think I can imitate. I even practiced her walk and her arm movements. That shouldn't be too difficult. It's the singing I'm afraid of, and standing up in front of all those people."

He patted her arm. "Don't worry, I have an idea of how to handle that. I'll speak to Corchran tonight and tell him you've decided that because you're ill you need me as a manager. Most of the entertainers who come through these towns have them. I can't think why Medora didn't unless she didn't want to bother."

116

"You don't suppose she had one who will turn up, do you? If that happens, we'd better leave town in a hurry."

"We'll have to take that chance, though I think if there was one in the picture we'd have seen him before now. I also think you'd better plan on making an appearance downstairs tomorrow. Say, for supper. It's time you met your public."

Ardeth felt the blood drain from her face. "Oh, dear . . ."

"Don't worry, I'll be right there with you. But you have to get better sometime, and it might as well be sooner as later."

"But my voice?"

"Oh, you won't get that back for several more days. That will give me time to work out my plan and also allow me to do all the talking. Think you can handle that?"

There was a brisk knock at the door as it was pushed open, and Martha came bustling in bearing a tray covered with a large white napkin. Ardeth nodded up at Nat and could not suppress a smile as Martha set the tray on her lap. The napkin was lifted up, and the delicious odors of steaming soup and fried steak took her breath away.

"I'd better be going," Nat said. "You stay and see that she does justice to that meal, Martha."

But Martha was already beaming as she watched Ardeth dig into the food.

117

* * *

By the next afternoon Ardeth had practiced Medora's movements alone in her room so thoroughly that she felt certain she could make them seem authentic. In spite of her confidence, as the evening hour approached she had so many butterflies in her stomach that at times she felt almost ill. At four-thirty Martha appeared to help her dress, bearing orders from Nat as to how she should look down to the smallest detail.

"That corset shouldn't be so tight," she fussed, lacing Ardeth up at the bedpost. "Anyone who has been as sick as you doesn't need to be trussed up like a chicken ready for the oven!"

"It will help me get through the evening," Ardeth mumbled, struggling to breathe in the confines of bone and lace that fashion required. Next came the bustle frame, the petticoats and then the yards of ribboned silk in shimmering shades of cornflower blue, and a necklace of rhinestones with a choker of pearls, all of it set off with a delicately worked white lace shawl. Martha proved to be more of a hair dresser than a nurse as she piled up Ardeth's black hair in curls, rolls and puffs and deftly placed two small rhinestone fan-shaped ornaments where they added just the right touch.

Ardeth stood in front of the long, framed mirror, hardly daring to believe she was actually seeing a reflection of herself. When she heard a brisk rap on the door, she turned, her hand at her throat, and

118

waited for Nat's reaction. It was all she had hoped for.

He stood, mouth open, astonished. Seeing her as she had been before—disheveled and shocked at the cabin; lying pale and distressed on her bed—had not prepared him at all for the transformation brought about by a beautiful dress, a flattering hairdo and the adornment of shimmering jewels. She was simply the loveliest thing he had ever seen, and his heart turned over at the sight of her. But he was careful after the first shock not to let his admiration show too much.

She gave him a brilliant smile. "What do you think?" she mouthed, twirling the long train of her skirt and turning her shoulders from one side to the other.

He rubbed at his chin in a characteristic gesture. "You'll do," he said casually and offered her his arm. "Ready?"

She nodded but leaned on his arm to help support her knees which had suddenly gone a little weak. Giving Martha a last grateful smile, she let him lead her out into the hall where they paused briefly at the top of the stairs. Nat gripped her hand. "Remember, I'll do all the talking. You just smile and nod and look beautiful."

"I will," she whispered back, feeling a slight flush at his compliment. The stairs yawned before her like a descent into hell, the place she felt sure to be sent for the trick she was about to play on the men of

119

Fireweed. But it was no use thinking such thoughts now. She had made her choice, and now she must see it through. Besides, it might even be fun!

They had not reached the last steps before the people in the saloon began crowding around her. She recognized the rotund, beaming countenance of Jasper Corchran right away. Several of the other faces pressing in on her were familiar, but she could not recall their names. Jasper elbowed the crowd aside and stood at the bottom of the stairs, reaching for her hand which he pressed to the lips that were hidden under his huge moustache.

"The divine Miss Medora," he intoned. "How wonderful to see you back on your feet and among us. Oh, I know you still have not regained the use of your voice much to our sorrow, but just to see you looking so well again is comfort enough for now. Come, let me lead you in to supper. . . ."

Ardeth shot Nat a worried glance, but he only smiled and handed her over to Corchran, who led her across the crowded room to the other side where a round table covered with a white linen cloth waited in an alcove. Ardeth nodded and smiled and mouthed "thank you" to the men who were swept along in her wake. Though the table was set for six, it appeared that the whole mob was going to crowd into the alcove alongside her. At the last minute most of them fell back, leaving Ardeth, Nat and Jasper Corchran to take their seats. Three other men filled the remaining chairs, all of them familiar to Ardeth from the day she arrived. As Corchran introduced them to Nat, she made a mental note of their names; Lucius Clay who owned the one and only bank in town, stocky, tanned Sheriff Meeker, and Aloyicius Fradin who ran the general store. Clay was a balding, shrewd-eyed fellow who barely came to Nat's shoulders yet exuded an air of confidence that came from the knowledge that when he stood on his money he was the tallest fellow in the room. Fradin, on the other hand, was pale and freckled and meek, as though he spent too much time among the goods in his store and not enough time out in the sun. Aside from Sheriff Meeker, he was the quietest man at the table, but Jasper Corchran and Banker Clay more than made up for his reticence.

In a very short time Ardeth began to feel more at ease. Since she was not supposed to talk, she could sit back and allow Nat to carry the burden of conversation while she examined the saloon spread out before her just outside the curtained alcove where they ate their dinner. It was so noisy, what with all the loud conversation, occasional arguments and eternal thumping of a piano, that she was grateful she did not have to try to talk above the din. She had not expected quite so many people either. It was early evening, yet the place was alive with people milling about. Farmers in dingy smocks nursed their drinks; cowboys who bore the odors of leather and horse embedded in their clothes sat at the tables or stood along the bar. Among them moved youngish men in dapper plaid waistcoats and spats, smart-fitting coats and large Spanish-style hats. These, Corchran informed her right off, were the gamblers and card sharks who roamed the saloons of the West looking for easy marks. Moving among the crowds of men were several women, most of them young in years but with ages of experience in their faded eyes and worn faces. They wore long skirts and tight-fitting blouses, and their hair was braided or roped high upon their heads. Occasionally one or two of them would move to the center of the room in a small space surrounded by the tables where they would dance lethargically to the thumping of the piano. More often, Ardeth noticed wonderingly, they would wander up the stairs to the rooms above, hand-in-hand with one of the cowboys or local patrons. Corchran pointed out a few of them to her, those with names like Billy, Roxie, Bertha and Dakota Lil.

"They come and go, you know," he said in a quiet, conspiratorial voice. "We can't keep 'em long. They're always looking for a better stake somewhere. It's just as well, though. If they're around too long, they get diseased, and then you've got nothin' but a parcel of trouble."

Nat caught Corchran's remarks even though the genial saloon keeper meant them for Ardeth's ears only. He threw Corchran a severe glance. "Remember you're speaking to a lady," he said without smiling.

Jasper shrugged. "I'm sure Miss Medora's been around enough saloons in her day to know whereof I speak. Haven't you Medora?"

Ardeth nodded with enthusiasm. "Oh, yes," she mouthed, even though she was not really certain what Corchran was talking about. The truth was she was so filled with the overpowering sensations of the saloon and so comfortable from the heavy meal and the heady wine that she could not think straight. The table groaned under its load of dishes, each one more delicious than the last. The clink of the cutlery, the cresting and ebbing noises of the many voices around them, the tinkling of the piano, and the occasional holler from an aggrieved card player were all such an assault on her senses that it was difficult to concentrate on anything.

They were halfway through the dessert course when applause suddenly cascaded through the room. Ardeth looked up in surprise at the bare stage near their table and saw that an entertainer had appeared, bowing to the raucous catcalls and clapping in the saloon. He had some kind of hand instrument under his arm which he pulled out and began yanking back and forth, singing an accompaniment which was lost under the noises of the audience.

"For God's sake, Jasper," Banker Clay intoned, thrusting his spoon into a bowl of blancmange. "Couldn't you have found someone better than a

123

hurdy-gurdy player to entertain Miss Medora. You'll have her thinking we're a bunch of yokels!"

"I kind of like hurdy-gurdy music," Fradin said in his slow, quiet way. "And besides, we are yokels, aren't we? Fireweed is a long way from Denver."

"That fellow still owes me twenty dollars," Corchran exclaimed. "Until he's paid it, he'll work it off, even if he's drummed off the stage."

"The way he butchers that poor instrument, he may well be drummed out of town. Seems like you could have found something more refined for Miss Melindez. Especially on her first night down after being so sick," Clay complained.

Sheriff Meeker toyed with his spoon over his dessert. "Have you ever played Denver, Miss Medora?" he asked, his shrewd eyes on Ardeth's pale face. She looked quickly at Nat.

"No," he answered for her. "Medora has not played many towns out West at all yet. Fireweed is almost the first. Her reputation was made back in St. Louis. However, we anticipate that before she is through she will be as famous west of the Mississippi as she is east of it."

"I don't doubt that she will be," Meeker added. Ardeth gave him her warmest smile but inwardly felt her blood run a little colder. The hurdy-gurdy player was having a hard time of it up there on that stage. Though he gamely went on performing, his voice was lost in the increasing uproar of the audience. When a bottle went flying through the air and creased his hat, knocking it to the back of the stage, the saloon erupted with hilarious laughter and catcalls. The miserable performer slunk off the stage while Ardeth's hand went to her throat, fingering her choker.

"What this town needs is a real professional entertainer," Nat said, leaning back in his chair and fingering the watch fob in his coat pocket. "You'll show them, won't you, Medora, once you get your voice back?"

Ardeth shot him a stinging glance. It was all too clear to her that she herself might be slinking off that stage in a few days. Would these barbarians throw whisky bottles at a woman, she wondered. She wouldn't put it past them.

"Why, we had a Shakespearean fellow through here just a few weeks ago," Fradin said. "He performed in the barn over by the livery stable 'cause Corchran here wouldn't allow him in the Diamond Ring."

"Can you see this crowd listening to that gibberish!" Corchran said with great feeling. "I'd lose half my custom."

"He wasn't half bad, though I found him hard to follow. All those 'thees' and 'thous' and words you never heard of before. Bad as reading from the Bible."

"Don't blaspheme, Aloyicius," Banker Clay intoned. "I, for one, think Fireweed ought to have more culture. In the long run it'll attract more decent folks and less riffraff like those cowpokes who shoot up the place every Saturday night."

"Those cowpokes are the life's blood of this town," said Meeker quietly. "Until the railroad started shipping cattle from here, we were nothin'."

"Well, sometimes I wish we had stayed that way," Banker Clay mumbled.

"That's kind of a strange comment coming from a man who has made a lot of money from those shipments," the sheriff observed.

There was an undercurrent in the conversation that grew increasingly sharper. Ardeth glanced nervously at Nat while Jasper Corchran picked up the wine bottle and began refilling glasses.

"Now, now," he said soothingly. "We've all made money on those cattle drives, hard as they are on Fireweed. They put money in the bank, bring money into the saloon, sell goods from the store and give you, Sheriff Meeker, more to do than sit around watching the dust settle. I think we can all be grateful for them."

"Did you know there is one on the way?" Meeker asked, still toying with his spoon. "Ought to arrive within the next few days if I calculate correctly. I heard it's about three thousand head, up from San Antonio."

"Well, Miss Medora. That ought to give you a first-hand look at what the West is really like," said Corchran, still all geniality. Ardeth clutched her choker and tried to smile. "And you too, Mr. Varien," Corchran went on.

"I'm afraid I may miss the fun," Nat answered. "I have to go to Abilene for a few days tomorrow. Too bad."

"Maybe they'll still be here when you get back," Meeker drawled. "These 'celebrations' tend to drag on awhile. After the long trek those fellows have endured, they like to have a chance to blow off steam."

"And spend their money," Fradin added.

A loud fracas erupted across the saloon, noisy enough to distract the people at the table. Cochran stood and peered across. "Looks like that Shannessy is at it again," he muttered. "He's one of our more notorious local drunks, Miss Medora. Usually he's pretty quiet, but if somebody says something he takes as an insult, his temper blows sky high. Don't know how much damage I've had to repair in here because of his outbursts. You'll excuse me a moment. . . ."

He bustled off across the room where a crowd had already gathered, eager for the sport. Nat took the opportunity to jump up and mutter Medora's apologies. She was looking white and tired, and it seemed the evening had been long and successful enough not to risk a faux-pas at this point. Ardeth smiled and nodded all around as she allowed Nat to lead her from the alcove and across the room to the stairs, carefully avoiding the crowd nearer the door. In the darkened hall upstairs, lit fitfully by one gas lamp near the stairwell, he hurried her to her door, making sure there was no one about. Though they could hear the dim undercurrent of voices in one or two of the rooms they passed, no one was in sight. Ardeth thought perhaps Martha might be waiting inside her room to help her undress, but when they entered and lit the kerosene lamp on the table near the bed, the room was empty. She was both surprised and glad that Nat stepped in with her, closing and locking the door behind them.

"What do you mean you're going to Abilene!" she said furiously, whirling on him.

"For God's sake, keep your voice down. Who knows what can be heard through these walls."

Ardeth lowered her voice, but her anger still made her words intense. "You can't go off and leave me here by myself. You promised you'd be right with me. You said you'd stand behind me all the way. I'll never be able to—"

He stopped her words with his lips, grasping her shoulders and pulling her to him with an intensity to match her own. She was so surprised for a moment she did not react. Then the sensation of his mouth burrowing in on hers sent her senses reeling. His hands tightened painfully on her shoulders, then slipped up to her neck, then to frame her face. Still his kiss went on, drawing the breath from her body. When he finally drew back a little, allowing her to breathe, his hands still framing her face, her knees had grown so weak she could hardly stand.

"I've been wanting to do that all night," he whispered, seeking her lips once more, drinking of their sweet nectar. Ardeth felt herself swept along on a rising warmth she had never experienced before. Only dimly did she recall that this was not what she wanted from Nat Varien right now. She slid her hands up his chest, splaying them against his coat, and shoved him away.

"You're just trying to distract me!" she accused under her breath.

He grinned at her, a smile so full of mischief and gaiety that her heart turned over. "I guess you could say that."

"Well, it won't work. Why are you leaving? Are you abandoning me here? What will I do . . . how will I manage. . . ."

"I'm not abandoning you," Nat said gently, slipping his arms around her waist. "I'm going to Abilene to help you, and I won't be gone more than two days at the most. Trust me, Medora . . . Ardeth . . . whatever your name is!"

Ardeth felt some of her fear and anger slipping away. His body was so close she could feel the firm contours against her. His arms were strong and hard. "But if I have to go through another dinner like this one tonight, how will I manage? And if they make me sing. . . ."

"They can't make you sing until you're ready. You still don't have a voice, remember? And you won't have one until after I get back. As for another dinner, well, you did beautifully tonight. You might have had me convinced you were Medora if I didn't know better. You look the part, your gestures were just right and you even seemed confident most of the time. As long as you can't talk, you'll do fine."

Ardeth was finding it increasingly difficult to concentrate on Nat's words with his lips gently coursing her cheeks and neck and his hands lightly stroking her back. "But it was so wild down there. That drunken brawl . . . and the way they jeered that hurdy-gurdy player. . . ."

Nat searched out her earlobe, tasting it, darting into the darkened cavity of her ear. His blood surged with warmth as he explored the planes and lines of her face. "It's a typical saloon. You must have seen many like it in St. Louis."

"I've never been in St. Louis," Ardeth breathed, floating on the sweet sensation of his skilled hands and tongue.

"I forgot. . . ."

He reached behind her neck and began to unfasten her pearl choker, his fingers lightly tickling her skin. It slipped to the floor, and he worked at the clasp of the rhinestone necklace.

"I think Martha is supposed to come in and help me . . . undress. . . ."

Nat bent to lick the softness of her throat. "She's not coming. I told her not to bother."

"It's not going to be easy getting out of all this."

His hands were already working at the tiny but-

130

tons at the back of her bodice. "Perhaps I can help."

Ardeth laughed throatily, carried along on the easy grace of the sensations he aroused in her. She felt the release of the tight bodice as the buttons came undone and let her body go slack, allowing him to do what he wanted with her. He lifted the bodice free and dropped it on the floor, giving a start of surprise at the sight of the swelling fullness below the lace edge of her chemise. It was cut low to reveal the shadowed cleavage that dipped beneath the cambric, framed on either side by the round globes of her breasts, the hard, taut nipples visible through the thin fabric.

"You're beautiful . . ." he breathed, burying his head in the fullness of her breasts and lightly tasting their softness. Ardeth gave a shudder, weak in his arms as he kissed every inch of exposed skin and nudged aside the cloth edges to go deeper. She felt his hips thrusting against her, his male hardness swelling into her skirt. His hands slipped to her waist where he deftly unfastened the yards of blue silk, allowing them to fall down around her feet. The petticoats followed until she was standing there, upheld by his firm grasp, wearing only her chemise, corset and pantaloons. Nat lifted her, light as down, and pulled her from the swath of silk and cambric on the floor. Her arms slid around his shoulders as she felt herself cradled in his arms, and for the first time, she kissed him back, her lips

131

lingering on his own.

Silently he carried her across the room and laid her gently on the bed. So warm and deliciously content, Ardeth stretched her arms above her head and arched her back like a cat waking from its nap. Sitting beside her, Nat ran his hands up and down her sides while she lay limp in his arms. Very slowly he slid the edge of her chemise downward just above the darkened areola of her left breast. Then bending over her, he began to circle with his tongue, lightly working away the cloth until the nipple rose upward, joyously encircled by his lips. Ardeth groaned, moving languidly beneath him as he deftly sucked and darted on the growing fire of her breast. His fingers gently kneaded it until she was consumed by such heat that a suppressed cry broke from her. Growing more inflamed himself, Nat pushed down the cambric, freeing both her breasts for his increasingly fiercer use. Then, wanting this moment to last longer, he forced himself to go easier and more slowly. He turned her over on the bed and worked away the laces of her corset, throwing it aside.

"I don't know how you women ever learn to wear these things," he muttered, turning her over again to unfasten her chemise and throw it after the corset. Ardeth tried to answer but was diverted as she felt his hands slide down her waist, over her hips and along her thighs. The fire within her was becoming a consuming torrent as Nat's hands slid between her legs, working upward to clasp her where the heat was most intense, gently massaging. Even through the thin cloth she writhed beneath his hands. When he fastened on her breast with his mouth, at the same time working his fingers into her body, she felt carried along on a whirlwind, bound for the stars.

She was not aware of how he got out of his clothes. All she knew was the sensation of her last piece of clothing being pushed down and off her legs, leaving her to lie naked on the bed. Then Nat was over her, kissing her wildly, thrusting her legs apart, his arms tight around her body, and there was this hardness entering her, thrusting upward over and over while they both gasped and groaned and flew above the world until the whole universe erupted in such bliss as she never knew was possible.

Ecstasy eased, carried on the wave of satisfaction, leaving her limp and weak on the sands of fulfillment. She lay with his arms tight around her, listening to his breathing slowly subside as her own pounding heart grew quiet.

When she could speak, she murmured in his ear, "I always wondered what it would be like to make love, but I never dreamed it was this wonderful."

Nat chuckled and rolled onto his side, carrying her with him in his arms. "Why, that was just the basics. There's lots more."

Ardeth ran her finger lightly down his dark

133

cheek. "How could there be more?"

"Take my word for it. I'll teach you all about it."

"When you get back from Abilene?"

He took her face between his hands and kissed the softness of her lips, the hollows of her cheeks, her eyelids, his lips making light traces on her skin that sent shudders of pleasure along her spine. "Don't be angry about that. If it works out as I think it might, you'll be glad I went. Trust me."

How could she not? She was like putty in his skilled hands. She couldn't even think straight, he created such turmoil of delight and anticipation within her. Abruptly she pulled away from him and sat up in the bed, yanking the sheet up under her armpits and encircling her knees with her arms. "Look at my clothes strewn all over the floor! What on earth will Martha think when she comes in here in the morning?"

"She'll think you're no better than you ought to be," Nat said dryly. "And why shouldn't she. After all, Medora was no Sunday School teacher. I think Martha won't even be surprised."

Ardeth caught her long hair and pulled it back behind her neck to trail down her back. Nat reached out to stroke its wavy thickness as she shook it out. "But that's terrible! My reputation. . . ."

"It's no more than people expect of saloon entertainers," he said, lifting her hair to kiss the back of her neck. Waves of pleasure coursed through her.

134

She reached back and lifted her hair as he bent over her. The sheet fell away and her back arched, lifting her full, ripe breasts as Nat reached around to cup them in his hands.

"Oh, dear . . ." Ardeth sighed as he gently worked her breasts in his fingers. "Oh, my goodness. . . ."

"Goodness has nothing to do with it," Nat whispered in her ear as he sat up behind her, his knees on either side of her hips, his hands cupping her breasts as his lips pushed away her long hair to kiss her neck, her ears, her throat, her shoulders. His hands slipped around her waist, and he pulled her against his hard body.

"And now, for my next lesson . . ." he said, quietly chuckling.

Chapter Seven

When Ardeth woke the following morning, Nat was gone. It was not until an hour later that she learned that he had left Fireweed for Abilene before dawn without saying goodby, but she was still basking in such a warm, lazy glow of satisfaction from the night before that she could not be angry even at what she still considered his desertion.

She had planned to spend the time he was gone "ill" in her room, but she soon found she was far too happy to stay so confined. She ordered Martha to make her up a hot bath in her room—a great luxury when she might have gone down the street to the public bathhouse—and then dressed in one of Medora's more sober but stylish gowns. She had Martha pile her hair in a chenille net leaving wavy tendrils to frame her face, touched up her cheeks and lips lightly enough to bring out their natural color, put on a straw hat decked with artificial daisies, tucked the handle of a ruffled sunshade under her arm and sallied forth below.

The saloon was almost as busy in the early hours

of the afternoon as it had been the evening before. The youngest and handsomest of the professional card hustlers, a dapper man named Owen Salter, tipped his hat to her politely.

"Glad to see you about, Miss Melindez," he said in a thick Southern drawl. "Ah do hope you're feeling well."

Ardeth smiled and mouthed a "thank you." Awkward as it was not to be able to talk, it was far better than being scheduled to sing before Nat got back, and she was determined to keep up the pretense of a sore throat until then.

"Are you sure you ought to be up, Miss Melindez," Eddie Lathrop, the piano player at the saloon, asked as she passed him on her way to the door. Ardeth gave him a wan smile and nodded, forcing herself to appear as if she was struggling against weariness when she actually felt like skipping and dancing. Eddie was a thin fellow with a permanent stubble of gray on his jutting chin. He ran to push open the door for her, and she stepped out into the bright sunshine. It was her first view of Fireweed outside the saloon since the day she arrived, and the glare of the dusty street and reflection of the whitewashed buildings on the other side almost forced her back inside the Diamond Ring. Ardeth paused, her hand over her eyes.

"You oughten to be up like this," Eddie said solicitously and helped her open her sunshade. "If there's something you need, I can get it for you."

137

Ardeth shook her head and mouthed, "It's all right." Leaving the piano player by the door, she started off down the wooden walk toward Kenneth's Dry Goods. There were not as many people on the street as there had been inside the saloon, but she recognized one or two: Sheriff Meeker, who always seemed to be hovering on the edge of things, and the dark, cadaverous form of Baskin Sawyer, the town undertaker, who politely tipped his hat to her. There was the occasional cowboy, his spurs jingling as he walked with seemingly permanent bowed legs, and several women in poke bonnets and calico dresses who pointedly ignored her even when she gave them a friendly smile. Three young boys in smocks and flat "pancake" hats ran up and down the walkway shooting each other with mock guns, and one little girl in a dirty apron sat in front of the dry goods store playing with a homemade cloth doll.

When she walked through the door of the dry goods store, Kenneth Dabney looked up from the back where he was stacking bales of fabric and came forward to meet her, obviously pleased. There were two other women browsing near the rear of the store who, when they saw her approaching, turned their backs and concentrated mightily on their purchases. It seemed a curious response to Ardeth, who up until then had been fawned over and coddled by all she met. But Dabney more than made up for their coolness by hovering over her while she selected a few purchases.

She was just reaching into her reticule to pay for her selections when there was a loud uproar outside in the street. Horses came pounding down the main road, raising clouds of dust, urged on by their riders who were whooping and shouting. Ardeth had only just looked questioningly at Dabney when guns began to roar.

"Everybody, down!" Dabney hollered as the women in the store ducked behind the counters. Surprised, Ardeth stared at the clouded window as the riders, who had reached the end of the street, turned and came roaring back.

"Get down, Miss Medora," Dabney cried as he squirmed over the counter to pull her to the floor, crouching beside her.

The report of the guns was so loud and steady that she covered her ears with her hands. Suddenly gunshot shattered the large front window of the store, sending shards of glass everywhere. Ardeth ducked as Dabney pushed her down and bent over her. The firing went on for what seemed like an eternity but was actually less than five minutes. Then as suddenly as it had started, it stopped, and the clatter of horses could be heard receding from the town.

Ardeth, her eyes as large as saucers, looked up into the angry face of Kenneth Dabney.

"I beg your pardon, ma'am," he said politely as he got to his feet. "But if you hadn't got down, you might of been hurt bad. Damned rabblerousers!"

She scrambled up to stare in horror at the ruin of the front part of the store. All around her feet the glass lay like shattered ice. Dust and shards covered all the neat stacks of clothing and bales of fabric. Dabney had a long cut on his cheek that streaked red against the ruddiness of his skin. He dabbed at it with a handkerchief as he stepped angrily over the broken glass to stare at the street. Ardeth had never regretted so much that she couldn't talk.

"It was that Tuchman gang, damn them," Dabney muttered, finally noticing the question in Ardeth's eyes. "They come through here like this just about twice a month when they been paid or taken a grievance of some sort. God knows what brought it on this time. Are you ladies all right back there?"

He left Ardeth to help the women at the rear of his store while she moved to the shattered window and peered out. People were beginning to trickle out of the other buildings, nervously inching into the street. Down near the Diamond Ring there was something dark in the middle of the road, attracting several men who hovered around it.

Ardeth grabbed up her packages. All she wanted was to get back to her room at the Diamond Ring and stay there. She left more than enough money on the counter and hurried out the door and down the walk to the saloon. The orderly street she had passed only moments before was a shambles. Hardly a window was whole, and those buildings without them were dotted with bullet holes. At the door of the saloon, she stopped long enough to recognize Baskin Sawyer bending over the inert form lying in the street. It appeared to be the body of a man, but the crowd moving in around it blocked her view. She shuddered and fled into the saloon, now almost empty since everyone had gone to view the body in the road. The Ring's windows were shattered too, but since they were not large to begin with, the debris was minimal.

When he saw her come through the swinging doors, Eddie Lathrop came running to her side from the rear of the building. "You all right?" he asked, taking her arm.

Ardeth nodded but was glad to lean on him for a moment. She motioned her head toward the street.

"Oh, that. I don't doubt it's one of the Lindemans lying out there. The Tuchmans been feuding with them for a couple of years now. Burton Tuchman's got a big cattle spread, and he don't like farmers interfering with his water rights. The Lindemans came here with a bunch of other Swedes with some kind of claim from the government, and they don't think anybody has the right to tell them they can't use it. This kind of thing happens a lot out here. You get used to it."

The horror on her face stopped him. "Don't let it bother you, Miss Medora. They ain't after the likes of you or me. Here, sit awhile and have a little dab of Wister's Redeye. It'll give you your courage

141

back."

Ardeth shook her head vigorously and moved toward the stairs. Eddie, thinking she was still unwell, mumbled something about getting Martha Higley to help her as Ardeth hurried up to the second floor and into her bedroom, locking the door behind her. She sat down to let her nerves calm before stepping to the window to look down on the alley below. Baskin Sawyer was moving ponderously along toward the back of his shop, accompanied by several men carrying the dead body of one of the Lindemans on a flat pine slab. Feeling sick, Ardeth turned away to throw off her clothes and climb back in her bed.

By evening she had recovered enough to venture back downstairs for supper. Corchran, seeing how pale she was, put her in the alcove by herself and had a meal sent over from the eatery across the street. She had planned to rush back to her room once she was finished, but she soon found that the other employees of the saloon liked to wander over to talk to her in a friendly fashion which was tinged with curiosity. It proved to be a pleasant diversion for her, even though the conversation was one-sided, and by the time she went upstairs for the night, she had a much better idea of the people she was living among.

John Wister was the barkeep, a big, beefy man with a huge handlebar moustache and a booming voice used mainly to bring rowdy customers back

142

into line. Only one of the dancing girls was friendly to her. Roxie, who said she had come west from the coal mines of Virginia, had a few years too many to be doing this kind of work. It showed on her face and in her green eyes which appeared faded from having seen too much of the world. But because she was experienced, she was the least threatened of all the girls by Ardeth's beauty and supposed talent, and she went out of her way to be kind. Owen Salter, the gambler, came over to pay court, as did Sheriff Meeker when he wandered in and Corchran himself.

There were a few loud altercations during the evening, the loudest caused by the infamous Shannessy, but on the whole, it was a quiet evening. Ardeth had thought that the dead Lindeman would be on everybody's tongue, but she found that the horrible events of the morning had only shattered her own nerves. Everyone else seemed to take the rampage and murder in stride, as though it was an everyday occurrence.

And then, as she was heading for the stairs, she passed a table where Salter sat playing faro with three other men, all of them looking hard and tough in a way that reminded her of Turnbull's gang. One of them rose to his feet, his tanned, leathery face scowling with black rage as he pointed a gun at Owen Salter.

"Cheat!" he said as with his other hand he swept the table clean of counters and cards. They clattered to the floor as the other two men scrambled away. A silence enclosed the space around the table while in the background the piano went on tinkling and a girl gave a brittle laugh.

"You calling me a card cheat," she heard Owen murmur in a cold voice. Though he had not stood from his chair, his eyes were fastened on his accuser with a malicious coldness.

"That's exactly what I'm callin' you. . . ."

Ardeth froze with her foot on the first step. She was right in the line of fire should the gun go off, and yet it was the thought of the pleasant Salter being killed in front of her eyes that filled her with horror. The man with the gun reached out quickly and hauled Salter to his feet by his neckerchief. At that same moment the sharp report of a pistol sounded. Screams echoed around her, and Ardeth slumped on the stairs as her knees gave way. She half expected to feel a pain in her chest until she saw that it was the man with the gun who had been hit. His pistol had been knocked from his hand, and he wheeled around, gripping his wrist. Sheriff Meeker, his six-shooter still smoking, walked up to the table and pulled the man away.

"That ain't the way we settle disputes in Fireweed," he said grimly. Salter picked himself up off the green baize cloth and made a big show of straightening his vest and cravat. "Git on your horse and leave town," Meeker went on.

"That card shark cheated me," the man cried as

144

he wrapped his neckerchief around his wrist. "It ain't right!"

"It's a lie," Salter said. "He lost fair."

"You might of settled it peaceable if you hadn't pulled a gun. Now git!"

Ardeth stayed long enough to see the man kicked toward the door where he turned to glare back at Salter. Then she fled upstairs once again, to lock her door and feel safe, at least for a few hours.

The next day the cattle drive arrived.

The first thing she noticed was the noise. Though the actual thousand-head herd was driven in nearer the train depot than the main street of Fireweed, the roar and rumble rolled over the town like a summer thunderstorm. It was an ear-splitting mélange of wailing beasts, thundering horses, and shouting cowboys, punctuated by the sharp snap and crack of many whips. Dust rose like a cloud of locusts to choke the air inside the stores and saloons of the town. Most of the action that day centered on the corrals near the railroad lines, but by evening the first of the cowboys began their rush into town to taste the joys of civilization.

They hit the saloons first as a prelude to the bathhouses and restaurant. Then later that night they were again making the rounds of the saloons. The population of Fireweed ballooned with the new arrivals, and the Diamond Ring all but burst its walls with the crush. Ardeth inched her way downstairs for a late supper, hoping she would be able to

145

eat it with the heightened odors of horse and leather lying pungent on the stale air of the saloon. She squirmed her way across the room, responding with angry glares when her bottom was pinched or a friendly arm was draped across her shoulders. Her icy demeanor did little to discourage her admirers, and it was with relief that she was finally able to break free for the comparative solitude of the dining alcove. Even there, the din was enough to ruin her meal. Roxie was up on the stage, cavorting to the sounds of Eddie's thumping piano and croaking some kind of song which was inaudible over the raucous crowd. Although the laughing and talking were ear-splitting enough, it was the frequently shouted orders to the barkeep across the room that made the din unbearable.

She was left in peace long enough to consume her meal. By then one of the wandering cowboys had discovered her in the shadows and descended on her, drawing some of his friends along with him. He was a tall, lanky man with a fringe of dark beard above his tanned, leathery skin. His hair had been combed but still hung listlessly to his shoulders from a rim on his forehead that appeared to be permanently pressed in place by his hatband. He wore a clean shirt of checkered calico with tight gray hairs erupting from underneath the first fastening. Ardeth pulled away in disgust.

"Come on, little lady," he said with great good humor. "Anythin' as pretty as you can't sit here on

146

the sidelines while there's dancin' goin' on. Let's us have a reel or two."

She shook her head vigorously, wishing she dared to talk. It did not phase the cowboy in the least. His arms had the strength of iron, and he pulled her away from the table and out onto the crowded dance floor like she had no weight at all. Gripping her waist, he began bouncing her around the floor, careening into the others with a wild abandon. Ardeth found herself clinging to him just to keep from being squashed by the other bodies pressing in around her.

"My name's Jack Prentiss," he said with a lisp that resulted from one missing front tooth. "What's your'n?"

Ardeth glanced frantically around for Jasper Corchran.

"Oh, too shy to speak, are you? Well, you'll soon get over that. We're a right friendly group as you'll soon learn. Only watch out for those fellers leanin' on the bar. They're the mean ones. They aren't interested in havin' a good time. They only want to fill up with whisky a hole that's been made dry by months on the trail."

Ardeth was so busy trying to keep her balance amid all the jostling that her partner was doing that she barely caught half his words. He went on, merrily shouting at her and bouncing around the floor, enjoying himself enormously while she searched the crowd for Corchran, or Salter or Meeker or anyone who might rescue her.

To her great consternation none of them stepped forward. Instead it was yet another cowboy who broke in, determined that Prentiss should not keep the pleasure of dancing with the prettiest girl in the room all to himself. Ardeth was released for a moment while the two men began jabbing at each other with their fists. When several others joined in, she took advantage of the chaos to slip between the crowd and head for the stairs.

She had reached the steps and started up when her arm was grabbed. Looking up into the sunburned face of yet another cowboy, she felt an arm slip around her waist as she was pulled against a hard male body.

"I been watchin' you, sweetie," the cowboy breathed into her ear. "You're my kind of woman. Pretty as a waterhole in the desert. And I been waitin' a long time." He nuzzled her neck as she drew back in horror, pushing against his chest. He had her bent over the railing before she could shove him away and regain her balance.

He was younger than the others, with black, dancing eyes alive with the determination to have a good time. Ardeth tried to step past him, but he grabbed her arm and pulled her back in the tight circle of his arms. She was standing on the step above which allowed him the opportunity to nuzzle at the shadowy cleavage between her breasts.

"Mmm," he murmured. "Will fifty cents be

enough?"

Furious, she shoved him back and swung her hand, slapping him on the side of the face. He only smiled more broadly.

"A gal with spirit! I like that. Well, ordinarily I wouldn't do it, but I just got paid. I can go up to a dollar."

Ardeth pressed her lips tightly together, her eyes flashing. She shook her head vigorously and tried to get up the stairs again. This time he caught her and kissed her, burrowing his wet lips into hers. When she was able to yank her head away and free her arms, she shoved him with all her strength, sending him careening down the four steps to the landing, where he sat, legs splayed out before him. The saloon exploded with laughter.

Not the least bit chagrined, the cowpoke got to his feet to start up the stairs again. To his surprise he was pulled back by a tall townsman wearing a silver star on his shirt.

"Go get one of the other gals, cowboy," Sheriff Meeker said calmly. "This lady's here special. She's not interested in your attentions."

"Well, she's here in a saloon, ain't she. What's that supposed to mean?"

"Like I say, she's here special. Take my word for it; she's not one of the dancing girls."

Something about the star on the sheriff's breast and the firm, no-nonsense manner in his speech finally got through to the amorous young cowpoke.

He picked up his hat, slapped it against his legs once or twice and headed back for the crowded floor. Ardeth waited only long enough to throw Sheriff Meeker a grateful glance, then dashed up the stairs to her room. She had to thread her way through a crowd of people coming and going in the hall, an unusual circumstance but not unexpected considering what was going on below. She hardly looked their way as she hurried to her door, not even daring to return the more than casual glances directed at her. Once inside her room, she turned the lock and sank on the bed to catch her breath. When the doorknob began to rattle from the other side, she picked up a chair and placed the back beneath it to reinforce the lock. Even then she found she was too nervous to sleep.

Had she been calm, the noise would have kept her awake anyway. It went on all night, often erupting into the streets, where the guns would blast away amid hooting and hollering and horses pounding along the road. None of it seemed malicious or even dangerous. It was more like a lot of overgrown boys determined to have a hell of a good time, no matter what. It reminded her of her brothers back home on the few occasions when they were given time away from their chores and they went at their fun time determined to make the most of it while it lasted.

She was more disturbed by the frequent shaking of her doorknob than the noises in the street. This went on all night, occasionally accompanied by a loud pounding on the door and good-natured calls to make herself available. While none of the men appeared to be really bad-natured, she did not want to imagine what might occur if her door gave way and there was no Sheriff Meeker around to save her. She spent the night listening to the racket outside and the laughter and creaking springs in the rooms next door and across the hall while she cursed Nat Varien.

Two days later Ardeth was sitting on her bed in the early morning hours, her knees drawn up to hold a tattered copy of *Love Among the Sagebrush,* one of Martha's collection of dime novels. She had found these tepid little books her only relief from the self-imposed exile that had kept her in her room since the cattle drive arrived in Fireweed. The noise, the wildness and the explosion of high energy had shown no sign of abating, and while the celebration continued, she was determined not to venture back downstairs. Martha had brought her her meals and kept her abreast of the latest outrages against civilized townsfolk, but the four walls of her room seemed to be constantly enclosing, making it each day seem a little smaller than the day before.

A brisk knock at the door brought her head up. The voice on the other side was muffled but managed to be audible.

"Open up, Miss Medora. It's your manager, returned from the wilderness!"

Ardeth threw down the book and dashed to the door, pulling away the chair beneath the handle. Then he was in the room, shoving the door closed behind him and swinging her around in his arms.

"Nat!" she exclaimed before his lips closed over hers. He filled the room with his big frame, his wide-brimmed hat, his fringed leather jacket and silver-spurred boots. He enclosed her in his arms, covered her face with his kisses, and laughed aloud to see her again.

"Oh, but you smell clean and good. And how I missed you!" he cried, sweeping her up in his arms to carry her to the bed. She laughed too, her heart brimming with the joy and security he represented. He dumped her on the bed in a swirl of skirts and petticoats and fell over her, holding her tightly in his arms and drinking the sweetness of her lips. Ardeth kissed him back, reveling in the feel of his body, the warmth of his arms around her.

"Did you miss me?" he asked, lifting his head and smiling mischievously.

That brought her back to earth. She scowled, doubled up her fist and swatted him on the back three or four times. "Nat Varien, you skunk! You went off and left me here in the middle of all these wild animals. I could have been killed, or . . . even worse!"

He kissed her on the tip of her nose. "My poor

girl. You weren't, were you? Worse, I mean?"

Ardeth pushed him off and sat up on the bed, throwing down her skirts. "No thanks to you. I couldn't even go downstairs. I haven't left this room for two whole days. And I haven't slept either with all the guns going off and the wild races through town. I couldn't walk across the room down there without being pinched or grabbed or propositioned! And I couldn't even scream or protest because I wasn't supposed to be able to talk. It was horrible."

He pulled her back down into his arms. "But you had Corchran to protect you."

"Much good he was," Ardeth said, turning her face to avoid his lips. His hand slipped up over her breast, and her blood stirred. "Now, don't distract me. You were horrid to leave me here like that!"

"But I did it for you, my love. I brought the answer to our problems back with me. Besides, you don't look like you suffered too much. In fact, you look beautiful."

Ardeth could sense his ardor rising. Twisting away from him, she tried to roll out of his grasp, but he pulled her down, burying his head in her bodice.

"Only because of Sheriff Meeker. Now Nat . . . don't do that. . . ."

His hand slipped up her leg. "It's all I've thought about or wanted for three days," he murmured as she slipped beneath him.

There was a rat-a-tat on the door.

"Damn!" he said, suddenly still. Their eyes were

153

only inches apart, and Ardeth's were wide with question.

Nat sat up and swung his legs over the side of the bed. "Straighten yourself, my love. I think that is the answer I brought back with me from Abilene. Trust him to appear at the most inconvenient time."

He reached back long enough to give her another lingering kiss. "We'll continue this later," he murmured, winking at her. She smoothed her skirts and hair and pulled down her bodice while Nat went to the door and threw it open.

"Medora, my love, meet Drury Templeton."

Ardeth rose to peer up at the tallest, lankiest young man she had ever seen. He loomed over her like an elongated fence rail, adorned at the top with a shock of wavy blond hair that spilled to his shoulders.

"Charmed, I'm sure," he intoned and swept up her hand to plant a very wet kiss upon it. Ardeth looked over the mass of blond hair and caught Nat struggling to keep from laughing.

"It's all right. He knows you can talk. Master Templeton is your new voice coach."

"And greatly honored I am to be so appointed, I must say. Indeed yes. It isn't often one's career is graced with the opportunity to be of service to an entertainer of such grace and fame. . . ."

"Put it in your hat, Drury," Nat snapped. "You don't have to perform in front of us."

Templeton laughed nervously and stepped back,

allowing Ardeth her first good look at his face. She was surprised to realize he was not so young after all. He had a long, thin face heightened with a thin, anemic blond moustache streaked with gray. His complexion was ruddy and blotched in sharp contrast to the faded gray of his eyes. His natty clothes, seen close up, were actually rather shabby and showed evidence of amateurish darning in several places.

Nat pulled up a straight-backed chair and straddled it. "Mr. Templeton was until recently a member of the Lyceum Four."

"One of the finest barbershop quartets ever to grace the planet," Templeton added.

It was obvious Ardeth did not know what a barbershop quartet was.

"There are several of them, sent out every year from Chicago by Hamilin's Wizard Oil to promote their sales," Nat went on.

"The Blood Pills and Cough Balsam people?" she said, suddenly remembering.

"You mean they've even heard of the stuff in the sod houses of Nebraska?"

"My mother was never without it. It was the cure for all sorts of ills, from colds to insect bites."

"One of the most famous medicines in existence," Templeton added in his theatrical voice. "Can't touch it for—"

Nat broke in. "Anyway, they send out these dapper quartets every year to entertain at the carnivals

155

and medicine shows. Fortunately for us, Mr. Templeton here left the show and was available for hire."

"A slight disagreement with the management, Madam Medora. After three years of touring with Hamilin's the ungrateful wretches had the unadulterated gall to replace me with a powder pigeon tenor! Three of the best years of my life, of my singing career—"

"He was thrown out for drinking too much redeye," Nat said laconically, just as Drury was beginning to get wound up.

"Unjust! Manifestly unjust!"

"You're too fond of the stuff and you know it. They warned you if you turned up too drunk to perform one more time you were out. Fortunately I arrived in Abilene before he sobered up enough to move on." He turned back to Ardeth. "Their loss is our gain. Templeton will teach you to sing, and in return I shall pay him enough to get him back to Chicago where he can convince the moguls of Hamilin's Wizard Oil that he is trustworthy again."

Ardeth sidled near Nat's chair and said in a quiet whisper, "But Nat, if he drinks too much, how can we trust him not to tell. . . ."

"Because Mr. Templeton is more anxious to return to Chicago and his old job than anything else in the world. If he wishes me to help him get there, he knows he has to do what I say. Right, Mr. Templeton?"

Drury bowed, sweeping the floor with his hat. He was such a preposterous figure that Ardeth could only shake her head in wonder that Nat would even consider trusting him. She only hoped he knew what he was doing.

"Now," Nat said, rising. "Drury and I are going to amble downstairs, have a little quick drink and hire him a horse. You, my love, had better get started."

"Get started on what?"

"Oh, I didn't tell you, did I? We are moving out of Fireweed for a few days to a little ranch I know of a few miles away. Pack a few clothes—nothing elaborate. It'll be very quiet. Lots of time to work on your—" he tipped up her chin and kissed her lightly on the lips—"your voice."

"Nat Varien," she spluttered, "you come waltzing back in here after three days away, ordering me out God knows where, and with this . . . this 'teacher.' I don't know why I ever listen to you!"

Nat already had Templeton by the arm, steering him toward the door. He threw her a look over his shoulder that melted her indignation.

"I'll show you why when we get to the ranch."

Chapter Eight

On the morning of their second day at the Casa Verde Ranch that Nat presented Ardeth with the gift he had brought her from Abilene. It was a skirt that on closer inspection proved to be actually a pair of trousers, allowing her to ride astride with an ease and fashion she had never known before. There were leather fringes around each leg hem while the waist was studded with small silver buttons forming a deep V. Though utilitarian, it was lovelier to her than Medora's shimmering silks, and she wore it on their long rides in the early morning or in the evening, before and after her all-day workout with Drury Templeton.

Those rides were the only thing that made her days bearable. Drury proved to be a demanding taskmaster when sober, driving her beyond her limit or desire. Of course, she admitted on reflection, he was trying to turn a rank amateur into a seasoned professional in the space of a few days, and that would be enough to drive both of them to drink. He had been relieved to discover that she could carry a tune and had a natural sweet, lilting vocal timbre. But her repertoire of songs being limited to a few lullabies and a folk song or two left him with the huge job of teaching her a raft of new songs as well as how to sing them and how to present herself on stage. For Ardeth, to ride off with Nat into the low hills around Casa Verde was like being released from prison.

It soon became their custom to stop at a small pond nestled among low hills of sage and scrub and surrounded by a fringe of cottonwoods. Though not tall, the trees afforded a scattering of cool shade, heightened by the elongated shadows they threw across the muddy water as the afternoon waned.

Ardeth leaned back against one of the narrow trunks and sighed contentedly. Drury had worked her hard that day but at last she felt she was beginning to show signs of progress. She knew four songs now and sang them with a flair that might pass for showmanship, at least to the yokels of the Diamond Ring. More important, she was beginning to feel more sure of herself. Drury might be a drunk, but he had been around the theater long enough to know all sorts of little tricks she could use to draw attention away from her lack of experience. With a little more self-assurance, she might even enjoy putting them to use.

"You're looking very pleased with yourself," Nat said. He stretched out beside her, leaning on his elbow and absently working tiny mounds from the cottonwood seed down that littered the bank. He hesitated to add how beautiful she looked, staring out at the pond, her black hair framing her face and spilling down over one shoulder. Life at Casa Verde had been good for her, he thought. She exuded a healthy glow that came from rest, happiness and appreciation of the out-of-doors. It was probably as far from anything a seasoned professional like Medora—who was long in the tooth to boot—would have ever wanted to experience.

"I actually got a compliment out of Drury Templeton today," Ardeth said, laughing. "It was so unexpected I had to sit down for a few minutes."

"I should think he would be the last person to be sparing with his compliments. If I hadn't picked him up out of that gutter I found him in, he'd be there yet, drowning in booze and wallowing in self-pity."

"That's probably true. But you know, he does have a quite beautiful voice. And he's very knowledgeable about performing on the stage. He thinks I'm an utter nincompoop, of course, with a voice little better than a sparrow's, yet he's taught me a lot these last few days."

"You think it was wise then to bring him back?"

She was surprised that he would ask for her approval. It didn't seem like Nat Varien. "I think it was the only thing to do. I would never be able to get up on that stage and try to pass myself off as Medora without some kind of professional help."

"I just hope we can trust him. He's chafing at the bit now to get back to civilization and the comforts of whisky. I've promised him a goodly sum to buy his help and his silence, but he won't get it until he's sitting on the train on his way out of Fireweed. We'd better pray it works."

"I feel more confident now that it will than I have since you first put this crazy proposal to me. It might even be fun."

Nat rolled over on his stomach and rested his head on his arms. "I'm disappointed you didn't find Medora's map while I was away. If we had that, we wouldn't need to worry about staying in Fireweed any longer than it took to placate Jaspar Corchran and the others."

"Well, I looked everywhere there was to look. And heaven knows, I had plenty of time to search, buried in my room alone while the town was going to hell and back around me. It's not among her things; I'm sure of that."

"All the same, I'd like to have a look myself when we get back. She must have had it with her. She wrote me that she would."

"Is that why you were near the train that day it was robbed? To meet Medora?"

"No. As a matter of fact that was only coincidence. I knew she would be on it of course, but I was there to catch Toad Turnbull and string him up to the nearest tree. A job at which I was singularly unsuccessful."

His head was close to her waist. Absently she reached out and smoothed the sandy lock of hair that fell across his wide forehead. "I've heard of

161

bounty hunters. Is that what you are?"

Nat smiled up at her. Normally he would answer a question like that with something noncommittal and vague. But over the last few days he had shared such moments of passion and closeness with this lovely girl that he thought perhaps he owed her more than that. And in a way, it was a relief to speak of all he had carried within him in silence for so long.

"No. I'm not interested in any reward for hanging Toad Turnbull. I want revenge. Vindication." He took a deep breath. "I used to own a lot of land down in New Mexico that had been in my family since the days of the conquistadors. After my father died, I started a successful ranch with my closest friend, Kit Randall. We did well enough to bring in a third partner, a man named George Wellington. I never cared much for Wellington, but he had good business sense and was valuable to us. We succeeded beyond our wildest dreams and seemed on the way to becoming as strong an outfit as Chisholm, or King, down in Texas.

"Then Turnbull showed up. At first he passed himself off as a possible investor, but actually he was looking us over. After one of our most profitable cattle sales, he and his gang hit our place. I wasn't there, but George and Kit were. Turnbull gunned them both down in cold blood. He took all the cash, burned the house and outbuildings, and ran off the stock that was close by. I came back to a ruin."

Ardeth sat very still. The casualness with which Nat spoke was belied by the burning rage in his eyes and the flush on his cheeks. "How terrible for you," she whispered.

"I wanted to rebuild, but we had too many debts to start over from scratch. The land was sold to some corporation—that hurt almost as much as seeing Kit's body. I had enough from that sale to stake me for a while, and I vowed I'd use it to find and kill Toad Turnbull. And I will."

Abruptly Nat rolled over on his back, his hands laced beneath his head. Through talking about the past, he had relieved a little of the tension he carried within him, yet he realized he did not really want to open up this old wound too far. It might take the edge off his determination to get his revenge. That was the one thing he was never going to give up.

"But why bother with Medora, then? I should think it would be a distraction to go searching for an old map."

"It's a necessary distraction. You see, that map is not just an interesting antique. It contains a diagram showing where a cache of Spanish gold was hidden away many years ago. Medora knew I'd be too fascinated by it to pass it up. Besides, my stake from the sale of the ranch is almost gone and I need a new one. A treasure such as she described would allow me to follow Turnbull to the ends of the earth and back."

Ardeth thought of the money and jewels sitting in

her room above the Diamond Ring. It would be easy for either one of them to use Medora's valuables, especially since they both knew she was dead. Yet neither one wished to. It would be too much like stealing.

Nat reached up to pull her down into the circle of his arms. "Now, that's my past. What about yours. You've said little enough about it."

Ardeth shrugged and nestled her head in the delicious hollow where his neck and shoulder met. "There is little to tell. A farm on the Nebraska plains. Too many children, too little money, sometimes too little food. No neighbors, no friends, nothing but endless work and flat prairie. Before I was ten years old, I vowed I'd get away. I was never really sure that I would be able to until my mother helped me. I will always be grateful to her for that."

Nat's fingers brushed her breasts with a tingling light touch. "Running away never works," he murmured.

"I'm not running away. I'm running to! I want to experience everything there is to experience. I want to be surrounded by beauty, light, excitement, adventure. . . ."

"Is that why you hid in your room during the cattle drive?"

"Now, that's not fair. It was the first time, after all. And you weren't there to give me any protection. I couldn't talk, and they treated me like I was one of those . . . those . . ."

"Loose women like Roxie and Dakota Lil. You'd

164

better get used to that. Most cowboys think women on the stage are only one cut above whores. Most of the time they are."

"But . . . but . . ." she spluttered.

"I know you're not, my pretty," he said, laughing as he kissed her. "I've been around enough women to recognize a decent, well brought up girl when I see one. Though I must say you have surprised me with the passionate way you've returned my amorous advances."

"Would you rather I was cold and prim?" Ardeth said, pulling away from him and trying to sit up. "Should I slap your face and order you to unhand me like they do in the melodramas?"

Nat pulled her back into his arms and nuzzled her ear. "I like you just like you are. Please don't change a thing."

Her arms slipped around him in spite of her half-wish to remain insulted. His proximity always had that effect on her, turning her bones to water and her reluctance to vapor. "It's getting late," she whispered as his lips sought her throat and slid enticingly lower. With an easy grace, he undid the buttons on her blouse and slipped his hand inside to cup her breast, lifting it in his fingers.

"I know. We'd better stop this useless talking and get to the real purpose of this ride."

Ardeth gasped as he released her breast from the confines of her blouse and closed his lips over the taut nipple. Her back arched in his enclosing arm.

"Nat Varien," she murmured, "you're nothing but

an animal!"

Nat made little wet circles on her breast with his lips, then lifted his head just long enough to answer, "Thank you."

It was a week before they returned to Fireweed. Even with all the work Drury Templeton had put her through, there was an idyllic quality to their stay at the ranch that Ardeth found hard to leave behind. For the first time in her life, she had enjoyed the sense of being isolated from the world, alone much of the time with Nat, sharing the exquisite pleasure of making love beside the pond, even cooking the simple meals which more often than not were eaten by the two of them since Drury tended to want his privacy when his work with Ardeth was finished. She suspected it was not going to be easy to go back to the frenetic activity of the cattle town. One hour there and she knew she had been right.

Jasper Corchran was delighted that Medora Melindez had recovered her voice and was now ready to perform. At Nat's urging, he was finally convinced to postpone the debut until the following night instead of her first one back, but he went about drumming up an audience with all the enthusiasm of a circus promoter. Signs appeared everywhere around town; tickets were hawked at the saloon. Ardeth found a terrible, sick stage fright gnawing at her until she forced herself to ignore all the hoopla and concentrate on the things she had learned. She now knew a few good songs, could sing them with enough breath to be heard at the back of the saloon, and was adept at using a few smart tricks with which to keep her audience's attention away from deficiencies of her voice. There were even a few moments when she looked forward to stepping out on that stage.

When she returned to the Diamond Ring, she found a letter waiting for her. Her first reaction was to assume it came from her mother until she remembered that such a letter would be addressed to Ardeth Royce, a name that meant nothing to the people of Fireweed. This letter was addressed in a sprawling, flourishing hand to Medora Melindez, care of the Diamond Ring Saloon, Fireweed, Kansas. She opened it with a mixture of curiosity and guilt.

It was from a gentleman she had never heard of before, Garth Reardon, of the Silver Sage Ranch in Green Valley, Wyoming. It was a very polite, friendly letter in which Mr. Reardon invited Medora to visit his ranch for a few days of relaxation and rest which, he proposed, might also include making her talents available to his other guests at a sum that Ardeth had to read twice to believe. It was obvious from the way the letter was written as well as the fancy paper and letterhead that the Silver Sage was no Casa Verde. The dates suggested for her visit were two weeks ahead, and under other circumstances she might have been intrigued enough to go.

But on closer thought, she decided that would not be wise. Surely in two weeks she would have earned enough as Medora to stake herself a new life somewhere far away from Fireweed, possibly along with Nat Varien. If her performances went at all well, she might even continue them somewhere else as herself. By then Nat would surely have found the map he wanted, and she could allow Medora to slip into oblivion in a decent and orderly fashion. It would be the best thing for all involved.

She soon forgot about the letter and Garth Reardon as the time for her first performance began to loom closer. She went over the songs with Eddie in a kind of soft half-voice, but even that was enough to draw the curious stares of the other women in the saloon and even a few of the men. Nat had convinced her that if she was going to bring this off, she had to get out on that stage with a certain amount of self-confidence, for certainly a performer as popular as Medora would have been very sure of herself. As the evening drew closer, Ardeth grew more determined that no matter how frightened she was, she was going to do a good job of it, just to please Nat if nothing else.

Yet later she stood in the narrow wings off the stage with Drury still fussing over the folds of her dress and listened to the noisy crowd with a sinking heart. The place was full, jammed to the very corners, and the atmosphere was extremely raucous. The poor hurdy-gurdy player had been pelted off the boards, and cries of "Medora, Medora" ended every act.

"You're going to be wonderful," Drury gushed. Ardeth glanced back at Nat's grim face as he stood behind her dapper teacher. Was he having second thoughts now after bringing her so far? Her lips tightened, and she drew in her breath. She would not let him down. Nor herself either!

There was an effusive introduction by Jasper Corchran that led into a bombastic fanfare on the piano. Picking up the long train of her dress, Ardeth gave Nat a wink and swept out onto the stage.

The row of gas lights framing the edge of the stage were blinding, preventing her from seeing anyone in the audience, though she could hear them well enough. She let the train of her dress fall gracefully around her feet as Drury had taught her, gripped her hands at her waist and waited for the noise to subside. The piano went into a long introduction to "A Rose with a Broken Stem" and Ardeth began to sing. It was a tentative, small voice at first. Then, closing her eyes, she concentrated only on the words and the sounds from her throat and began to enjoy herself. With the last note, a hushed silence fell over the saloon. Ardeth gripped her hands and waited, half believing a delegation might mount the stage any moment to drive her off.

Then the applause began to ripple, growing into a ground swell, punctuated with loud hollers and foot stomping. She knew most of these men did not understand a song like the one she had just given them any more than they appreciated the performances of Shakespeare's plays presented by the traveling troupes of actors that wandered through Fireweed. But they knew it was supposed to be "culture," and they were kind enough to give her the benefit of the doubt. It was not going to be so difficult to fool them after all.

She followed with two songs along the same line, old fashioned ballads with sentimental appeal: "The Rival Cavaliers" and "I Loved You Better Than You Knew." By then Ardeth was beginning to enjoy herself, and when she swung into "Was There Any Harm in That" and "The Bell Goes A-ringing for Sai-rah," with jaunty rhythms that allowed her to cavort a little on the stage, she had the audience eating out of her hand. The last two songs were shared with Drury, "Pretty as a Picture" and "Take Back the Ring"—one of the lures they had used to buy his silence. One was pretty, one was funny and both were received with gusto. Ardeth bowed in the best tradition Drury had taught her, received a large bouquet of flowers from a beaming Jasper Corchran and left the stage to collapse in Nat's arms.

"You were wonderful!" he whispered, whisking her upstairs for a rest between performances.

"Do you think they were convinced?" she asked, falling into one of the chairs as her knees gave way beneath her.

Nat poured her a drink of lemonade—the strongest thing allowed. "If there had been a real critic in the audience, he might have known this was your first time on stage, but these yokels never had an inkling, I'm certain. I told you all you had to do was look beautiful and show an ankle now and then and they would love you. And you did both to perfection."

He leaned down and kissed the top of her head. "Careful," Ardeth cried. "You'll destroy my fancy hairdo, and I have to go on again, you know."

Nat backed away. "Two performances a night—we're going to have to get Drury to teach you a few more songs. Do you think you could learn them?"

"Right now I think I could do anything! What a feeling to be out there facing all those people, knowing all those eyes were fastened on you, feeling that you could move them to tears or laughter or anything you wanted. It was magical. Wonderful!"

"I think you've found your calling," Nat muttered. "But don't get too carried away. It's Medora's career, you know. Once we find that map, all this will be over."

Ardeth stretched her arms above her head and smiled up at the ceiling. "I don't want it to be over," she exclaimed. "I hope we never find the map. I want to go on and on and get better and better until it's *my* career!"

Nat shook his head. "I've unleashed a monster!" he muttered beneath his breath.

Of course the early euphoria Ardeth felt over her singing career did not last long. In two days' time, she was beginning to realize just how limiting her repertoire of songs and lack of experience actually were. She simply did not have that reservoir of talent and knowledge that years on the stage give a performer, a well they can draw from when things do not go as planned or when routines grow tired or the unexpected happens. But she looked beautiful under the lights, and she enjoyed herself in front of an audience just enough to keep up the charade, she hoped, for at least the two weeks she was scheduled to perform.

She was rehearsing on stage one afternoon when Nat sauntered in and took a seat in the darkened alcove off to the right where she was accustomed to eating supper. He slouched in one of the chairs, watching her with a kind of bemused wonder. It was amazing to him how she had grown in self-assurance in just two days. She was obviously enjoying herself and stretching the limits of a new-found talent. He must remind her to throw a tantrum or two, in the best tradition of the prima donna. Medora would do so, he felt certain.

He was concentrating so on Ardeth's movements on stage that he did not see the figure slip into a chair beside him. Conscious of someone there, he turned to see Roxie placing her elbows on the table and leaning close.

"Mr. Varien," she said in her husky voice.

"Hello, Roxie. It is Roxie, isn't it?" He hadn't really paid much attention to the other women who worked at the Diamond Ring, but this one appeared

172

to be friends with Ardeth, and he thought he remembered her calling her by name.

Roxie seemed pleased by the recognition. "That's right," she said, giving him the full blaze of her smile. "I don't get to talk to you much alone—you're always with her." She gestured a hand toward the stage. "But I've seen you about. I thought . . . well, maybe it would be nice to get better acquainted. We might have, well, a few friends in common. Who knows."

Nat doubted that. It was the closest he had ever been to one of these women, and he hardly thought they would have anything in common. Roxie had been a pretty girl once, in a pleasant, ordinary way. Seen close up, she was older than she looked from across the room, and those vestiges of youth and beauty were fading fast. Beneath the rouged cheeks and darkened eyes and brows, there lurked the first signs of a flintiness forged by the life she had led.

Nat smiled politely and pushed back in his chair. Roxie only leaned closer, allowing him the full view of her white breasts ballooning above the low decolletage of her tired satin gown.

"I don't have much time for anything these days but managing Medora's career," he muttered. Roxie laid her hand lightly on his arm.

"Oh, I can understand that. But a gentleman like you oughtn't to give all his time to one woman, especially when she's as young and inexperienced as that little lady. I mean, she's my friend and all and I like her, but you got to admit, she don't know much about the world out here."

"Inexperienced . . ." Nat said, his heart sinking. If Ardeth's lack of experience was so obvious to a woman of Roxie's limited sensibilities, how could they expect to get away with this masquerade for two weeks.

"Well, I mean she knows her business and all on stage, but off of it, why she's a regular prude. You should of seen her when the cattle drive came through. Why, she hid out in her room for three days, scared silly one of those cowpokes might lay a finger on her. And she never takes a drink of whisky or redeye or anything stronger than a little wine. Now, it seems to me, a man like you might appreciate a woman who can handle the world better than that."

Nat breathed a sigh of relief. "A woman like you, you mean."

Roxie shrugged. "Now that you mention it, yes. I mean, I could show you a real good time and all. And I'm not talking business or anything. I mean, this would be for free. I like you, you see. You're kind of, well, my kind of man, I think. I bet we would be something together."

"I'm flattered you think so," he said, trying to look pleased. Out of the corner of his eye, he noticed that Ardeth had stopped moving on stage and was peering at the alcove with a quiet intensity. "Really, Miss . . . Roxie, I appreciate your offer and I'll think about it. But right now I have all I can handle with Ar—Medora's career. She's a bit more demanding than you'd guess from her youth." In fact, Roxie might be quite surprised if she knew just how exciting Ardeth was between the sheets.

Roxie's painted face darkened. She sat back in her chair, away from him. Her initial anger at being sluffed off was softened a little when she remembered he hadn't yet actually turned her down. "Think about it then, if you want. I'm willing anytime you are. In the meantime . . ."

Nat waited. She appeared to hesitate but did not move from her chair.

"That mutual friend, I mentioned . . ."

"Yes?"

"It might be he has the initials T. T. That he goes by a nickname that also starts with T. That maybe it's kind of close to a frog."

Nat sat straight up in his chair. Roxie smiled, knowing she now had his full interest.

"You know Toad Turnbull?"

"I might," she said with a ludicrous coyness.

"There's no 'might' about it. Either you do or you don't."

His voice was so stern that Roxie wilted under it. "All right. I do, then. I knew him way back, down in Arizona. We kind of keep in touch."

Now Nat leaned toward her over the table, his eyes darkened with intensity. "Do you know where he is?"

Roxie looked away. "Well . . ."

He reached out and grabbed her wrist. "If you know where he is, tell me."

"Ouch! Let go. I don't know. Sometimes I hear from him, or from friends of his who go through. But I haven't heard in a while. That's the God's truth."

Nat realized he was taking the wrong tack with this woman in allowing his strong hatred for the Toad to spill over onto her. He dropped her wrist and apologized, forcing himself to sound friendly. "Look, I got a little carried away there. I'm sorry. I've been looking for Turnbull a long time, and since the last job he pulled, I haven't been able to learn anything about where he went. To tell the truth, there hasn't been much time to find out, what with Medora's needs and all. But if you could tell me anything, I'd be, well, very grateful."

Satisfaction spread over Roxie's face. "I don't know, honest. I haven't heard anything lately about where he is. But I might be able to find out for you. That is, if you really mean what you say."

Nat felt himself gritting his teeth. But perhaps if he didn't spell out just what form his gratitude would take, he might still be able to get some information out of this woman. At least it was better to keep his options open.

"Roxie," he said, patting her arm, "I think we can be good friends. If you want to please me, you'll find out anything you can about Turnbull. And in return, I'll do what I can to help you."

"Friends? Well, yes. I'd like that. I'll see what I can do. And meantime, when you've had enough of Miss Prim up there, and decide you want a real

176

woman, remember me. OK?"

"OK." Nat gave her his friendliest smile and watched as she slipped out of the chair and moved toward the bar at the far end of the saloon. Then glancing up, he saw that Ardeth was glaring at him from the stage, her blue eyes blazing with a quiet fury.

Chapter Nine

Shortly after speaking with Roxie, Nat left the saloon, murmuring under his breath at the perversity of women. Eddie Lathrop swirled his piano stool away from the keyboard and watched him leave, wondering that Medora had cut short her rehearsal, not to follow Varien but to stalk off upstairs to her room.

"If you ask me, there's too many preemer donners in this town," he muttered. "Fireweed ain't big enough for all of them."

"Didn't ask you," the bartender, Wister, answered, sloshing a wet rag along the gleaming counter. "Don't even know what it means."

Eddie ambled over to the bar and leaned against it. "Give me a little of that tarantula juice, Wister. All this rehearsin's left me dry."

"Kind of early in the afternoon, ain't it? You got a long night."

"S'never too early for whisky." He took the glass Wister placed in front of him and downed it in two gulps. Then he wiped his arm across his mouth and adjusted the elastic bands on his shirt sleeve. "How about finishing that game we started yesterday while things is quiet. I picked up a little loose change last night, and I figure to get back what I lost."

Wister glanced around the saloon. Aside from Shannessy sitting in one corner, well on his way to his daily inebriation, and two of the girls lounging dispiritedly two tables away, the place was dead. No better time to relieve Eddie of his loose change. "Why not," he said and threw the rag below the counter.

By the time the money had changed hands twenty minutes later, two other men had entered the saloon. One of them Wister recognized as a farmhand from the Swedish colony outside town who ambled in to visit the girls when he was sent into Fireweed for supplies. The second man, who had pushed through the swinging doors just as Wister won the last pot and reached for Lathrop's coins, was a stranger. He was a short man with long muttonchop sideburns and so nattily dressed that he almost took Eddie's mind off losing the game.

"Mother of God!" Eddie muttered. "What a dandy. He must have just rolled off the stagecoach."

"Coach ain't due till tomorrow." Wister gave the man a long appraising look, taking in the striped waistcoat, the fawn-colored frockcoat, the tall hat of gleaming brown suede, the checkered trousers and the spats. "Won't Roxie have a fit to see this dude!"

Spotting the two men staring at him from a table

179

on the side, the stranger smiled broadly and made his way over. Though short of stature, he walked with such a straight back and such mincing steps that he might have been an operatic tenor, Lathrop thought. Sweeping off his hat, he made them a highly theatrical bow.

"Am I addressing the proprietor of the Diamond Ring," he asked, smiling even more broadly. Both Lathrop and Wister saw at once that he sported one brightly gleaming gold tooth, and it was as much as they could do to pull their eyes away from it.

"No you ain't," Wister finally answered. "I'm the barkeep and this here's the piano player. Jasper Corchran owns the place, but if you want to see him, you'll have to wait till tomorrow when he gets back from Hays."

The man's face fell. "You can run a game here anyway," Lathrop added helpfully. "Corchran don't care even if you cheat, long as you don't get caught at it. You could get shot or strung up, but it's on your own head."

"That's right," added Wister. "Do what you like, just don't expect us to help if you get in trouble."

"My good sirs," the stranger said haughtily. "You are making a gross mistake. I am not a card barracuda!"

"You ain't. I would of sworn you was a shark. Wouldn't you have sworn, Wister? Why, from the looks of you, you could put old Owen Salter to shame."

"We do see a stream of gamblers come through here, though not many so fancily dressed as yourself," Wister replied.

"Professional gambler! Merciful heavens, has it come to this! Is this such a one-horse, provincial backwater town that anyone suitably dressed is taken for a professional poker player!"

"Oh, we have other games besides poker. Faro, Keno—"

"Please, sir! I do not indulge in games of chance of any kind. I am an impresario." Laying his hat on the table, he delicately placed his chamois gloves along the brim and took a chair, crossing one leg over the other. Wister and Lathrop exchanged mystified glances.

"A who?" Wister asked.

"If that means you want a job singing or playing the hurdy-gurdy organ, we already got all the entertainers we need," Lathrop said, leaning over the table and assuming a superior tone because he knew a little more of the world of music than Wister. "In fact, we already got the best singer this side of the Mississippi."

"I do not sing. I manage. I manage singers' careers. Who is this golden-voiced paragon you have already hired?"

"It's Miss Medora Melindez. And she's been knocking 'em dead here every night for almost two weeks."

There was an abrupt change in the stranger's demeanor. Sitting bolt upright, he pulled a large linen handkerchief from his sleeve and dabbed at his brow. "Here? Still? Oh, thank heaven. I was afraid I must have missed her and would have to go off on another of these endless searches through these dreadful, dusty collections of ramshackle buildings you people call towns. Thank God!"

"You know Miss Melindez?" Lathrop asked, suspecting that somewhere in all those words there was buried an insult to his town.

"Know her! Why, sir, I am the one who brought her here, who made the arrangement for her triumphant tour of the Great West. Allow me . . . my card . . . Mortimer Yancey, Musical Impresario and Agent to the Golden Voices of the World! Not only voices but entertainers of all kinds: child acrobats, comedians, snake charmers, song and dance. You have heard, no doubt, of Master Wille Sidney, the Champion Light-Weight Roller Skater of the World. My creation. Old Rubber Face, whose contortions have delighted millions from the bowery to the Painted Desert—I set him on his road to fame. Just name what you want, be it a drove of camels or an Arabian belly wobbler, and I'll produce it for your edification and, incidentally, profit."

Wister rose to return to the bar. "We don't need no more half-baked entertainers at the Diamond Ring. We're in the business of selling whisky, not entertainment."

Lathrop leaned on the table. "Oh, I don't know. That Arabian belly wobbler sounds pretty good."

"Good sirs," Yancey intoned, "I have journeyed far in my search for Miss Melindez. Pray, tell me where to find her and I shall be on my way, eternally indebted to you."

Lathrop had his mouth open to tell him the lady

182

was upstairs when Wister broke in. "She's not here. She was earlier, but she left after going over her songs for tonight."

"But where would she go in such a limited place? Surely I can find her."

"Well, she has rooms at the boardinghouse across the street," Wister said blandly, ignoring Lathrop's mystified stare. "You might find her there. It has pretty good food, so she'd probably be there waiting for supper."

Yancey gathered up his hat and gloves, sighing with resignation. "Would this boardinghouse also have extra rooms? Perhaps I might take of one myself. It would be most gratifying to divest myself of at least one layer of this eternal dust."

"Could be. Why don't you go over and ask?"

"I shall do so at once. Good day, gentlemen. And thank you for your information." Yancey snapped his shoes together and bowed formally before setting his hat on his head and starting for the door. It had barely swung closed behind him before Lathrop was bending over the bar into Wister's face.

"Why'd you do that? You know Medora's upstairs. And Ma Combley's food would kill a rattlesnake."

Wister wiped at a bottle with a damp rag. "Don't really know. Something about him bothered me. I guess it's that 'cock o' the walk' attitude, like he was somethin' great and we were nothin'. Besides, I kind of like Nat Varien, and I think he ought to know this fellow's in town trying to take over his territory. He won't appreciate seeing somebody else move in

183

on Medora, and can't say as I blame him."

Lathrop nodded, though it would never have occurred to him to send the cocky impresario off on a wild goose chase. Yet Wister generally knew what he was doing. "Maybe I ought to go out and find Nat Varien," he said in what was more of a question than a statement.

Wister placed the bottle back on the shelf with the others. "Maybe you should," he answered. "And hurry. Fireweed's not big enough to keep that fellow away from Medora for very long."

Eddie caught up with Nat at the stables where he was supervising the daily grooming of his sleek roan stallion. It was some satisfaction to Lathrop to see Nat's face fade to two shades lighter when he told him of Yancey's arrival, though he could not know the real reason for it.

"And he's over at Ma Combley's now?" Nat asked in a strange voice.

"That's right. You could probably catch him there if you've a mind to."

"No. I think I'd better see Medora first. And thank Wister for me, will you?"

He was off at once, thinking to take the back stairs up to Ardeth's room, but halfway there, he changed his mind and headed into the Diamond Ring to slip Wister a small gratuity and inquire about Roxie.

"Up in her room, I believe," the bartender said, gratefully pocketing Nat's money.

"Alone?"

"Far as I know."

"I'm obliged to you, John," Nat said and made for the stairs. Roxie's room was at the opposite end of the hall from Ardeth's, but the distance was close enough that he moved quietly and knocked gently as he recalled Ardeth's murderous glances earlier that afternoon. All the same, as Roxie's door opened a crack, so did Ardeth's down the hall. He caught a quick glimpse of her white face staring at him for an instant before she closed the door a little more forcefully than was called for. "Damn!" he muttered as he slipped into Roxie's room.

It was sparsely furnished and littered with all manner of clutter that revealed none of the feminine touches of Ardeth's. Roxie's eyes widened at the sight of him. She pulled a wilted feathered robe around her chemise and slid up against him, thinking he had changed his mind about wanting her much quicker than she had expected.

Nat put his hands on her shoulders and pushed her away. "Roxie, I need your help."

Her arms slid around his neck. "Oh, sweetie, you know you can have anything you want from me."

He pushed her away again. "No, it's not that kind of help. Maybe later but not right now. I've got another problem now that you can help me with."

She was disappointed, but she put on a brave face. After all, any kind of attention from Nat Varien was better than indifference and might just lead to something better.

185

"You just name it."

"There's a man just arrived in town. He's over at the boardinghouse and probably will be staying there. I want you to . . . divert him."

"You mean get him into bed?"

"Yes. Make a big fuss over him. Keep his mind off . . . other things. Take up all his time. Think you can do it?"

Roxie shrugged and allowed the neckline of her robe to slip down over one shoulder. "In my sleep. But . . . you realize it will cut into my working time."

"Oh, I'll pay you for it and pay you well. But you have to keep him occupied and away from the Diamond Ring as much as possible."

"Who is this man? A gunfighter? Running from the law?"

"No, no. In fact, he's quite straight. Even a dandy, I'm told. Probably has lots of money, so you can get paid two ways."

"A dandy! Is this that dude who was in the saloon a little while ago? I watched him from the stairwell. Why, he looks like he wouldn't know what to do with a girl like me!"

"Then, teach him. It ought to be a challenge for you."

"Why, he's got a little pursed mouth and walks with these mincing tiny steps. God A'mighty, you ask a lot."

"I'll pay you for it."

"It's goin' to cost you more than I thought at first."

186

"All right, all right. Just keep him busy and away from this saloon. Believe me, I'll be very grateful."

Roxie looked at him through her slanted eyes. "How grateful?"

Gritting his teeth, Nat reached over and gave her a peck on the cheek. "Extremely grateful. Now, I have to go. Get dressed and get over to Ma Combley's as quick as you can."

He was out of the door before she could protest further, closing it after him with a sigh of relief. He stopped on the landing a moment to consider where to go next. At all costs this Mortimer Yancey must be prevented from coming face to face with Ardeth, or their whole elaborate scheme was doomed. Though they had not yet found Medora's map, he was more certain than ever that it was somewhere among her belongings. Not only was it important for them to look further, but there was even some hope that Roxie might help him discover the Toad's whereabouts. And Ardeth was doing so well in impersonating Medora on stage that it would be a shame to have to throw away all their hard work. He had enjoyed this time with her more than he ever thought possible. Besides, he was very unsure about how the townspeople of Fireweed would react once they learned they had been duped into laying out the red carpet for an impostor. No, if Roxie could keep Yancey occupied for the rest of the afternoon and evening and he could keep Ardeth in her room until time to perform, it might at least buy them a little time. He would think of some way out eventually.

He went downstairs long enough to order a supper to be brought up to Ardeth's room in an hour, then made his way back upstairs to knock lightly on her door.

"Who is it!" a very unladylike voice inquired from the other side of the door.

"Medora, it's me. Nat. Open up. I need to talk to you."

There was a shattering crash as something broke against the other side of the door. "Go away!" Ardeth yelled. "Go see your fancy woman. I don't want to see your miserable face!"

Nat rattled the handle, trying to keep his voice down. "Medora. It's not what you think. Believe me, it's *imperative* that we talk. Now please open up the door."

"I can't think of anything I have to say to you!" Her voice was nearer, as though she was standing right next to the door.

"Believe me, you do," he said in a loud whisper. "Your *manager* has arrived in town."

There was a pause then a rattle as a key turned and the door cracked. Ardeth peered out at him without giving him room to enter. "My manager?"

"That's right, *Medora*," Nat said. The dark look on his face was enough to convince her he was serious, and she opened the door just far enough for him to slide in. He locked it behind him while she took off across the room.

"You . . . you bastard! Why don't you go back to that whore down the hall since you like her so much. Flirting with her and playing up to her and

188

right in front of me. You're nothing but a . . . a RAKE!"

"That's mild compared to some of the names I've been called."

"It's only because I'm a lady that I can't call you what you deserve. Go on. Get out of here! Go back to your slut!"

She grabbed the first thing to hand, one of the pillows off the bed, and threw it against his chest. "I don't think you'll want me to leave when you learn why I'm here," he said, picking it up off the floor. It was followed by a second pillow and, hard on the heels of that, a bone-handled hairbrush. Nat dodged the brush and started across the room toward her, fending off an ivory comb, a bottle of scent, an inlaid mahogany chest and a porcelain, round picture frame. All these missiles were interspersed with her vehement comments: "Get away from me! I never want to see the sight of your ugly face again! Go away and don't ever come back! It was a mistake to ever get involved with you!" When she reached for the painted lamp on the bedside table, he was close enough to grab it from her hands.

"Calm down, for God's sake. What's the matter with you? Have you gone crazy!"

Deprived of her weapon, Ardeth began beating on his chest with her fists, so angry now that all she wanted was to inflict some of the same hurt on him as he had on her. Nat grabbed her fists, painfully gripping them, his own fury spilling over. "Will you stop this for a moment and just listen!" he roared.

"No, I won't!" she yelled back and, working one hand free, swung her arm and slapped him across the face.

That was too much. Lifting her, he threw her across the bed and, before she could scramble off again, was over her, pinning her arms with his hands and staring down into her contorted face. She struggled helplessly in his grip.

"Let me go, you . . . you bastard!"

"I'll let you go when you stop this thrashing and listen for a minute."

"I don't want to hear anything you've got to say. Get away from me!"

"Damn it! Be still!"

Ardeth writhed beneath him, twisting her legs until she managed to raise one knee, thrusting it up between his legs. She was so encased in petticoats and skirts that it did little damage but was the last indignity Nat was willing to suffer. He shifted his weight, wedging his knee between her thighs and spreading her legs. Her twisting, writhing body inflamed his desire, spiraling his anger into a white-hot need. He released one hand to grab her chin, pulling her lips up to his, kneading against them, forcing them apart with the blade of his tongue. Ardeth shoved her fist against his chest, but he was much too strong for her. She found her mouth opening to his, receiving him, welcoming him, even as her sense of outrage swelled within her. Her hand stilled as spiraling waves of heat consumed her. She felt him wrestling furiously with her skirts, felt the coolness of his fingers tearing at her clothes

190

until they searingly gripped her hot thighs, thrusting upward into the moist receptacle of her body.

"Let me . . . go. . . !" she tried to say vainly, tearing away her lips from his flaming tongue.

"No!" she heard him mutter. His arm went around her shoulder, pinning her to him as her struggle began anew. The force of her body caught him off balance, and they rolled completely over on the bed in a swirl of her skirts.

His hand on her groin imprisoned her against him, kneading, thrusting, violently massaging her. She felt her body tremble and go slack. She wasn't even aware when she began kissing him back, thrusting her own tongue into the cavity of his mouth, tasting, exploring. She never knew how he got free of his pants, but suddenly she felt his hot masculinity fill her, thrusting home with a violent intensity. She gasped as they rolled over again to lay poised on the edge of the bed, hanging dangerously over the edge.

Waves of heat swept over her, carrying her on spiraling streaks of ecstasy. The hammering thrusts of his body surged within her, and she rode with each wave, moving in concert with his urgent need. Yanking her skirts up higher, she spread her thighs wide to receive him deeper and was just conscious enough to smile with delight at the mumbled cries that escaped his lips. He was desperate for her now. Pushing her over on her back, he thrust home just as they both went careening off the bed onto the floor, soaring on an exploding firestorm of delight so strong that they hardly noticed they had fallen.

Gasping, they clung to each other as the frantic pounding of their hearts subsided and their breathing eased. For a long moment neither moved. Ardeth nestled her head against the hollow of his neck and reveled in the warmth of his comforting arms. At length Nat raised his head and looked around.

"How the devil did we get on the floor!"

"You were being violent. Don't you remember?"

"I remember you wouldn't be still." He raised up, lifting her with him, and she saw they were lying in a bundle of her clothes at the edge of the bed with half the bed covers pulled down with them. It was so ridiculous Ardeth began to giggle.

"It's not funny," Nat said with mock seriousness which quickly erupted into laughter.

"No, it's not," Ardeth said when she could stop giggling. "As a matter of fact, you very nearly raped me!"

"I seem to remember you being willing enough there at the end."

"That was later. I wasn't at first."

"Well, if you hadn't been so blasted violent yourself, I might have kept better control. You're so damned beautiful when you get angry." He gently pushed back the long strands of raven-black hair that had slipped over her white forehead. "You're beautiful when you're not angry, too," he said, kissing her lightly on the lips. "You drive me crazy. You know that, don't you?"

Ardeth pulled back. "Is that why you were so thick with that slut Roxie? You didn't appear very aware of my charms then."

For an answer Nat reached behind her and pulled her face back to his. "For God's sake, don't you know I wouldn't give an old broad like Roxie a second look? That was pure business, as I would have told you if you had given me a chance to explain." He dropped his lips of the curve of her neck and nuzzled there.

Ardeth felt her body tremble with the tickling waves of his caress. "Business? What kind of business?" Her arms slid around his neck. He bent his head, baring his brown neck to her lips. She traced patterns with her tongue on his skin as she felt his lips move lower, making gentle swirling patterns on her breasts.

"Confound these clothes!" Nat exclaimed and set about methodically untying her stays. Ardeth lay slack and warm as he pulled the bodice and corset away, reveling in the feel of his strong hands sliding up her waist to cup her breasts and lift them to his lips, each in turn.

She forced him away long enough to help him get out of the remainder of his own clothes. They both lay sleek and naked on the floor beside the bed, half on the crumpled bed covers. His hands drifted over her body with feathery softness, lulling her into a dreamy, sensual fog. He traced her knees, her thighs, the moist mystery between, then lightly up her abdomen to her waist, cupping one breast. He bent to take its stiff point between his lips, thrusting, and tasting with his tongue while she writhed in pleasure.

Suddenly she felt him lifting her. He set her on

the edge of the bed and knelt before her, sliding his hands along her thighs. She looked at him in confusion, not knowing what he had in mind. Then he kissed her inner thighs near the knee and slowly began working his way up her leg. Gently forcing her silken thighs apart, he placed his lips on her most intimate parts, delighting her with a forbidden sensuality she had never known existed.

Ardeth moaned, arching her back, her hands on the bed. She was drifting again on a spiral of sheer pleasure, almost beyond thought. Then, just as she drifted close to the edge, he moved again, laying her back on the bed and bending over her. She felt his body move along her lips, his chest, his abdomen, the tufts of hair, and then, in a gesture she hardly understood, she took his hard, male shaft between her lips, sucking on the delicate, rounded tip. She heard him groan with pleasure as his shaft began to throb within her hands. Then he moved again, sliding her beneath him, taking her in his arms and burying his face in her neck as the delicious need within him took over, shoving its way to a joyous fulfillment.

They lay quietly, clasped together, for a long time. Ardeth thought Nat had gone to sleep, he was so still. She herself was completely relaxed and happy. *He loves me,* she thought. *He must love me to share all this with me. And I was so worried he would abandon me for a slut like Roxie!*

It was not until later when they were having supper together in her room that Nat told her about Mortimer Yancey. It almost ruined the sleepy, contentment that had been left from their afternoon of making love.

"But if he knows Medora . . ." she said, her hand going to her throat.

"Exactly. Once he sees you, he'll know something strange is going on. That's why we have to keep him away from the Diamond Ring until I can figure out a way to get him out of Fireweed."

"But I'm supposed to perform tonight."

"Roxie will keep him busy tonight. It's tomorrow that worries me. I can't keep you locked up here in your room forever."

"Is that the business you had with Roxie?"

"Yes," Nat said without hesitation. No point in going into the rest of it.

"Well, if we spend all our time locked up like we spent this afternoon, I won't mind too much." She looked at him archly and smiled.

"My love, if we do that, I won't survive to see Mortimer Yancey leave town. I think we'd better find a more practical way of avoiding Mr. Yancey."

"Of course," Ardeth answered meekly. "But what?"

"I don't know yet, but I'll think of something. If only we'd been able to find that map! We could have been long gone from Fireweed by now and not have to worry about managers turning up. Oh, well, at least we don't have to worry about tonight."

He remembered those words later that evening when, as he was standing in the wings watching Ardeth going through her performance in high style, he saw a short, dapper gentleman who could only be Mortimer Yancey push his way through the swinging doors of the saloon and approach the stage.

Chapter Ten

With a flourish of skirts Ardeth came dancing off the stage into the wings where Nat grabbed her arm.

"You can't go back out there!" he exclaimed.

Ardeth stared in amazement. "But I've got to take my bow. Listen to all that applause."

"No! Yancey is in the house. I just saw him come through the door."

Ardeth went white beneath her makeup. "Yancey! What are we going to do?" Her comment was almost lost under the thunder of stomping and clapping with which the audience summoned her back on stage.

Nat glared around the curtain as the noise level rose even higher. "You'll have to take one bow but make it quick. Keep your eyes on the floor. Whatever you do, don't look directly out into the audience."

Ardeth nodded and ran back out on stage, bending almost to her knees and staring at the floorboards. Then she rose, fixed her gaze on the ceiling and threw kisses to the house, trying vainly to look pleased. Once back in the wings, she clung to Nat.

"Wait here a moment then go straight upstairs," he said quietly as the hurdy-gurdy man went bouncing by him onto the stage. "Lock your door and don't let anyone in but Martha. I'll try to head him off."

Ardeth nodded and watched him leave. After a few moments, she peered around the curtain just far enough to see Nat's tall form heading for the bar on the opposite wall accompanied by a short, straight-backed man in a tall, gleaming felt hat. Since their backs were to her, she used that moment to dash out and head upstairs, keeping one hand up to shield her face. Once upstairs, she ran down the hall to her room and dashed inside, leaning against the door to calm her pounding heart.

As she was standing there, she noticed a letter lying on the floor, half buried beneath the fringe of the washstand table. It must have come during the afternoon, and she had not seen it what with the distractions Nat had created. Absently she reached down to pick it up, glancing at the ornate handwriting as she began pulling at her buttons.

Downstairs, Nat leaned on the shining brass rail of the bar and ordered two whiskies. "It's really too bad about Miss Melindez," he said sympathetically, "but you see she's had a difficult time since she arrived in this town. For the first two weeks, she could not perform at all because of a morbid sore throat. She's still inclined to suffer the vapors quite frequently and only made it through tonight's performance out of sheer professional willpower."

"Oh, yes, a thorough professional," Yancey said, taking a swig of his whisky. "But it is too bad. You cannot imagine what I've been through trying to see this lady. The horrors I've had to endure in this godforsaken country. Trying to travel from one half-baked, uncivilized outpost to another, suffering the primitive trains, stagecoaches, even, at one time, forced to ride a horse myself! I tell you, sir, it's more than a gentleman of gentility and culture should have to endure!"

"Mmm," Nat agreed. "You're out from St. Louis, then?"

"St. Louis? Oh, no, that is, yes, of course, but some time ago. Distances are so great in this part of the world. Such a long time . . . so far, you see . . . so difficult to get from one place to another. Been traveling quite a long time."

Nat pushed his glass toward Wister for a refill. All this hemming and hawing on Yancey's part made it obvious that Yancey was not inclined to say where he had seen Medora and when. For the first time, he began to wonder if Mortimer Yancey was quite the threat he had seemed. But it was better to be sure.

Yancey went on before Nat could frame his next question. "Why, even in Fireweed I've had to overcome obstacles trying to see Medora. Just this afternoon, a woman in the boardinghouse—a damn fine-looking woman, too—why, she would have had me in bed with her all afternoon and evening if I'd had a mind. But I learned long ago that you can't get ahead in this world that way. No, sir, Mortimer Yancey never allows pleasure to come before business."

"Too bad," Nat muttered.

"What's that?"

"Oh, I was just thinking that since you were unable to see Miss Medora anyway, you might want to go back and take advantage of this woman's generous offer. It might be a pleasant way to wile away the hours until tomorrow."

This thought obviously had not occurred to Yancey. "Mmm. Not such a bad idea at that," he said, downing the rest of his whisky. He reached for his hat and gloves as Nat laid a hand on his shoulder to encourage him toward the door. "You're certain I can't see Miss Melindez?" Yancey stopped to ask. "I wouldn't keep her long, and I'd be careful not to upset her. But I've been waiting so long."

Nat patted his shoulder sympathetically. "No, no. It's quite out of the question. Believe me, you wouldn't want to see her when she's feeling this ill. She's a regular terror. It would be much better to wait until tomorrow. We'll make certain you can interview her first thing in the morning."

"Well . . . if you're sure. . . ."

"Believe me, I'm sure." He pushed open one half of the swinging door. Resigned, Yancey clapped his hat on his head, thrust out his chest, pulled himself up to his full five feet and went out the door, his thoughts already on Ma Crombley's boardinghouse. Once the doors swung behind him, Nat sank into the nearest chair and loosened the collar of his shirt. "Thank God!" he muttered, grateful to be reprieved at least until morning. What he was going to do then, God only knew.

By this time Martha Higley had come upstairs to Ardeth's room to help her undress. Relieved of her corset, Ardeth slipped on a soft, sky-blue silk robe with ecru lace ruffles at the wide sleeves. As she sat at the dressing table to allow Martha to brush out her long glistening locks, she saw the letter lying on the table where she had thrown it earlier. Idly she picked it up. Of course she had recognized the ornate handwriting the minute she saw it as another letter from Garth Reardon in Wyoming. Curious, she broke it open and glanced down the contents.

He refused to be discouraged, although he had not received an answer to his first letter. No doubt it had been lost somewhere in transit—mail was so undependable in the West. So here he was again, earnestly pleading with her to accept his invitation to visit the Silver Sage. Further, he wished her to know that he would be in Cheyenne on the twenty-fourth to meet her and escort her himself to his ranch. He felt certain she would enjoy her stay there since his estate included all the amenities of civilized living. Furthermore, his distinguished group of visitors would be most entertaining for her as well as possibly offering her the opportunity to enhance her career. He remained her most obedient and admiring servant, etc. etc.

Ardeth folded the letter and laid it in her lap, dreamily letting her mind wander while luxuriating in the good feel of the brush stroking through her

201

hair. It was tempting, this invitation to a fine, wealthy ranch in Wyoming. It was a part of the world she had never seen, it included meeting obviously well-to-do and cultured people of a sort she had never known, and it was bound to offer her new, exciting experiences of a kind she had never hoped to have. Her stay in Fireweed was almost up anyway. She had made enough money here to be able to establish herself and still send some back to her family in Nebraska, but there would be a lot more to be made in Wyoming if Reardon was as well off as he appeared to be from his letters. How impressed her father would be at her success!

But no. It was too risky. She had gone on with this playacting at being Medora about as long as she could. It had been successful so far, but her luck could not last much longer. Even if she managed to avoid coming face to face with Mortimer Yancey in the next few days, there was bound to be someone coming through Fireweed someday who had known Medora. Better that she and Nat should leave Fireweed and go off together to some other life where she could once again become Ardeth Royce.

How casually she assumed that such a life would include Nat. The truth was, she suddenly realized, that life without him had become unthinkable. Though he had never mentioned the word "love," she knew that he cared deeply for her just as she did for him. She could no longer imagine a life without lying in his arms, feeling his lips on her cheek, his lean, hard body against her own. Their lives were intwined together now, deeply and inseparably.

"Why have you got that silly smile on your face," Martha said as she watched Ardeth in the mirror over the dressing table. "As if I didn't know."

Quickly Ardeth got her emotions back under control. "I don't know what you're talking about."

"Oh, I seen the starry-eyed looks you give that Varien fellow. I tell you, you got to watch out for men like that. I seen 'em come through Fireweed more often than you could count, good lookin', smilin', arrogant as the devil himself. Why, they'd take a girl's heart and stomp on it as easy as they'd jump on a rattlesnake. I tell you, they ain't to be trusted. None of 'em are no better than they ought to be, and all of 'em are nothing but trouble!"

"That's enough!"

"You're too young and pretty and trustin', I say, for a fellow like that. It'll do you no good, no good a'tall."

Angrily Ardeth grabbed the hairbrush from Martha's hand. "I won't hear any more. Mind your own business!" How haughty she sounded since she had become Medora. Ardeth Royce, farm girl from Nebraska, would never have spoken so rudely to her elders.

Martha was not the least offended, chalking up Ardeth's response to her artistic temperament. "All right, but remember what I say," she muttered as she began picking up Ardeth's clothes which were lying in heaps around the room, reserving those that needed washing and pressing. As she headed for the door, Ardeth called to her. "Wait, Martha. I'm sorry I spoke so rudely. The truth is I'm not

203

feeling so well."

"There now, I thought you looked a little sickish."

"Would you do me a big favor and let me sleep in the morning. Don't let anybody bother me before I call you, would you, please?"

Martha walked back to her and stroked her hair. "Do you want a tonic, then? I've got some Hostetter's Stomach Bitters. Nothing puts the starch back in your bones quicker than that medicine. I swear by it."

"No, thank you. I'm just tired. It's nothing a good night's sleep won't fix. But you will keep everyone away from my door?"

Martha gave her shoulder a quick squeeze. "The United States Cavalry itself couldn't get past me."

The next morning Nat was careful to keep well out of sight of the Diamond Ring Saloon, and Mortimer Yancey. Though Yancey was inside asking for Ardeth shortly after sunrise, he did not get even as far as the stairwell, it was so well guarded by Ardeth's friends. He sat nursing his frustration until noon and, when Medora had still not appeared, finally went across the street to the boardinghouse for dinner.

Nat saw Yancey's short, portly form disappear into Ma Crombley's, then dashed up the walkway and into the saloon. In the distance he heard the whistle of the train arriving at the depot outside of town and briefly toyed with the thought of knocking Yancey on the head from behind and bundling him into the train as it rolled out again. There were too many people who ate Ma's cooking to make that idea practical, however, so instead he ducked into the saloon and kept watch through a small peephole in the clouded window.

"Well, you look like your mind's a thousand miles away," said a bright voice behind him. "What's the matter? Expecting the Toad to come riding in?"

Nat turned and saw Roxie coming toward him from the stairs. She was wearing a long blue skirt and a white blouse that had seen better days. Her hair was carelessly piled on top of her head, and the shadows on her face made her look several years older than she was.

"You look rather the worse for wear yourself. Have a hard night?"

Roxie shrugged and pulled a chair. "No worse than usual. I did what you asked and kept your friend occupied. There's more life in that little fellow than you'd think to look at him."

"Looks are often deceiving. But I'm grateful. I trust he made it worth your while."

She leaned toward him over the table. "Oh, yes. But it's you making it worth my while that I'm interested in."

Before Nat could frame a reply, his concentration was drawn to the street where a wagon had just drawn up, disgorging passengers who had come in on the train. His words froze on his lips as he recognized a shock of blond hair on a tall frame that was unbending itself from the wagon frame. "No!" he breathed, bringing Roxie up beside him to look through the window.

"What's wrong? You look like you seen a ghost

. . . Hey, ain't that the teacher you brought back from—"

He clapped his hand over her mouth. "Yes. But you don't need to advertise the fact. The truth is, you see, Medora has suffered a recurrence of the morbid sore throat. That's why she hasn't come down this morning. You won't say anything to anyone, will you? I'll let them know in due time."

Roxie removed his hand and ran her fingers lightly down the palm. "Anything you ask, love. But don't forget our bargain."

"I won't, I won't," Nat whispered as several of the passengers from the wagon began to stream through the door. "Now, excuse me, I've got to go speak to . . . my friend."

He bounded off, not even noticing that Roxie had frozen, staring at one of the men who had just entered the saloon. Cutting off Drury Templeton before he could reach the bar, Nat took his arm and dragged him to a table far back against the wall near the stage.

"What the devil are you doing here!" he said through clenched teeth. "I told you to stay away from Fireweed."

"Why, Mr. Varien, I was hoping to see you again. I was mighty afraid you and Miss Melindez would have moved on by now. Much relieved to see you're still here. That is—" he glanced around—"I presume she is still here."

"Yes. She's got one or two more performances, then we're out of here. I didn't think to see you back again before we left."

Templeton ran his hand through his thick shock

of blond hair. He was looking very grubby, Nat thought, as though he was just coming out of a long, extended drunk. In fact, that's probably exactly what he had been doing since he left Fireweed. His chin was covered with ragged blond fuzz, his clothes were dirty and disheveled and even his fingernails were grimy. First Yancey and now Templeton! The recipe for disaster!

"The fact is, Mr. Varien, I ran into a spot of trouble. Robbers, you know—they're everywhere out here—and a poor man traveling alone is nothing but a lure. They took everything I had, every cent."

"Not before you managed to drink up most of it, I trust."

"Well . . . yes, I had enjoyed a snort or two. But when the rest was stolen, well I thought, why not seek Mr. Varien's help again. After all, I helped him when he was in need." He looked slyly around. "I presume, you see, that since you are still here, Miss Medora must have learned what I taught her quite well."

"She's done well."

"A great success, in fact?"

"You might say that."

"Indeed, her fame has traveled. I heard a weathered cowpoke at the bar in Hays bragging about what a wonderful entertainer she was. He had heard her here and was singing her praises up and down Kansas."

"So you thought you'd come back and get in on the pickings."

"How crass! Surely you can't think so lowly of me. . . ."

"Now listen here, Templeton. Let's stop all this poppycock and speak plainly. You're here to blackmail me, and we both know it. You probably drank up all I gave you and are back for more." Nat's face was close enough to Drury's to see the flecks of saliva on his thin lips. Reaching out he grabbed him by his grimy collar and pulled him closer. "You slimy bastard!"

Panic flared in Drury's pale eyes. "Please. I detest violence of any sort. I'm an artist!"

"You're a drunk and a blackmailer. But I'm going to buy your silence one more time." Releasing Templeton, Nat sat back and pulled out a small leather purse from inside his coat. "Here's enough to get you started on your daily dosage. I'll have the rest tonight."

Drury reached for the coins Nat slid across the table. "Most grateful . . ." he muttered, his eyes lighting up with the prospect of a drink. Nat slapped his hand over the coins.

"Just one thing more. You're going to be out of here on the first stage or train, whichever comes first. And, if I hear one word around town about Medora not being all she's supposed to be, I'll know where it came from. I'll find you and shoot a hole right through that classic white forehead. Is that clear!"

The coldness of his voice and eyes added weight to Nat's words. Drury nodded, licking his lips nervously. The truth was, he had been very fearful of confronting Nat Varien once more but had no place else to go. He cared nothing in the least about Medora's true identity as long as he got the money he needed for his addiction.

Nat watched him pocket the coins clumsily and wobble over toward the bar. He drummed his fingers on the table. Of all the people to show up just when Mortimer Yancey was sniffing around Medora. How was he going to keep them all apart and fight off Roxie, too?—though Roxie seemed uninterested in him at the moment, occupied with two of the new arrivals at the opposite end of the bar from Templeton.

It was too much to figure out right now. He would go up and see Medora and try one last, desperate time to discover what in hell she had done with that map!

Yet, since the two of them had already searched three times in every conceivable place the map might be hidden, he ended up striding up and down the room, slamming his fists one against the other, trying to figure a way out of this dilemma.

"For heaven's sake, sit down," Ardeth snapped. "You're wearing out the carpet."

"I've got to find a solution for this. I can bundle one of them out of town perhaps, but two . . . impossible! How am I going to keep Yancey away from this saloon and get rid of Templeton at the same time?"

"I don't know, but you've got to think of something. I can't stay cooped up in this room for the next five days pretending to be sick again. I'll go crazy."

"Yancey and Templeton must be kept apart at all costs, yet they are both drawn to the Diamond Ring like a magnet. And you can't leave until you finish the last two performances. A second-rate promoter, a drunken has-been of a tenor and a farm girl masquerading as a singer. God, what a mess!"

"I wish those performances were over and we could leave today. Have you thought about where we're going next?"

Nat seemed distracted. "No. Anywhere away from Fireweed."

"It will be so lovely to be myself again and not have to worry about being unmasked. We can finally lay poor Medora to rest."

"Not until we can find a way to keep these two men apart."

Ardeth picked idly at the ruffles on the sleeve of her robe. "Perhaps that's it," she said quietly. "Yes, perhaps that will solve everything. . . ."

He stopped in midtrack halfway across the room. "What is," he said, staring at her lounging on the bed.

"Well, it's just a thought, but you're trying so hard to keep them apart when perhaps bringing them together might solve all our problems. Drury is a performer after all, and Yancey handles performers. . . ."

Nat started to protest that Drury Templeton was not much of a performer any longer. But the possibilities in her suggestion grew as he thought it over. "Listen," he said, sitting down at the foot of the bed. "Is there anything in Medora's belongings in her handwriting?"

"There's a short letter to a theater manager in St. Louis and one or two bills. Why?"

"Do you think you can copy it?"

"I think so. It's not particularly distinctive."

"Good. Now, is there anything in this room you can write on."

Half an hour later Nat was downstairs dragging Templeton out the door of the saloon by the frayed collar of his coat.

"I protest!" Drury cried as he struggled against Nat's iron grip. "This is lunacy. I don't need a bath. I had one two weeks ago!"

"All the same you're going to have another one. And a shave and those clothes pressed," Nat muttered as he pushed and shoved the unwilling singer toward the bathhouse. "Then it's three cups of coffee to sober up some of the effect of that redeye you've been guzzling all morning."

"Barbarism! Despotism! Overhanded brutality . . ." Templeton spluttered until Nat tightened the grip on his collar so tight he couldn't speak. By then they were inside the crude, raw-pine shack that served as a bathhouse for the cowboys who needed soap and water after months on the trail. Standing behind a screen, Templeton was divested of his outer clothes until he stood in his long johns. Then the bucket of water that was suspended above his head was dumped on him. Throwing the clothes to a woman who would take them to the laundry to be pressed, Nat then grabbed up a brush and a handful of lye soap and began scrubbing, underwear and skin together. The cold water went a long way toward sobering the unwilling bather. Spluttering and choking, Templeton jumped around trying to dodge

211

the wire-stiff brushes until Nat was satisfied the top layer of dirt was gone. Then he was doused with the bucket of water once more, given a towel to dry off with and directed toward a bench behind the bathhouse to allow the hot afternoon sun to steam the rest of the dampness away.

When his clothes came back looking far more presentable, though still not exactly debonair, he was hauled off to the barbershop for a haircut and shave.

"What a difference," Nat muttered, looking the final product up and down. "You look almost handsome."

"I'll have you know I was the central attraction for the ladies on the Lyceum circuit. Why—"

"Spare me your triumphs," Nat said, guiding him toward the door. "Now that you are back among the human race, we're going to pay a call on Mr. Mortimer Yancey."

Yancey was back in his room at Ma Crombley's boardinghouse, nursing his frustration over being kept away all day from an indisposed Medora. It was compounded by the fact that neither had he once seen Nat Varien, who had assured him the day before that he would be able to meet with Medora. He was more than a little surprised then when Varien himself showed up at his door accompanied by a tall, distinguished-looking fellow in a frayed suit whose pale, esthetic face Yancey instantly recognized as that of an artist.

"Gentlemen . . ." Yancey said opening his door a

crack wider.

"We have business to discuss, Mr. Yancey," Nat said officiously, pushing his way into the room.

Yancey stared up at the tall form looming over him and was suddenly very annoyed with Mr. Nathaniel Varien, this arrogant cowboy who had managed to prevent him from meeting with his rightful client. He pulled himself up to his full five feet and puffed out his chest.

"Unless you have Medora Melindez behind you in the hall there, I have no wish to talk with you further."

Nat sauntered into the room, unperturbed by Yancey's anger. "You know Miss Melindez is not well."

"I demand to see my client! Well or not, I have the right—"

"Calm down, Mr. Yancey," Nat said, sinking into one of the round-backed chairs that flanked a table near the window. "I've come to explain everything."

"I don't want an explanation; I want to see my client. You've kept her from me ever since I arrived. I don't believe she is sick at all. I think it is you who invented that story just to put me off, for reasons of your own, no doubt. I wouldn't be surprised if you are keeping her a prisoner in her room. Well, it won't work, Mr. Varien. I'm on to you."

Nat motioned Templeton to the other chair, crossed one long leg over the other and drummed his fingers on the table. When the color had subsided a little from Yancey's choleric face, he said levelly, "I am not the one keeping you away from

Medora, Yancey. The truth is, she doesn't want to see you. She hasn't wanted to see you ever since she heard you were here. Naturally, I tried to spare your feelings — "

"Poppycock! I don't believe you. Why wouldn't she want to see me, her manager, the one who arranged her triumphant tour. . . ."

"Because you are no longer her manager. She hired me for that position a good four weeks ago. I know it must be a disappointment to you, but that's the way it is."

Yancey spluttered incoherently a moment more, then sank onto the edge of the bed. "I don't believe you."

"Oh, it's true," Nat replied, reaching into the pocket of his coat. "I have her letter to prove it to you. I'm sure you'll recognize the handwriting."

"But . . . but we have a contract. Ten percent. . . ."

"Oh, I don't think you have a contract, Mr. Yancey. A loose agreement, perhaps, but no contract." Nat watched the little man closely. The truth was, he suspected there was no written contract, or it would have been among Medora's things. He wasn't certain that his guess was correct until the pause lengthened without Yancey producing a copy.

"It was as good as a contract. And I contacted Jasper Corchran at the Diamond Ring. I arranged the schedule. . . ."

Nat rubbed his finger along his nose, trying to hide his obvious relief. "True, and for that you do deserve your percentage of her appearances. I have no quarrel with that. But once you have them, you can leave Fireweed. You'll have no further business here."

Yancey threw Ardeth's letter on the bed, relieved to know he would receive something for all his miserable travels among western towns and convinced more than ever that performing artists were the lowest form of human life, just one step above traitorous, cutthroat, self-serving managers.

"Ahem . . ." Templeton coughed to remind Nat he was still there. Yancey's gaze fell on the long blond hair, the esthetic face, the flamboyant, shabby bow at the throat. He looked questioningly at Nat.

"I see we understand each other, Mr. Yancey," Nat said, smiling pleasantly. "And just to show you there's no hard feelings, I've brought you another client by way of consolation."

"And that was all there was to it," he told Ardeth later in her room. "As easy as falling off a log. So ends the threat from Mortimer Yancey."

"But surely he didn't just walk off with Drury without some kind of verification."

"Oh, he heard him sing one or two songs and was much taken with his vocal prowess. Drury's not bad when he's sober, you know. In fact, he's damned good. I think by the time I drove them to the depot to wait for the two o'clock train, he was already mapping out a 'grand tour.' And this time it'll be in writing, you can bet."

"I'm so relieved he didn't have a written contract with Medora. How did you know that, anyway? I would have just assumed one existed somewhere."

"That was a lucky guess. I figured if Yancey had an air-tight agreement with Medora, he would have been a lot more forceful about seeing her face to face. And surely a copy would have been somewhere among her papers. But even though I was pretty certain none existed, I was very relieved when he gave up the fight so easily. I knew then that he didn't have anything more to go on than a verbal agreement."

Ardeth jumped to her feet and gave him a light kiss on the lips. "Well, I'm vastly relieved to know the threat is gone. Now I can go down and rehearse with Eddie for tonight. There are a few new little steps I thought of to add to "The Cowboy's Lament" which ought to make it more effective, and I want to practice them first." She headed for the door.

"Do you think you should go downstairs yet? The train's not due for another twenty minutes."

"But they're already at the depot, aren't they? It's too far to come back into town. It'll be safe enough." Her hand was on the knob when she paused, turning back to Nat. "By the way, did Yancey say anything about where Medora was to go next?"

"No, and I'm sure he would have if he had anything planned. So, after tonight and tomorrow, your professional appearances are over."

"Thank heaven. We can go quietly away, and I can become Ardeth Royce once again."

Languidly Nat unbent his long frame from the chair where he had been sitting and walked over to slip his arms around her waist. She was looking very pretty in a simple, rose-colored gown with a graceful round neckline that showed off her white throat. He bent to kiss her. "Are you so anxious to bury Medora?"

Ardeth slipped her arms around his neck. "Yes, I am. It's been an interesting experience playing her, and I'm grateful for the money I've made. But there's something so . . . well, dishonest about it all. I'd rather just be plain old me."

"Living at Ma Crombley's and waiting tables in her dining room? That's what you'd be doing, you know, if you hadn't taken on Medora's identity."

She leaned against his broad chest. "I wouldn't want that, no. That would only be a little improvement over Pa's farm in Nebraska. No, I love all this comfort and these nice things, and I'm glad I've had them. But I can't get rid of the nagging guilt that they don't really belong to me."

"They don't belong to Medora, either, anymore. In fact, without any of her relatives about, they don't belong to anyone."

Ardeth looked up into his lean, thoughtful face. "Are you satisfied with the way things have worked out? Did my disguise please you?"

He kissed the end of her nose. "How can you doubt it. I think you have discovered a real talent for entertaining that you would never have known you had if we hadn't done this."

"And a few other talents as well that I didn't know I had," she said, chuckling.

"Which surprised no one more than me! No, the only regret I have about this whole scheme is that I never found Medora's map."

Ardeth gave him a quick hug. "We'll find it yet. We just need to think of new places to search, and we can do that better once we are away from Fireweed. Now, I must go downstairs and corral Eddie Lathrop into helping me rehearse."

"I'll come too. I'm curious as to how anybody can liven up 'The Cowboy's Lament'!"

Ardeth laughed and kissed him again before opening the door to walk arm in arm with him down the hall, which was empty for a change, though they could hear the low murmur of voices and an occasional clink of glasses from below. Lifting her skirts, she moved down the stairs, stopping at the last one to call to Eddie, who was sitting at a table near the door. When she told him that she wanted to rehearse, he rose listlessly and crossed the room to the piano to run his fingers across the keys. Nat, standing behind Ardeth, paused to pull a cheroot from his waistcoat pocket, all set to enjoy the sight of Ardeth prancing around the stage. She had just walked toward the steps to the proscenium, her back to the hall, when a voice came ringing from the swinging door at the other end of the saloon.

"Miss Melindez, Miss Melindez! At last we meet!"

Nat's hand froze on his pocket. Peering over her shoulder with a startled gaze, Ardeth saw Mortimer Yancey's short frame bounding toward her from the saloon door.

Chapter Eleven

Her heart stopped beating. One hand went to her throat as the color drained from her face, leaving it stark white against the frame of black hair. She glanced over at Nat still standing in shock by the stairs.

"My dear Miss Melindez," Yancey said, his face wreathed in smiles. "You cannot know how I have looked forward to this moment or what I have endured to make it possible." He reached out to take her hands, peering into her face.

By this time Nat had recovered. Bounding over, he elbowed Yancey aside to get between the two of them and block Yancey's view of Ardeth's white face. "Why aren't you on the train!" he exclaimed. "You're going to miss it."

"No, no. It's an hour late. A telegram came while we were waiting. And since I had the extra time, how better to use it than to make one last attempt to see my famous Medora. Besides," he went on, glaring at Nat, "it offered me the opportunity to hear from her own lips that she had changed managers."

He peered around Nat's large body, then nimbly side-stepped so as to once again face Ardeth. "I'm so relieved to see that you are feeling better, my dear. Now we can have a nice, long talk."

There was nothing to do but brazen it out. If Yancey denounced her here in the Diamond Ring, it would soon be all over the town. Jasper Corchran was not around, but Lathrop and Wister and even Owen Salter were watching them now and listening to every word. But she would not admit defeat without a fight.

"Perhaps we had better go up to your room, Miss Melindez," Nat jumped in, making some of the same deductions Ardeth had. If they could get this pompous little troublemaker out of sight before he realized Ardeth was not Medora, it might give them time to come to some understanding. Then his heart sank as out of the corner of his eye he saw Drury Templeton enter the saloon and head straight for the bar.

"We have nothing to say to each other," Ardeth said with all the haughtiness she could summon. "Mr. Varien is my manager now."

"So he told me," Yancey replied, staring at her intently. "Yet I do think we should discuss the matter. Considering the letters we exchanged, the arrangements I made for your tour. . . ."

"What arrangements? Except for this engagement at Fireweed, I know of no such arrangements."

"Did you say 'letters'?" Nat asked. But Yancey ignored him.

"Well, I'm still working on that. It's not so easy, you know. But I'm certain the Opera House at Denver would love to have you. I've already made preliminary advances and all that is needed—"

"I don't want to discuss it," Ardeth said, tearing her hand away from Yancey's grasp.

"Wait a minute," Nat said, gripping her arm to hold her there. "Are you saying you only corresponded with Miss Melindez? You didn't have a verbal agreement?"

"Well . . . I meant to have such an agreement, but by the time she reached St. Louis, I was already out here setting up the schedule for my other performers. However, as any lawyer will tell you . . ."

Nat and Ardeth exchanged glances as Yancey went rambling on. The relief that settled over them could almost be felt. However, the one person who might have been most interested in noticing it— Yancey himself—was too involved in his defensive explanations to see anything.

Ardeth at once became more charming. "My dear Mr. Yancey," she said, taking his arm to lead him to a nearby table. "Although we no longer have a professional arrangement, there is no reason why we cannot have a pleasant drink together before you leave for your train. For old time's sake, so to speak. I would be interested in knowing more about these other performers you manage and some of the towns where they are scheduled. Tell me more about them."

Yancey beamed and followed in her wake, glancing back only long enough to throw a "there, you see" look at Varien. Nat headed for the nearest chair, dabbing at his forehead with his checkered handkerchief. He would give the two of them just enough time to down a glass of wine, then bustle Yancey and Templeton off again to the station where, with any luck, they would be gone for good.

"Haven't seen you alone much lately," a seductive voice said softly as Roxie slid into the chair opposite him. She was wearing a drab gray blouse and long black skirt that made her look like one of the housewives of Fireweed. Though her lips were rouged, she wore no other makeup, and her years as a saloon girl were in stark evidence.

"Shouldn't you keep out of sight?" Nat said, motioning toward Yancey.

"I've got my back to him. Besides, how would he recognize me without my fancy duds and makeup. I've been looking for you. Some friends of mine stopped by the other day and told me a few things you might be interested to hear."

Nat was suddenly alert. "That so?"

"Very interested."

"Look, I can't talk now. I've got to get these fellows to the train in a few minutes. I'll stop by later."

"Upstairs?"

He did not at all like the predatory look on her ravaged face. Yet, remembering Ardeth's reaction the last time she saw Roxie pushing herself on him, he decided the sooner he got rid of her now, the better.

"All right. Upstairs."

She rose languidly, one hand on her hip, the other twisting a strand of hair that had escaped the wide bun that framed her neck.

"I'll be waiting."

* * *

Ardeth was mildly surprised that evening when, after the performance, Nat did not come to her room. There had been a few times when he was preoccupied with what she considered his "cowboy affairs" and had stayed away for brief periods, so she was not too concerned. The following day he was again nowhere to be seen, even when she gave her last performance as Medora that night. By this time she was beginning to wonder why he had not told her he had to go away or at least left her a note. Yet even the few nonchalant inquiries she made to Wister behind the bar or to some of the gamblers who often played cards with him got her no information. Nat had vanished. His horse was not in the stable, but that meant little. Wherever he had gone, he would have ridden his roan stallion. It was more upsetting when, on the third morning of his absence, she ambled over to Ma Crombley's and discovered he had paid his bill and cleared his room of all his belongings. She walked back to the Diamond Ring, alternating between waves of confusion, hurt and fury. Slamming the door to her room, she sat down on the bed and tried to think of all the places he might have gone and all the reasons he might have left.

But it was no use. She could come up with nothing to explain his disappearance except that now, when she was at last free of Medora, he had decided he did not want her.

The thought was like a knife through her heart, yet she determined she must face it. It did not seem possible given the strong physical passion they had shared that he would desert her, but what else was she to think. She decided to give him a few more days to return before she would begin to believe he had deliberately gone off and left her.

Keeping up a brave front, she hung around the saloon, trying to look as though she expected Nat back any moment. She did not miss the suspicious looks thrown her way, the pitying glances, the question in everyone's eyes. Corchran was very kind and even offered to allow her to begin giving performances again for as long as she wanted, but she declined his offer and, with a burst of inspiration, said that Nat was off setting up her next appearance. Why he had not taken her with him when her time in Fireweed was finished was tactfully left unquestioned.

The week dragged on, and by the end of it Ardeth was beside herself with anger and desperation. Doggedly she tried to hold on to the possibility that Nat had some plan in mind for the two of them, but with every passing day that hope became fainter. And teasing unmercifully at the back of her mind was always the taunting question: If he did not come back for her, what on earth was she to do? Where was she going to go? She had become so accustomed to depending on Nat for guidance and emotional support that she was unsure as to whether or not she could even make it on her own. And yet the thought of going back home to Nebraska was unbearable.

She was sitting at one of the tables by herself early one afternoon near the end of the week, mulling over her unappealing future, when she saw three of the dance hall girls come into the saloon. She recognized Roxie at once. It took her a moment to recall the other two—Dakota Lil and Bertha Timms. Although they were laughing at some private joke, all three women seemed to Ardeth to look hard, shabby and shopworn. She had never been comfortable around them, and now, with their whispers and giggles and surreptitious glances in her direction, she was even less so. She hoped they would ignore her and head for the bar, but to her dismay she saw all three of them bearing down on her table.

"Still waiting around?" Roxie said as she slid into one of the chairs. "I thought you'd be long gone by now."

Dakota and Bertha stood close by, giggling.

"What's it to you," Ardeth snapped, glaring t the three of them.

"Nothing to me. Only when your time was up, I figured you'd be off to some opera house or something to knock 'em dead in the aisles. Ain't that right, girls?"

"Yeah," Dakota drawled, "don't know why anyone famous would hang around Fireweed."

"Mind your own business," Ardeth said and started to rise. Roxie laid a hand on her arm and pulled her back.

"Just a minute. Why don't you two girls go have a drink or something and let me talk to the 'Great Medora' alone."

Ardeth's dislike spilled over. "I have nothing to say to you. Let me go."

"Oh, I think you do. For instance, what if I

could tell you where your handsome cowboy's gone? You'd like to know that, wouldn't you?"

Ardeth glared at her and yanked her arm away. She watched the other two women amble across the saloon, still giggling to themselves, torn between her desire to flounce away from Roxie and her curiosity. "How would you know where Nat Varien has gone," she finally said quietly.

"Because maybe I'm the one who sent him away," Roxie said, obviously enjoying her triumph. "I got friends, you see. And them friends came through town and told me about another friend, a man Mr. Varien is most anxious to talk to. Once Nat knew where to go looking for that friend, why, he just took right off to find him. It's as easy as that."

"I don't believe you," Ardeth said between clenched teeth. And yet, even as she said it, she knew it was the truth. Toad Turnbull! Nat wanted to find and kill Toad Turnbull even more than he wanted Medora's map, and so he had gone running after him the first moment he knew where to look. Had he even given her a passing thought?

"He would have told me," she added, to Roxie's obvious delight.

"Why, I'm surprised that he didn't. Of course, I never saw a man so happy to get that information or so anxious to be on his way. He was all fired up, he was. Of course . . ." she paused to fluff up the straggling hair on her neck, "he did stay with me awhile before he left. Long enough to make me powerful sorry he had to leave. Yes, indeed. Powerful sorry!"

Ardeth jumped to her feet, glaring venom at the

226

woman whose smug arrogance was almost too much to bear. She longed to smack her right across her rouged cheeks but refused to make such a spectacle of herself. Instead she drew herself up to her full height and, with all the dignity she could summon, declared again, "I don't believe a word of it!" Then she stalked through the swinging doors and out onto the street.

It was a blistering hot day, so there were few people on the boardwalks that lined the road. In her haste, she had come out without even a bonnet and had to shield her eyes from the glare with her hand. She walked up the road to the edge of the stores that lined the street where a tree shaded a water trough and sat down on the stone edge, dabbling her hand in the cool water and thinking hard.

It was true, of course. Nat had gone bounding after Toad Turnbull without so much as a goodby. Perhaps she could forgive him for that, given the terrible desire for vengeance he felt toward this man. But to spend his last night with a trollop like Roxie! To not even bother to write her a word of explanation or take the time to tell her where he was going! He might at least have told her where to go next or even suggested that she wait for him here in Fireweed.

There was only one explanation for such cruel, unfeeling conduct: he cared nothing for her and wanted to get away from her before any more romantic complications could develop. Perhaps he had been put off by the very fact that she told him how much she loved him. All the ecstatic lovemaking they had shared had meant nothing to him. He had gotten what he wanted and left her high and dry.

She wiped at a treacherous tear that slipped down her cheek. She would not cry! She would not wither away over Nat Varien or any other man. She would learn a lesson from this never to be vulnerable again, never to give her heart so willingly. And if she ever accidentally ran into Nat Varien again, she would pick up the nearest object she could find and pound him into the dust with it!

Yet as she made her way back to her room, she knew that now she must leave Fireweed for good. No more waiting around, wondering what to do with herself. She would go to Denver, not as Medora but as herself, and try to get work singing in some kind of establishment there. She still had money. And she had Medora's things. They would both tide her over until she got herself established.

She had hoped to get through the Diamond Ring without seeing Roxie again, but the woman and her two friends were still there, lolling around a table where several new arrivals had started a faro game. They all smirked as she passed, ignoring the daggers Ardeth sent their way. Ardeth did not linger but hurried up the stairs to her room to begin packing the trunks and carpetbags that held Medora's clothes. She had the trucks half-filled and the bags spread on the bed when she reached for the jewelry box and opened it. Peeking under the tray was a corner of white paper. Only then did she remember Garth Reardon's letter.

She took it out and unfolded it to scan its contents again. The twenty-fourth was only a few days away. It ought to take about that much time to pack up and make the trip to Cheyenne.

She plopped down on the bed with the letter in her hand. Should she go? It would mean being Medora Melindez a little longer. But it would also mean going to a secure place where she would be taken care of, meet fascinating new people, and live in high style. Best of all, she would never be likely to see Nat Varien again.

"Why not!" she exclaimed and began folding more of her clothes into the trunks.

She sat on the train as it rolled away from Fireweed, filled with conflicting, warring emotions. There was relief to be away at last from the pity and snickers of the people there, who knew very well that Nat Varien had gone off without her. There was also the satisfaction of knowing that if by chance Nat came back looking for her he would find her gone, no one knew where.

But there was also sadness, a feeling of loss at leaving a place where great things had happened. She had given her heart and her body totally to a man who had seemed to return her passion. And she had achieved a professional triumph she had never dreamed of having. She had lived in what was luxury compared to her days on her father's farm and had loved it. She had made friends of all kinds of people whom she would never have known had she not left home. On balance, it seemed her time in Fireweed was a success, and yet she could not rid herself of a nagging misery, a feeling of betrayal and hurt.

She also felt some trepidation about what lay ahead. Garth Reardon seemed pleasant enough from his letters, and he obviously was well off. But she could not be certain he had never actually met Medora and would recognize an impostor at once. Was he perhaps expecting someone more sophisticated or accustomed to wealth than she? Though there might be wonderful possibilities in this visit to the Silver Sage, there was also the chance of dreadful calamity. She would not know which to expect until she was actually there.

The train lumbered across the prairie and into the foothills of the mountains surrounding Denver without incident, much to Ardeth's relief. She had not forgotten the trauma of that robbery on the way down from Cheyenne, and in fact, being on a train again revived all the horrible details she had managed to suppress during her stay in Fireweed. She waited at the Denver station long enough to find out when the trains to Cheyenne would be running and which one would take her there on the correct day. Then she took a cab to the best hotel in town and booked a room for the two nights she would have to lay over.

She had expected to be lonely being in Denver by herself, but she soon found she enjoyed the town immensely. When she remembered the frightened, cowering girl who had come through here such a short time before, it raised a smile to her lips. So much had her confidence been increased by all that had happened since then that she found herself ordering waiters around in the dining rooms, booking a box at the opera house and even shopping in the stores with the same aplomb Medora herself might have shown. Several times she found people watching her admiringly and suspected they were asking themselves who this lovely stranger might be. One of the young fellows hanging about the doors of the opera house even asked her if she was famous! It was very satisfying to Ardeth to tell him in her best professional voice that she had indeed performed on the stage.

But her confidence melted away once she boarded the train for the trip north to Cheyenne. Once again she was acutely aware that she was alone, without Nat to depend upon. All the questions about this venture came roaring back, and she took out the two letters to reread them in the hope they would fortify her courage. She imagined Reardon as an elderly rancher, probably showing in his lined face the signs of a hard life spent building up a thriving cattle business. His letters had made it sound as though his visitors were a genteel group, and yet how much culture could there be out in the wilds of a territory hemmed in by mountains where one had to still look for Indians behind every bush. No doubt he had exaggerated in order to entice Medora there, probably out of desperation for some trifling particle of civilization. She only hoped it would not turn out to be too primitive, though judging from what he said, it *had* to be better than the sod house in Nebraska where she had grown up.

By the time the train finally rolled into Cheyenne, she had worn herself out with worry and anticipation. She smoothed her skirts and straightened her hat; then with her purse over her arm and her parasol in one hand, she descended to the platform, trying to appear more confident than she actually felt.

There were surprisingly few people moving along the walkway. Ardeth recognized several of them as fellow passengers greeting a coterie of men and women who had obviously come to welcome them. She stood looking around, seeing no one who might possibly fit her picture of Reardon. Then she spied a very tall man in a large cowboy hat about twenty feet away. He had his back to her, and she could see long strands of white hair curling from beneath the brim and over the collar of his coat. Long leather fringes hung along the collar yoke and down the sleeves, and he wore boots with high heels and silver spurs.

She took a deep breath and walked up to this dazzling epitome of the Great West. Touching him lightly on the shoulder, she said, "Mr. Reardon?"

Startled, he turned, looking down on her.

"Mr. Reardon," she went on, "I'm Medora Melindez."

The hat was swept off revealing a mane of silver hair. He could not speak at once for a great wad of tobacco in his mouth. Spitting a stream of amber juice to one side, he smiled at her, showing a few gaps in his yellow teeth. "Ma'am," he said, bowing politely.

Ardeth took a deep breath. "I'm Medora Melindez. I've just arrived on the train. My boxes and trunks have already been taken off if you have any kind of conveyance for them, as I'm sure you must . . ." She was talking breathlessly, and sounding inane. Her dismay was making her appear a fool, so she got a good grip on herself.

Turning the hat brim in his gnarled hands, the white-haired gentleman gave a low laugh, his faded eyes twinkling. "Why, ma'am, though you are just about the prettiest thing I seen in a month of Sundays, and much as I might wish I was the richest fellow in the territory, I got to tell you the sad truth is you've made a mistake. I ain't Garth Reardon."

A deep crimson flush began to make its way up Ardeth's cheeks. "Oh, my goodness, I do beg your pardon."

"Why, that's all right. In fact, if these old eyes serve me right, that there's Mr. Reardon comin' down the platform right now. And judging from the way he's travelin', he's a mite late."

Ardeth turned to face the man hurrying up behind her. She had a quick vision of long, shoulder-length dark hair and a spotless white cravat with a glimmering diamond stickpin nestled in its folds. Exquisite lace framed the strong hand held out to her. Her gaze fastened on gray eyes fringed with heavy lashes and sauntered down to a wide mouth, sculptured in its delicacy yet made strong by the firm line of the jaw and resolute chin.

Garth Reardon was the most beautiful man she had ever seen!

Chapter Twelve

For a moment Ardeth was too stunned to speak. Then she found she didn't need to because Garth Reardon plunged in, taking her parasol from her hand and steering her by the elbow toward the open doors of the depot.

"I do hope you'll forgive me, Miss Melindez. I had every intention of being here before the train pulled in but I was held up at the Cattleman's Association office. Business, you know. It has a way of pushing all other considerations aside, at least momentarily. But it is utterly unforgivable that I wasn't here to hand you down, and I do beg your forgiveness."

"It's quite all right," Ardeth muttered, glancing back at the bemused old codger she had assumed was Reardon, who was watching them with amusement. Garth nimbly opened a way through the crowd with such aplomb that royalty itself could not have done it any better.

"No. It's not all right at all. But it happened, and now we must push on. Here, Phillips . . ." he

234

called, waving a hand at the melange of carriages and wagons grouped around the entrance to the depot. A man materialized from the crowd, running up. Here was the cowboy she had expected, wiry frame, whiskered chin, checkered shirt and high-topped boots and all. He whipped off his hat and stood politely while Reardon rattled off instructions.

"Have Miss Melindez's boxes loaded on the buckboard," Garth said with brisk efficiency. "We'll be in the carriage."

"You want I should drive you? Patsy can take the buckboard if you want me to drive you."

"That won't be necessary. I'll drive her myself. Just be certain you're close behind."

"Yes, sir," Phillips said, touching his hat and bobbing to Ardeth before he loped off into the crowd.

Garth picked up Ardeth's cloth bag. "I presume you have everything in here appropriate for an overnight stay," he asked, patting it with his long, lean hand.

"Well, yes, but —"

"It is quite a distance to the Silver Sage. I plan to take it in easy stages which will give you an opportunity to see something of our Wyoming Territory as well as afford us the chance to get better acquainted. Once we reach the ranch, I usually find that concerns of business and other guests interfere with my privacy to a great extent."

Ardeth was bundled to the street hardly knowing what was happening. Suddenly in front of her was the most elegant carriage she had ever seen. Its

235

sleek black sides shimmered in the hot sunlight. The tufted velour upholstery in a luscious shade of burgundy red invited her to lean back and luxuriate in its comfort. Standing in harness were two sleek bay horses, perfectly matched, whose long tails and silky manes gave them a beauty the like of which she had never seen before. Even Nat's Spanish stallion paled in comparison.

She was not surprised when Reardon stopped by this elegant equipage and handed her up. He moved quickly around, climbed aboard and took the reins, then snapped them against the horses' broad backs, setting them briskly into their paces. "We'll have lunch at the Cattleman's Club, and then we'll start off. There ought to be just enough time to reach the Broadman Ranch near Laramie, where we'll spend the night."

The carriage glided smoothly along the crowded street, but Ardeth found herself clinging to the seat frame all the same. She felt as though she was being swept along in a whirlwind over which she had no control. "You mean it will take more than one night to reach the Silver Sage?"

"Oh, yes. It will take several nights. However, there are one or two towns along the way where we can find accommodations, and where there aren't, I have made arrangements for us to stay with friends. Don't worry about a thing. You will be completely comfortable."

She mulled this over as the carriage rolled in and out of the heavy traffic. Any other time she might have been fascinated by the town itself which had a reputation as "hell on wheels" in the western territories. But it was difficult to be so objective sitting next to this attractive, dominating man whose firm authority enveloped her so completely. It also gave her a disturbing sense of not being her own woman anymore. But that, she felt, would be sorted out as they went along. More troubling was the tiny nugget of excitement growing like a seed within her. The brief, shy glances she got of Reardon from beneath her hat brim revealed more clearly the strong, classic lines of his face. His chin was perhaps too broad and dominating, but it only slightly overshadowed the sculptured mouth, the long, aquiline nose, the sharp brows with a tantalizing tilt in the center, the thick lashes—strangely heavy for a man—and the high forehead, almost eclipsed by his sleek, expensive hat. She was more and more conscious of his wide, firm shoulders and the muscles of his arms against the tight cut of his coat as he worked the reins. His legs were long and firm in their tight-fitting plaid pants, and the high, tooled-leather boots might have been fashioned for a Spanish grandee. His feet were surprisingly small for a man of such height, their size accentuated by the pointed toes and high sloping heels of his boots. But then she remembered Nat telling her that next to his hat, a cowboy prized small feet above all. In fact, to call a man "big-footed" was a terrible insult.

The thought of Nat gave her a pang of guilt until she remembered how he had abandoned her alone in Fireweed. With his sandy hair, good-natured grin and soft green eyes, Nat almost faded into obscurity beside a dark Apollo like Garth Reardon. The attraction a man like Reardon awoke was both disturbing and delicious, and she would not allow the enjoyment of it to be ruined by hopeless memories of Nat Varien!

She glanced up to see Reardon studying her and felt a slow crimson blush creep up her face, as though her every thought had been open and obvious.

Reardon smiled. "Forgive me," he said politely. "I don't mean to stare. It's just that I expected someone . . . well, older. You are much younger than I thought you would be . . . and far more beautiful."

Ardeth looked away as she felt the blush deepening. She tried to smile and nod in the sophisticated manner she imagined Medora might have assumed, but her crimson cheeks, she knew, gave her away. "I am older than I appear," she finally managed to say. "And part of an entertainer's job is to continue to appear young even when the years take their toll."

"Then permit me to congratulate you on your excellent deceit. Ah, here we are at the Cattleman's Club. I hope you are hungry. They serve the best beef steaks in Wyoming."

By now Ardeth was back in control. "I'm starving," she said, as Garth handed her down. She swept up the steps with all the assurance of Medora herself, conscious of the heads turning as she crossed the porch and passed through the open double doors. She was also conscious of Reardon following in her wake, for the first time not in charge. It was rather satisfying.

* * *

As Garth had promised, the journey to the Silver Sage was made in easy stages, and Ardeth soon became accustomed to its leisurely pace. The Reardon entourage formed its procession like a royal pilgrimage across the dun-colored landscape. First came the carriage, which Garth always drove himself, followed by two buckboards, one of them piled high with her trunks and boxes. Several smaller wagons rode behind them, with a small group of horses bringing up the rear. Men on horseback framed both sides of the convoy, sometimes riding close by, other times ranging far out onto the brown grass prairie. She never had a chance to learn their names because they always kept a polite distance, but she could tell from the way their eyes roamed constantly over the horizon and the manner in which they kept their shotguns at the ready across their saddles that they were there to guard, whether from Indian attack or wild animals, she wasn't sure.

The country grew more fascinating as they went along. Rolling hills, like undulating brown waves grew in size as they continued west. She found a stark desolate beauty in some of the strange sandstone formations rising up like prehistoric monsters from the plateau. Shallow riverbeds reminded her of her Nebraska home, but there was nothing at all familiar in the way the rolling hills at times gave way in the distance to soaring, shadowy mountain ranges.

"Will we be going through those," she asked wistfully, pointing to the distant hills.

Garth laughed. "No. But once we reach the Green River, you will find enough mountains and canyons around you to last you for a lifetime."

Ardeth started to reply that someone raised on a flat, Nebraska prairie could never get enough of soaring mountains. But then she remembered just in time that Medora was not from Nebraska.

There were one or two close calls of that kind as the days progressed, even though Garth was not a man to encourage constant conversation or to press her to talk about herself. When she gave vague answers to such questions as he did ask, he seemed to respect her need for privacy and never pushed her for more complete answers.

In fact, she mused, he was almost too polite. He treated her with a courtesy and respect that was almost frustrating. At the same time there were countless little tantalizing touches: a brush against her ankle with the toe of his boot; the light tattoo of his fingers on her back when he was guiding her along a street or into one of the ranch houses at which they stayed; the linger of his hands on her shoulder when he helped her into her short pelerine. Too often these brief contacts sent an electric warmth coursing through her that she hurriedly brought under control. It was foolish to grow so fluttery just because a handsome man paid you a few courtesies, she chided herself. But it did no good. The next moment, when Garth would lean closer to her face than was needed to point out some landmark in the distance, or his shoulder would brush hers as he handled the reins, once again she could almost feel the air come alive between them.

And yet, at the same time, he never went any farther. In the several days it took for the leisurely trip across the territory and during the pleasant nights when they stayed at the various ranches belonging to his friends, he remained unfailingly courteous and polite but nothing more. With her reluctance to talk about her past and Garth's unwillingness to tell her much about himself, their conversations still managed to be lively and interesting. Reardon was not one of the most successful ranchers in Wyoming for nothing. His knowledge of the territory, its people, animals, flora and fauna was deep and far reaching, and he was always ready to share it with her. Once, during the night they spent in Laramie, he took her for an evening walk a short way out into the countryside. The brown hills were bathed in a copper glow of moonlight that threw fantastic shadows from the grotesquely shaped sandstone monuments, like huge cloaks lying on the ground. There was a wild, primitive magic in the ghostly light, and Ardeth was glad when Reardon laid his hand on her arm to guide her. She thought perhaps this once he might forget his courtly reserve and at least kiss her, but it did not happen. When they returned to the fort, he left her at her door more frustrated and confused than ever.

As they neared the Green River Territory where Reardon had his ranch, Ardeth's anxiety began to gnaw at her with growing strength. The pleasant trip had involved a minimum of discomfort, traveling as they had between ranch houses and small towns, and she had been fascinated by the newness and beauty of the country through which they traveled. She had also been captivated by Reardon and had enjoyed the attentions he paid her. Never in her life had anyone been quite so assiduous in looking out for her comfort, and she found she rather liked it.

But now that the end was in sight, Ardeth was reminded that soon she would be surrounded once again by strangers who would expect her to perform at a level she knew she could not reach. Once more she would be forcing herself into Medora's skin, trying always to remember how Medora would have answered that question, what comment Medora might have made. And, worst of all, she would be constantly having to guard herself against the smallest mistake that might give away her true identity. She wished they could go on crossing the Wyoming Territory forever!

"Tell me about the people who are staying at the Silver Sage," she asked Reardon on the last day of their trip. He had warned her they would reach the ranch by that evening, and already he was driving his team with an urgency she had not seen before.

"Oh, they're the usual assortment. Well, perhaps not so usual, since most of them came from England and one is even an earl."

Ardeth's hand flew to her throat. "A real English earl! What on earth is he doing out here?"

"Hunting, mostly. There are quite a few of the English nobility out here in the West, as well as a number of well-heeled eastern millionaires. They've discovered that chasing foxes or shooting quail is no sport at all compared to riding down a bison or one of our gray wolves."

"But it's such a long way to come just to shoot at

a poor animal."

"As with most things, there's money involved. A lot of it. Most of these men have invested in cattle ranches, hoping to add to their already considerable fortunes. They are entrepreneurs, anxious to make big profits."

"Has the earl invested in the Silver Sage?"

Garth gave a dark chuckle. "The Silver Sage does not need an infusion of foreign money. It does quite well on its own."

"You must be a clever businessman," Ardeth said archly. To her surprise, for the first time he actually began telling her something of his past.

"I was among the first ranchers to come into this territory, but I wisely came with a very large stake. I also came after learning everything I could about raising cattle. The people on the first wagon trains to come through this territory could see only poor farmland when they looked at these bleak brown hills. Then one bitter winter one of the trains on the Oregon Trail was forced to release its oxen into the wild, fully expecting them to die over the winter. When they were found the next spring fit and healthy, men began to see that this land afforded excellent grazing for cattle. I took advantage of that fact as well as the government's generous offer of free land, up to one hundred sixty acres to anyone with the ten-dollar filing fee who was willing to develop and improve it."

"But surely your ranch is larger than a hundred sixty acres."

Garth laughed. "It's nearly fifty thousand acres. I made sure I filed for the river land, then I paid my men to file other claims nearby. It's not an uncommon practice out here. The river serves all our water needs, and the fact that the valley is surrounded by mountains means it does not suffer the extremes of temperature found in other parts of Wyoming."

"It sounds ideal."

Reardon gave a small shrug. "It has proved very profitable." His nonchalance did not fool her for a moment. He was extremely proud of his success and of his wealth—that much she had learned just from watching him these past few days—but perhaps he had a right to be.

"Of course, my interests are not merely confined to ranching. I am involved in a number of concerns. Mining, for instance. There are vast fortunes to be made off the mineral rights as well as the discovery of valuable ores. Silver, gold, copper—"

The coach was all at once pulled to a stop. Ardeth, who had been intently listening to Garth, looked up over the broad backs of the horses to see several figures standing in the road, blocking their path. The carriage had barely pulled to a halt when two of the guards raced past them to clear the road.

"Who are they?" she asked Garth in a whisper.

"Savages." The violence with which he spat out the word surprised her. Immediately she thought of wild, painted faces and tomahawks. Yet she could see they were not on horseback.

"I want to see," she said, gathering up her skirts to step down.

"That is not a good idea," Garth said coldly.

"But they don't appear to be dangerous. I'd like to get a closer look."

244

His hand closed over her arm, the nails digging into her flesh. "No! Stay here. My men will handle it."

She looked up into his dark eyes, charged now with a black intensity. His fingers relaxed a little, and he tried to smile, though still gripping her arm. "Trust me. They are only a brief diversion."

One of the cowboys came riding back, pushing his hat up on his forehead. "It's a Shoshone squaw, boss, with a parcel of naked kids. Says she hungry."

"Why isn't she up at Wind River where she's supposed to be? There's plenty of food there."

"She says she left because there wasn't no food there neither. You know how they lie though. Probably just didn't want to stay. Wouldn't be surprised if most of those kids weren't half-breeds."

"Tell her to get out of the road or we'll ride over her, wagons and all."

Ardeth gasped. "But Garth . . . Mr. Reardon . . . surely we have something we can give her for her children."

"I can see you are not familiar with the ways of these creatures, Miss Melindez," Garth answered coldly. "They will beg you into poverty if you let them. They don't belong here, and the sooner they are discouraged from being here, the better for the territory."

Ardeth, whose experiences with Indians had been learned mostly from horror stories told by others, nevertheless had surmised long ago that they were a people whose culture had been destroyed and usurped by the flood of white immigrants taking over the plains. "But they were here first," she re-

245

minded Reardon.

Garth studied her for a moment before turning back to the cowboy. "Give her a little food from the last wagon. But tell her she had better head back to the reservation. If I see her within twenty miles of my ranch, I'll have her run off or shot."

The rider took off, leaving Ardeth to sit with pursed lips and her hands clenched in her lap. After a few moments, she saw the creatures shuffling off to the side of the road, allowing the carriage to pass. Garth took off in a hurry, allowing her only a brief glimpse of a thin face huddled inside a dirty blanket, surrounded by shadowy small, half-naked figures. For a long time she did not speak but concentrated on watching an immense soaring eagle against the sky and the prairie dogs cavorting in the fields that lined the narrow road.

"Forgive me," Garth said at last in a pleasant voice. "I did not mean to seem unduly harsh back there, but, you see, my experiences with the Shoshone and other tribes has taught me you have to use a firm hand."

"They were only a woman and her children," she answered tightly.

"They were savages. Two years ago a band of Shoshone went on the rampage and cut a swath of destruction and terror throughout the territory the like of which had not been seen since the sixties. It was their way of protesting being sent to Wind River, but the only result was to deepen the determination of the settlers here that they must be run off these lands forever. They are their own worst enemies."

"They know no other way. Their culture, after all, is so very different from ours."

"I think if you had lived through those few weeks and seen firsthand some of the sights I saw, you would not be so charitable. However," he added cheerfully, "how can I expect someone who has lived mostly in St. Louis to understand the ways of the frontier."

Ardeth found herself resenting his patronizing attitude almost as much as his cold meanness to the Indian woman and her children. But she wisely kept her mouth shut, determined not to pursue the subject any further since it would only make a rift between them which might carry over into her stay at the Silver Sage. She knew she would need his support and sympathy if she was to bring off her visit there successfully.

That evening when the dark shadows of the cluster of buildings that made up the Silver Sage finally came into view, she found she was more glad to see them than she had expected to be. The rest of the day had not been so pleasant after their experience with the Shoshone woman. After a few attempts at lightly passing it off, Garth had become formally polite while she had lapsed more and more into long periods of silence in which she mentally prepared herself for the ordeal ahead.

Reardon pulled the coach to a stop on the rise of a hill overlooking the valley. "There is it," he said, the reins resting in his long, supple hands. "The Silver Sage."

Ardeth shaded her eyes with her hands. The sun was beginning its descent below the yellow buttes

far in the distance, but it bathed the valley in soft
rosy hues interlaced with long gray shadows created
by the house and outbuildings. Long thick ridges of
trees separated the clusters of buildings and lace-
work of fences from the sloping dun-colored hills
beyond. Even at this distance she could see that the
ranch included a multitude of low clapboard buildings, a high, imposing barnlike structure and scores
of fences scattered around its perimeters. Far to the
west, somewhat apart from the working buildings,
stood a two-story house, flanked on one side by a
one-story addition and on the other by a huge stone
chimney reaching far above its sloping roof.

"I'm impressed," she said simply.

"You should be. It's one of the largest and finest
ranches on the frontier."

He was not bragging, he was simply stating a fact
which she could not deny. She was surprised when
he reached over and took her hand very gently.

"But you must be tired after this long trip. I
shan't keep you here admiring my handiwork any
longer. You'll soon have your own room and a comfortable bed."

Ardeth tried to smile. "I'm looking forward to it,"
she replied as Garth urged the carriage forward one
last time. The bays, sensing home, took off at a
brisk trot.

As the ranch drew nearer, Ardeth's admiration
grew. By the time they were gliding smoothly among
the myriad outbuildings and barns, skirting the
fenced corrals and small pastures, her awe was beginning to burgeon. When, at last, they pulled up
before the overhang of the porch along one side of

the imposing house, she was ready to allow Reardon his pride in the Silver Sage. It was the finest complex she had ever seen. Indeed, after the sod houses and wind-swept farms of Nebraska, it was almost palatial.

They had barely pulled to a stop before they were surrounded by people. A ranch hand appeared to hold the bridles of the bays. Two men in dark clothing hurried down the porch, one to hand her down, the other to scurry around to the far side of the coach and speak to Reardon. On the porch stood three women, each wearing a black blouse and skirt, whose fronts were almost obliterated by an expanse of spotless starched white aprons. All three bobbed a curtsy as Reardon started up the steps.

Garth spoke briefly to the three women, then turned to Ardeth. "Medora, this is Antonia, Maria and Juanna. You'll soon get to know them. For now, however, Antonia will show you to your room and see to your needs. Don't hesitate to ask for anything you do not see. I imagine you would like to rest before dinner which will be at eight o'clock."

Ardeth only nodded, wondering which of these women was Antonia. When the youngest one smiled at her and bobbed another curtsy, she smiled back.

"Welcome, madam," the girl said. "If you'll just follow me."

"Oh, and by the way, dinner is formal," Garth added as Ardeth started into the house. "I like to observe the niceties of civilization, even out here. I'm sure you're accustomed to it."

Ardeth smiled, thinking of the alcove table at the

Diamond Ring in Fireweed. But she merely nodded and went on. She hoped Antonia would be willing to show her just how formal and civilized Garth liked things to be.

The interior was cool and dark. She had an impression of heavy ornate furniture, but Antonia was moving too quickly and efficiently to allow her time to look more closely. She followed the girl down a long hall, up stairs carpeted in thick, lush burgundy, down a hall lined with gleaming mahogany doors, all tightly closed, to one at the end where Antonia threw open the door and stepped aside for Ardeth to enter.

It was not a large bedroom and was made even smaller by the enormous furniture that filled every space. The bedstead reached almost to the ceiling and was one huge, carved slab of wood, larger than the family table in her kitchen at home. Wardrobes, chests of drawers, an elaborate stand with a thick marble top for the porcelain washbowl, and long windows draped with crimson velvet and tied back with thick gold tassels—the ponderous heaviness of it all gave the room the semblance of a cave. And yet, she recognized the expensive quality of these furnishings from the magazines she used to devour at home. All in all, she was surrounded by more luxury than she had ever dreamed possible.

"Would madam like me to put her things away now," Antonia asked politely.

"To tell you the truth, Antonia, madam would like a bath more than anything in the world. Is that possible?"

Antonia smiled, and Ardeth realized she was even

more young than she had appeared at first. "Of course it is. I will have the tub and water brought up right away."

Ardeth reached up to pull the long pins out of her hat. "Hot water. Lots and lots of hot water!" She shook out her hair.

Antonia was already at the door. "It shall be done, madam. And when I return, I'll help madam undress."

Ardeth watched her leave, thinking that madam did not really need help in undressing. Yet after five days on the road, she felt as though every thread she possessed was crusted with dirt. How wonderful to shed them and get clean again!

The bath came more quickly than she imagined. The two men who had met them on the porch appeared in minutes bearing a large tin tub on splayed metal feet. No sooner was this set up than two other men, obviously Mexicans, began a procession of large copper water pots, half of them steaming. When they were gone, Antonia helped Ardeth out of her clothes and into the tub, then stood silently by, supervising as a Mexican woman scrubbed Ardeth's back and washed her hair. It amused Ardeth that there apparently was a hierarchy even among servants, but she said nothing, simply lay back and enjoyed the pampering.

Wrapped in a soft, warm robe, she rested for a while on the big bed while Antonia saw that one of her dresses was shaken out and pressed. By then it was time to dress for supper. Ardeth allowed the girl to fix her hair in rolls and curls, fasten the brocade skirt around her waist and button up the low-cut embroidered bodice. She stood back, looking at her reflection in the long standing mirror. There were shadows beneath her eyes that testified to her lingering fatigue, but her black hair against her pale face perfectly set off the eggshell blue of her shimmering dress.

"This seems terribly fancy, Antonia. I won't be overdressed, will I?"

"Madam looks beautiful. You will outshine all the others."

"Does Mr. Reardon really wish his guests to dress so elaborately for dinner? Does this happen every night?"

Antonia paused as though searching for words. "The master likes everything to be always correct. Those were his particular orders while the English guests are here and especially after the great Medora arrives. You will not be overdressed, I assure you, Madam."

Nevertheless, Ardeth kept her jewelry simple. She put on Medora's long white gloves, picked up a fan whose delicate blue color matched her dress and started the long trek down the hall to the stairs. Antonia followed along after her like an obedient puppy. When she began to turn the wrong way at the bottom of the stairs, the girl politely redirected her to the front parlor where the master liked his guests to gather before going in to supper.

Then they stood before the closed doors, and Ardeth found she was fighting down the butterflies that were rioting in her stomach.

How foolish, she thought. *I'm elegantly dressed, I'm accustomed to being Medora by now; I can bring it off.*

Antonia reached out to slide the doors back. The darkened hall was at once lit up by the brilliance of the light spilling from the room. Ardeth had an impression of several groups of people standing inside, all of them turned toward the door, staring at her with curiosity and expectation on their faces.

Chapter Thirteen

She almost turned and ran. Then, getting a grip on herself, she paused to think how Medora would have entered this room. Of course, she would soar in like the confident performer she was. That was all Ardeth needed. Her head went back, and her arms went out in a lovely, theatrical gesture that included everyone in the room. She glided smoothly forward, smiling around.

Reardon broke away from the group of men he had been talking to and came to meet her. The admiration in his eyes was evident as he took Ardeth's hand and brought her fingers to his lips, holding them there perhaps a little longer than was seemly.

"You look very beautiful, my dear. Charming. . . ."

"Thank you," she replied, beaming under his approval. Suddenly all the fussing upstairs was worth the time it had taken.

"Come. I want you to meet my other guests."

He turned to the tallest of the men standing nearby and, with a gentle hand on Ardeth's back, eased her forward.

"Medora, may I present Neville Carmichael, Lord Berry. Madam Medora Melindez, my lord."

The introduction could not have been made with more grace. Ardeth bent a curtsy, then looked up into the pale blue eyes of the earl. He was older than he had seemed at first glance. Like many very tall men, he had a pronounced stoop, and he sported a rotund potbelly which his fashionable waistcoat could not disguise. His face was long and lean with graying blond hair swept back from a broad, high forehead. His thin lips were partially hidden by a narrow blond moustache.

"Charmed, my dear," he said, bending over Ardeth's hand as Garth had done. "My conscience, Reardon," he said in a loud, grating voice, "but from where out in this wilderness have you produced this lovely young thing. Are there more like her hiding beneath the sagebrush? Why hasn't she been presented before? Keeping her to yourself, eh!" He poked a long finger at Garth's vest. "Why, she quite puts all the other ladies to shame, if I do say so."

Ardeth gave a quick embarrassed glance at the two other ladies in the room, who were sitting on a settee near the window, taking in every word. "You are too kind," she mumbled, reclaiming her hand from the earl's clammy grasp. Garth came to her rescue by taking her arm and leading her around the room to introduce her to the other guests. Ardeth was concentrating so on her performance that she barely heard their names, and it wasn't until they went in to supper and sat around the table that she began listening to the conversation in order to sort them out.

It was difficult for her to believe that such magnificence as Reardon's dining room could be found in a pioneer territory like Wyoming. The room was a blur of candlelight, gleaming silver sconces and tableware, freshly cut flowers and creamy porcelain. Sumptuous dishes appeared nestled in silver urns and bowls of gleaming bone china: raw oysters, glazed sweetbreads with French peas, roast beef, quail larded with jelly, English plum pudding and orange ices. Her fatigue left her with little appetite, but she tasted something of each as she concentrated on sorting out the other people at the table.

It was easy to pick up on who the two women were. The youngest one was quite lovely with a delicate purebred kind of beauty that reminded Ardeth of an Arabian colt her father had briefly owned. She had the beautiful complexion of a true Englishwoman, but her figure was more like a child's than a woman's. Ardeth wondered if she starved herself to stay that thin. She was the earl's cousin, and her name was Lavinia Patton. "Lady" Lavinia Patton.

The older woman was Lavinia's exact opposite. Also a lady—Ardeth hoped she could keep all these "ladys" straight—Charlotte Teague had obviously come along with the earl's party as Lavinia's chaperone. While Lavinia, still miffed at the earl's slur in the parlor, was cool and unsmiling toward Ardeth, Lady Teague made no attempt to soften the fact that she thought it was beneath her dignity to sit at the same table with an *actress!* She was arrogant, proud and rude, and her lips seemed to form themselves into a perpetual sneer. To be fair, Ardeth noticed, her haughtiness was not merely directed at Ardeth her-

256

self but was generously spread around to encompass every American at the table. It was obvious that Lady Teague, in coming to Wyoming, had found herself among the barbarians and was taking no pains to hide the fact.

Sir Lawrence Appleby was the only other gentleman to make up the earl's party. A longtime friend of Neville Carmichael's, he was jovial and friendly and seemed to enjoy his strange surroundings. In fact, Ardeth thought, he was probably the kind of man who would enjoy any place in which he found himself. Utterly unpretentious, never a deep thought, never analyzing anyone or anything, he simply went along, good-naturedly taking part in whatever came his way. Of all the English visitors, she liked him the best.

She was more ambivalent about the other American at the table. Mr. Cameron—no one mentioned his first name through the entire meal—was from New York City, and it did not take Ardeth long to figure out that here was the fellow who Reardon thought could further her career. He appeared to be immensely wealthy if the huge diamond stickpin on his cravat and the gold rings on his fingers meant anything. He was a large man, tall and heavy with a big paunch of a stomach. He had heavy jowls and long sideburns which, from the way he absently stroked them, suggested they were a point of vanity with him. His voice was only slightly less booming than the earl's, and with it he dominated the conversation, talking endlessly of his holdings in the city, his stock investments, the boards on which he served and the fledgling entertainers he had brought to stardom in the New York theaters. She did not care for him at all but realized she was hardly seeing him at his best.

All at once she realized someone was speaking to her.

"Miss Melindez . . ."

She looked around at Larry Appleby, who was sitting beside her and saw Garth leaning across that table.

"I'm so sorry," she murmured. "What did you say?"

"You are, of course, going to join us on the hunt?"

"The hunt. . . ?"

The earl broke in. "My dear, the very reason we have come so far. You must be familiar with the hunt."

Ardeth vaguely recalled a picture in one of her mother's books of men and women in bright red jackets sitting on very large, very sleek horses. There were dogs milling about at their feet, and if she remembered right, they were there to chase down one poor, vulnerable red fox.

"Oh, I don't think so. It's not something I've ever enjoyed very much."

Lavinia Patton gave her an arch smile. "Don't tell me you do not ride, Miss Melindez. Why, I thought girls out here on the frontier were practically born on the back of a horse."

"Lavinia, my child," said Lady Teague, "there is a vast difference between galloping around on the back of one of these half-wild western ponies and riding a thoroughbred to hounds. Miss Melindez has no doubt not had the opportunity—"

"I've had the opportunity," Ardeth lied. "I simply do not enjoy it."

"Oh, but you must try this Wyoming style of the hunt, Miss Melindez," the earl broke in again. "it's superb. White wolves, elk, bison . . . real sporting game. And so many of them. Why, one can barely go out without bearing home several trophies. It's every bit as good as was promised."

Mr. Cameron leaned across the table toward her. "The earl's come out West here because we have some of the finest hunting in the world. That speaks of a true devotion to the sport, wouldn't you say? I myself tend to agree with you. Killing some wild animal is not something I find particularly invigorating, though I shall probably go along for the scenery if nothing else. I would suggest that you might go for that reason as well."

Ardeth looked at Garth, hoping he'd rescue her. "Perhaps Miss Melindez will feel different in the morning after a good night's rest," he offered. "One can hardly blame her for not wishing to get on a horse after the journey she has just made."

Lavinia smirked. "I'm sure Mr. Reardon has a few gentle old mares in his extensive stables that you might ride. There must be at least one you would feel safe upon."

Ardeth smirked back at her. "Perhaps you have already found such a one."

Garth quickly changed the subject, and no more was said about the hunt. Ardeth hoped it was forgotten, but when the interminable meal was finally ended and Garth took her arm for a walk outside along the porch that wound around the house, it was the first subject he brought up.

"You really mustn't feel you have to go if you don't want to. Miss Patton was just trying to annoy you because she thought the earl had paid you too much attention before we went in to dinner. She has her eye on him, of course."

"That old man! I should have thought he already had a wife and a parcel of children as well."

"He has the children, but the wife died not long ago. He hasn't been able to pry himself away from Lady Lavinia since. She's hoping to return to England solidly promised to him."

Ardeth was feeling much better now that they had left the rest of the party behind. The wine and delicious food had left her feeling tired but contented. She was grateful that Reardon had brought her outside and away from the others, singling her out for his attentions. The night was very beautiful, the air soft with a fragrant touch of honeysuckle that spilled over the roof of the porch. The moon was full and bronzed the odd shapes of fences and buildings and even the mountains in the distance. Far off, a horse snuffled in one of the corrals, sounding sleepy and homey.

She was very conscious of Garth's nearness, his fingers on her arm, his shoulder brushing hers in the darkness. When he paused at one corner of the porch, she leaned against the wooden post, her heart beating a little faster than before as he moved in close to her.

"I'll go on the hunt," she said, feeling more confident of herself. "I won't shoot at anything, but I'll ride. And I bet I'll keep up with Lady Lavinia, too."

Garth laughed, his teeth white in the moonlight. "I don't know. She's a superb horsewoman. I'll find you a suitable mount—one that's not too rambunctious."

"And let her think I don't know how to ride a horse! Never. I only insist on one thing. I won't ride sidesaddle. I have the proper kind of dress to ride astride, and I insist that I be allowed to use it."

"It won't bother me, though Lavinia and Lady Teague will probably be horrified."

"Good. I hope they will be."

He placed one hand on the post behind her head, leaning toward her. Ardeth felt her heart begin to race, and her skin warmed with a delicious glow that spread through her body.

"And how do you like the earl?" Reardon asked.

"He's pleasant enough. You didn't invite me here to be Lavinia's rival, did you?"

His face was very near her own. He reached out a finger and lightly traced a pattern on her cheek.

"Of course not. The earl's here to look over western lands as an investment. Strictly business. However, I do hope you'll get on with Cameron. He's a very important man back East."

"Oh, yes," Ardeth murmured, trying to keep her mind on Garth's words. She could feel his lips, light as the brush of a feather against her hair. His hard body slid smoothly against her own, pinning her to the post. "The man who is going to help my career. . . ."

"He's very anxious to hear you sing, but I told him he'd have to wait until you recovered from the rigors

261

of your trip. . . ."

His arms went around her. It was what she had been dreaming of, hoping for since the first moment she laid eyes on Garth Reardon in the Cheyenne depot. Ardeth went limp in his embrace, sighing as his lips scanned her cheek, down to the hollow of her throat, and up along the ridge of her chin, seeking her mouth. One of his hands slid smoothly up from her waist to cup her breast, a finger lightly stroking the taut damask over her nipple.

His mouth sought hers, and he leaned into her, forcing her head against the post. His lips were soft and moist and open. His tongue flicked back and forth, forcing her lips apart.

Ardeth gasped. Her body froze. The warmth vanished; the glow was transformed in an instant. All at once she was not drifting deliciously on a wave of sensuous pleasure. She was being pushed painfully against a shaft of wood, a hard, foreign body invading hers. She was conscious of wet lips, a violating tongue, hands that were cold against her skin.

Twisting her head, she forced her arm up between them and shoved Reardon away. For an instant she caught the black look of surprise and rage in his eyes before he stepped back and masked them with his hand.

"Forgive me. I've offended you. . . ."

Ardeth was embarrassed. "No, no. I'm just . . . tired, I suppose. not in the mood . . . I'm terribly sorry. . . ."

"It's entirely my fault. I should have waited. You are very beautiful, you see. Especially in the moonlight. Please say you'll forgive me."

262

Ardeth stepped away. "Perhaps I should go up. Can you give my regrets to the others? I'll see them in the morning."

"Of course," he said very kindly. "And why don't you stay in bed tomorrow and rest. Forget about the hunt. There will be others. I don't want you getting ill while you are here."

She smiled at him gratefully. "Thank you, Garth. I really don't know what is the matter with me, but I suspect it is fatigue. If you'll just show me the right staircase, I'll say good night."

"Of course." He did not touch her as he led her through a side door into the main hall outside the drawing room where the others sat playing cards. She hurried up the stairs and down the hall, closing the door behind her with relief. It was only much later as she lay in the darkened room that she thought back on the scene on the porch.

What on earth had happened? One moment she was in ecstasy to be in Garth's arms, and the next she was repulsed by everything about him. Had someone thrown a bucket of cold water over her, she could not have gone through a more dramatic transformation. She was certain she had deeply offended him, even though he had gone out of his way to be kind to her. But how could she explain to him what had happened when she did not understand it herself. He was still the beautiful, virile man she had found so attractive the first time she had seen him. For days she had dreamed of having him take her in his arms. What had come over her? And why?

She could find no answer. She only knew that the feeling lingered and now the thought of Garth

Reardon's hands on her body was utterly repulsive.

How was she going to get through the rest of this visit?

As it turned out Ardeth was spared taking part in the hunt, not just for the next day but for the whole week. She did not know how Garth had managed it, but all of a sudden everyone stopped urging her to join them, even though they made several jaunts without her. Though she enjoyed the rest, she found particular pleasure in ambling around the ranch, getting to know something about the way it worked and the people who kept it going. She pumped Antonia unmercifully about Garth, about the ranch, its size, the number of cattle and horses, the ranch hands and cowboys. Soon she knew all the servants by name and position. Then she set about becoming familiar with some of the men. It was a huge ranch covering several thousand acres, and there were many facets to its organization. She could only touch the surface of the activities around the ranch house, but she found a great satisfaction in that. She roamed the fenced corrals and pastures and drank in the distant vistas of the mountains, relieved that she did not have to mount a horse to inspect them closer. That would come in time.

In the long, slow evenings she sat with the others in the parlor playing whist or faro. Lord Berry taught her to play backgammon and insisted she perfect her skills through lengthy games while Lady Teague sat on the sidelines and glared at them both and Lady Lavinia flirted outrageously and rather desperately with Garth.

Twice she even sang for Mr. Cameron, nothing too grand, just a few of the more respectable songs she had learned at the Diamond Ring. Reardon had a Mexican hand named Alvarez who accompanied her on his guitar, adding a kind of soft, exotic touch to her performance. Cameron seemed impressed with the purity of her voice but was hesitant about promising to bring New York to its knees on her behalf, much to Ardeth's relief.

After two weeks of this pleasant dalliance, she began to sense that if she was going to keep her self-respect she would have to show Lavinia that she could ride a horse. When the next hunt was planned, she cheerfully asked to join even before anyone could ask. The men seemed very pleased, and Lavinia's tight-lipped disappointment only amused Ardeth.

She was pleased when the day dawned clear and bright, with just a cool touch to the wind that suggested summer would not last forever. Ardeth put on her fringed pant-skirt, a blue silk blouse and a soft leather jacket. She cinched a leather belt around her waist, caught her hair in a chenille net at the back of her neck, and set a black felt gaucho hat she had purchased in Denver on her head. Silver-tipped boots completed her costume.

She rather enjoyed the lifted eyebrows and shocked expressions on the faces of the others, already waiting by their mounts. Lavinia wore a typical velvet riding habit, complete with long gauzy scarf dangling from her pert little hat. One end of her skirt was tucked up awkwardly to enable her to ride side-saddle. After their initial shock, the men stepped forward to comment favorably on how lovely she looked, which only caused Lavinia's lips to purse even tighter.

Garth had prepared just the right horse for her, a beautiful black gelding whose gentle ways Ardeth recognized the moment she swung into the saddle. The hunters were accompanied by a large group of ranch hands—there to guide, collect the kill, and prevent any untoward accidents—and one large buckboard wagon loaded with supplies. It looked to Ardeth more as though they were setting out on another cross-country journey than on a three days' hunt.

They soon left the ranch far behind. As the tall hills grew ever closer, Ardeth found that the satisfaction of seeing them first hand was even more satisfying than the shock her outfit had given the two "ladys" earlier.

For a long time they rode at an easy pace, casually chatting and pausing now and then to admire some especially lovely distant view or unusually shaped outgrowth of sandstone rock. Ardeth was fascinated by the country through which they traveled. The hypnotic vision of ever closer mountain ridges, the thick forests of pine and fir that opened suddenly upon wide vistas of brown, gravel-strewn slopes, the shallow creeks vividly blue with the reflection of the sky, the riotous sweep of wild flowers—Indian paintbrush, Jacob's ladder, sunflower, rabbit brush, a broadcast of color against the green slopes—it seemed like her picture of what heaven must be like.

Once they entered the higher hills, they sighted a group of elk browsing among the trees, and the hunters took off at a run chasing them. Ardeth, who was not interested in running down an animal twice her size, hung back. To her surprise, Garth Reardon also stayed his mount.

"Don't you want to be in on the kill?" she asked as Garth eased into pace beside her.

"I'd rather keep you company. Besides, I've been there many times before. It's a novelty to them because they have nothing like our wild animals to hunt in England. But I can remember when the bleached bones of slaughtered bison covered the hills like stones as far as the eye could see. It hasn't been that long since the herds were so many thousand that they would bring a train to a stop and keep it waiting for hours while they crossed the tracks. It's all much too familiar to me. Besides, my men are along to make sure they enjoy it."

They rode in silence for a while, listening to the occasional gunfire in the distance. "I do find this country so very beautiful," Ardeth finally said. It had not been a comfortable silence, and she felt constrained to say something. "I've never seen hills or mountains or forests quite like these. It quite takes my breath away."

"Oh, we have much more interesting natural wonders than these. Up in the mountains of the north, there are places where the water bubbles up out of the ground, boiling hot like a bathtub. There are deep canyons and waterfalls and even a geyser that erupts from time to time, spewing water into the air. I must show these things to you sometime."

"They sound incredible. I'd love to see them."

"We even have a few local natural phenomena. For

example, look over there. What do you see?"

Ardeth pulled up on the reins and shaded her eyes to peer ahead. "The hills rise rather sharply, almost forming two walls. And they move in together, like a narrow opening. But the trail appears to move through and out into a kind of plain."

"Yes, it seems to go right on into a valley, doesn't it?"

"Indeed it does."

"Well, let me show you. . . ."

He began cantering off toward the narrow opening formed by the sloping rocks. Ardeth's mount, glad to have the chance to move faster, took off at a brisk pace that soon outdistanced Reardon. As they moved through the canyon opening and out onto the flat plain, the horse was almost running, Reardon's mount close behind. With the wind against her cheeks and the joy of a good horse beneath her, Ardeth was all of a sudden filled with happiness. Then, like a knife cutting through her joy, she suddenly saw looming up before her the dark shadow of a chasm. She cried out, pulling back sharply on the reins. Her horse dug its heels into the dirt and reared, sending her sliding backward in the saddle. She clung wildly to the reins as Garth reached to grab the bridle and turn her horse.

"I can't believe it," she cried, trying to steady her thumping heart.

"You came very close to the edge."

"Why, I never guessed it was there. Why didn't you tell me?"

"I wouldn't have let you go over." He sat with his hands resting on the pommel of his saddle while Ardeth caught her breath. "It's an old Indian trick. They used to chase the buffalo into this narrow canyon and over the cliff to their deaths. The poor buffalo never knew it was there either. You have to admire the Indian's ingenuity."

Ardeth dismounted and walked over to the edge. Close up like this, the yawning hole that broke the surface was apparent, though it had been invisible a few yards back. It was not a sheer drop; the ground sloped slightly. Yet anything tumbling over it would fall sixty feet to the floor below. And, going at a run, an unsuspecting rider would never see it until it was too late to stop. She shivered.

"I did tell you we have our local phenomena," Garth said smiling, trying to make a joke of it.

Ardeth remounted and turned her horse back toward the canyon mouth. "Are there any more like this one?"

"Nothing quite that dramatic," he answered, falling in place beside her.

Chapter Fourteen

By the time they caught up with the rest of the party at the rendezvous, the chuck wagon had been set up, and preparations for the midday meal were almost finished. Ardeth, having heard tales from the cowboys of what life on the trail was like, was astounded at the sumptuous meal which the cook soon set before them. Thick, tender steaks, roasted potatoes and tinned fruit, pots of boiling hot coffee for the hands and Garth's best wines for the hunters. It was certainly not the primitive dinner that she expected, but then she should have known Garth Reardon would never settle for that.

Satiated, they rested for a while, then set off once again. This time she joined the hunters, more for the joy of a swift ride than for the chase itself. For the rest of the afternoon she struggled to keep up, resting beside her horse when they dismounted to stalk game and bringing up the rear when they streaked after a herd of deer or elk. Evidently Lord Berry wanted more than anything to shoot bison and was disappointed that he had arrived several years after the great herds had been destroyed. However, near the end of the afternoon when he brought down an aged buck with the largest pair of antlers Ardeth had ever seen, his good humor was restored.

They camped that evening near a stream bordered on one side by a ridge of hills that rose sharply from the bottom land. She realized why it had been chosen when, later that night, the wind picked up, fresh and chilly. They sat around a huge fire for nearly an hour after supper, listening to the mournful songs of the cowboys and the noisy racket of the night insects. Far off in the distance they could hear the chilling wail of wolves in the mountains, a sound that brought visions of tomorrow's hunt to the men and shivers to the women. A bottle of Tennessee whisky was being passed around among the gentlemen, so Ardeth, tired after the day's strenuous riding, soon left them for the snug comfort of her own tent. She was thankful to have one to herself since sharing sleeping space with Lady Lavinia was not something she had looked forward to. That she was spared this, was probably due once more to Reardon's thoughtfulness.

She fell at once into a half-drugged sleep, dreaming wild dreams of horses and chasms and wounded animals. Deep in the night she woke suddenly from one of the more vivid dreams and realized there was someone in her tent. The night was so black it was like being blind, yet she could hear quite plainly someone shuffling near her cot, making low, quiet murmurs. She stiffened with fright, instantly wide awake, and strained against the blackness, trying to make out who or what was moving around near her.

Then she recognized a man's low voice, mumbling to himself. Garth? Would he have deliberately put her alone so he could come to her in the night? Ardeth pulled the blankets close around her throat and edged toward the top of the bed. At that moment the man plopped down on her cot, and she could see that he had lifted one leg and was pulling at his boot.

"Who's there?" she said in a loud whisper.

"Oh. Oh, my goodness. Did I wake you? So sorry, my dear. Meant to just slip in first, quiet like, you know. Wake you more gently."

With growing horror she recognized Neville Carmichael's voice, conspiratorial, slurred and quite drunk. Ardeth scrambled farther up the cot.

"My lord! What are you doing here. Please leave at once."

"Bloody boot!" the earl exclaimed as he finally got it off. "Pardon the language, my dear. Don't mean to offend. . . ."

"You offend by being here," Ardeth said in a loud whisper. "Go away!"

Paying her no mind, the earl tugged at his other boot and yanked it off. "Can't make love with these confounded boots on, now can we? Not a bit sporting. . . ."

To her horror he threw himself across the bed. "Now, where have you got to?" he said, scrambling at the covers. "Ah, here we are."

By this time Ardeth was up against the side of the tent, trying vainly to push away the earl's hands which seemed to be everywhere. His big body half covered hers, and the cot groaned under their com-

272

bined weight. His hands worked beneath the covers and found her waist, then slid up beneath her warm nightdress to clutch at her breast.

"Can't know how I've longed to do this," the earl grunted. Finding her face he began lavishing wet kisses over her cheeks while Ardeth struggled to push him away. Her wish not to insult his lordship was quickly drowned under the swelling onslaught of her fear and outrage.

"Stop it!" she cried. But the narrow cot left her little room to maneuver away from him. She began to scratch and claw, reaching for any surface she could find. When she got hold of a cheek, she raked her nails down it.

"Bloody hell!" the earl exclaimed, releasing her long enough to slap his palm against his wounded face. "Why, you've stabbed me. I like spirit in a woman but this goes beyond—"

With his grip on her relaxed for a moment, Ardeth was able to shove him away. With a cry he rolled off the cot and fell sprawling onto the floor. She jumped up, wrapping the blankets around her and, leaping over him, scrambled to the door of the tent, standing there, watching.

"I tried to tell you to leave me alone."

A little sobered, Neville staggered to his feet, struggling to recoup some of his dignity. "Well, really. I'm not accustomed to being welcomed in such a fashion by the ladies."

"I'm sorry but I did not invite you here, you know. Please leave."

He reached down, swept up his boots and tucked them under his arm. "It's the outside of enough!" he mumbled and started across the tent, hit his knee against a chest and nearly went down. Cursing under his breath, he staggered past her, threw open the tent flaps and went weaving out into the night. Ardeth groped her way back to her bed and sat there, trying to quiet her thumping heart. She was half amused and half appalled by the earl's appearance. Most of all she wondered how he had gotten the idea he could saunter into her bed whenever he felt like it. Perhaps it was the whisky, she thought, trying to be charitable. But she got very little sleep the rest of the night.

The next morning she delayed making an appearance at breakfast as long as she could. She half expected everyone to know what had happened during the night, but there was no sign from their greetings that anything was different. The earl treated her with a stiff formality when he looked her way at all. For her part, she carefully avoided glancing at the long, red streak that furrowed his cheek.

The day went much as the one before had gone. It wasn't until some time in the afternoon that Ardeth found herself riding quietly beside Lawrence Appleby, a little apart from the others. She had almost forgotten the incident in her tent and was caught by surprise when Appleby brought it up.

"You mustn't be offended by his lordship. He's a good sort of chap actually, and was a little inebriated after all that strong whisky."

Ardeth felt a slow flush rising in her cheeks. "I had hoped no one knew."

"No way to avoid that, I'm afraid, with such a small party as ours. But I especially hope that you will not hold a grudge against Berry because of this little incident. You see, he is accustomed to women welcoming him into their beds. Indeed, he is even more accustomed to being the unwilling partner."

"But I never gave him any indication that I wanted him. I've barely got to know him."

"Yes, but you are an actress."

"I'm not an actress. I'm a singer."

"It's all the same. Most ladies of the stage would welcome the opportunity to form a liaison with a rich, titled gentleman like Neville. And he is not exactly unattractive, you know."

Ardeth caught back her exclamation. Tripped up again by Medora's reputation! How could Berry or Appleby, either one, know that she had had a proper upbringing in a Nebraska family. "You are very kind to explain all this to me," she said, smiling at Appleby. "And I appreciate it. I would like you to find a way to inform the earl that even though I am a singer, I am not interested in forming a liaison with anyone at the moment. Perhaps we can avoid any more unhappy incidents in the future if he knows this."

"How unfortunate. But you'll not hold it against him?"

She smiled again, sending Appleby's admiration soaring. "As you said, our party is small. Too small for grudges. It will all be forgotten."

Nevertheless, she was awake most of the following night, listening for footsteps, straining for any sign that someone was inside her tent. All passed quietly however, and she joined the others the next morning relieved yet feeling sluggish from lack of sleep.

275

Though the earl was politely cool when circumstances threw them together, he avoided her most of the day as he had the day before. That was all right with Ardeth, who wished to have as little to do with him as possible.

This was the last day of the hunt. The plan was to take a path that morning that would swing them back toward the ranch, then set out in the afternoon for the trip home. As luck would have it however, they spotted a small group of bison grazing on one of the wide plains, and the ride that ensued took them far out of their way. It was almost worth it for the delight it brought to the earl, who, at last, had a chance at the game he really wanted. Even Ardeth enjoyed it at first. The wild dash across the flat plateau, a good horse beneath her and the wind in her face all added up to a thrill of excitement she knew she was unlikely ever to experience again.

It wasn't until the shooting began that she pulled up to fall back away from the party. This was not easy to do since the loud report of the guns frightened her horse. Tugging at the reins, she managed to turn its head from the pursuit and make a wide half-circle away from the others. She was actually slightly behind them, slowing her mount, when she heard the whine of a bullet graze her ear. Her horse reared, nearly unseating her. She grabbed frantically at the reins, tightening her knees against her mount's flanks, desperately holding on. Then the frightened animal gained its foothold and took off wildly in the opposite direction, away from the hunting party.

Ardeth had no control over the gelding now. All she could do was bend over its neck, clinging desperately to its mane with the reins tightly intertwined in the horse's hair, and hope the animal would soon be winded. She had no idea where they were headed or what lay ahead. Then she became conscious of another rider alongside, drawing near her horse's head and reaching for the bridle. Gradually they both slowed as the other rider pulled her frightened mount in to finally stand, its head drooping, its exhausted sides covered with foam and heaving from its exertions.

Ardeth slumped over the animal's neck, straining to get her own breath.

"What happened?" Garth asked, breathing heavily beside her. "I never expected you to lose control of that animal."

"Something spooked my horse," Ardeth replied between gasps. "Maybe the guns."

"He's heard plenty of guns before this."

She gave him a long, hard look, debating with herself how much to say. "Perhaps not so closely," she finally answered. "This was the first time I've actually been so close to the others when they were chasing game."

"Maybe that was it." He glanced off at the horizon. "They're almost out of sight. I hope Berry has shot one of those buffalo by now. It's the only thing that's going to satisfy him. Shall we try to catch up with them?"

Ardeth threw one leg over her saddle and slipped off her mount. "Just give me a moment to catch my breath. There's a shady spot over there by that group of pine trees that looks too inviting to pass up."

"You go ahead. I'll just check the horses and then

join you."

On unsteady legs she made her way over to the pines, glad to leave Garth behind fussing with the horses. Her hat had long ago fallen back on her head but was still fastened around her neck by its strings. She slipped it over her head and sat down to lean against one of the tree trunks, turning it in her hands. The bullet hole was clean and neat, a trim little opening right through the hatbrim. Ardeth studied it, amazed at her reaction. Somewhere deep down inside she felt a slight tremor but quickly willed it away. With a detached objectivity she poked at the tiny hole with the tip of her finger. Just a little closer. . . .

Garth was walking toward her. Turning the hatbrim, she set it in her lap and forced herself to smile up at him.

"Do you think we'll be able to catch up with the others?" he asked. "They were going like a locomotive after those bison. Maybe it would be better to stay here awhile and wait for them to head back."

Ardeth reached up for his hand. "Oh, no. I feel fine now, and I'm sure they'd worry if we didn't catch up. Besides, in this wild country we might miss them entirely."

He pulled her to her feet. "You needn't worry. I know the way back," he said, circling her waist lightly. Ardeth glided nimbly away.

"Oh, but I wouldn't want the others to be concerned. And, after all, you're their host. You can't just absent yourself to escort me home. I'd never live it down. And I wouldn't want to give Lady Lavinia the satisfaction of thinking I was too weak to stay with the party."

Garth shrugged. "I suppose you're right. Very well. Mount up and we'll find them. I only hope they didn't go too far off the trail."

But by the time they finally caught up with the others, even Ardeth realized they had gone very far indeed—so far that they were going to be several hours later than they had planned arriving back at the ranch. And since the supply wagon had been sent on ahead, it was necessary that they reach the Silver Sage soon after dark at the latest. Lord Berry had at last killed his bison. Leaving a group of his ranch hands, who were quite capable of spending the night on the plains without the aid of a supply wagon, to skin and cut up the game, Garth led the rest of the group at hurried pace back toward the ranch. Ardeth rode near the rear, lost in her own thoughts. The earl was full of exuberant good spirits. He almost never stopped talking, reliving the hunt over and over during the ride. Garth sat his mount quietly, staring ahead. The English visitors and Mr. Cameron listened to the earl, occasionally breaking in with comments of their own, pointedly ignoring her.

Which of them could it have been, she wondered over and over. Had a stray bullet come her way, one of many that the hunters and the hands were shooting in the air to run down the buffalo? That seemed unlikely since she had been behind the others when that shot was fired. It would have had to have been deliberately fired in her direction. But who would have done such a thing?

She looked at them, each in turn. Would the earl, in spite of his polite demeanor, be seething at her re-

279

jection and have tried to get even with her? That seemed unlikely, considering his great delight at finally spotting a herd of bison. Would Lady Lavinia have grabbed at a chance to get a rival out of the way? She was an excellent shot as well as a fine horsewoman, and Ardeth would not put it past her. Yet there had been other times more convenient. Why not then?

Mr. Appleby and Mr. Cameron both seemed not to care that much about her to bother with shooting her. And Garth? He had never been anything but polite to her, and, after all, he had come after her to stop her frightened horse. Yet he was an enigmatic man. One never knew what he was thinking beneath that attractive facade. On the other hand, he had invited her out here. Why would he want to shoot her?

She could find no answers that seemed plausible, and by the time they finally reached the outskirts of the ranch, she had decided it had to have been an accident—an accident that with the variation of an inch or two might have left her dead out there on the prairie.

It was this unsettling thought that nagged at her beneath the weariness she felt when the party finally rode into the fenced corral of the Silver Sage. It was completely dark by now, and had they not been so close, they could not have continued on. Exhausted and thick with layers of brown dust, the weary hunters dragged themselves out of the saddle and trudged up the graveled walkway to the house.

Ardeth had never been so glad to see civilization again. All she wanted was to get out of these dusty clothes and sink into a comfortable bed behind the locked door of her bedroom. A bath would have to wait until tomorrow, but she was so tired she did not even mind.

Antonia met her on the upper landing. "Oh, miss," she started. "I wasn't sure you'd get in tonight, it being so late and all. . . ."

"Go to bed, Antonia," Ardeth said wearily. "I don't need you. I don't even want you. I'm just going to throw off these clothes and fall into bed."

"But, miss—"

"I would like a good hot bath first thing in the morning, however. Could you arrange that?" She was standing with her hand on the door handle of her room. "But Miss Medora. There's—"

Ardeth gave her an indulgent smile. "Go to bed, dear. That's what I'm going to do."

She slipped inside and closed the door behind her. The room was dark with only two bronzed patches on the flowered rug where the moonlight filtered through the lace curtains. Ardeth began pulling at the buttons of her shirt, then slipped it over her shoulders. She dropped it on the floor, tugged at her belt and let it fall beside the blouse. She unfastened the buttons on her dusty riding skirt and stepped out of it, leaving it to join the other garments, then sat on the bed and began tugging at her boots. Only then did the hairs on her neck suddenly come alive as she began to realize there was someone else in the room besides herself.

A low chuckle sounded in the shadows near the far corner of the room. She jumped to her feet, the boot in one hand, staring into the darkness.

"Who's there?" she cried, terror surging in her

281

chest.

"I'm glad to see you look as good as ever, even with one boot on and in your underwear!"

The words came from the shadows surrounding a chair in the corner. Relief surged through her body as she recognized their full, mocking timbre.

"Nat!"

Chapter Fifteen

She flew across the room and into his arms. Still chuckling, he crushed her to him, lifted her off her feet and swung her around. Her arms went tightly around his neck, and she felt his lips hot on her cheek, her neck, her mouth. Then she remembered.

Trying to pull away from the tight clasp of his arms, she began pummeling his chest. "You weasel! You swine! You snake in the grass!"

"Whoa, hold it there . . ." he said, grabbing at her fists.

"You walked off and left me in that dreadful town absolutely alone. And without a word of explanation or apology. I hate you! How dare you come waltzing back in my life!"

"Just a minute!" he cried, trying to dodge her blows. "Damn it, Ardeth, be still and listen."

"I don't want to hear anything you have to say. Get out!" She managed to break his grip on her and ducked out of his arms. Grabbing the cushion on the chair, she slapped it against his chest. "Get out and stay out! You're nothing but trouble!"

Nat grabbed at the cushion, then caught her wrist, holding her in his grip while her eyes blazed at him.

"Will you be quiet for a minute. You're going to wake the whole house. How will that look when the great Mr. Reardon comes roaring in to find a strange man in your bedroom."

"I don't care what Garth Reardon thinks, or any of the rest of them. Just go away."

"No, I won't. What's the matter with you anyway? Didn't you read my letter?"

"What letter? There wasn't any letter. There wasn't anything except that loathsome tart, Roxie, smirking long enough to tell me you had gone. That was the worst part of the whole thing. I'll never forgive you!"

"But she had the letter. I gave it to her myself. She promised to put it in your hands the next morning. You mean you never saw it?"

Ardeth's massive wrath began to wane slightly. "I never saw anything. As far as I knew you just walked away without a word."

"Why, you poor girl. No wonder you're ready to murder me."

"That's not a bad idea, come to think of it."

Nat took the cushion away from her, laid it back on the chair and sat down, pulling her down on his knee. "It was too bad I had to leave so suddenly, but there was no other way. Roxie had learned where Toad Turnbull was hiding out from some friends traveling through Fireweed. I had to take off after him or risk losing his trail. I thought the letter would explain everything."

"She never gave me any letter. And she certainly

did not explain in full why you had to leave so suddenly. In fact, she enjoyed my misery and confusion. I thought you had just grown tired of me."

His arm tightened around her waist, and he pulled her down against him, nuzzling the hollow of her neck. "Grown tired of you! Never."

"Don't do that, Nat," Ardeth said, struggling against him. "I'm still not sure I forgive you. After all, you certainly thought more of the Toad than you did of me."

"Well, there are some things even more important than love. A lot of good it did me anyway. He was long gone by the time I got there. I went back to Fireweed because I expected you to wait there for me. How do you suppose I felt when I found you had picked up and left, bag and baggage and no one even knew where you had gone."

"I'm sure Roxie made you very welcome."

"Bother Roxie! You can't for a minute imagine I'd give a shopworn old tart like Roxie a second look, can you? All I ever wanted from her was information about Turnbull."

Ardeth laid her hand along his lean cheek. "Is that really true?"

"Of course it's true. Good God, Ardeth, can you imagine me taking up with the likes of her after having you! If would be like going from steak to jerky!"

"I'm not sure I appreciate the comparison," she mumbled and went limp in his arms, melding with his body. With her anger gone, she could savor once again the delicious feel of his hard, firm body, the clean smells of soap and leather, the soft flannel of his shirt, and the crispness of his chest hair against her cheek below his open collar. All at once she knew how much she had ached for him, something that her hurt and anger had prevented her from acknowledging for so long.

"Mmm," Nat said, nuzzling her shoulder. "God, how I've missed you!"

She leaned against his arm, and he bent over her, kissing her face until he found her lips, gentle and warm beneath his. Her arms went around his neck, and her heart swelled with happiness. "Oh, Nat. I've missed you too," she murmured as his insistent lips lightly swept her face, searching the little hollows of her ears, down her throat and across her shoulder. She felt the warmth growing within her, like a tiny flame increasing in strength. While one arm cradled her shoulders against him, he slipped his free hand along her ankle and up her leg.

"Do you know you've still got one boot on?" he mumbled.

Ardeth gave a low laugh, arching her back, her throat bared to his kiss. "I don't think I care," she whispered.

"It might prove . . . cumbersome, to say the least."

She could feel his fingers sliding gently along her knee, silkily moving up her thigh. With an almost imperceptible movement, she shifted her weight, allowing his insistent fingers to move higher. Though she could feel the swelling hardness of his body beneath her thin cotton petticoat, she knew it was she who was being swept along a mindless cascade of feelings — not him. He was in firm control, working on her gently, firmly, like a musician with his beloved instrument, drawing her along to the brink of a need that flamed with desire.

"Nat," she groaned, writhing slightly under his unceasing, exploring fingers. His lips slid along her throat, tasting through the thin cloth of her chemise the sweetness of her breast. He shifted his arm, lifting her breast to meet his kiss and she fell back on the arm of the chair, so filled with fire that she herself pushed away the lacy edge to bare the taut nipple for him to take between his lips. His tongue was cold on her flesh but so teasingly insistent that she could hardly bear it. His other hand moved up her thigh and grasped at the firmness between her legs, already moist with expectation. He worked beneath the enclosing cotton to her yielding flesh and began with increasing fervor to massage her into a frenzy of desire.

Ardeth gasped, crying for him, desperate for him. When she thought she could bear it no more, he slid suddenly to the floor, stretched above her, fumbling with his clothes until he laid aside the encumbrances, and thrust deep into her, pulsating with his own overwhelming need, again and again until together they went crashing into that timeless void where all was sensation realized, wholeness attained.

They lay in silence while their hard breathing subsided. "I didn't mean that to happen quite so quickly," Nat finally managed to mumble. "Somehow I always seem to lose control around you."

Ardeth chuckled softly. "I thought your control was pretty good."

"I didn't know until now how very much I missed you," he said, pulling her against him. "But I do wish you'd get rid of that other boot."

"Do you think we can make it to the bed?"

"We'd better if we don't want to spend the night on the floor."

Stifling their laughter, they managed to cross to the bed where, giggling, they threw off the rest of their clothes and ducked beneath the covers, warmly clasped together. The intoxicating feel of Nat's bare skin against her own sent Ardeth's senses reeling all over again, but she subdued the incipient flame of passion. There were things they had to face before giving themselves to the enclosing, delicious night.

"Mmmm, you feel so good," Nat murmured, pulling her against him and running his hand down her waist and along the cool sweep of her hip. "We have a lot of times to make up for," he mumbled, nuzzling the shadowy cleavage between her breasts.

Ardeth maneuvered her hands between them and pushed him a few inches away. "You feel good too, but that can wait for a few minutes. We have some very important things to discuss first."

"Nothing is more important than this," Nat whispered, pulling her back inside the tight circle of his arms. Ardeth wiggled away once again.

"I don't even know how I'm going to explain your sudden appearance to the others. Come on, Nat. Help me figure that out at least."

"Oh, very well," Nat said with a sigh. Scrunching up against the headboard, he plumped a pillow behind him and leaned back, both hands laced behind his head.

"So, who are these others who have to have an explanation? Tell me something about them."

Ardeth nestled against him. "Well, there's an English earl who's quite obsessed with hunting and a friend of his, also from England, who is rather friendly and nice. Then there are two women with them, both 'Lady Something or Other.' The younger one has her cap set on becoming the next 'Mrs. Earl' and the older one, a dragon of a woman, is her chaperone, though why Lavinia should need one has so far escaped me. They both dislike me because I'm a lowly actress, and Lavinia also sees me as a rival for her nobleman's affections, and that puts an even sharper edge on her animosity.

"There's also a wealthy gentleman from New York, who I suspect is here to help my career. He hasn't exactly offered to take me back East and make me famous, but I think he might with a little encouragement."

"The Toast of Broadway, eh?"

"Something like that. It's not anything I'm interested in. I didn't want to go on being Medora at all, but after you left so suddenly and Garth Reardon sent me a second invitation to visit his ranch, it seemed the only way to survive."

"Tell me about Garth Reardon. What do you think of him?"

Ardeth rested her head against Nat's chest. His soft hairs tickled her cheek, and she could hear the quiet thumping of his heart beneath her ear. "What is there to tell? He is one of the most attractive men

I've ever seen, on the surface. Yet underneath there is something not quite attractive at all, though I can't really tell what it is. It took me a while even to learn that. He exudes power, yet it is a kind of manipulative thing, as though the people around him all had strings like puppets and he's above them pulling them up and down as he wishes. I guess that sounds kind of silly, but it comes closest to what I feel about him."

"No, it's not silly. I had heard of Reardon, of course. Like Kohrs and Littlefield, he's well known in the West as one of the men who has made a fortune out of cattle. I never thought much about him though until after I started looking for Turnbull. Everywhere I've gone, his name has cropped up. Never directly, just somehow involved. It began to make me very curious.

"After I left Fireweed it happened again. When I lost Turnbull's trail outside of Cheyenne, it was one of the reasons I decided to come on to the Silver Sage. That, and the fact that I heard in Cheyenne you were visiting here. But isn't it an interesting coincidence that Reardon has cropped up yet again?"

"Well, for all his authority and wealth, Garth does not strike me as the kind of man who would indulge in anything illegal. He's too shrewd."

"You'd be surprised. There isn't much law and order out here in the western territory, you know. A clever man can get away with almost anything once he has enough power. You haven't noticed anything strange going on here, have you? Any strangers about? Any disappearances on Reardon's part?"

"Not really. Except . . . there was this one thing. . . ."

Abruptly Ardeth hopped out of bed, crossed the room and began rummaging in the clothes on the floor. The moonlight cascading from the window bronzed the smooth patina of her bare skin. Nat watched her more with approval than curiosity.

"Look at this," she said, climbing back into bed and handing Nat her black felt riding hat. "I finally went out on one of those hunting expeditions the English visitors like so much. Nothing much happened aside from having to convince his Lordship that I didn't want him in my tent. Until the last day. They sighted a group of bison and took off after them. I only followed for a while to run my horse. By the time I turned to fall back, there was a lot of shooting going on. Then—look at this. Clean through the hat brim. An inch closer and it would have been my head."

Nat took the hat, studying it in the dark. He poked the tip of his finger in the hole in the hatbrim. "Are you sure it wasn't just an accident. I know from experience that when a group of cowboys are trying to turn cattle, sometimes the bullets go where they aren't intended."

"I would think that except that I was behind the others when this happened. All of them were ahead of me. It makes me think that a bullet in my direction would have had to be intentional."

"Did you tell anybody else about this?"

"No. It spooked my horse, and it took off in the wrong direction. Garth came after me and caught

291

the animal. I almost told him about it, but somehow it didn't seem like a good idea until I could figure out what really happened."

"Good thinking. Don't tell anyone. But I do think we ought to learn a lot more about Mr. Garth Reardon. You'll have to do some nosing around. Look into his papers, perhaps, ask a few questions."

"I think he keeps everything pretty much under lock and key."

"Then, you'll have to find the key, won't you?"

Ardeth swelled with indignation. "That's easy for you to say. Who are you anyway? What's your excuse for coming on the scene so suddenly. How am I going to explain having you in my room all night?"

"Calm down. I'm your manager, didn't you know? I was detained in Fireweed but followed you as soon as I could get away. I'm here to work out some kind of deal with your wealthy eastern friend. As for this," he added, pulling her back into his arms, "well, everybody knows that relations between actresses and their managers are often more than they should be. They won't think anything of it."

Ardeth giggled as he nuzzled her neck, tickling her with his tongue. "You'd better watch out for Lady Lavinia. She may decide you're a better catch than the earl and lure you away just to annoy me."

"And would you be jealous?"

"Jealous! Of course not!"

"No more than you were of Roxie," he said slyly.

Ardeth grabbed a pillow and slapped it against his chest. "It's not the same at all!"

Laughing, Nat pulled her against him. "I promise

not to encourage Lady Lavinia. Besides, I'm too destitute for her to take me over a landed nobleman."

"I thought you had a lot of money."

"I did. But I've used up a lot of it traipsing around looking for Turnbull and following you around the country. That's one of the reasons I'd like to find Medora's map. I don't suppose you've had any luck finding it?"

"None. You know how thoroughly we looked in Fireweed. I'm beginning to think Medora didn't even have it with her."

"She must have. I know she did."

"How do you know?" Ardeth sat up and fluffed the pillow behind her head. "What is there about an old map that can be so important? I don't think you've been honest with me about it."

Nat crossed his arms over his chest and stared into the darkness. "Well, I may not have been completely honest. I suppose after all this time I owe you some kind of explanation. I'm sure Medora had the map because she wrote me she was bringing it. As you already know, she had offered to sell it to me. I was to meet her in Fireweed with the money."

"But how could you have known it was real? She might have been leading you on to get money from you."

"No, there was more to it than that." He hesitated. "Well, I suppose I might as well tell you. Medora was the mistress of my uncle, Flores de Lago. My mother came from one of the old *hidalgo* families of New Mexico, and Flores was her elder brother. The de Lagos came to the new world with the first conquistadors and once were quite well-to-do. All my life I've heard the legend how once, when the Apaches and Comanches were on one of their rampages, the Franciscans near our home took all the gold from their church and all the bullion the de Lagos had accumulated from their mines and hid it in the mountains. No one has ever known where, but the legend has been passed down for over a hundred years.

"Flores unearthed a map of the area where the gold was hidden shortly before he died. He gave it to Medora to bring to me, but looking out for her own interests, she offered to sell it to me instead. The description in her letter had too many details to be faked—things she could not possibly have known unless Flores told her. Of course, the map might prove to be a fake, but it was just too tempting. I had to know."

"But why didn't your uncle go look for the gold?"

"He was sick and old when he found the map. He trusted her to bring it to me. But she had been on the stage a long time and was nearing the end of her career. She put herself first."

Ardeth sighed. "But we've looked through everything she owned, and it's not there. She had no home, so she must have had it with her. I suppose she could have left it in St. Louis, but why would she when she expected to sell it to you?"

"Exactly. It has to be here somewhere. We just haven't looked in the right place yet. We'll simply have to go over everything again."

He reached out and pulled the pillow from behind Ardeth's head. Then scrunching beneath the covers, he slid her down alongside his lean, hard body. "But that can wait till morning. We've had enough talking for tonight. We've still got to make up for a lot of lost loving, and we've only just got started!"

When Ardeth awoke the next morning, Nat was already gone, and it was only later that she learned he had been given a room of his own in the rear of the house. He appeared at breakfast clean shaven, neatly dressed and smiling like a cat who had been at the cream. Most of the English contingent were already at the table. They looked up in surprise as Ardeth rose to link her arm in Nat's and introduce him around. She got some satisfaction from the raised eyebrow on Lady Lavinia's face and the startled, disapproving frown on Lady Teague's. Though the earl barely acknowledged Nat's presence, Lawrence Appleby gave him a friendly welcome and seemed delighted to have someone new added to their group. Once he knew Nat had come from New Mexico, he steered the conversation to that part of the country and was full of questions about its heritage and landscape.

The two men and Ardeth were the only people in the group left at the table when Garth Reardon walked into the room. He had, of course, heard of Nat's arrival the night before and was not surprised to see him sitting at the table. His handsome face was impassive as Nat stood to introduce himself and thank him for his hospitality. Without shaking hands, the two men faced each other off, outwardly polite and mentally trying to size each other up.

"I was not aware Madam Melindez had a manager," Garth said lightly, as he helped himself to the food on the sideboard. Though he was impeccably dressed, it was obvious he had been up for some time and had already been out on his horse around the ranch.

"It's the usual custom," Nat answered. "Particularly when performers are arranging to appear in out of the way places like our western towns." He leaned back in his chair, one arm over the back, regarding Garth with glittering, hard eyes. Ardeth began to feel a nervous twinge in her stomach.

"Strange I did not hear from you when I was making the arrangements for Medora to visit the Silver Sage," Garth casually commented as he moved to the table and took his place at its head.

"Oh, that was my fault," Ardeth said quickly. "Nat was very busy at the time, and I was pretty sure at first he would not be able to come. Then we had a slight . . . disagreement, and I decided to come without him. But that's all over now."

"Yes, all is forgiven," Nat said, smiling at her. "Of course, had I known of your invitation, I would have urged her to take advantage of it." He observed Garth toying with the food on his plate. "I understand you have a guest here who might be able to arrange some appearances for her back East."

"Mr. Cameron, yes. There has been some discussion about it."

"Well, now that I'm here, we can discuss it in earnest. Can't we, my dear Medora?"

Ardeth nodded and tried to smile, even though she felt like a minnow caught between two pike. Thankfully she was distracted by one of the men servants who came gliding softly into the room to bend down and whisper something to Garth. Though both Ardeth and Nat exchanged glances and strained to hear, the message was delivered with such practiced finesse it was impossible. They both noted, however, that the message brought a sudden flush to Garth's handsome face. He quickly excused himself and left the room. At an almost imperceptible nod from Nat, Ardeth suddenly remembered she had neglected to bring down an important letter she was keeping for him and went off to retrieve it.

For once the hall was empty of maids. She swept lightly down the carpeted hallway toward the rear where Garth had his office. Peering around the corner, she could just see him standing by the door, reading what looked like a telegram. The ranch foreman, John Glover, was with him, his back to Ardeth.

"Come inside," Garth said grimly and began to unlock the door.

Ardeth hastily retraced her steps to the front stairs, ran to her room and grabbed the first thing she could find that looked like a letter. By the time she reentered the dining room, Lawrence Appleby was leaving.

"I believe I'll just have one more cup of coffee," Nat said casually as Ardeth sat down at the table. "I'll meet you in an hour for that ride."

"Good enough, old chap." When Appleby had got

far enough away Nat leaned over the table toward Ardeth.

"What was that all about?"

"I'm not sure. Garth had John Glover with him. I think he had received a telegram. Whatever it was, he looked pretty serious."

"Who is John Glover?"

"The ranch foreman. He's a typical cowboy—hard as nails but very efficient. I don't see much of him, but when our paths have crossed, he's always been polite."

"Sounds like someone I should get to know. Listen, my love. You've got to find out what that telegram was about. It might explain a few things. I've got to go out riding this morning with your friend, Appleby, who has graciously offered to show me around. Some of the others may be going as well. Can you use the time while we are gone to nose around a bit?"

"Nat! I don't want to be a sneak! It's very distasteful."

Nat smiled at her, rubbing his chin with his finger. "Think of it as part of your impersonation of Medora."

"Oh, thank you," Ardeth commented, her cheeks warming.

Nat reached out and took her hand. "I'm serious, my love. My instincts tell me this Reardon is up to no good, no matter how grandly he lives. But perhaps my instincts are wrong. I hate Turnbull so much that perhaps I've come to see his evil taint on everyone. Help me find out the truth."

"You make it sound nicer than it is, however it's still sneaking around. But all right. I feel there is something not right about Garth Reardon, just as much as you do. I'll do what I can, but don't expect too much."

"Does he always keep that study door locked?"

"I'm not sure, but I'll find out. Just make sure you keep Appleby and the others out of the way."

He leaned over and kissed her cheek. "That's my girl."

Ardeth waited in her room well beyond the hour that Nat had planned to leave. When she finally went back downstairs, she wandered the rooms, making certain they were empty and asking the occasional cleaning maid where the others were. Nat, Appleby, Cameron and Lady Lavinia had all gone riding, she learned. Lady Teague was upstairs with a sick headache and "the master" had gone off with Mr. Glover. When she wandered down the back hall and saw the study door standing open, she began to think fate was playing right into her hands.

She stepped inside one of the smaller rooms off the hall which had been designated, somewhat grandly, "the music room," and peered around the door frame to see why the study was open. A few moments later one of the maids came out carrying a broom and a dustpan, closed the door and took off down the hall toward the kitchen. Ardeth made certain no one was watching, then slipped down the hallway and turned the study doorknob. It moved under her hand. Furtively she slipped inside the small room.

It held little of interest: a large oak desk near the one window, several massive chests along the walls, one huge elk's head on the wall, its sightless eyes staring down at her accusingly. She tried the chests first and found them all locked. The desk proved to be locked as well. Her heart was beginning to thump a little too loudly, and she was about to slip out of the room when she spotted a yellow edge of paper under the books lying on top of the desk. She grabbed it up, realizing with some excitement that it was the telegram she had seen in Garth's hand. She read it through, folded it and put it back exactly as she had found it. Then she hurried to the doorway and slipped out of the room, closing the door behind her. Turning, she careened straight into the cleaning maid.

"Oh, good heavens! You startled me," she cried, suppressing the urge to turn and run in the opposite direction.

"I'm sorry, miss. I didn't mean to."

"I . . . I seem to have lost my way around here. I was looking for the music room. I left some of my music there, and I need to study it. This house is so big, it still gets confusing."

"The music room is over there, miss," the girl said sullenly. She was new to Ardeth, young, and appeared none too bright. Her broad face was sprinkled with a band of freckles, and her eyes were so light blue they appeared almost white. "This here's the master's office. I'm giving it a cleaning."

"Yes, of course. Well, I'm sorry I disturbed you. Thanks for showing me the right room." She hoped her excuse did not sound as lame to this stupid girl as it did to her. Edging along the hall, she then darted inside the music room once more, closed the door and sank into a chair. Her heart was pounding in her chest. She was going to have to get stronger than this if she hoped ever again to get beyond those locked doors of Garth's office, she told herself. At least she had read the telegram. Now if only that stupid girl would accept her explanation and forget to mention that she had been inside Garth's office.

Grabbing up a pile of music, she went back into the hall just in time to see the cleaning girl locking the study door. There was another bit of interesting information, she thought. The maids had keys to all the rooms. She would have to remember that.

"So, what did it say?" Nat asked.

Ardeth glanced around, making certain they were alone. She was sitting with Nat in a small, ornate gazebo set in a pool of shade trees behind the main house of Garth's ranch. Ardeth had discovered it as a quiet, private island of calm long before Nat appeared, and now that he was here, it proved the safest place for the two of them to talk without being overheard.

"Nothing terribly important, at least as far as I could tell. I don't think it had anything to do with your Toad Turnbull."

"I might decide that for myself if you'd only tell me what the telegram said."

"It was about some herders coming through the

Rockies. It mentioned an estimated arrival time and a very large number of cattle. That was all."

Nat rubbed a finger along his chin. "Did it actually say, 'cattle'?"

"No, I don't believe it did. I just assumed that's what it meant."

"But it did say, 'herders'?"

"Yes. I remember that distinctly."

Nat rose, placing one booted foot on the seat and leaning on his knee. "Not cattle, my love. Sheep. The cattleman's worst enemy. Someone is trying to force grazing lands for sheep from Reardon's empire, and I have a notion he will never stand for it. Lesser men have gone to war over this matter. The last few years there has been an exodus of sheepherders from California trying to lay claim to the grazing lands east of the Rockies. Garth must have a pretty good system of communication for someone to telegraph him that they're coming."

"But why should he care? There's plenty of land here. Surely there's room for both."

"Ardeth, you may have learned how to perform on a stage since you left Nebraska, but you've still got a lot to learn about raising cattle. Sheep crop grass down to the roots, leaving the fields bare until next year's rains. The cattle that follow find no grass at all. Sheep can move on to higher ground where cattle cannot go. It works well for the sheep but is disastrous for the cattle.

"Besides, a man like Reardon, who carved this valley into a great ranch, is not going to stand idly by and see his grazing lands stolen from him. I'll be

302

very interested to see what he does about it."

Ardeth suddenly remembered the ragged Indians who had stopped Reardon's carriage on their journey from Cheyenne. "Garth can be hard. I saw it once myself."

"I suspected as much. Well, it's his problem, not ours. What matters for us is for you to open up those chests in his office and have a look at some of his papers. My instincts tell me there is a lot more to Garth Reardon's business dealings than even we suspect."

"But Nat. You've no idea the terror I went through just to read that telegram. And even though I got inside the room, the chests were locked. How am I ever going to get my hands on the key?"

Nat reached out and tipped up her chin, brushing her lips with his own.

"Don't worry about it. I'll find a way."

"I hope you can find a way to shore up my courage, as well."

He laughed. "I'll work on that tonight!"

Chapter Sixteen

Garth Reardon was gone for four days. It was amazing how smoothly the routine of the ranch carried on, with all the comforts and concerns for the guests being as well arranged as if the host himself had been there. They might not have missed him at all, Ardeth thought, except that his presence was so strong and all-prevailing that it created a sense of unease not to see him at the tables or in the rooms. She had expected to feel more relaxed and confident without the possibility of his walking in on her as she moved around the house, learning everything she could about it. Instead, it was almost as though his unseen presence followed her around, peering over her shoulder. Perhaps, she thought, that was not so surprising after all. He had his servants so well trained she felt certain they would go straight to him when he returned with a detailed account of her every movement.

In spite of that, she persevered. She discovered that the master keys were kept in the pantry cupboard near the kitchen. There was one ring, not marked, but containing smaller keys such as might unlock a padlock or a desk. That had to be the one she needed, she felt certain. But how to find an excuse to get inside the room with time to unlock the chests and examine their contents—that she could still not imagine.

And then, two days after Garth's return, fate itself raised its erratic hand to solve her problem.

From an upstairs window, she spotted the two men riding up the long trail toward the ranch. Like two tiny toy soldiers, their silhouettes were dark against the brightness of the sun rising behind them. Ardeth watched them until they drew close enough for her to be certain they were strangers. By the time they had ridden up to the porch, she had ambled to the top of the stairs and was peering down, being careful not to be seen from below.

One was tall with a thick brush of a moustache on a long, narrow face, burned dark and leathery by the sun. The other was shorter and better dressed in a suit and string tie. The tall one spoke curtly to the housemaid and sent her scurrying for Garth. They waited impatiently in the hall, muttering low comments to each other until Reardon appeared from the dining room.

"Marshal Connely," Garth said, wiping at his mouth with a napkin. "This is a surprise. What are you doing so far east."

The marshal turned the brim of his hat in his leathery hands. "This here's Samuel Blamey, land agent from Montana Territory. We need to have words with you, Mr. Reardon."

"I can't imagine what a land agent from Montana would have to say to me, but you're welcome to come in. Have you had breakfast?"

"Thanks, yes. We ate on the trail."

"You must have been traveling pretty hard to get here so early in the morning."

"We have important business, Mr. Reardon. I suggest we get to it as soon as possible."

Reardon shrugged and threw his napkin on a nearby table. "Come into my office, then."

As the three men disappeared down the hall, Ardeth looked around to make certain no one was watching her, then scurried down the stairs and along the back hall to the music room. She could see the study door was not completely closed, but though she strained to hear, she could not make out what was being discussed.

Then a dark figure slipped in beside her.

"Nat!" she gasped. "For heaven's sake, you gave me a terrible fright."

"Sssh," he said, motioning for her to stay quiet. Then he whispered, "I saw those men riding up. One of them is wearing a badge."

"He's a marshal from somewhere west of here. The other one is a land agent."

"A government man. This could be very interesting."

Nat cracked the door, and they both leaned against it, trying to make out what the voices from the room across the hall were saying. At first it was impossible, but then, as tempers apparently began to fray, the voices increased.

"This is absurd!" they heard Garth saying. "You haven't the slightest bit of proof that I was involved in any way. You're just trying to get back at me because I drove off a few farmers last year."

There was a low, indistinct murmur that they recognized as the marshal's voice. Then Samuel Blamey's high pitched tones took over, loud and clear.

"This has all the earmarks of your high-handed style, Reardon. But this time you've gone too far. Rim-rocking twenty-five hundred sheep to death! Murdering two Basque herders in cold blood. Even the dogs slaughtered, and in the most cruel manner. You're not the law here, Garth Reardon, no matter how much you think you are. This time justice will be served!"

"Tell this man to curb his tongue, Marshal, or I'll have him thrown off my land."

"I'm afraid I can't do that, Garth." The marshal dropped his voice.

"What's rim-rocking?" Ardeth whispered in Nat's ear.

"Driving them over a cliff. It's very effective."

"That telegram. Surely that shows he was involved."

Nat laid a finger lightly on her lips as the voices from the study rose in a crescendo.

"Why should I go with you to answer a lot of ridiculous charges that you can't possibly prove. You have a hell of a nerve to come here and suggest such a thing."

For once the marshal spoke clearly. "I'm not suggesting, Mr. Reardon. These are serious accusations, and you're going to have to answer them. And not here on your ranch, either."

"Why, you half-baked gunslinger. I know what you were before you took on the respectable role of a lawman. And don't think I can't destroy whatever credibility you've built up since you put on that star. As for you, Mr. Blamey, it would take only one telegram to Washington to have you relieved of your appointment. I have influential friends—"

"It'll do you no good to threaten me, Reardon. You can have me relieved of my appointment any time you want. I'm still going to make sure you answer for that massacre in the Salt River Pass."

"You'd better collect your things, Garth," the marshal intoned. "After all, if you're innocent, what have you got to fear."

There was a short silence as Garth appeared to be thinking this over. When he spoke next, his voice was lower and more calm. "I have several house guests to see to first. Then I'll come. But I won't forget this, Connely. You'll regret it someday."

Nat eased the music room door almost shut as they heard the men move into the hall. He kept one eye to the thin sliver of the opening while Ardeth pressed against the wall, hardly daring to breathe.

When they had passed the music room door and turned into the next hall, he whispered to Ardeth, his voice thick with excitement.

"He forgot to lock the door!"

"Are you sure?"

"I watched him. I guess he was too insulted to think straight. Quick, run to the kitchen and get those keys to the desk. This may be our best chance to see what's in those chests. Our only chance!"

"Wouldn't it be better to wait until we're sure he's gone? He'll probably be away several days."

"Then you'd have to lift two sets of keys from the pantry, and somebody down there might miss them. Hurry. I'll go inside the office and wait for you."

Ardeth was still not convinced, but since time was important, she gave in. While Nat slipped inside the study, she hurried down the back halls to the kitchen, trying to devise some excuse for being there. But she was lucky. The Chinese cook Garth employed was outside on the back porch overseeing two of the kitchen helpers as they peeled vegetables. The kitchen was dappled with shadows from the long row of windows that overlooked the patio outside. Keeping in their dark pools, she slipped along the wall to the pantry, lifted the small set of keys from the bottom corner and, clutching them in her pocket, hurried out. She had been so lucky not to run into one of the servants that she began to think perhaps Nat was right. This was the best time.

When she slipped inside the study, quietly closing the door behind her, Nat was already rummaging through the items on Garth's desk. Without a word, he took the keys and motioned her to stand by the door and listen, just in case one of the maids passed by and found the door unlocked. With her breath tight in her throat, Ardeth kept to her place while Nat opened one drawer after another, going quickly through the papers there and murmuring to himself.

"Hurry," she finally whispered, wanting nothing so much as to get away from this dangerous room and back to the comparative dullness of daily life.

"Very interesting . . ." Nat whispered. "Who would have thought. . . ."

"Please, Nat."

Nat leafed through a sheaf of legal-looking yellowed papers he lifted from one of the bottom drawers. "I'm hurrying. There's a lot here."

The silence in the room and in the hall outside was oppressive, as though fate, which had played into their hands, was galvanizing itself to drop a huge disaster on them. Ardeth tried to calm her taut nerves, telling herself that so far they had managed everything perfectly.

Then she heard voices in the adjoining hall, growing louder.

"My God! He's coming back!"

She felt the color drain from her face as she turned to Nat. He stuffed the papers back inside the drawer and pushed it shut. "Get back to the music room," he ordered. "And stay there."

"But you—"

"Never mind me. Go!"

She didn't argue. Closing the study door behind her, she ran across the hall and ducked inside the music room just as Garth turned down the back hall. She could clearly hear him ordering two of his men to wait for him at the front of the house. The spurs of his boots jingled merrily as he passed her door and stopped before the study, the clink of the keys he carried in his hand ringing loudly in Ardeth's ears. Ardeth watched through a slit in the doorjamb as he fit one of the keys in the lock. He paused a moment, reconsidered, then opened the door and went into his office.

Without thinking, she flew after him.

"Oh, Garth!" she cried with a forced nonchalance. "I'm so glad I saw you. I've been looking for you everywhere. You're very hard to find, you know, especially in the mornings. I suppose it's because you have so much to do to run this great, large ranch."

He had only managed to take a few steps inside before Ardeth was framed in the doorway. In one glance she saw that the room looked normal and empty. But it wouldn't do to let him stay too long.

"What do you want, Medora," Garth said in a voice lacking its customary polite tones. "I'm very busy. I'm going to have to go away again for a day or two."

He moved around the desk and began pulling at the drawers, making sure they were locked. Ardeth dashed inside, leaning over the desk.

"Oh, well, I'm sure it's nothing important, at least not to you with all the really important things you have on your mind and all. Though, I admit, it does have a lot of significance to me. Maybe even for my career—"

"What are you talking about?" Garth moved to the chests and pulled on one or two of the drawers. To Ardeth's great relief, they did not slide open. She slipped up beside him, putting her arm through his and talking nonstop.

311

"Why, I just thought that since Mr. Cameron was here and all, and now that my manager is here as well, that it would be such a fine idea to let me put on a real show for your lovely guests. You know, give Mr. Cameron an idea of what I can really do on stage. Now, don't you think that would be a fine thing? It would entertain the earl and all his party, and it might convince Mr. Cameron to offer me a contract as well. It came to me in the early hours of this morning, and I just couldn't wait until I found you to put it to you."

Garth gave a cursory glance around. "I thought you were not anxious to perform for my guests. You certainly haven't been up until now."

"Well that was because I didn't have my manager with me. It makes all the difference, don't you know." She practically led him to the door. "I didn't know," he answered absently. "But we'll talk about it later, after I get back."

"Well, that's just fine. It will give me lots of time to practice my songs and get my program ready. Really, Garth, you're so wonderful to do this for me. It's just what I need to get my career going."

She had him in the hall now, watching as he fitted the key in the lock and turned it. "It's nothing," he murmured, dropping the keys back into his vest pocket. Ardeth hung on to his arm all the way down the hall.

"But I'll never forget it. I'll always be grateful . . ." she went on blabbing shamelessly, ignoring his obvious desire to be rid of her. Finally, near the stairs he could take no more. He stopped and gently but firmly unattached her arm from his.

"We'll discuss it when I return. Now, really, you must excuse me."

"Why, of course," Ardeth said, smiling inanely. The smile faded to a grimace as she watched him walk heavily out the front door and onto the porch. Several saddled horses were waiting before it, the marshal and Blamey already mounted, four of Garth's men standing beside their own mounts. Ardeth forced herself to wait by one of the parlor windows, watching them until they were all mounted and cantering out of the yard. Then she turned to sink into one of the velvet-backed chairs standing near a table. She only gave herself a minute to catch her breath, then took off, running out the front door and around the side of the house where she was just in time to catch Nat climbing out of one of the study windows at the rear of the house.

As his feet touched the ground, he was grabbing her by the hand to run out of the shadows of the house and toward the shady grove behind it where the gazebo stood hidden.

"Not so fast," Ardeth cried. "Someone might see us from the house and wonder why we're in such a hurry."

Realizing she was right, Nat forced himself to slow down and walk at a normal pace. "I was so anxious to get away from that office that nothing else mattered," he muttered.

It was the first time he had admitted he had shared some of her nervousness, and it gave Ardeth

313

some satisfaction. "Where were you? I couldn't see any sign of you from the door."

"Behind the window drape. If Garth had stayed longer or looked closer, he couldn't have missed seeing me."

"That's why I followed him. Oh, Nat, was it really worth all this anxiety? Perhaps our suspicions are foolish and Garth is perfectly innocent."

"Our suspicions are right on target," Nat answered grimly. "That's one thing I learned from nosing about those locked drawers. Reardon is into every kind of land swindle these territories offer. He's bought lawmen from Kansas to Colorado. He even has files on various individuals and groups that look like fodder for blackmail. In just the short time I had to snoop around in there, I could see that he has a finger in all kinds of questionable pies."

"He must be pretty ruthless as well, if what that land agent said was true."

"Why wouldn't it be? Reardon has a vested interest in keeping sheepherders out of this valley. You can bet your last month's wages he was involved in that massacre at the Salt River Pass. He probably planned the whole thing."

They reached the dappled shadows of the gazebo where Ardeth sank onto the circular wooden bench, resting her elbows on her knees. "It's still hard to believe. Outwardly he just doesn't seem like that at all. He's attractive, pleasant, graciously polite. . . ."

"Don't be misled by a handsome face and good manners, my love. You just haven't had occasion

314

yet to see the other side of him."

"I know. And I still haven't forgotten that bullet hole in my riding hat. But I'd feel better if we had some kind of proof."

"It's early in the day yet. There's more to this Silver Sage Ranch than appears on the surface, and I haven't finished looking around it, not by a long shot!"

It took Ardeth most of that day to settle down after the excitement of the morning. That evening passed pleasantly with Lavinia flirting mildly with Nat, trying to entice a little jealousy out of the earl, and the gentlemen accepting Nat's presence among them as though he had been another invited guest. The following day they received word from John Glover that Garth would be back the following morning. Ardeth and Nat went riding alone that afternoon and returned in time for supper with the others. It seemed a long, slow evening with most of the English contingent playing cards while Ardeth and Mr. Cameron passed the time at the backgammon board. She noticed that Nat seemed restless and bored, so she broke off the game while the others were still playing cards and suggested they take a walk around the porch.

It was a warm night, and the soft breezes rustling the leaves that hung like a canopy over the wooden porch felt refreshing on her throat and arms. Not content with merely strolling the porch, Nat suggested they walk out toward the corrals and barns.

There was a round, buttery moon that lay a soft gilt coverlet over the yards and threw shadows from the branches of the trees in dark relief. Once again Ardeth felt the contentment and ease that lay over the ranch when Reardon was absent. With her arm in Nat's, the ruffles of her long skirt rustling in the grass, they ambled toward the largest of the barns, pausing beside one of the seven-slat fences to slip their arms around each other.

Ardeth leaned against him, drawing strength from his body, reveling in the feel of his embrace. His arms tightened around her. In the barn they could hear the quiet snuffling of the horses punctuated by an occasional neigh. To the side of the barn and a little behind it, a lantern beside the bunkhouse door created a little pool of light on the ground, like a tiny golden pond. The rattle of the night insects and an occasional lowing of a cow added a peaceful undertone to the lovely evening.

Ardeth sighed. "I didn't realize until this moment how glad I am you followed me here."

He lifted her chin and kissed her soft, moist lips. Laying his hands on both her cheeks, he gently explored her face with his lips, lightly kissing her eyelids, the tip of her nose, her chin and, finally, drinking deeply from her lips again. "I don't think I realized it myself," he murmured, pressing her against him. "Ardeth . . . Medora . . . I don't think I ever meant you to matter to me quite so much."

"Oh, Nat. I never meant it either. I don't even know what I'm going to do—or be—once I leave this ranch. I only know that a life without you becomes more unthinkable every day. And I think you feel the same."

Nat smiled down at her. He was about to answer, about to speak the words she wanted to hear so much and knew were true, when the sound of voices came drifting over from the bunkhouse. Nat lifted his head, peering through the dark.

"It's all right," Ardeth murmured. "They can't see us here in the shadows."

Suddenly she felt him stiffen. Even in the darkness she could see the frozen concentration on his face as he stared toward the bunkhouse.

"What is it? What's the matter?" She turned, straining to see through the darkness, but all she could make out were two men standing half in the shadows of the lantern, talking to one of the ranch hands who had come to the bunkhouse door. "Nat," she whispered, trying to reclaim his attention. "What is it?"

His hands went to her shoulders, but his eyes never left the figures by the bunkhouse. "Go inside," he snapped.

"But why. . . ?"

"That's Turnbull. I'd swear it."

Ardeth gasped as disappointment swiftly replaced ardor. The ranch hand had come outside now and had turned back toward the rear of the barn with the other two men. "How can you tell?" she whispered. "You can't see them in the dark."

"I'd know that stocky, short physique anywhere." Roughly he shoved her aside. "Go back in the house."

Ardeth clung to his arms. "No, Nat, please listen. Don't go over there. You're not even wearing a gun. If that really is Turnbull, you won't have a chance against him. Use your head, Nat!"

He tried to push her away, but she clung stubbornly to him. "This is not any of your business, Ardeth. Let go of me. Get away!"

"Nat . . . please!"

He half dragged her along the fence. "What's he doing here, anyway? I knew there was something about this place. He's probably in cahoots with Reardon. . . ."

Ardeth watched in dismay as he shoved her away and took off toward the barn, keeping in the shadows. She almost followed but thought better of it. Her long trailing skirts, corseted jacket and ruffled bustle were not fashioned for running around darkened outbuildings. Instead she waited by the fence, listening for the sound of loud voices or even gunfire. The minutes dragged by, leaden with apprehension. And then, all at once, Nat materialized once more out of the darkness to stand by her side.

She could see how taut and grim the line of his jaw was in the moonlight. "Well?"

"I couldn't find them. It was as though the night swallowed them up. There must be some kind of hiding place back there."

"Perhaps they rode away."

He looked down at her absently. "I would have heard that."

"Oh, Nat, how can you be so sure it was the

road? I could barely make out that it was two men, much less who they were."

It was as though he had just remembered she was here. "Go back inside, Ardeth. I'm going to stay out here for a while."

There was so much she wanted to say. She wanted to rail at him for letting this Turnbull drive everything else from his mind. Nothing else mattered once there was a possibility he might come face to face with Terrence Turnbull. And just at the moment when he was about to speak of what he felt for her. . . .

Well, now she had a pretty good idea, at least, just how little she mattered to him. How foolish to let herself think he had come here for her. He had followed Turnbull here, and she happened to be close by. Like some romantic schoolgirl, she had let herself believe that he really loved her. Now she knew.

Without a word she turned on her heel and started back toward the house. Let him stay out here in the dark, chasing his demons. She would lock her door and go to bed alone!

Ardeth did go to bed alone, but she did not lock her door. She was sound asleep when he came to her, slipping underneath the covers to take her with a violence that left her sore and breathless. His lovemaking awakened a response in her that matched his intensity, feeling hurt and angry with him as she did. Gone was the gentleness, the tender

319

concern. There was a kind of subdued fury in the way his fingers dug into her flesh, in the tiny nibbles he took at her breasts, in the plunging, driving force of his body into hers. From sleepy surprise, to shock, to furious return, Ardeth matched him, step for step, until they both fell back on the bed, panting and spent. They were lying across its expanse, the covers on the floor, and Ardeth could not even remember how they had got there.

Yet she felt a deep satisfaction. Nat had vented some of his frustration and anger on her body, but it had somehow brought them closer together. He needed her, whether he was ready to admit it or not. And now that the fury had passed, the gentleness would come again.

Chapter Seventeen

Ardeth was late going down stairs the following morning, and she found that all the other guests had already had breakfast and gone about their day's activities. When she casually asked the dining room maid whether or not Garth had returned, she learned he had been back for several hours. On her way back upstairs, she ran into him in the hall. He was coolly polite, but she did not miss the unusual scowl on his face and the preoccupation underneath his customary manners. Evidently things had not gone so well with the marshal and the land agent.

Yet, as Nat later confirmed, they had gone well enough to allow Garth to return to his ranch. Blamey had been disappointed in his hopes of getting Reardon into jail, because ultimately Marshal Connely refused to go through with it. "Garth must have finally convinced him he would have no job if he pursued the matter," Nat commented dryly.

"I only hope no one saw you climbing out of that study window. The servants would go straight to him with the information. He hasn't said anything to you, has he?"

"He's been excessively polite. He even offered to ride out with me in the morning and show me some of the surrounding ranges. If there's any malice there, he's certainly concealed it well."

"I'm probably imagining things again. Are you sure you can trust him?"

"There will be other people along. Besides, I want to be around Mr. Garth Reardon for a while. I still can't put the man we see as our host together with the man I saw in those papers in his office. An excursion like this might help sort him out."

"Just be careful," Ardeth added and squeezed his arm.

By the evening meal, Reardon had resumed his usual pleasant demeanor. He entertained them with stories of his early days on the range and carefully drew out reminiscences from the English gentlemen about their own experiences of hunting in England. Later, in the parlor, he deliberately took Ardeth aside and asked her about her plans for putting on an elaborate concert to impress Mr. Cameron.

She had forgotten all about the excuses she made when she pushed her way into his office, and she found herself stumbling a little before finally launching into a long list of suggested songs.

"I'm sure whatever you do will make a favorable impression," he answered, never losing his pleasant smile.

"I'll begin practicing my routines tomorrow morning," Ardeth said, trying to look enthusiastic.

And the following morning she actually did go down early to the music room and begin sorting out her songs. While she was mostly play-acting, the role did offer her the opportunity to be close to Garth's office. But the door was closed and all was silent, and she soon realized there was nothing here to learn.

She made an attempt at pulling out several songs that might be used in a concert but soon felt too restless to go on with the charade. She was completely unable to concentrate, but half an hour had passed before she realized that this came from an overpowering sense of anxiety. Finally she lumped all her music together, threw it aside and walked through the house and onto the porch.

There was some kind of activity going on at one of the corrals. Curious, she ambled over to the fence where most of the ranch hands were lined up, leaning on the rails. Inside the corral another man stood holding a young horse by a rope while a second hand pulled at the cinch on the saddle. The horse snorted and reared against the taut rope, its white eyes ranging wildly around the area.

"What's going on," she asked one of the men.

He quickly pulled at his hat and smiled. "Got a few tenderhorns here we're breaking in, ma'am."

"You mean that young horse?"

"The horse and the men, ma'am." He laughed, displaying yellowed teeth. He straightened the kerchief around his neck. "Here, make room for the little lady," he said and shoved aside the other men so that Ardeth could stand on the lower rail and look into the corral.

There was a lot of shouting as one of the cowpokes was pushed forward to place his boot into the stirrup. He took a moment to pat the horse's damp neck, then vaulted into the saddle. With a whoop, the man holding the rope let it go, and immediately the horse began to buck, throwing its rider backward and forward like a limp doll.

Even Ardeth had to smile as the men around her went into gales of laughter, half railing at the rider, half cheering him on. When he finally went careening over the pony's head and into the dust with a thump, there was a general hilarity. The corral filled with a film of yellow fog from the churned dust. The chagrined cowboy stumbled to his feet and hobbled to the fence while the triumphant pony went bucking, riderless, around the ring.

"Let Patsy try him," one of the men called.

"Yeah, Patsy can ride anything, if you believe him!" another responded.

As the dust settled and a second rider came forward to try his hand, Ardeth glanced across the corral and for the first time noticed the men lined up on the other side. It took her a moment to realize who they were—Lord Berry, Lawrence Appleby and Kenneth Cameron—all of them as engrossed in the proceedings as the cowboys themselves. For a moment Ardeth wondered why she was so surprised to see them there. Then she remembered.

She struggled to recall the name of the ranch

hand standing beside her. "Mell—that was it. She tugged at his sleeve.

"Mell, I thought the English gentlemen went out riding with Mr. Reardon and Nat Varien this morning."

With difficulty Mell pulled his concentration away from the corral. "No, ma'am. They decided they would rather stay here and see the fun."

"But, some of the ranch hands went along, didn't they?"

Mell pulled the brim of his hat down on his leathery face. "I don't believe so. Mr. Reardon says he don't need nobody."

"Then, they went alone? Just the two of them?"

"That's right, ma'am. I seen them ride out myself, about an hour ago."

Ardeth felt her chest constrict. It might be all right, just a casual ride together. Pleasant . . . convivial. . . .

"Mell, could you saddle up a horse for me? I think I'll join them. I'll go and change while you get the horse ready."

"But, ma'am. They got a good head start. . . ."

"Never mind. Please just do what I ask. And make it a fast horse."

She was already running back to the house.

Later Ardeth could barely recall throwing off her morning clothes and pulling on her riding skirt and jacket. Of course she was being foolish. She would look like a half-wit rushing out to search for Garth and Nat and would probably come upon them hav-

325

ing a pleasant canter across the prairie. Yet she simply had to go. She could not sit here at the ranch knowing they were out there together, knowing that Garth might possibly take advantage of the opportunity to be rid of Nat once and for all. There was no real indication of any kind that Garth distrusted Nat or suspected he was not really her manager. There was just this overwhelming anxiety, growing like a cancer within her, choking off her breath. She had to go. Perhaps her presence would curb Reardon's dangerous inclinations.

When she reached the stable, she found that Mell had saddled up two horses and intended to go with her. "Can't have you riding out alone, miss," he said, touching his hat. "It wouldn't sit well with Mr. Reardon if he knew I'd done that."

Ardeth smiled her gratitude and jumped on her horse. The animal was ready for a good jaunt, having been penned up for two days, and it was all she could do to hold her mount as they cantered out of the yard. Once they were away from the house, she realized she hadn't the foggiest notion which way to go.

"You didn't hear Mr. Reardon say where he was taking Mr. Varien, did you?"

"I heard him say something about the canyons. That's a pretty kind of ride, and lots of newcomers at the ranch like to see it."

"Good. We'll head for the canyons."

It was a beautiful morning. Had she been less concerned, she might have enjoyed the colors and the bright sunshine. As it was, she kept straining to see two dark figures in the distance. Because Mell turned out to be a good tracker, they were able to pick up the trail the two men had taken earlier and follow it for a long way. When they reached the higher ground, Ardeth decided to follow the crest of the hills as much as possible, hoping to see them below.

The farther they rode, the easier she began to breath. If Nat had come to any grief, they would surely have found some sign of it by now. An hour later, when she finally saw the two dark figures ambling along the canyon floor, she really did begin to feel foolish and silly.

"There they are, Mell," she said, resting her mount and pointing ahead. "It's not going to be easy to get down there with them though, is it?"

"Oh, yes, ma'am. There's a trail through those rocks there. It shouldn't take us too long."

As he spoke Ardeth heard a whoop and holler far down below and saw both men take off, galloping across the canyon floor. They were engaged in a race of some kind which, if the way Nat pulled up his mount was any indication, her manager had won handily.

Just like two little boys trying to out-do each other, she thought. All the same, she was vastly relieved. Following Mell's lead, she kicked her horse to begin picking its careful way along the difficult footing of the trail. She soon lost sight of Garth and Nat, but the loud whooping from down below suggested they were into another race. The trail brought them around a cluster of large boulders as they neared the canyon floor where Ardeth again had a vista of the narrow, flat length of land between the rising walls on either side. She could see Garth and Nat sitting their mounts directly below her and Garth pointing ahead, gesturing. *Yet another race,* she thought absently, wondering if Garth was deliberately allowing Nat to win. Reardon rode the best horses at the ranch, and it seemed unlikely he could be beaten so easily.

Ardeth stopped and looked ahead. There was something familiar about that stretch of flat land. She raised in the stirrups, peering over her mount's neck. What was it?

It came to her just as Nat took off with a loud whoop, Garth at his heels. "My God," Ardeth breathed. "The buffalo trap. . . ."

She slapped the reins on her horse's back. Startled, it reared a bit, then took off, racing down the trail and out onto the flat surface between the canyon walls. Nat was ahead of her, but he would be forced to follow the curve of the path. She might be able to cut him off before. . . .

She was unaware of Garth's lagging behind or of Mell racing after her in confusion. All her concentration was on reaching the edge of that precipice before Nat reached it and she drove her horse mercilessly to get there first.

Nat had not seen her coming. All at once a dark form loomed up in front of him, forcing him to move to one side. In fury and frustration he pulled his mount around, following a broad semicircle until the winded beast slackened. Then he pulled up on the reins while his horse dug in its heels and neighed in protest.

"What the devil are you doing!" he raged at Ardeth. She rode up beside him, slumping in the saddle and gasping for breath. "Where did you come from, anyway. You've got some nerve. There was a lot of money hanging on that race, and I would have won it!"

"Go over and look," Ardeth said between gasps. "You would have been at the bottom of that drop."

Anger mingled with confusion in his eyes. He yanked off his hat, wiped his arm across his brow and thumped the hat back on his head. Then, casually, he walked his horse over to where the floor fell away into a steep drop.

"Well, I'll be damned," he muttered. "You can't tell this is here at all from back there."

Behind him, Ardeth looked up as Garth came riding up to her. "Why did you do that?" she cried, her eyes blazing. "He might have been killed."

"Nonsense," Garth said, smiling. "He would have seen it in time. Besides, I told him to run that way."

Nat came back up to join them. "So you did. But you didn't say why. It might have changed my mind for me."

"Tell him about it, Garth. Like you told me."

"Of course. We can discuss it on the way back."

It was just about the only thing that was discussed on the long, easy ride back to the ranch. Both Ardeth and Nat were lost in thought most of the way. Reardon made attempts at conversation but soon gave up when he got so little response. His attitude, that nothing out of place had occurred at all, was so infuriating to Ardeth that she could barely bring herself to look at him. Nat, too, seemed very pensive.

They dismounted at the stables, and, leaving Reardon there, walked together back to the house.

"The bastard," Nat muttered. "He would probably have left me there at the bottom of that hole and told everyone I got lost."

"He meant you to go over it. I just know he did."

"And I would have, but for you." He laid an arm around her shoulder. "It's just too much, isn't it? The bullet in your hat and my intended 'accident.' Now do you believe he's dangerous?"

"Yes, I do. Oh, Nat, let's get out of here. I'm sick of playing a part, and I'm frightened of Garth Reardon. Can't we just leave the Silver Sage and go someplace where we can just be ourselves?"

"You forget, my love. I have some unfinished business left to do. Before I leave this ranch, I want to be very certain that it has no more answers."

"Well, I don't see how we could do more than we've already done."

They were nearing the porch steps. Nat dropped his voice. "There is one thing more. But I'll need to get back inside that office to be sure."

Ardeth felt a tremble deep inside. "Not that," she

groaned.

"Yes, my dear Medora. I'll need you to get the keys for me one more time!"

There was an undercurrent of strain beneath the polite camaraderie among the guests that evening which Ardeth sensed came more from Garth than anyone else. Though outwardly pleasant and full of concern for the comfort of his visitors, there was a falseness about him she could not shake off. Once or twice she caught him staring at her with veiled eyes that harbored a hostility she had never seen before. It disappeared almost at the moment she caught it, replaced by the usual smiling, "aren't we all friends" benevolent grin. She suppressed a shiver and concentrated on the backgammon board.

"You seem a trifle preoccupied, my dear," Lawrence Appleby commented after a second stupid move had allowed him to win her disks.

"Just a little tired," Ardeth answered, glancing nervously at Nat, who was standing over them, watching the play. At a table across the room, the earl, the English ladies and Cameron were engrossed in a game of bridge while between the two groups Garth sat on a sofa, legs crossed, puffing on a Spanish cigar.

The earl and Lady Lavinia were losing, much to that lady's chagrin. Finally Berry threw down his cards petulantly. "A boring game, bridge. Don't know why I bother with it."

"I suppose I oughtn't to have bid no trumps," Lavinia said lamely.

"No, you oughtn't to have. I say, Reardon, what about another hunt tomorrow. I'm getting restless again to have a shot at some more bison. It's been several days, after all, since we went out."

"Good idea," Appleby joined in. "And let's make this a good long one. A week ought to take us far afield. I have a notion to see those bubbling hot pools you told us about."

The earl, full of enthusiasm once again, bounced up from the card table and walked across to Garth's sofa, helping himself from the cigar humidor.

"It would take more like two weeks to really explore Yellowstone," Garth said, tapping the ash from his cigar. "But I suppose it could be done. However, it may have to wait two days. I have to go into Caribou for supplies tomorrow. I thought perhaps the ladies might like to come along. Do a bit of shopping."

Ardeth remembered Caribou from the trip out to the ranch. It was a town of four drab stores lining a wide dirt street with a few shacks scattered around the perimeters. Any shopping it might offer would be primitive in the extreme.

"Perhaps you gentlemen would like to come along as well," Garth added, looking directly at Nat.

Lavinia spoke up. "Well, I'm for it," she drawled, following the earl away from the table. "It would be divine to have a change of scenery, and there are a few things I'd like to pick up." It would also postpone the rigors of the hunt for a couple of days. Though she would never admit it to Berry, she was not looking forward to a week or more of primitive conditions out on the prairie.

"I too, might enjoy the change," Lady Teague quickly put in, thinking it wouldn't do at all for Lavinia to go along unchaperoned.

"I think I'd rather stay here," Nat said without looking at Ardeth. "I had enough riding this morning to last me for a while."

"Well, I certainly don't care anything about shopping," Cameron said. "Here now, we can't break up the game just yet. Come along, Medora. How about you and your manager having a game."

Ignoring Lady Teague's belligerent glare, Ardeth moved to the card table. "I think I'll forgo the pleasure of a trip into town. But I'd love to try my hand at bridge. Come on, Nat. Be my partner."

Nat ambled to the card table. "I'll give it a try," he said picking up the deck and shuffling it. "Though I'm better at poker or faro than bridge. I think you should go into town tomorrow, Medora. It would do you good. And you might pick up a few things for me if they have a decent store."

Ardeth tried not to glare at him as she picked up her cards. "I feel the need of a day's rest," she mumbled.

"Nonsense. You'd just be bored sitting around the ranch with half its people away for the day. Go and enjoy yourself." He spread the cards in his hand and frowned in concentration as he looked them over. "I should have stayed with backgammon."

"I bid one heart," Cameron said enthusiastically on Nat's right.

"Pass," Ardeth murmured, glaring at Nat.

At the end of the evening, Nat walked Ardeth to the door of her room. "You're just trying to get me out of the way," Ardeth hissed, looking around to make certain no one else was in the hall. "I know what you'll be up to while I'm off to that stupid town."

"I'm counting on you to keep Reardon occupied. It couldn't have worked out better. Besides, you won't be alone with him. He wouldn't dare try to hurt you with the English ladies and Appleby around. You'll be safe enough."

"And what about you. He's far too shrewd to leave you here alone without some kind of safeguard. You know you'll be watched. Nothing goes on in this house that he doesn't know about."

"I'll take my chances. This is the best opportunity I'll get—maybe the last opportunity. If we have to go along on that Yellowstone excursion, I have doubts about either of us coming back. It offers too many excellent chances for an 'accident' or two."

"You know where the keys are? They'll be missed if they're gone too long."

"Don't worry. I've figured out the best way to get

into that office. They won't be gone long enough for anyone to notice."

She reached up and kissed his cheek. "Oh, Nat. Be careful. There's no telling what Garth has planned."

He smiled and tipped up her chin to return her kiss. "Don't worry about me. Just enjoy your shopping."

Once the party got under way the next morning, Ardeth began to think she really was going to enjoy the trip. It was a beautiful, clear day with the air so clean and brilliant the horizon might have been painted by an artist. The fields and rolling plains, the gigantic, awkwardly shaped buttes, the glowing rim of mountains in the distance, even the meandering groups of cattle they passed along the way, all might have been pictures from a book, they were so enchanting.

Even the grubby little town of Caribou seemed more picturesque than she remembered. When she had come through it before, its one main street had been churned to mud by a recent, infrequent shower followed by a drover's herd of cattle running through. Today it was hard-packed and firm, not even giving off the clouds of dust so frequent in Fireweed. Several more raw-pine buildings lined the street, thrown up since her last trip. Now, in addition to the general store, saloon, barber shop and bathhouse, there was a spanking-new pharmacy, a dry goods and clothing store, a doctor's and under-taker's office, and a real estate loan agency. Cari-bou, evidently, was growing by leaps and bounds.

Reardon deposited the ladies outside the clothing store, reckoning rightly that they would be more in-terested in it than any other. He had been coolly polite to Ardeth on the ride in, as he had to the other women. She could see no difference in his at-titude toward her, and gradually she lost her anxiety over being there with him. As Nat had pointed out, the presence of the others made the trip extremely safe.

She rummaged around the dry goods store for a while but found that most of its wares were de-signed with farm women in mind. There was little in the way of luxuries among the chintzes and cot-tons, though she did find some striking jet buttons and a length of wide pink satin ribbon that alone made the trip worthwhile. The ladies Lavinia and Teague bent over the counters together, talking to each other and pointedly ignoring her, and she soon grew weary of trying to be polite. Gathering up her parcels, she informed them she was going to walk along to the general store and stepped out onto the wooden walkway. She opened up her parasol and pulled up the ruffled hem of her skirt to prevent it from dragging along the dusty walk. At the other end of the walk, in front of the store, she could see Garth standing beside the buggy talking to two men from the town. Across the street Mr. Appleby was standing in front of the barber shop, inspecting its window as though undecided whether or not to go inside. Ardeth started along the walk, passing the doctor-undertaker's office just as a short, rotund gentleman came through the door, almost careening into her on the walkway.

"Oh, I do beg your pardon, miss. . . ." His hat had been knocked ajar. As he straightened it and looked up at Ardeth, his round face broke into a grin.

"Why, bless my soul. Bless my soul. It's a miracle! That's what it is. A miracle from heaven!"

Ardeth balanced her parasol on her shoulder and looked blankly at the man. "Have we met before, sir?" He was a total stranger as far as she could see.

"Why, yes, indeed, though it was a long way from here. Don't you remember? We shared a coach on the way to Cheyenne."

Her stomach turned over. "Oh . . . oh, my goodness. You were the dentist!"

He beamed at her and swept off his hat. "That's right. Roland Picket, DDS and MD . . . though," he lowered his voice, "we won't say where the MD came from. I have a practice here in Caribou now. Yes, indeed, Dr. Roland Picket it is now. Practitioner to ranchers and ranch hands and farmers and their families. Doing very well at it, too."

Down the walk Ardeth saw Garth watching them. "Well, how surprising. It was nice seeing you again, Mr. . . . Dr. Picket, I'm sure. If you'll just excuse me. . . ."

"Oh, but you can't go running off. Why, this is

such a coincidence, running into you like this. We've been looking for you, my girl. Never really thought our paths would cross again, but now, here they have. It's a miracle, isn't it. A regular miracle."

Ardeth stood frozen hearing only one word out of his effusive tirade. "We. . . ?"

"Why, yes. Bless my soul, I'd almost forgotten." He stepped quickly to the door of his office and threw it open. "Come here, my boy. You won't believe this. Come quickly." With her heart in her throat, Ardeth stared at the doorway as a lanky, shambling figure suddenly filled it. Her eyes rounded in shock and disbelief as the boy's face lit up in delighted surprise and a grin split his freckled cheeks. He gave an excited whoop.

"Why, hello, sis!"

Ardeth's voice was choked. "Ebal!"

Chapter Eighteen

"Whoo-ee, sister, don't you look grand, though. You musta done pretty good fer yerself."

"Ebal, what are you doing here?" Ardeth said weakly when she finally recovered her voice. "You're the last person I ever expected to see."

"Ma sent me looking fer you. When we didn't hear nothin' no more and got no more money or such, well, she got worried."

"But how on earth did you ever find me here?" Down the walk she caught sight of Garth Reardon eyeing them curiously. She dropped her voice. "I mean . . . I went to Kansas. . . ."

"Ah, that was my doing, I'm afraid, young lady," the dentist spoke up, beaming. "Your good brother and I reached Fireweed at about the same time. I had come there to . . . ahem, set up a practice. When I heard he was in town asking about a young woman of your description, I immediate recognized the charming lady who had shared my coach on the way to Cheyenne."

Ardeth closed her parasol as she saw Garth stepping away from the other men on the walkway in front of the general store. "Why don't we step inside and discuss this in comfort," she said to the dentist. "I'm still in rather a state of shock and would welcome the chance to sit down."

"Of course, dear lady. Forgive me that I didn't think of it myself. Do come in, I pray you."

Opening his office door, the good doctor ushered them inside a small, dark, stuffy room with several chairs, a square table black with age and a long, horsehair cot along one wall. A cabinet hanging near the one window was crammed with bottles and medical implements neatly arranged in rows. Ardeth gratefully lowered herself into one of the chairs. She had not been making excuses by wanting to sit down. Her knees were still trembling.

Ebal Royce followed the other two inside the room but remained standing near the table. He suddenly remembered he was still wearing his floppy canvas cap and yanked it off. He was having difficulty merging this lovely creature swathed in ruffled silk and a pert, flower-decked bonnet perched over one eye with the drab, serious girl in homespun whom he remembered as his older sister. Ardeth was almost as confused as her brother to see a member of her family suddenly materialize in this strange, fabulous world so far from her Nebraska homestead. Ebal's scrawny frame, freckled face and shabby, country clothes were like an apparition from another world—one she had never thought to see again.

The round little dentist pulled up a chair and straddled it. "Is there anything I can get you, my dear. You look quite pale."

"No, I'm all right, thank you. I just need a moment to get accustomed to . . . to really believing my brother is here."

"I went looking for Cousin Emma," Ebal said. "I was that surprised when I learned she had died. Ma don't know it yet."

"Yes, I learned she was dead while I was on my way to Fireweed. I didn't want to go back home, so I went on. I found a . . . a job, and everything worked out."

"I should say it did. I never saw anything so pretty and so grand as you look. Ma would bust with pride if'n she could see you now."

Ardeth turned to the dentist. "Dr. . . . I don't believe I got your name. . . ."

"Dr. Picket. Roland Picket."

"I still don't understand how you found me."

"Why, we learned you'd left Fireweed for the Wyoming territory, so we came along this way too. It did not take me long to discover that Fireweed was not so congenial as it seemed at first, and I had the thought to try my luck elsewhere. We were in Cheyenne for a while . . ."

"Whoo-eee, what a town, sis. Like nothin' I ever seen!"

". . . then moved on. Of course, we had no idea which way to go, but I had been told medical men are scarce the farther west you go. When we

341

reached Caribou, they were delighted to have some one of my talents stay for a while. Their last doctor took off for California over a year ago. But we never expected to just stumble across your path as we have today. This is truly an astounding piece of luck."

"A regular miracle," Ebal intoned.

"Oh, Ebal," Ardeth sighed. "What in the world am I going to do with you!"

A short rap on the door frame interrupted her. Ardeth turned and saw Garth Reardon standing in the doorway, smiling benevolently at them all.

"I saw you enter the doctor's office, Medora. Are you well? Is anything wrong?"

Ardeth tried to smile. "No, no. Nothing is wrong at all. It's just the most extraordinary coincidence. I came across my brother here in town."

Genuinely surprised, Garth smiled at the dentist. "Your brother? How amazing."

"No," Ardeth said, getting quickly to her feet. "This is my brother. Ebal Royce. This is Mr. Reardon, Ebal."

Garth's eyes grew round as he fastened them on the boy. Ardeth could imagine what was going through his mind. This young, lanky, unkempt, farm boy with his sandy hair flopping in all directions and the myriad freckles adorning his face — the brother of an established concert singer.

"Royce?" Garth said curiously.

But she had already mentally solved that problem. "Melindez is my stage name, Garth. It's not ncommon to have one, you know."

"Of course. Welcome to Wyoming, young Mr. Royce."

"Reardon . . . Reardon. I've heard of you," Dr. Picket cried, bustling up to shake Garth's hand. "You have the biggest ranch in the territory. In fact, the story of your success out here has spread as far as Kansas. My, what an honor it is to meet you, Mr. Reardon."

Garth looked down his aristocratic nose at the dentist. "My pleasure . . ."

"Dr. Picket," Ardeth volunteered. "Dr. Picket brought Ebal out here."

Garth turned back to her brother. Ardeth could almost see the wheels turning in his fertile brain as he looked at Ebal . . . all the questions that were forming.

"Well, Ebal Royce, my young friend. I trust Medora has told you about my ranch where she is staying."

"Medora. . . ?"

"As a matter of fact," Ardeth jumped in quickly, "Ebal is on his way back home. He is just collecting a few remembrances I intend to send back to my parents, and then he'll be on his way, won't you, Ebal? We wouldn't want to worry Ma any longer than necessary."

"Well, Ardeth, the truth is, I ain't all that anxious to go back home so soon. I mean, I never knew there was so much of interest outside Nebraska. I'm kind of enjoyin' seein' it all."

343

Ardeth saw Garth's eyebrow inch upward as Eba[l] spoke her name. But he said nothing. He jus[t] smiled his enigmatic, smugly satisfied smile at th[e] both of them while she went on writhing inwardly[.]

"Your young brother is most welcome to sta[y] with me," Dr. Picket broke in. "In fact, I've come t[o] enjoy his company so much I almost regret havin[g] found you at last."

Not half so much as I regret it, Ardeth though[t] bitterly.

"Nonsense," Garth said. "I won't hear of the bo[y] staying anywhere but at the Silver Sage. He shall b[e] as welcome there as you yourself, Medora. You ca[n] reminisce at your leisure, and when he's ready, I'[ll] send him back to . . . Nebraska, was it? . . . in fin[e] style. You'd like that, wouldn't you, son?"

Ebal beamed. "Well, to tell the truth, I'd lik[e] mightily to see a fine ranch."

"Really . . ." Ardeth cried.

"It's all settled, then. Gather up your things, an[d] we'll make room for you in the wagon. Come, Me[dora, my dear. We ought to be getting back."

"Really, Garth. You don't have to do this."

He smiled down at her with what Ardeth saw fo[r] the first time was malicious satisfaction. "It's m[y] pleasure."

"I don't suppose you'd be needing a doctor or [a] dentist at the Silver Sage," Dr. Picket said as he fol[-] lowed them onto the walkway. "No, I thought not[.] But don't forget me if you do. Caribou is not tha[t] far away."

Ebal came bounding out the door clutching a blanket roll that held his few possessions. Smiling broadly, he shook Dr. Picket's hand and thanked him for his help while Ardeth stood watching, dying inside. Her worst fears were being realized. She could not even imagine what Nat would say.

While Garth went ahead to make a place for Ebal in their caravan, Ardeth gripped her brother's arm as they walked slowly toward the wagon. "You'll do exactly as I say, Ebal," she hissed under her breath, "or, so help me, I'll put you on the train to Cheyenne myself."

He looked at her in amazement. "Ardeth you're pinchin' my arm."

"I'll pinch more than that if you don't do just what I tell you. And don't call me Ardeth! They all think my name is Medora."

Ebal said suddenly, "What kind of a name is that." This dominating, pinching, demanding woman was all of a sudden very familiar as his sister even if the clothes were much more fancy.

"You'll smile and nod at everybody and say nothing! Don't you tell a soul about our family or our farm. Not a word, do you hear me!"

"I never heard of such going's on. It don't sound right."

"You do it anyway or so help me, I'll make you sorry you ever saw me today!"

"You ain't changed much, except for the clothes. I don't know how you ever got linked up with a nice man like that Mr. Reardon."

Ardeth clicked her tongue in exasperation. "I'll explain it to you someday. Right now, just do what I tell you. The Silver Sage is a very fine place, and if you behave yourself, you might learn a few things there about ranching. But if you forget what I've told you, I promise you won't stay long enough to tour the outbuildings. Remember that." They had reached the end of the walk where Lady Lavinia and Mrs. Teague stood watching them curiously.

"Lady Lavinia," Ardeth said brightly. "The most amazing thing has happened. You'll never guess . . ."

"Just tell me one thing—how a hayseed like that ever got to be your brother!"

Ardeth gave an anxious glance to the door of her room. Though it was shut, she felt certain Nat's angry bluster could be heard clearly to the end of the hall.

"We have the same parents. For heaven's sake, keep your voice down. You're no more distressed about this than I am, but we needn't let the whole house know how we feel."

"You don't even talk alike. How can *you* be so intelligent and cultured while he sounds like he just stepped off a compost pile. And looks like it too!"

Ardeth firmly took Nat's arm and led him to a chair near the window. "I told you once before, my mother schooled me in the culture I know because she wanted me to get off that farm. My pa would never allow her near the boys. He figured it was bad enough to fill a girl's head with such non-sense."

"Well this is all we need. And just when I was beginning to really learn a lot about Garth Reardon."

Ardeth sat on the arm of the chair and draped an arm over Nat's shoulder. When she thought back to the look of incredulous stupefaction on Nat's face while Ebal babbled downstairs about the wonder of the Silver Sage, she was still inclined to laugh — except that in several important aspects, the situation was really not very funny.

"Did you get into Reardon's office, then?"

"Oh, yes. It was easy. While you were being reunited with your long lost brother, I was discovering that Reardon was behind the corporation that bought my land in New Mexico. I wouldn't be surprised if he wasn't behind the robbery as well. He's probably working hand in glove with Toad Turnbull!"

Ardeth felt her chest tighten. "Nat, you won't do anything foolish, will you?"

"Not until I have the last few pieces of Reardon's puzzle. It was all I could do today not to meet him at his door with a gun in my hand. But that would be giving away my advantage, and I'm not ready for that yet. But soon . . ."

She felt her shoulders tense even as he talked of revenge and was all at once consumed with fright. Slipping to her knees in front of him, she knelt, her arms around his waist, and looked up into his determined face.

"Listen to me, Nat. It would be suicide to try to face down Garth Reardon here at his ranch. You'd never live long enough to question him. He's surrounded by people who will do anything he tells them. All they have to see is someone coming at him with a gun, and that would be the end of you. Promise me you won't do anything so foolish."

Nat's preoccupation was so intense that for a moment she was not sure he had even heard her. Then he looked down into her pleading eyes and shrugged. "Don't worry, love. I won't be so open about it as all that. But I'll get the truth out of him somehow, and when I do, and if he really did have anything to with Kit Randall's death. . . ."

His eyes got that hard, distant look once more, and Ardeth's fear flamed higher. "Nat, can't we go away from here? Leave this ranch and strike out for California or some place where we could start again, all on our own? You'd love to have your own ranch again, wouldn't you, and I'd love helping you build it. Let's go now, tonight!"

He looked at her as though she were speaking another language. "Leave? Now — just when I'm about to learn who ruined my livelihood, stole my land and killed my best friend? Never! It's an insane idea."

Ardeth flounced to her feet and paced the room, twisting her hands, feeling more hopeless by the minute. Then, as quickly as it had come, his fierce concentration was gone. Nat rose and caught her in midstride, clasping her in his arms.

"Don't be so solemn, love. Come, we've got even bigger problems right now than Garth Reardon, and we'd better think of a way to solve them."

Ardeth relaxed against him, reveling in the light touch of his lips on her cheeks. "Such as. . . ?"

"Such as what in the world are we going to do with your hayseed brother!"

But after Nat left her, she found the lingering dismay she had felt before was still very strong. She looked frantically around the room, feeling for the first time the closeness of it, almost like a prison.

Forcing herself to sit down on the edge of the bed, she rested her chin in her hands and thought over the alternatives. Unless she could get Nat away from this ranch, he would certainly confront Reardon and probably be killed for his efforts. Yet there was no way he would leave.

Unless . . .

Medora's map. It was the one thing that was certain to lure Nat off this ranch and away from Garth Reardon's evil presence. It was the *only* thing. If only she could find it! They had already searched every inch of Medora's things, and yet, perhaps they had missed something. Some tiny, obvious hiding place that had been under their noses all the time.

She would simply have to look again. Jumping to her feet, she began pulling open the chest drawers.

It was no use. Though Ardeth went painstakingly over each and every item that belonged to Medora, she could not find anything resembling a map. She even went over the hems of all her gowns, thinking perhaps it might have been sewn within one of them, but there was nothing. Completely discouraged, she rang for Antonia to help her dress for dinner. She had spent so much time scouring the room, she was already late.

Even Antonia's customary cheerfulness had no effect on her sagging spirits. When one of the laces broke as she was being tied into her corset, it was just another disaster in a day of disasters.

"What shall I do, Miss Medora," the girl wailed, feeling as though it was somehow her fault.

"Don't worry about it, Antonia. Get the old one from the chest. It'll do for tonight."

"I pulled too hard. . . ."

"I asked you to, remember. It's these thin waists we women force on ourselves in order to look fashionable. Though why I should care. . . ."

"Oh, you always look done up like a bandbox, Miss Medora. The prettiest lady in the house, I'm sure."

Ardeth tried to smile. "Lady Lavinia would not appreciate your sentiments."

"Well, that English woman might have fancy gowns and jewels, but they don't really do anything to keep you from seeing her long nose and stringy neck. Besides, her eyes are too close together. Now, what you wear is set off by your own pretty face and figure. You'd look better in a potato sack than she does in one of her silk gowns."

Ardeth grabbed hold of the bedpost and hung on for dear life as Antonia began choking her into the strangling confines of her corset. If she had been able to breathe, she might have even chuckled at the thought.

There was a strained formality among the people at the table as they went about consuming the excellent dinner Garth's Chinese chef had prepared for them. It took Ardeth only a few moments to pin down the source—a grim-faced Nat Varien and a beaming Garth Reardon whose good humor was blatantly contrived. It did not take long for the masks to drop.

Lawrence Appleby asked innocently about the feasibility of investing in mining rights in the western territories, and Garth answered at some length with a description of the rich lodes that had been discovered in Colorado, Nevada and even Wyoming. Up until then Nat had sat silently eating his dinner. When he interrupted Reardon's garrulous reply, even Ardeth was startled.

"You're familiar with everything in these western lands that makes money, aren't you, Reardon?"

Garth turned his gaze from Appleby to Nat without changing his fixed smile. "I've invested in some of these mines, yes. Why not? It takes a lot of money to run a ranch like the Silver Sage."

"I suppose you own land in other territories as well. Say, even as far south as New Mexico?"

Garth beamed around the table. "As far south as Texas. The government back in Washington has made it fairly easy and profitable to procure lands out here."

"The Homestead Act, of course. Though I don't think that law was intended for rich men to add to their holdings."

"I say, Reardon," the earl spoke up. "I've heard a little about that Homestead Act. Do you think I might put together a sizeable acreage out here by filing a few false claims? Wouldn't mind owning my own . . . spread, as you so quaintly put it. Could hunt at my leisure, you know, and as often as I want."

"Excellent idea," Appleby said. "And one that's increasingly popular, so I've heard. Lots of foreigners, I'm told, buying up these great prairies for their hunting grounds. And why not. There's hardly any open land left in England anymore."

Garth tore his eyes from Nat's furious scowl. "Why not? I might even sell you a few hundred acres from my own spread."

"Yes, why not?" Nat said bitterly. "You'd have plenty left over, wouldn't you? You'd never miss a few hundred. Naturally, they wouldn't include any water, so his lordship here would have to pay to use yours."

"But surely, my lord, you don't intend to spend that much time in America," Lady Lavinia said weakly, with visions of dreary years spreading before her eyes.

352

Nat went on, ignoring her. "That Homestead Act was meant to encourage small farmers. Don't have much use for farmers, do you, Garth?"

Garth's voice went cold. "Not much."

"Nor for sheepherders either, I suspect."

"Sheep ruin the pasture for cattle. The two cannot live together. Fortunately, we haven't been much bothered by an influx of sheep in Wyoming."

"Now, I wonder why that is," Nat said, absently drawing the tines of his fork along the linen tablecloth. "How have you managed to hold them off when every other state and territory has had to endure them?"

"Perhaps they knew they would not be welcome here," Garth said, once more beaming at his other guests. Looking at the smug satisfaction on his handsome face, Ardeth suddenly realized that he was enjoying this. He was toying with Nat, waiting for his temper to give way so that he could be dealt with.

"Perhaps I could sing for you after supper," Ardeth said quickly. "And we really ought to discuss our plans for a performance. Remember? The one I asked you about. . . ."

"For Cameron's benefit," Garth said, nodding at that gentleman, who was totally absorbed in his supper. "Since you hadn't mentioned it again, I rather thought you had decided against it."

"Oh, no. It was just that my brother's unexpected appearance put it out of my mind," Ardeth answered.

"Where is your brother?" Lady Teague asked, seeing a chance to needle her precious charge's rival. "I notice he has not joined us."

Ardeth mentally flailed herself for being so stupid as to remind them of Ebal. "He wants to learn all about how a ranch like this is run, so he's spending most of his time with the hands." It was not much of an answer, but it was preferable to the horror of putting Ebal at the table with these sophisticated people.

"You have some very experienced ranch hands, don't you, Garth?" Nat said, commanding Reardon's attention once more.

Don't let him mention Toad Turnbull! Don't let him mention Toad Turnbull! Ardeth prayed silently. That would lose them the game once and for all, assuming there was anything left of their "game" that Reardon did not already know about.

But Nat kept silent. Perhaps it had occurred to him as well.

"They are a very loyal and efficient group of men," Reardon answered.

"Don't you mean henchmen!" He had the satisfaction of seeing Garth's eyes narrow.

"They do what I tell them. That's a characteristic of a good employee."

"Yes, and that makes the employee only as good as the employer, doesn't it?"

Garth was still smiling. "I'm not certain I know what you mean."

Nat sat back in his chair. "Only that if they rob,

cheat, murder and steal it is a reflection of the man who gave them their orders, more than of themselves."

Ardeth flung down her napkin and stood up. "Nat, we really must begin thinking about this concert. I need your help. Come along now and let's get to it. We've wasted too much time on more pleasant occupations, and now we really must begin thinking about my career once more."

Garth turned easily to her. "But you haven't had your coffee yet, Medora."

"I'm not in the mood for it tonight. Really, I'm more and more wholly consumed with the need to begin performing again. Come along, Nat, dear. We really must face this while I have these strong inclinations."

For a horrible moment she was afraid he was not going to come. Finally, languidly, maddeningly, he dragged himself up out of his chair. "All right, Medora. I suppose you're right. I've been enjoying the pleasantries of Mr. Reardon's 'hospitality' too much to think about work."

"Exactly," Ardeth said, sweeping around the table. "I'm sure you will all excuse us," she said, taking Nat's arm. With a theatrical wave of her hand, she hurried Nat out of the room and up the stairway. It wasn't until they reached her bedroom door that she was finally able to speak.

"What the devil do you think you're doing!" She spat out the words but kept her voice low all the same. "Can't you see he's just toying with you, waiting for you to say too much so he can pounce. I never saw such a dumb display of vitriolic temper in my life!"

Nat seemed to pull himself out of his grim preoccupation. "I know. It's just that sitting there looking at his smug, satisfied face and knowing the things he's done . . . it just gets to me. I want to smash him to pieces right there among his silver and china and fancy furniture."

"Just make one move in that direction and you'll be dead before you know it. Then where will I be!"

Nat's eyes hardened. "Oh, forgive me. I didn't realize my death would be so hard on you."

Only her anger prevented her from throwing her arms around his neck. "That's not—oh, Nat, I don't want to see you killed. I love you. This terrible vengeance of yours has got me scared to death. Can't you put it aside for a while, at least until we get away from this ranch?"

He tipped up her chin, looking down into her eyes that had filled with tears. "My darling Ardeth. Can't you see that this may be my best chance to finally get even with the man who was behind Kit's death and the loss of my family's property. I can't just ignore that and walk away."

"But you don't *know* Garth was behind it. You have no proof."

"No. But there are too many coincidences. And I'll get proof if I push him hard enough."

"Damn it, Nat! All you'll get is a bullet in the back! Why can't you listen to reason?"

He reached down and lightly kissed her lips. "We're never going to agree on this, love. Go lie down and calm yourself. I'm going to have a walk around outside and sort out my thoughts. Maybe I'll check on Ebal. He's such an innocent he's probably being eaten alive by those experienced cowboys out there in the bunkhouse."

"You will think about what I've said?"

"Yes. I promise I'll consider it."

It was all she was going to get from him. Reluctantly she watched him walk off down the hall, went into her bedroom and began throwing off her clothes. The evening was young, but she had no heart to go back downstairs and face the others. Antonia had laced her so tightly she couldn't breathe, and the turmoil that raged in her chest made the constriction even worse. She let her clothes fall on the floor as they came off, not even caring how wrinkled they got. Petticoats were jumbled up with the satin skirt and beaded bodice. She pulled off her soft kid slippers and, in a burst of frustration, threw them across the room. Then, tugging at the laces, she finally got the corset off and threw it on the pile beside the bed. Flouncing on the edge of her bed, she sank her head in her hands and let the tears finally flow.

She was never going to get Nat away from this horrible place. He would stay here and snoop and needle and confront Garth until Reardon finally wearied of it and either shot him himself or had one of his henchmen do it.

What would he use as his excuse, she wondered. She was certain there would be no more "accidents" like the one that almost happened out in the canyon. He wouldn't bother with that when Nat was so conveniently provoking. A duel? A gunfight? Or just a careless shot is the dark, while Nat was out walking, like tonight!

All at once she realized she was looking through her splayed fingers at something on the floor. How long had she been seeing it, without even realizing? Wiping the tears from her eyes, Ardeth leaned down and peered closer.

The corset—Medora's old corset—was lying over the pile of petticoats and satin gown she had thrown down. It was a simple thing, linen, edged with fine layers of narrow lace, and stiff with thin, concave slivers of bone sewed within the inner and outer layers of cloth. No different from any other corset, not even the elegant thing she had purchased on her trip to Denver.

Except that one of the narrow strips between the pieces of bone was very white, not opaque as all the others were. It might be simply a fold in the fabric, or the way it was sewn. Or it might be. . . .

She grabbed up the corset and ran her fingers over the cloth. It was thicker than the other, definitely thicker. Ardeth felt her throat close as she ran to the press and dragged out a sewing basket, digging inside for a tiny pair of embroidery scissors. With the pointed edges she began working at the cloth, tearing it away when she could not find the minuscule stitches. Finally, she had one long rip in the cloth where she could work her finger inside.

She was almost afraid to do it, fearing to find only a doubled-over section of linen. But when she dug into the fabric with her fingernail, working it open, her heart began to pound as she realized there was something loose there, something that could be pulled out.

She stared down at the thing in her hand, almost too excited to breathe. It was a narrow bag of linen cloth, tightly sewn. Taking up the scissors again, she tore at the stitches until she was able to pull them apart at the top. Reaching inside, she managed to grasp the edge of its contents with her nails just enough to ease them out.

A narrow fold of yellowed paper, no thicker than a pencil, lay in her hand. Carefully she began to unfold it, easing out the creases until it lay open on the bed. She looked down at the faded lines, red and black smudges on a thin piece of parchment, worn and browned with time.

"Thank God!" Ardeth breathed. "Medora's map!"

Chapter Nineteen

With unusual self-control, Ardeth forced herself to wait until she was certain that most of the household had gone to bed before she slipped to the rear hall to knock softly on Nat's door. She wore her nightdress and robe so that if anyone saw her they might assume she was headed for an assignation. Actually, making love was the last thing on her mind at the moment.

It gave her some satisfaction that he was as flabbergasted as she had been to learn she had finally found the map.

"It's not very big, is it," he said, smoothing the parchment out on the table with his thick fingers.

"If it had been any bigger, she would never have been able to hide it so well. As it is, she folded it so thin I was almost afraid to smooth it out for fear it would tear." She looked up and saw Nat's worried frown. "It is the map, isn't it? The one you were looking for?"

"Oh, yes. It's my uncle's map all right. It's awfully faded, but I can tell enough about it to recognize some of the markings."

Together they bent over the table, keeping their voices very low, even though Nat's room was far from those of the other guests. "Can you read it," Ardeth asked, her head very close to Nat's.

"It's in an archaic kind of Spanish, but I recognize a few words. Look here—Sangre de Cristo—that's the Blood of Christ. There is a group of mountains south of here that are still called by that name."

"Very far?"

"I think so. That is about the only geographical symbol I recognize. None of the others make much sense. Perhaps I'll understand them better after I study it for a while." He reached over and planted a kiss on her forehead. "Bless you, Ardeth, my love, for noticing that corset. This might just make everything worthwhile."

Ardeth took a deep breath and steeled herself to ask the question that was uppermost in her mind. "Don't you think we should go look for the mine right away?"

Nat turned back to concentrating on the yellowed paper under his hand. "Of course we must. If we really find that treasure, it will give me the money I need to bring Garth and Turnbull to justice."

She breathed a sigh of relief. "I'm glad you agree. To tell the truth, I feel that the longer we stay here, the larger the risk of Garth learning about this map and taking it from us. He knows everything that goes on in this place. It's as though he has eyes everywhere, and ears. Even now I wonder how on earth we will ever be able to get away without him stopping us."

Nat reached for a chair and pulled it up to the table. "I don't know that myself yet. Give me a little time to work on it. I'll come up with something."

"Nat, what on earth are we going to do about Ebal. I can't just leave him here at Reardon's mercy. I feel responsible for him. If only there was some way to send him back to Nebraska."

"We'll have to take him with us. It makes things more complicated, but there's no help for it. We may even be glad of another pair of hands somewhere down the road."

Ardeth sat on the floor and laid her head on his knees, her long, black hair spilling over them. She was filled with a buoyant hope—the first she had felt in days. Not for a moment did she doubt Nat could work out a way for them to escape, now that it was what he wanted too. And once away from the Silver Sage, all his energies would be concentrated on following this map and finding whatever lay at the end instead of getting even with Reardon and Turnbull. Once again she said a silent prayer of thanks to Medora and her love of money.

Everything after that night seemed to run together in a blur of anxious and hurried activity. Methodically and carefully Nat made all the preparations they needed to slip off in the night, telling Ardeth only as much as was actually necessary for her to know. Even then, she found the hardest part was to go on pretending everything was the same in front of Garth and the others. By now she had been pretending to be Medora so long that she was very well practiced in the art of thinking before she spoke. Yet there were several times when she felt certain her eyes and her face gave her away.

But if they did, no one gave any sign of it. Then, a week after finding the map, Nat stole softly into her room and woke her in the darkest part of the night.

"It's time," he whispered. She was instantly awake and out of bed, fumbling with her riding clothes in the dark. They had already planned to leave everything of Medora's, partly so as not to be burdened down with useless luggage but mostly as payment for the horses they would have to "borrow" from Garth's stable.

"That ruby necklace alone would buy ten horses," Ardeth had complained, but Nat was adamant.

"I won't have him accuse us of horse stealing. It's bad enough to have to sneak off like this using his horses. He won't be able to say we didn't pay him for them."

She knew he was right, and she purposely boxed the jewels together and wrapped them in heavy gray paper with Garth's name on the outside. She did not want anyone stumbling into her room and helping themselves before the truth was known.

The biggest problem was Ebal. Nat had deliberately chosen a night when the boy was set to watch the stables with one of the other ranch hands. When they reached the barns, Ebal was half-dozing inside while the older man sat smoking by the door. Nat threw a rock to draw him away from the barn and into the darkness, where he could knock him out and tie him up. Then together, they woke Ardeth's startled brother and whispered directions. Though he was completely mystified, Ebal said little as he helped saddle Nat's horse and two others Ardeth had ridden. When they rode out into the darkness, Ardeth had never been so thankful that her brother owned so few worldly possessions.

Long before the first faint rays of dawn etched the dark horizon, while Nat dismounted to readjust their supplies, Ebal began quietly questioning his sister, keeping his voice low in spite of the fact that they were surrounded by endless, open spaces.

"Has this got somethin' to do with ranchin'? I mean, are we supposed to join a roundup later on?"

Ardeth looked cautiously around, straining to see through the half-light. "No, Ebal. We're leaving Mr. Reardon's ranch, and we don't want him to know it."

"How's he not going to know it when we took his horses?"

"We left payment for them. Don't ask questions now. I'll explain it all later."

"But, sis, Mr. Reardon's a nice man. How come we couldn't leave in daylight with his blessing and

364

all?"

"We just couldn't. I told you, I'll explain it later. Right now we've just got to get away from here as far as we can before they realize we've gone. Help Nat with that pack and quit asking questions."

Ebal dutifully lumbered down off his horse and over to where Nat was struggling with the supplies. The whole thing made no sense to him, but as he had often concluded in the past, it was another adventure, and for that he would gladly go along. Anything that kept him from going back to the hard drudgery of his father's farm was welcome.

It was the last conversation any of them had for several hours. Ardeth had never seen Nat on the trail before, and she was hard put to keep up with him. He drove both her and her brother relentlessly until nearly noon, pushing south and keeping as much as possible to the contours of the land that afforded them shadows and quick hiding places while avoiding the open range as much as possible. When he finally allowed them to stop and rest long enough to drink and eat, they had left the Silver Sage so far behind that it seemed impossible for Garth and his men to catch up with them.

She had grown so tired and was so mindlessly focused on putting more miles between the ranch and themselves that she never noticed Nat had changed their direction until she saw the dark outlines of buildings looming upon the horizon. Surprised, she said nothing until they were close enough for her to recognize the usual clapboard stores with their false fronts advertising the necessities of life to be found in the barren western lands. As they rode down the wide, dusty main road, she couldn't hold back her reservations any longer.

"This is a big place, Nat. Look, it's even got a church. Why on earth did you bring us here?"

"It's got a saloon, too, sis," Ebal spoke up with excitement. "How about stopping to wet our whistles. Mine's pretty dry."

"It's got a railroad depot, and that is all that matters," Nat snapped, finally allowing himself to slump a little in his saddle. "We'll find out when the next train leaves for Denver, and then, if there's time, we'll have a bite to eat. But no drinks."

"I don't understand. Why are we taking a train?"

"Because we want Reardon to think we followed the trail south. You didn't really think I was going to cross the Rocky Mountains on horseback, did you? Maybe by myself, but certainly not with a girl and a kid along. No, this is better. Let him think we're camping in the mountains, when in actuality, we'll go to Denver by train and head south from there."

It only took Ardeth a few moments to realize how much she preferred this latter arrangement. "But the horses. . . ."

"I'd like to take them with us, but if we can't, we'll sell them here and buy more in Denver. I'm afraid we're still close enough to the Silver Sage for their brand to be recognized, so you'd better say a little prayer that they can ride the train along with us."

Once they reached the depot, they learned that the train to Cheyenne was expected in an hour and that there would be a car for the horses. Ardeth was still too anxious to enjoy the substantial meal they had at the depot restaurant, and it was only when the train came wheezing along the track and she climbed aboard that she began to let go of a little of the tension that had been tight within her since dawn. For Ebal, riding a train was even more of a thrill than crossing the mountains on horseback. He sat in the seat behind them, eyes glued to the window, endlessly commenting on the wonders of engines and high-speed travel. Ardeth reached out and squeezed Nat's hand beside her. For the first time she felt a real hope that they would get safely away from the dangerous clutches of Garth Reardon.

It wasn't so much the fact that Nat and Ardeth had slipped away that sent Garth into a silent paroxysm of rage; it was the humiliation. For once he had been duped and by two people whom he had never thought would be able to outsmart him. From the moment shortly after dawn when he had been roused from his bed by one of the ranch hands, until the time he stood in Ardeth's room, tearing away the wrappings from the box of jewelry she had left as payment for their horses, his anger with himself for not sensing what they were up to was almost as great as his contempt and fury at the thieves themselves.

The people around him had, of course, not realized this. He had become very adept over the years at schooling his face and guarding his tongue, and when his only response was to order his horse saddled immediately, he could see the mounting incredulity in their eyes.

"Shall we go after them, Mr. Reardon," John Glover asked eagerly as Garth swung up into the saddle.

"Not until I tell you to!" he snapped and rode off furiously into the rosy dawn.

Twenty minutes later, his lathered horse was pulled up in front of an isolated cabin hidden in the canyons north of the ranch. A Mexican in a dirty serape that half hid the heavy gun belt around his waist ran out of the cabin and grabbed the reins. "Cool him down," Garth snapped, already on his way toward the cabin door. "He was ridden hard."

The interior of the cabin was so dark he had to pause a moment to adjust his eyes. Then he saw the dark shadow of a man across the room rising up from a cot standing against the wall.

"You're up early," growled Toad Turnbull, pulling on his shirt. "I ain't hardly awake yet."

"Get dressed. You've got a hard ride ahead," Garth said, striding to the square plank table that stood near a decaying fireplace on the opposite wall. Turnbull began yanking his pants over his long johns.

"Well, that's good news. I was goin' crazy lying around here. What's it about?"

"I want you to catch up with a man and a woman who left my ranch before dawn today. Their trail ought to still be fresh if you get out of here right away. I'm not certain where they're going, but it's got to be south. Take Sanchez with you."

Turnbull was already pulling on his boots. "How far should I chase them, just in case they're hard to catch?"

"As far as it takes. Just be sure to let me know before you make your move. The man is Nat Varien, in case you're curious."

Even in the darkened room, Garth could see the sudden glitter that entered Turnbull's eyes.

"Is that right. Well, now. I think I'm going to like this job."

"Just don't kill him before I get there. Those two have something I want badly, and I intend to get it. If you go rushing in shooting everything in sight like you usually do, I might never find out where it is. That's an order."

Turnbull buckled on his gun belt with more enthusiasm than Reardon had ever seen in him. "Are you certain they have this thing you want? Maybe they was just tryin' to get away."

"Oh, they have it all right. Otherwise they wouldn't have left. Now get going and send me word the minute you learn where they are."

The Toad reached for his hat. "Okay, Colonel. You're the boss."

369

"Wait a minute," Garth said, following Turnbull from the cabin. "There may be a third person with them—a young boy. I don't care what happens to him, but I want Varien and the woman alive. Don't forget that."

Turnbull reached in the pocket of his shirt and broke off a plug of tobacco, spitting out the remains of last night's chew on the ground. "Like I said, Colonel. You're the boss."

Ten minutes later Reardon watched the two men gallop away from the cabin spewing dust in the dry air of early morning. It still gave him some satisfaction to hear himself addressed as "Colonel," even though he had in actuality been only a captain during the late war. One of the youngest ever to serve in the 7th Tennessee. The increase in rank was in keeping with all that he had accomplished in the years since. His success had been hard earned and carefully built, and he was not going to allow this cheap little impostor and her vengeful cowboy to destroy it. On the other hand, if he moved carefully, he might even add to his wealth to a degree beyond his wildest dreams. Now, if Turnbull would only follow orders and not go off half-cocked on his own, those dreams were sure to be realized.

He climbed back on his horse and rode at an easy pace back toward his ranch, smiling to himself.

Denver was even more crowded and noisy than Ardeth remembered. After the peaceful, empty

370

plains around the Silver Sage, it was especially nervewracking to have to force her way along a crowded walk, pushing through flowing clusters of people so intent on their own business they rudely shoved her aside. The streets were congested with wagons, drays, men on horseback and horse-drawn trollies, giving off a raucous bellow of men and beasts that drove her at times to cover her ears with her hands. Added to it was the constant hammering of new buildings going up everywhere, pushing the perimeters of the town ever farther out onto the plain toward the high ground to the southeast. Many of the new buildings were three and four stories high, and nearly all were made of brick, even the sparkling new sporting houses. There were banks, hotels, rooming houses, homes and even parks, all of which seemed to have doubled themselves since her last visit.

With Ebal following behind, mouth gaping in amazement and wonder, Ardeth clung to Nat's arm and let him pull her along the walkway to the largest general store in town. It was only a little less frantic inside than the street had been, but it was cooler. Ardeth perched on an upturned barrel and caught her breath while Nat went purposefully around the store picking up purchases. It was not long before he began complaining to the clerk, a large man with long handlebar moustaches and a big belly that was covered with a canvas apron like a sail in a full breeze.

"What kind of a store is this? You don't have

half the things I need."

"We been cleaned out by them prospectors coming through. There's no end to them. Soon as we stock up, they come through taking everything. We got a new shipment of supplies coming in on the train from the east next week. If you get here early enough, you can find what you want."

"What prospectors?" Nat asked, glancing warily at Ardeth.

"You ain't heard? They struck a rich vein of ore in Leadville. Half the country's headed there by now."

"Gold ore?"

"Not this time. Silver. Lead-silver, to be exact. So rich all a man has to do is stick a shovel in the earth and start digging it out."

Nat laid the items he had been able to find on the counter. "I've heard that before. I wonder how many men have been ruined by rumors like that."

"No, no. It's true. Why, a friend of mine told me hisself that one of them miners died last winter and when the ground thawed and the undertaker went to dig a hole to bury him, he struck a vein so rich he forgot all about the corpse. Far as I know, the feller's still lyin' there. I guess you ain't headin' for Leadville."

"No," Nat said, reaching in his shirt pocket to pull out a list. Look, here're the things I need. Warm jackets, tinned fruit and beans, coffee, flour, salt, blankets, a coffee pot, and a compass. And some more ammunition. Oh, and a few sticks of dynamite. Can I get this stuff at any of the other stores?"

Reaching for a pencil, the clerk began totaling up the few items Nat had laid on the counter. "You'll find most of them if you shop around. But they'll be dearer than here—if we had them."

Carrying his packages, Nat led Ardeth and Ebal back out into the street, grumbling. "Damn prospectors! Nothing but gamblers, every one of them. This is going to take us longer than I wanted."

"I don't mind stayin' here for a while," Ebal said, dodging around a street lamp to keep up with Nat's long strides. "I never seen anything like this place. It's just . . . just wonderful."

"We didn't come here to see Denver. Remember that."

"Couldn't we stay one night, Nat?" Ardeth asked, dreamily imagining a comfortable bed. "We'll be on the trail for a long time."

"The longer we're here, the greater the chance that someone will remember us. It would be much better to head south at once."

Yet after fruitless stops at two more stores, and with the coming evening dropping the temperature dramatically, Nat gave in and found rooms for them at one of the hotels far away from the train depot. Though her room was simple and plain, Ardeth reveled in its clean comfort, knowing it might be a long while before she enjoyed such pleasures again. She was even more pleased when Nat knocked softly on her door. Though it was late into the

373

evening, the noises on the streets outside testified to the vibrant activity still going on there.

She held the door ajar for Nat to slip through, then locked it behind him. When she turned, it was to be encircled in his arms.

He bent to kiss her, gently and lingeringly drawing sweetness from her lips.

"I was so hoping you'd come tonight," she sighed when she could speak again. "What did you do with Ebal?"

"I sent him off to one of the fancy houses down the street. He might as well enjoy the big city while he's here. He may never have the chance again."

Ardeth giggled. "Are you sure that was wise? He's so innocent, and he might say something he shouldn't."

"He's not quite as innocent as he was before he went to Fireweed. And I impressed upon him that if he said anything out of turn I'd head straight for Nebraska in the morning and deliver him to his farm myself. Here, let me look at you."

The small, round oil lamp on the table beside the bed was turned so low that the light in the room was almost as bronzed as moonlight. Nat led her over to the bed and sat down, drinking in her beauty. She had let down her hair which cascaded over her shoulders and down her back in raven ringlets which he laced with his fingers. The golden shadows of the lamp set off her perfect cheekbones, full, ripe lips and the crescent fringe of heavy lashes along her cheeks. Even in the simple nightrobe which was all she had brought from Medora's silken robes, she looked more beautiful to him than ever.

She stood in front of him, her hands lightly on his shoulders. Opening his legs, he drew her slim body between his thighs.

"My vixen," he sighed. "Sometimes you make it damned difficult to keep my mind on maps and treasure!"

Ardeth bent over him, rubbing her cheek against his thick hair. "There will be plenty of time later to think of those things. With Ebal along, there won't be any privacy for making love."

"Then, we'd better take advantage of it now, while we've got the chance," he said, his voice hoarse with longing. His hands slid up her sides to pull her forward, then higher, one on each side of her breasts, gently pushing them together. He buried his face in the luscious mounds of sweet flesh, lightly tasting, tickling with his tongue. Lifting them from below, he moved as in a trance from one to the other, drinking in their nectar. With his thumbs, he slid the edges of the fabric her breasts strained against down over the taut, pointed tips of her engorged nipples and caught first one, then the other in his lips.

Ardeth flexed against him, her back arched to meld into his body. A slow, sensuous warmth, the glow of a growing ecstasy, swelled within her. His hands slid around her, over her back and down to knead her buttocks. Pressed against him, she slipped her own hand between them, seeking and finding the hard shaft that told her of his need for her. Gently she rubbed her hand along the taut fabric of his trousers, arousing him even more.

Pulling away slightly, she began to undo the buttons on his shirt until she could push it over his shoulders. Dreamily, Nat let her work at his clothes, enjoying the sensation for once of being undressed, all the while anticipating the moment when he would be free to take her. When the last piece of clothing was gone, he moved to slip her robe over her shoulders, then picked her up and laid her on the bed.

Her skin was cool and soft as a mountain stream. He lay beside her, his fingers drifting over the mounds and valleys of her body, delighting in the textures of her silken flesh, quietly rousing to life the flames of her desire he knew were there until they burst into raging need. Then slipping her beneath his hard body, he drove his own into those mysterious depths where they were linked together as one person. Her arms and legs encircled him, closing him together with her, and as one breathing, sighing creature they shared the harmonious unity that echoed a life before time.

In all their times together Ardeth had never before felt such a sense of belonging to this man. When her pounding heart finally eased, she rolled on top, clasped him in her arms and held him fiercely, tightly. Then looking down into his face, she said, "Whatever happens after this night, Nat, remember this. I love you and I will always love you. You are a part of me as I am of you. Wherever I go, some part of you will always be with me, as I shall always be with you."

He felt the strong emotions behind her words, but he had none of his own to reply with. Instead he smoothed her hair away from her face and looked into the dark pools of her eyes, smiling up at her. Then he drew her down, kissing her again.

The dark outline of horse and rider was barely visible in the shadows of the single, large tree. Garth Reardon spurred his horse and cantered toward the stand of pines that rose like sentinels on the flat, open plain. The ground was bathed in the soft rose of the setting sun, pale against the long strands of blue and gray that streaked the sky.

Toad Turnbull rode to meet him as he neared the trees. "I'd almost given you up," he muttered, furious at having been kept waiting so long.

Garth kept his horse moving until they were both hidden beneath the shadows of the tree's branches. "You're lucky I could get here at all. Haven't you ever heard of telegrams! Who is following those two while you came back here to tell me in person where they went?"

Toad's eyes flashed in the darkness. "Sanchez is waiting for me in Cheyenne. By the time I get there, he ought to know which train they took."

"So they did take the train. I thought as much. Only a fool would ride a pack horse into Colorado,

377

and Nat Varien is no fool."

"Well, he's not so smart neither. A dozen people recognized the Silver Sage brand on them horses. One cowpoke with a woman and a young boy ain't easy to forget."

Garth shifted in the saddle, fingering the reins. "But you don't know where they went from Cheyenne?"

"Not yet. We will, though."

"You needn't waste much time. They headed for Denver; I'll stake my life on it. If they didn't go west—and they wouldn't have gone to Cheyenne for that—then they'll go south. It's Denver that will be the problem. It's a big town and growing larger all the time. But if they spent any time there at all, someone will remember them."

"And if we pick up their trail there, do we follow it?"

"Yes. I'll be there myself in a few days, staying at the Munroe Hotel. Leave a message there for me. Whatever you do, don't let their trail grow cold. They could get away completely if that happens."

Turnbull leaned across his horse and spat a stream of tobacco juice on the ground. "I know how to track a man," he muttered.

Garth pulled his horse around, revolted, as usual, by Turnbull's vulgarity. He opened his saddlebags and handed Turnbull a small leather bag filled with coins. "This is for expenses. If you have to bribe information out of people, then do it. Just don't lose Varien."

Toad Turnbull grabbed at the coins a little too quickly for Garth's taste, stuffing them inside the pocket of his shirt. The heavy money pouch went a small way toward easing the resentment he had felt while waiting for Reardon to arrive. "You got nothin' to worry about, Colonel."

He pulled his mount around and took off, riding hard toward the horizon. Garth sat looking after him, his hands on the pommel of his saddle, his shapely mouth drawn tight.

"I wish I could be so sure," he muttered.

Chapter Twenty

"Couldn't we stop soon?" Ardeth's voice sounded plaintive even to herself.

Nat turned in the saddle to look back, smiling at her bedraggled figure. Actually she had kept up very well until they rode out of the mountains and onto the high southern plateau where the heat was stronger than any she had ever experienced. But this was no time to let pity influence his judgement.

"I think we should go a little farther. Do you think you can manage it?"

"You're worse than a slave-driver," Ardeth sighed, reaching for her canteen. The water, still cold from the mountain stream where she had filled it, was refreshing and delicious. "I guess I'll make it."

Behind her Ebal slumped on his horse. He was feeling the hotter weather as much as Ardeth, but he would die before mentioning it. If he hadn't finished his own canteen earlier, he would have poured its contents over his head now. But he had learned early on that Nat made the decisions on this trip, and if he wanted to push farther south, there was no changing his mind.

"See that ridge in the distance," Nat said, pointing. "I think we should try to make it there. We can set up camp and stay put for a couple of days while I scout out the area. How does that sound?"

"Heavenly. Does that mean we've gone as far south as we need to?"

"No. It just means I'm not sure where to go next. Come on. We might as well take advantage of the light as long as we can."

Reluctantly Ardeth spurred her mount to follow Nat's lead down a gravel-strewn hillock and onto the flat land that stretched ahead seemingly for miles. Her horse was no more anxious than she to continue plodding, and she had to give it several forceful kicks to encourage its obedience. The three riders and the heavily loaded pack horse straggled out single file with Nat in the lead, the only one to show any enthusiasm for the trek.

Actually, Ardeth thought, if it were not so hot, she was sure she would not feel so drained and weary. All the long way through the mountains after leaving Denver, she had kept up with the two men very well. The rigors of camp life had been difficult at first, but she soon grew accustomed to the long hours in the saddle and the peaceful solitude of campfires at night with riotous stars as thick as diamonds in the ebony sky above. Though Nat had kept them constantly moving, still they had developed a cosy camaraderie among the three of them that made up for the lack of creature comforts in the wild.

And the beauty of the country through which they passed more than compensated for comfort. Never had she seen such high peaks white-topped like frosting on a cake, such rolling forests, clear, singing streams, or land that swept downward to deep, green valleys one minute and upward to high cliffs stretching toward the sky the next. If heaven really existed, she concluded, it must look like these mountains of the Colorado Rockies.

But they were through all that now. This was a country of misshapen sandstone rocks and cliffs, of flat, hot plateaus, of subdued colors of buff and rose and brown. The trees were smaller, the grasses thinner. Its stark beauty was just as impressive as the mountains but in a more harsh, demanding way.

She was so absorbed in her thoughts she was brought up short when Nat stopped directly in front of her. Pulling her horse around, she saw him staring out across the flat plain. "What is it?" she asked, shading her eyes with her hand.

"Riders coming." He looked around anxiously. "And nowhere to hide. Damn."

Ardeth eased her mount up close to Nat's. "Do you think it's Garth?"

Nat raised in the saddle, peering into the dusk. "I don't think so. They're coming too fast, straight at us. I doubt if Reardon would be so direct."

"Why, them's soldiers," Ebal cried behind them. "I can see the blue of their shirts."

Nat smiled with relief. "Your young eyes are beter than mine. But you're right. Now I can make out their uniforms. I hope they don't detain us."

Since it was obvious the troop was heading their way, they sat and waited for them. Curiosity had by now replaced anxiety, and when the troopers finally pulled up to canter toward them, Nat rode to meet them.

An older man with an officer's chevrons on his shoulder, touched his gloved hand to his hat brim. "Captain McCormack, sir, of the Fourth Cavalry."

Nat extended his hand. "Nat Varien. I didn't realize there was a fort nearby, Captain. Otherwise we might have gone there first."

"There isn't, Mr. Varien. We're on special duty out here. May I ask why you're here?"

"Just passing through on my way to New Mexico. Why? Is there some law against that?"

"No law but that of common sense. You're rather vulnerable out here with just a girl and a young boy," the captain said, glancing at Ardeth and Ebal, who waited on their horses a few feet away. "There's Indian trouble. A party of Utes, unhappy with the way things were going on the reservation. They've attracted some other malcontents and have attacked several farms and ranches, causing a lot of destruction."

"I hope you're not trying to round them up with just these few soldiers."

The captain glared at Nat. "We've got a whole company camped twenty miles east. What about you? You won't have a chance out here alone. We'll escort you back to the nearest town, where you'll be safe."

Nat glanced quickly back at Ardeth. "No thank you, Captain. I think we'll take our chances and push ahead. Maybe by the time those Utes reach here, we'll be gone."

The officer gave Nat a long, grave look, wondering at the mystery of the stupidity of man. "Suit yourself," he said, pulling his horse's head around. "Don't say we didn't offer."

Nat touched his hatbrim. "Thanks for the warning."

As the soldiers hurried away back in the direction they had come from, Ardeth walked her mount over to Nat. "Was that wise? Wouldn't it have been better to go with them?"

"And be stuck in an army fort for God knows how long, like sitting ducks for Reardon when he decides to show up? I've had some experiences with Utes, and I know a little of their language. If we run across them, I think I can manage."

"I don't care much for savages," Ebal said quietly. "I heard tales—"

"We've all heard tales," Nat snapped, kicking his horse to move off. "Most of them are safely on reservations now. These are probably just a few renegades who will soon be rounded up by all those brave soldiers. Forget them and let's make for camp on that ridge. We'll certainly be safer there than out in the middle of this plain."

The shadows were growing very long, and the

ridge looked awfully far away. Ardeth also suspected that even a few renegade savages could be as bloodthirsty and destructive as a whole band of Indians if all she had ever heard about them was true. But she said nothing and simply prodded her mount to move a little faster.

They reached the ridge of high cliffs shortly before total darkness fell over the plateau. After Nat built a fire, Ardeth warmed up some tins while Ebal and Nat made camp. Once supper was eaten, Nat insisted Ebal go off to stand guard. He had been more influenced by the officer's talk of savages on the loose than he had let on.

It was so peaceful sitting around the fire with the light dancing on the shadows of the cliff that Ardeth was able to let go a little of her anxiety and weariness. When Nat pulled out the map and spread it on the ground in front of him, she leaned forward on her elbows, eager to examine it too.

"Does it make sense to you now?" she asked.

For the first time he actually answered her question. "Of course I recognize the Sangre de Cristo mountains. And this section here corresponds roughly to where we are—high cliffs, mesa, sandstone cliffs. I'm pretty sure we're in the general area."

"But what do these strange-looking figures mean? It looks like a town." Her finger traced a pattern on the paper. "And over here, some kind of tower?"

"I don't understand that at all. There are certainly no towns in this godforsaken country that I ever heard of. It's part of the mystery. But look here. Before you reach that, there are two other distinctive markings. I've been watching for anything resembling them, but I've seen nothing."

"Do you mean this?" she asked, pointing at several slashes of lines.

"Yes. It looks like a tree with one branch broken and trailing on the ground. That should be pretty obvious."

"What about this thing? It looks like a hat."

I think that's a rock formation and one that is so distinctive we ought to be able to spot it easily. But I haven't seen anything that would remotely resemble it yet."

Ardeth rolled over on her blanket and laced her fingers behind her head. Above her the stars were beginning to trace their diamond patterns on the ebony sky. "Do you really think we have a prayer of finding this cave in all this big country. It seems so unlikely that out of all the canyons and towns and caves in Colorado and New Mexico that we should stumble on that particular one."

"Well, we can pin it down to some extent. We're in the general area. Now, if we can manage to avoid trouble and have the time we need, I believe we can find it. We should begin looking for this rock formation. That's our best bet."

But the next day they traveled along the rim of the canyon, and though they passed many unusual rock shapes, there was nothing resembling a hat stovepipe or otherwise. Two more days of that and

Ardeth was beginning to grow discouraged as she saw their supplies running low. She found no comparable feelings in her companions. Nat continued to drive them forward with a single-minded forcefulness, entirely focused on looking for signs from the map. Ebal simply enjoyed being there—the new sights and sounds of a beautiful, strange country. Even his fear of running into Indians eventually added to the excitement of the journey.

And then Nat realized they were being followed.

He discovered it only when they came up against a canyon wall and, realizing they could go no farther that way, doubled back by way of a wide circle and came across the remains of a campfire near their own. It had been so nearly obliterated that only a sharp eye like Nat's could recognize the signs. He did not mention it to Ardeth until they stopped for a rest at noon.

"Garth?" she asked softly.

"I don't know. Possibly some of his men. I think we should move on quickly. I remember passing a narrow gap a little farther up that might take us through this wall of rock to the other side. We'll try that and hope."

The path was narrow and sloped abruptly downward, the walls of the canyon rising steeply up on either side like a tunnel. It was a dry stream bed chiseling its crooked way through the steep rock walls until it broadened out on a level plateau of rolling hills studded with small trees and shrubs. As the bed narrowed once more between jagged cliffs,

Nat was feeling very satisfied with himself at out-witting whoever was behind them. Then, all at once, Ebal pulled his horse up and pointed up to the cliff ahead and above them. Ardeth drew in her breath sharply as she saw four silhouettes of horses and their riders poised on the top of the cliff. Even at that distance Ardeth recognized the dark shape of feathers jutting from their heads.

"Indians! My God! What do we do now?"

"Don't panic," Nat said quietly. "Just keep riding. I wonder how many there are."

Even as they watched, other riders joined the group. "I count seven," Ardeth said, her voice full of unease. Nat sat passively in the saddle, but his eyes moved rapidly and anxious around at the terrain. "Keep calm. Don't hurry. There's a butte up ahead that once we get around it to the other side we can take off. Follow my lead."

It was almost as if the Indians read their minds. As they reached the wall of the butte, they heard behind them the horrible caterwauling yowls of the Indians as their ponies came tearing down the hill toward them.

"Now!" Nat yelled and dug in his spurs. Dropping the reins to the pack horse, Ebal went galloping behind him while Ardeth slapped her reluctant mount to keep up. The three of them tore across the uneven ground, glancing back to see if their pursuers were gaining. Ardeth bent over her horse's neck, her hair flying, more terrified than she had ever been in her life. It seemed as though they rode forever, dodging up steep hills, and careening down, with the canyon walls enclosing them in their engulfing arms, or at other times, dropping away to leave them vulnerable on the open, gravel-strewn plateau.

At one point Nat pulled up to give their lathered horses a moment to rest. Behind them the high-pitched yowls had stopped, as though the Indians were unsure which direction they had taken. Then they started up again, closer than before, and Nat drove his horse forward.

They entered a maze of canyons and, by taking circuitous routes through twisting paths, earned a little time to catch their breath. Finally, when Nat saw that their horses could go no farther, he pulled up. If they had not lost the Utes now, there was no hope of evading them.

Ardeth fell over her mount's slumped neck. "I can't go any farther," she gasped. "I feel as spent as my poor horse."

Nat slid out of the saddle, leaning against his horse's heaving sides.

"I haven't the faintest idea where we are, but I think we may have given them the slip. Ebal, you look as white as that rock behind you. Get down and catch your breath."

Nat moved to help Ardeth out of the saddle. She slumped against him, and he caught her under her arms, gently setting her on the ground where she could lean back against the wall of sandstone behind her. Her heart was pounding so loudly she felt it in her ears. Nat eased down beside her and pulled off his hat, wiping his brow with his sleeve.

"We lost our pack horse and all our supplies," Ebal moaned when he could finally speak.

Nat, too, could barely talk for gasping. "That's little enough if we managed to get away. Indians are not known for the kindness to captives."

Ardeth leaned her elbows on her knees and put her head down. She was relieved but also more tired and out of breath than she had ever been in her life. All of a sudden, it seemed foolish to go on with this crazy escapade. The map and the search had, back at Garth's ranch, seemed more important than anything in the world because it was a way to get Nat out of danger. Now this senseless roaming and searching and trying to deal with the problems it created just did not seem worth it.

She turned to Nat with her mouth open to ask him if they couldn't please go on down into New Mexico and work out their lives but held back her words when she saw the look on his face. He was staring off to the left, his cheeks gone suddenly white, his eyes glinting with amazement.

"What is it?"

"Look at that. . . ."

She had to move around him to see, and even then only gradually did the lights and shadows rearrange themselves so she could make out what he was staring at so intently. Several hundred feet away, across a rising patch of land, the canyon wall rose steeply above a huge yawning overhang. In the shadows of that overhang, full of silence and emptiness, was the unmistakable shape of square rock dwellings with blank, staring windows. They moved at irregular intervals all along the deep recess beneath the overhang of the cliff. And near the center, where the recess was highest, stood a small, square tower, three levels high.

"What is it?" Ardeth breathed.

"I've heard stories about places like this. They were built by ancient savages and abandoned long ago. I didn't even believe the stories were true."

"But . . . it's a town," Ardeth said with growing excitement. "The town on the map. . . ?"

Nat was smiling. "That's right. It's not a living town at all. It's a town of the dead!"

Chapter Twenty-one

In spite of the excitement they felt at stumbling upon the strange, silent town, Nat forced them all to wait until he was certain they had not been followed by the Utes before traversing the rugged, irregular basin that separated them from the cliff dwellings. As they climbed up the series of ledges that led to the ruined buildings, Ardeth grew increasingly fascinated and entranced. The quiet was so heavy it could almost be felt, yet it was not a somber, frightening silence one might expect in a city of the dead, but more a reverent awe in the face of a great mystery. Most of the first square, stone cubicles were missing their roofs, but the ones farther back, under the great slab of rock overhang seemed more like tombs than dwellings.

"Those at the back look as though they were carved out of the cliff wall," she said to Nat, keeping her voice low even though there was no one else around.

"They probably were. It's amazing, isn't it, that

anyone could create such structures out of adobe and rock. And out here in this wilderness, too. Some of them must have been two and three stories high."

Ardeth looked up at the uneven windows that stared blankly out, like the eyes of the dead. Broken shards of pottery, yellow with dust, bore evidence that life once existed here, but there was little else except the structures themselves to suggest people had once walked these stones.

"Do you think the friars really came here with their gold?" she asked.

"It conforms to the map, doesn't it? What else could their drawings mean? There are no living towns within miles of this place." Nat poked at the walls, running his hands over the stones. With the pointed toe of his boot he dug into the soft sandstone at his foot.

"What are you looking for?"

"Look here at the map," he said, smoothing it out against the stone wall. "This suggests a hole of some sort. Perhaps a cave behind one of these rooms. That will be where the gold is hidden."

Ebal, who had kept close to his sister and now crouched behind her, peering at the map, gave a small gasp. "Gold?" he whispered. "Real gold?"

Ardeth had forgotten they had not included her brother in the reasons for their search. "Yes. That's what we've come all this way to find."

"You mean, we're going to be rich?"

"Don't get your hopes up too soon," Nat cautioned. "We aren't sure yet that this is the town on the map. I think we should split up and search the place. Ebal, you take the far end to our left. Ardeth, you take the other. I'll search the middle."

"What should I be looking for?" Ebal asked.

"An opening of some sort. A cave, a tunnel, even a hole in one of the back walls that a man could squeeze through. If you come across anything like that, give a holler."

Ebal did not move. "But, sis, this place makes my skin crawl. Couldn't we go together?"

"Do what Nat tells you," Ardeth answered, giving him a good-natured shove toward the far end of the cliff. "What are you afraid of? Ghosts?"

"Well . . . now you mention it. . . ."

Nat was already heaving his body up on the next ledge. "A ghost won't take your scalp," he said briskly. "On the other hand, if we don't find what we're after before those Utes discover where we've gone, we might all lose our hair."

That was enough to galvanize Ebal. He went loping off toward one end of the overhang while Ardeth began picking her way in the opposite direction.

The interiors of those rooms that still had their roofs were dark and cool, a welcome relief to the heat outside. Although Ardeth tried to hurry, she found she was too fascinated with the ruins to simply poke her head inside long enough to make certain there were no openings to caves and then move on.

Who were these people, she wondered. How had they managed to carve such elaborate dwellings out of the face of a cliff? Some of the rooms went far back into the cliff wall, one cubicle leading to another. Several had stone steps that led to a higher level where other rooms were grouped. She found several splotches of red paint on the walls, like a sign left by the ancients to make contact with her. She touched these spots with her fingers, longing for that reach across the ages that would tell her something of the people who had lived here before. But there was no sound. Only silence and wondering.

She began at the far end and worked her way toward the center. In a short time she had completely lost track of her brother and Nat, engrossed as she was in her own explorations. She came out of a complex of several rooms back into the blinding sun and shaded her eyes to look for the others but saw no sign of them. Above her, a narrow, rising path, worn in the center by the passage of ancient feet, led to a ledge bordering two more cubicles tucked far back under the jutting edge of the overhang. Their blank doors gaped darkly in the sunlight. She walked up the ledge and peered into one of the rooms. It was empty and bare and had nothing faintly resembling an opening in any wall. She moved on to the other door and bent to look inside. The interior was darker than the other since it nestled more closely to the end of the cliff wall, but it was just as bare and just as empty.

Ardeth straightened to retrace her steps, when she suddenly felt her waist circled by something hard and thick that tightened around her with such force the breath was pushed from her body. In an instant she realized she had been grabbed by a man, his arm tight as steel around her waist. She gasped and tried to cry out, but his hand covered her mouth, jerking her head back viciously. She felt herself lifted completely off the ground, carried like a sack of grain and hurled into one of the rooms. She was slammed up against a wall with such force that for an instant everything went black. Then, her eyes wide with shock and fear, she felt his body push up against hers on the rough stones, and he spat out in a thick, low voice: "Make a fuss and I'll kill you right here!"

From the sound of the voice, she knew it was not an Indian who was holding her with such cruel force. But that was little comfort as she felt her hands viciously roped with some kind of rawhide thongs that bit into her flesh. A rag, grimy with sweat, was pulled around her face between her lips and tied at the back of her head. The horrible, strong hands slid down her body to grasp her ankles, whipping them together with another leather thong, leaving her trussed as helplessly as a young calf. Her knees buckled, and she would have fallen but for the iron grip of that thick arm. With one arm around her, he dragged her across the room to stand beside the door, peering around the entrance. She saw that the other hand now held a long revolver, pointed out at the white, glaring sunlight, threatening anyone who might approach.

Her mind raced frantically, trying to think who the man could be that would want her as a prisoner. Then he stepped back inside and shoved her against the wall, facing her.

She stared into the gross, swollen features, the bulging eyes and fat lips. He was no taller than she, but his stocky girth was iron hard and strong as steel. She slumped against the rocks as she recognized Toad Turnbull. And she was his helpless prisoner.

He was so intent on making sure no one had followed her that for a moment he ignored her. Then, when he felt certain she had been alone, he turned back to her, pinning her to the wall with his body hard against hers. The smile that broadened his thick lips was as evil as anything she had ever seen.

"So," he said in a breathy voice. "The great Medora! And all mine. Maybe you'll sing for me, hunh?" He gave a crazy, malicious giggle.

Ardeth turned her face away, struggling against the tight gag of the cloth in her mouth. She felt his hand slip up her waist to cup her breast, squeezing it painfully. She winced, tightly closing her eyes.

"I know ways to make you sing." He giggled as his hand slid down her stomach, his fingers thrusting between her legs. "Sing like you never done before. Want me to show you some?"

The room began to swim around her, then grow mercifully dark as she fainted dead away.

* * *

Nat was sitting on his haunches, studying the rubble-strewn floor of one of the ruined houses when Ebal finally caught up with him. The lanky boy, covered head to toe with yellow dust, sank down close by and leaned back against the mortared stones.

"Well, I didn't find nothin' that looked like a cave. That is, if you don't count this whole place, which is a kind of cave itself."

Nat got down on his knees, running his hands across the rubble. Up until a few moments before, he too, would have said he'd found nothing. Nothing, that is, but broken shards of pottery, dust-covered baskets, lying askew as though thrown aside by an angry housewife, and a few stone implements, most of them broken or worn past recognition. But just as he had been about to give up and go searching for Ardeth, he had noticed more closely the circular pattern of the stones on the floor. It was a pattern repeated in several places, and it suddenly occurred to him to wonder if it could mean anything.

"Course, I did pick this up," Ebal said, holding something out in his long fingers. Nat looked up into the vacant grin of a small human skull.

"Good God! Put that back."

Ebal's pale eyes widened in surprise. "Why? I found it fair and square. Ain't nobody around here who'd care."

"It was a human being once. Besides, we're not looking for ghoulish souvenirs. Bury it someplace."

Ebal sniffed loudly. "Don't seem right . . ." he muttered and walked out to the edge of the rock ledge to pitch the skull down into a shallow ravine clustered with scrawny trees and bushes, looking after it wistfully.

"Come look at this," Nat said behind him. "Notice how these stones are laid? You can't see them all, but enough are still uncovered to make out the shape."

"It's a kind of circle, ain't it?"

"That's right. An almost perfect circle. I've seen several of these. There must have been a reason for them."

"Maybe they just liked the shape. Indians like to make pretty things with different kinds of shapes. I've seen a lot of them on their clothes and shoes."

Yes, but they usually have a reason for choosing one over another. It often has something to do with their religion." Even as he spoke, Nat was crossing the interior of the circle, thrusting a stick he had found into the rubble, pushing aside small rocks with the toe of his boot. Then he stopped, looking around the full diameter formed by the stones.

"The center. Of course."

Ebal looked at him blankly. Grabbing his arm, Nat pulled him to the center of the circle and shoved the stick in his hand. "Start digging. If there's nothing here, then it won't be anywhere and I'm on the wrong track."

399

"You can't dig with this puny thing," Ebal said, throwing down the stick. "This is better."

He pulled out the long knife he had carried all the way from Nebraska and, falling to his knees, began prying at the pile of rubble on the floor. Using his hands, Nat helped, pushing aside the loose dirt as Ebal worked apart the debris of centuries.

Look," Nat said excitedly. "It's a stone. A large, square stone."

"That'll be heavy. I don't know if'n we can lift it?"

Grabbing the knife from Ebal's hands, Nat pried at the mortar around the single large stone that sat in the middle of the circle. When he had loosened it enough, he took the knife and cut a staff from one of the larger stunted trees in the ravine. Using this as a lever, the two men worked it up far enough to get their fingers beneath it. Then, with a heave, they slid it out of its place.

"That moved easier than I thought it would," Nat said, dropping to his knees. "It was probably a cover and meant to be moved. And look . . . there's our hole!"

Bending down, he peered into the musty blackness below.

"Is it the cave?" Ebal asked, dropping down beside him. "Do you see the gold?"

"I can hardly see anything, but I think it's a room of some sort. It doesn't appear to be too deep. Here, give me a hand."

"You're not going down there!"

"Yes, and so are you. But first move back. You're blocking the light."

With a nimble leap Nat jumped down inside the hole. He landed on the dirt floor of a small circular room reeking with the closed air of centuries. He waited a moment for the dust to settle, then moved slowly around the circle, feeling his way until his eyes adjusted to the light.

There was the usual litter plus a few faded feathers lying half-buried in the dust. But nothing else. By the time Ebal had screwed up his courage and jumped down to join him, Nat was staring around dejectedly, wondering if he had not been wrong about this entire place. He should have kept looking for a cave and not been sidetracked by this ancient deserted city.

Ebal looked around cautiously, standing close to Nat. "There ain't no cave here. Nor no gold."

"I know. It seemed so promising. Well, perhaps we'd better clear out. Give me a hand up and I'll pull you out."

"There's another of them stones."

For a minute Nat did not realize what the boy had said. Then he saw Ebal staring at the floor directly beneath the opening where the light made a pool of gold on the floor. He hadn't seen it before, but there it was, a faint outline of a rounded stone. With his hopes rising once again, he dropped to his knees to examine it.

"Are we goin' to have to dig this one out too," Ebal asked, already pulling out his knife.

"It's our last chance." Nat took the knife and worked the point into the loose earth around the stone. "It's not mortared like the last one. It ought to be easy. Here, help me move it. . . ."

Yet the stone proved to be heavier than expected and more deeply embedded. It took them long minutes to work it loose enough to get their fingers beneath it and pry it up. Even then, it was almost too heavy to lift. Exerting all his strength, Nat pried up one corner until he could get enough of a grip to slide the lid to one side. With Ebal working in the same direction, they managed to shove the heavy lid along the floor until they had worked it away from its bed. Even before it was completely free, Nat caught the shimmering flame of yellow that leaped to life as the sun fell upon it. His heart went soaring in his chest.

"The gold," Ebal breathed, leaving the stone to bend over the depression in the earth.

"Don't touch anything!" Nat cried, and grabbed the hand the boy had thrust at the glittering light. "Look first. . . ."

The two of them bent over the hole. It was not large and was composed mostly of packed earth. But in the center, lying serenely in the dirt, its bright shaft reflecting the shimmering rays of its first sunlight after years of darkness, glowed a golden object.

"It doesn't look like very much gold," Ebal said quietly. "Maybe this wasn't the right place after all."

Nat sat back on his knees, a smile playing about

he corners of his wide mouth. "Oh, it's the right place, all right."

Ebal's pale eyes glinted in the darkness behind him. "How can you tell?"

Nat ran his finger along the cool, golden shaft. "Because, my dear Ebal, that object we have just uncovered is a Spanish crucifix!"

She was swimming in light. It ebbed and flowed around her as consciousness came sweeping back, now achingly bright, now dappled in shadow. Arleth fought against it, unwilling to lose the blessed unknowing for the terrible reality that pricked at her mind. Then it all cleared, and she remembered.

She lifted her head, her eyes half-open. A surge of fear reminded her of where she had been when she had lost consciousness. She looked wildly around.

She was outside, sitting on the ground, her back against the scaley bark of a juniper tree. Her hands were tied behind her back, and the awful gag was still in her mouth, straining against her cheeks.

Across a clearing, standing on the far side, were the blurred shapes of three men. One of them turned and started toward her, and she recognized the stocky, misshapen form of Toad Turnbull. Scrambling back against the tree, her eyes wide with terror, she made strangling sounds against the kerchief that bound her mouth.

"She's awake," Turnbull muttered.

"You don't seem to have left a very pleasant impression," a familiar voice behind him said. Ardeth's terror turned to incredulity as she saw Garth Reardon walking toward her. "Take that thing away from her face. She could scream to high heaven here and no one would hear her."

Turnbull leaned down and jerked away the gag, leaving her with the dry, stagnant taste of cotton in her mouth. She ran her tongue over her lips. When Garth bent down, pressing a canteen of water to her lips, she drank greedily.

"You'll forgive me if I'm not grateful," she murmured. He screwed the top back on the canteen, smiling down at her.

"Under the circumstances, I understand completely. I regret the force that had to be used, but the Toad here is not known for subtlety. He gets the work done, however, and that is what matters."

"I'd of used a lot more if I could've had my way." Turnbull spat out the words, glaring at Ardeth and leaving no doubt about the kind of force that would have been. For the first time she was glad Reardon had shown up. She glanced around the clearing and saw the other man there, lounging on the ground. He wore a large Spanish-style sombrero with a striped poncho over his shoulder and had the unshaven, slovenly look of a desperado. She suppressed a shiver as she recognized the bandit who had taken her from the train, and her eyes went back to Garth. "I didn't expect to see you here."

He squatted down beside her, his long fingers

404

pulling at a leather thong. "I'm sure you didn't. You'd be more surprised to know that my friend, the Toad here, has been on your heels since you left my ranch. I only joined him when we felt certain you were nearing the end of your search."

"Then you know. . . ."

"About the map? Of course. Why do you think I wrote to you in the first place? Medora wrote me about it before she left St. Louis, offering to sell it to me. God knows how many others she had made the same offer to; she was out to get the most she could get for it. Of course, I never thought of her offering it to Varien. Not until I learned he was related to her lover, anyway. I should have realized that sooner."

"You seem to know everything."

"I do, sooner or later. Occasionally some little fact gets by me, but not often."

Turnbull, who had been standing sullenly listening, kicked angrily at a decaying branch at his feet. "This is a waste of time. While we're standin' here jawin', that lousy cowpoke is digging out the gold. When are you goin' to let me kill him?"

Garth threw him a withering glance and rose to his feet, hitching his fingers in his gun belt. "That's your way, isn't it, Toad? Go blundering in, letting Nat Varien know you're on his trail. Let him do all the work. Once he's found the gold, we'll take it and get rid of him."

"I can read a map good as Varien," Turnbull muttered, giving Garth a look of smoldering rage.

"Not this one, you can't. He's obviously onto something or he would have been out here looking for our lovely captive long before now. However, we probably ought to make sure. Sanchez, go and see what Varien and the boy are doing. And don't let them see you."

The Mexican sitting across the clearing rose to his feet, nodding at Garth, then went loping off through the trees. Ardeth watched him with mixed emotions. She felt it was all too typical of Nat to be so engrossed in his search for the gold to even realize she was missing. When he did, would he come for her? Or would he be so busy trying to keep it or trying to settle his old score with Turnbull to ever worry about what was happening to her? For an instant her heart failed her. Had he ever really told her he loved her? Had he ever shown in any way that she was more important to him than anything else in his life? That she was worth more than wealth or vengeance?

Perhaps he had never said it in so many words, but surely the love they had shared would mean more to him than carrying off a treasure or killing an old enemy. It had to!

"What about this one?" she heard the Toad say angrily. "She knows too much to let her go."

Garth looked down at her, smiling evilly. "What shall we do with you, Miss Ardeth Royce? I admit, that's a puzzle."

Ardeth met his eyes boldly. "I suppose you knew about that, too."

"Oh, I knew right from the beginning you couldn't be Medora. She had to be older, and . . . shall we say . . . of a different temperament. Life on the wicked stage doesn't leave one as young and innocent as you. I realized that the first time you turned away my advances. Medora would have fallen in bed with me on that trip to the Silver Sage, if only to assure that she got the most money possible out of me. I admit, I couldn't figure out at first how you came to be impersonating her. But I knew in the end I would learn, so I simply went along with it.

"Of course, I was a little surprised when Varien showed up. That fellow, he keeps turning up like a bad penny. I thought I was rid of him when I won his land in New Mexico."

"And killed his friends."

Garth glared at Turnbull. "That was not in my plans. Unfortunately, my lamebrained associate here will jump at any opportunity to shoot down a man or two. He never seems to learn that it only complicates what would have been a clean, profitable situation."

"I should of killed Varien, too. It would have saved us a lot of trouble."

"You'll get that chance yet, if you can possibly control your neanderthal impulses until the right time."

Ardeth glanced from one man to the other. She was beginning to realize that Garth had a way of tossing off insults about Turnbull without noticing

their effect. The stocky outlaw stood silently, neve
contradicting him, but glaring at Reardon with nar
row, smoldering eyes that betrayed his fury.

"You don't seem to think much of the men yoʋ
hire to do your dirty work," she said, hoping tɾ
stoke that fury a little.

"I learned long ago that the way to become ricᴉ
and successful out here is to let the less intelligen
carry out your violence for you. Turnbull here loveˢ
violence. The more I give him, the more he likes it
Besides, he gets paid well for it."

"Less intelligent . . ." Turnbull muttered.

"Dumb, Toad. Dumb, dumb, dumb. I'm thɛ
brains and you're the brawn. That's why we work sɾ
well together."

"I ain't dumb." It was spoken so softly that Gartᴉ
barely heard it. He turned back to Ardeth, morɛ
concerned about what to do with her than abouɬ
the feelings of the man he had used for so long.

"I could give you to Turnbull . . ." he said. Turn·
bull's anger suddenly faded, and he stepped forward, almost licking his lips. Garth laughed
amused by the Toad's lascivious lust and by Ar·
deth's sudden loss of color. Her eyes widened iɾ
fear.

"But I won't. She's a bit too fine a morsel for thɛ
likes of you, Turnbull. We'll take her back with us
If we run into those Utes, she'll make a useful bar·
gaining tool." Reaching out, he grasped Ardeth'ˢ
chin and lifted her head painfully.

"You wouldn't!" she cried. She wanted to cry thaɬ

he was too civilized, too cultured, too conditioned by the wealthy society he moved among. But she was beginning to see that Garth Reardon was only civilized on the surface. Beneath that handsome, cultured facade, there lay a completely self-centered ego, focused solely on its own gratification. She doubted he had the ability to wonder, much less to know, what anyone else was feeling. Once again her heart quailed.

"It's a shame, really." Garth smiled down at her. "I think I might have found Medora infinitely more useful. What did you do with her, anyway?"

"She died. Accidentally."

"And so you took her place. Well, you can drop the act now, Miss Royce. There won't be any need for singing and posturing among the Utes. You'll be the lowest squaw performing the hardest chores and used by the men as often as they want. See how you like pretending then!"

"It won't happen. Nat won't let it—"

She was interrupted by Sanchez, hurrying back into the clearing. "I think he has found something, Colonel," he said, excitement in his voice. "They are digging again."

Ebal winced as Nat dug his fingers into the soft flesh of his wrist. He pulled back his hand. "Don't you want to see it closer? See if it's really made of gold?"

"It's real gold all right. And old gold, too. But I

don't want to pick it up yet. There may be a reason that it was put there just that way."

"But maybe there's more gold underneath it. You said there was lots buried here, not just one little piece."

Nat looked up into the boy's thin face, gone all eager and greedy. He, too, was anxious to pick up the crucifix, turn it over in his hands, hold it up to the light and watch the play of sunlight on its glimmering surface. That was the effect gold had on men. It was something almost mystical, harking back to kings and emperors, power and wealth. And yet at the bottom, it simply came down to greed. Not even its fabled ethereal beauty could diminish that basic, innate desire for all that gold could buy.

Carefully Ebal worked the point of his knife into the soft packed earth in which the cross lay. "I don't feel anything else. Just dirt."

Taking the knife from him, Nat poked at the ground with the point until he, too, was certain there was nothing there. Then he sat back on his haunches, studying the glimmering cross.

"It was put there for a reason; I'd stake my life on it. It can't be all there was. Why come all this way and go to all this trouble? Suppose . . ."

Ebal ran his tongue over his lips. ". . . it was put there to tell us something else?"

"Exactly. But what would it be?" Nat got to his feet and moved to stand directly behind the cross, holding out his arms in the direction of the shorter crossbar. As if he was reading Nat's mind, Ebal moved in the direction of Nat's outstretched arms, first to one side of the room, and then to the other. But though he felt carefully around the stones and even tried to pry the mortar out from around them, they were too firmly cemented to move away from the wall.

"They look as though they haven't budged from the day they were put there," Nat said after examining the two places.

"Maybe that was not where we're supposed to look?" Ebal offered. "Maybe they meant the top of the cross."

Nat went back to stand above the circular depression in the floor. "No, I don't think it's the top. It's the long part of the shaft that's pointing, isn't it? Like an arrow. Here, Ebal," he said, pointing his arm above the trajectory of the shaft. "Try that section of the wall."

Ebal eagerly dug around the stones where Nat pointed, but they were as solidly entrenched as the others had been. Finally he stepped away. "Maybe that cross is all there is," he said dejectedly.

"I can't believe it." Absently Nat reached into his pocket, fingering the battered compass that had brought them across the mountains. He pulled it out and held it over the cross, studying it. "North by northwest. Curious." Glancing up through the hole in the roof, he suddenly smiled. "It's not down here at all! Ebal, give me a hand up."

"Aren't you going to take that with you?" Ebal

411

said worriedly, pointing at the crucifix.

"Not now. We'll come back for it."

With Ebal's help, Nat climbed out of the low room then bent to pull up the boy. Once on ground level, he stood holding the compass until the wavering needle pointed in the same direction as the long shaft of the cross. Then he took off, following it.

Ebal came loping behind him, dodging haphazard piles of rubble and stone, circling cubicles and climbing ledges until they could go no farther. "It's the back wall," he moaned. "It doesn't go nowhere."

"No," Nat said, running his fingers along the stones placed flush up against the rock wall of the alcove. "Give me your knife. If these stones aren't easier to move than the ones in that lower room, I'll be very disappointed."

With the first jab of the knife point, the dried mortar began to flake away. Seeing it, Ebal rushed to help, using the sharp point of a piece of a worked-stone artifact he found lying on the ground nearby. Their excitement began to grow as they worked away the first of the stones and glimpsed a tiny, dark hole near the bottom right corner. Nat put his hand against it and felt a cool draft of air.

"I think we've found our cave!" he crowed. "Hurry, Ebal. Let's get these stones out of the way."

Egged on by their growing excitement, they quickly had the wall apart, leaving a hole just large enough for Nat to squeeze through. Though he was anxious to climb inside, Nat cautiously kept working until the entrance was one they could climb in and out of it with some degree of ease. He poked his head inside, trying to see through the cool darkness.

"It appears to go far back. I hoped it would be a simple little hole. Well, come on, Ebal, let's see what we've got here."

"We might need a light," Ebal cried, and ran off to the nearest ledge to pick up a juniper limb lying on the ground. "This ought to make a dandy pine knot."

"Good thinking," Nat said as he put a match to the top of the stave. Carrying it before him he climbed into the cave. The flickering light fell against the rock wall, bringing out the streaks of ore and highlighting the uneven surface, suggestive of sands on a beach. The bottom sloped downward as Nat stepped cautiously deeper into the cave. He was disappointed at how mundane it appeared, and how far back it went. It was not going to be a simple business, he thought as the roof sloped down, narrowing the tunnel. Even now he could not stand up to his full height.

The path appeared to round a slight projection in the wall. Once they moved around it, they came up against a solid wall of earth blocking their way. "Damn!" Nat muttered.

"Is this the end of it?" Ebal asked, peering around Nat's shoulder.

"I don't think so," Nat answered as he handed the torch to Ebal and began examining the barrier.

413

"It looks like a cave-in. It may be natural or it might have even been caused by the friars to protect their treasure." He dropped to his knees and began digging at the earth. In a short time he had an opening large enough to work his hand through. "It's clear on the other side, here at least," he said, lying on the ground and shoving his arm through the hole. "And I feel something. Wait a minute . . . I've got it. . . ."

He pulled his arm through the hole, dragging with it a heavy bar whose golden surface reflected the wavering light of the torch.

"Look at that!" Ebal breathed, bending to stare at the gold bar. "It's the treasure, sure as anything. We're rich!"

Nat tried to temper his satisfaction. "Not yet. We've got to get through all this dirt first. It'll take us days to dig it out."

"What about the dynamite? That would be a lot quicker."

Nat looked up at the barrier of rubble that blocked their path. "It could be dangerous. We don't want to make this any worse than it is already. But a little, carefully placed. . . ." He made a sudden decision. "Ebal, go get my saddlebags. I'm going to try it."

Ebal gave a small whoop and started off. "And fetch Ardeth while you're out there," Nat called. "She ought to be in on this too."

Ebal was gone a long time, but it gave Nat a chance to examine the cave carefully and decide just where he should try to blast a path through the rubble. He tried again to reach through to recover a second gold bar, but there was nothing close enough for his fingers to grasp. He had just finished a third attempt when Ebal came crawling back into the cave, carrying the saddlebags.

"Where's Ardeth," Nat asked as he began unwrapping the sticks of dynamite he removed from the leather bags.

"I couldn't find her. That's what took me so long. I called and called, but she didn't answer."

Nat felt a sudden anxious twitch which he forced himself to ignore. "Did you look at the other end where she was searching?"

"Yes, but there wasn't any sign of her. I don't know where she went to."

He paused, looking up at the boy's face. "But she has to be there. She hadn't fallen, had she? She might be hurt."

"I looked pretty good. If'n she was hurt I'd of seen her."

Nat laid the dynamite on the ground and started up. "We'd both better look again. She couldn't have got far enough away to be lost. We have to find her."

Ebal wailed. "Not yet! Can't we do this first? It won't take that long, will it?"

Nat looked from the bright opening far down at the end of the cave and back to the wall of earth that separated him from the goal he had sought so long. Blast Ardeth, anyway, going and getting her-

415

self lost just when success was within their reach!

He dropped to his knees again. "Hand me one of those sticks, Ebal. We'll just take care of this, then go look for your sister."

Chapter Twenty-two

Garth Reardon lifted his gun from its holster and checked the cartridges until he was certain it was fully loaded. "Come along, Sanchez," he said, slipping it back. "We'll check out what's happening over there. It's just possible they've found the gold for us by now."

He started to walk toward the trees. "Don't leave me with him!" Ardeth cried, as the Toad moved toward her, his eyes following Garth.

Reardon stopped, glaring at Turnbul, "Don't touch her or you won't live to regret it. That's an order."

Turnbull glared at him through his narrowed, smoldering eyes. "How do I know you won't take that gold and leave me here."

"You fool. Would I leave the girl here if I planned to do that. Use your limited wits, Toad."

"Then, let Sanchez stay. I want the chance to kill Varien."

"What is this? Rebellion in the ranks? You'll do what I tell you, just as you always have. You've done well enough by it in the past."

"But this is different. There may be a lot of gold out there. Enough to make a man like me fixed for life. You've already got everything you need."

"How little you understand me, Turnbull. No matter how much money I get, it only stimulates the need to have more. This fortune was offered to me, not you. I got you involved only because you wanted to track Nat Varien. You'll get some share of the total, but it's mine to give or withhold as I please."

Turnbull took a step toward Garth as Sanchez faded back into the trees, recognizing the signs of the Toad's growing fury. Just as alarmed, Ardeth pulled at the bonds on her wrists but could not work them loose. She looked imploringly at Garth, trying to will him to be more cautious in his dealings with the dangerous Toad, but if he saw her, he ignored her warning.

"That's always the way it is, ain't it," Turnbull said in a low, guttural voice. His eyes were bulging as he stared his hatred at Garth. His shoulders were leaning forward, his body poised. "It's all yours to dole out to us who gets it for you, piece by piece. Well, maybe I'm tired of it."

Impatient to see what Nat was up to, Garth almost turned away. "Oh, for God's sake, Turnbull, get hold of yourself. What a time you picked to start growing sensitive. There's too much at stake here for these theatrics."

418

"Garth, please . . ." Ardeth cried as Turnbull leaped forward, blocking Garth's way.

"Well, maybe I'm sick of your orders," the Toad said, crouching in front of Reardon. "Go here, go there. Do this, do that, and always so you can get richer."

"I've kept you from the hangman's noose for years," Garth snapped. "Get out of my way, you ignorant ape!"

"And that's another thing. Dumb! Ape! Always bad-mouthin'. I'm sick of it. I'm sick of you."

Reardon's sculptured lips tightened with his anger. "You fool. You couldn't survive a week without me. You can't think that far ahead."

"Maybe it's time I found out. . . ."

He lunged, quick as a snake striking, shoving Reardon to the ground and diving on top of him. Ardeth watched, frozen as the two men rolled struggling on the ground. Reardon was taller and in better shape, but Turnbull had the advantage of his enormous strength and smoldering fury. With his hands on Garth's throat, he rolled him over until they were almost lying at Ardeth's feet, Reardon pinned below Turnbull's heavy body. Ardeth watched as the color left Garth's face and his eyes began to bulge as Toad's thick fingers dug into his neck, closing off his windpipe. Garth worked his hands up his assailant's neck and pushed upward on his chin, shoving his head back until a lesser man's neck might have cracked. Ardeth kicked out at

Turnbull, slamming the toe of her boot against his side, but it might have been the bite of a flea for all the effect it had on that rock-hard body. Then, as he was about to lose consciousness, Garth was able to shift his weight just enough to obtain the leverage he needed to throw Turnbull to one side. He rolled out from beneath him, swinging his fist against Turnbull's chin with a sharp crack. Turnbull slumped slightly, long enough for Garth to get to his feet where he crouched before slamming his boot into the other man's side.

With a loud swoosh, Turnbull grabbed at his side and fell on his back. Furiously, Garth kept kicking him, knocking him halfway across the clearing. Then, when he was certain he had no breath left, he grabbed him up by the collar and slammed his fist against the Toad's face, over and over until the man fell in a heap at his feet, gasping.

"See how well you can do without me now," Garth said in a rasping voice. He rubbed at his throat, waiting for his heavy breathing to subside. Then he walked over to pick up his hat, slapping the dust off it against his knee.

"Come on, Sanchez," he snapped to the Mexican, who had been hovering back among the trees while the fight raged.

Ardeth watched him walk away, her heart sinking. Then she glimpsed the Toad, on his knees on the ground, one hand moving swiftly to his gun belt.

"Garth!" she screamed. The gun blared, its loud

report covering her cry. Garth's body arched as he clutched at his back, poised for a moment, frozen in midair. Then he turned, sinking slowly to the ground. She couldn't see his face, but she knew he was dead, and her heart froze within her. She watched in horror as Turnbull staggered to his knees and hobbled over to Garth's body lying on the ground. He kicked at it savagely, over and over until his rage was spent.

"That'll show you," he muttered and giggled in a way that set the hairs on her neck rising.

"You coward," she cried. "You shot him in the back!"

He looked up, his head jutting forward on his thick neck. "So what." He came lumbering over to her, and she shrank back against the tree trunk.

"Give you to the dirty Utes, would he? Well, we'll see about that." Furiously he began working at the rope that bound her to the tree. "Not fit for Toad Turnbull but fit for the lousy savages, hunh." He jerked her away from the tree, twisting the ends of the rope around her hands and across her chest. "I guess he won't be givin' no more orders. Nor no more insults either!"

He looked up to see Sanchez standing on the edge of the clearing, watching him, still with fear. "What are you lookin' at!" he yelled. "Get out of here. Go on, before I kill you too!"

The Mexican took off between the trees, followed by Turnbull's mocking laugh. Ardeth heard the clatter of his horse a moment later as he galloped away from the area. She felt utterly lost, at the mercy of a crazy man who would kill without compunction or thought.

"Why don't you shoot me, too," she said defiantly.

He pulled at the ropes that bit painfully into her chest. "Oh, no. I got better things to do with you. But first, I gotta get my hands on that gold."

"Nat will never let you have it."

"He will when he sees what I got with me. You're gonna be my ace in the hole." He gripped her chin with his tight fingers and squeezed her face into his. "And no funny business or I'll kill you right in front of him."

Ardeth spat into his face. He laughed, wiping his cheek with his sleeve, the gun still dangling in his hand.

"Ha. I like a woman with spirit. I like seein' how long it takes to beat it out of her. We're gonna be a good team."

She never had time to reply. Jerking her around until he had one arm around her in a vise, he dragged her off through the trees, sidestepping Garth's body on the ground. Ardeth caught a glimpse of Reardon's handsome, white face, the eyes still staring up into the dappled leaves, full of surprise.

"I told you she wasn't here." Ebal sank down on a pile of stones that was all that was left of a wall. "I don't see why we couldn't have got the gold out first, anyway. It's her fault if she goes and gets herself lost."

Nat stood, hands on hips, looking out over the tangled ravine just below the ledge of dwellings they had only just finished examining. His sandy brows were knitted closely with an anxiety that was growing stronger by the minute.

"The gold can wait. It's not going anywhere."

Of course the truth was that he was too embarrassed to explain to Ebal just why he had abandoned the cave with the gold to go searching for Ardeth, especially after he had decided not to. It seemed so sensible, so practical to make sure he completed the quest he had come so far to complete. After all, how far could she have gone in this isolated place? But though he had tried, he found almost at once that his concern for her would not allow him to put aside her possible need for him. He was astounded at himself to realize all at once how precious she had become to him. Like a curtain rising in his mind, he saw suddenly and clearly that nothing or no one in this world mattered more to him than this black-haired, blue-eyed, fascinating, infuriating, lovely girl. He wasn't even sure when it had happened. All he knew was that now she was so much a part of him that he could never put her welfare aside while he went about searching for his family's gold. It was a stunning realization, a little incredible and a little frightening, that his love for her far surpassed his love for anything else. He could hardly believe it himself.

"I'm sure that was a gunshot we heard," he muttered, trying to focus on the practical.

Ebal, who would have preferred to be opening up the cave, slapped at the yellow dust that covered his boots. "I don't see why you won't let me call her some more. She's bound to hear eventually."

"No. She would have answered by now if she could have. And if there is anyone else out there, it'll only tell them where we are." *As if they didn't know already,* he added to himself. The hairs on the back of his neck seemed alive in the dry heat. He was certain there *was* someone out there, and Ardeth was probably in their hands. It might be the Utes, of course, but his intuition told him it wasn't. It didn't feel like Indians. But it didn't quite fit Garth Reardon, either. This ominous silence wasn't his style.

"Come on," Nat muttered, jumping down to the next ledge. "We'll work our way back into the cave."

Ebal jumped eagerly to his feet.

"And try not to make so much noise," Nat snapped, as he stepped over a low wall of broken stones. Ebal had opened his mouth to reply when the sudden shriek of a gunshot came zinging near his face, ricocheting off the stones behind him.

"Goda'mighty!" he cried, frozen in place.

424

Nat dove back behind the wall, crouching. "Get down!" he yelled as Ebal fell to his knees and began crawling frantically back toward him. Reaching over the wall, Nat grabbed him by the collar and pulled him across the broken stones as a second shot went flying past. He felt the wind of that one as he fell down behind the wall, Ebal sprawling beside him.

"Who . . . what. . . !" Ebal spouted incoherently.

Nat reached for his Peacemaker revolver and checked the cartridges. "Don't ask questions. Just keep down."

"But who would be shootin' at us out here? I ain't even got a gun!"

Without answering, Nat slid down along the wall toward the end where the stones were built up higher and he could crouch to look around them. He barely had time to examine what lay ahead before another shot rang out, digging into the wall just above his head. He fell to his knees. What he had been able to see was not encouraging—a jagged landscape of cubicles and holes, great slabs of rock and several different edges all at different levels. But if it afforded a wide choice of hiding places to whoever was shooting at them, it offered the same to them.

"I'm going to try to get closer," he whispered to Ebal, who had come squirming along the ground toward him.

"You're not goin' to leave me here!"

Briefly Nat considered giving Ebal one of his pistols to protect himself but quickly decided against it. He might need all his ammunition before this was over.

"While I try to get down there, you divert him somehow."

"How. . . !"

"Throw stones, run close enough to the wall to let him see you without making yourself a target. Anything you can think of. I've got to try to get behind him."

"But Nat . . ."

Nat didn't bother to argue but went scrambling along the wall to the other end where he looked back. Ebal had started to follow him, then thought better of it. The wall was very short at that end.

"Now," Nat snapped.

Grabbing up a handful of good-sized rocks, Ebal threw two of them out across the wall. Another gunshot shrieked in their direction as Nat tumbled over the wall and scrambled down the ledge to drop four feet below. Throwing himself flat on his stomach as another shot went zinging above his head, he crawled forward until he was able to crouch behind a cluster of ruined stones about three feet high. He looked back at Ebal's wall, praying the boy would have the sense to act. As though his prayers had been heard, a second barrage of stones went clattering over the wall. A shot rang out. Nat got to his feet and, in a crouching run, scrambled across an open patchwork of stones, through a door into one of the roofless cubicles and threw himself flat down against the inside wall. One of the shots that had followed him had come close enough to singe his shirt. Whoever was out there must have an ample supply of ammunition to be so free with it, he thought absently. And he must have also positioned himself in an excellent place, to be able to spot them so clearly.

He began working out in his mind what he remembered of the cliff complex, trying to figure where his assailant was. There was a circular half-ruined tower near the center where, if he remembered right, the stones left from the interior could serve as ledges near the top for a gunman to stand on. Reasoning that the gunman had to be there, he decided his best course was to dive for the ravine and use it as a cover to get on the other side. It might serve to lure the man out of his fortress and also put Nat closer to the entrance to the cave where the gold lay. Waiting a few moments in the hope that the silence might mask his intentions, he drew a deep breath and ran through the cubicle door, across a short open terrace and dived down a four-foot drop to the next level. Gunshots traced his progress, digging into the stones around him.

Catching his breath, he dove again for the next level, seeking the barrier of ruined walls until he could finally throw his body into a roll down the slope into the tangled trees of the ravine. He knew by the pursuing gunshots that he had been seen and had lost his best advantage. But now, crouched among the trees, he would be able to work his way back toward the opening to the cave without being followed. He hoped so, anyway.

"Goddamn!" Turnbull muttered, as he saw Nat roll out of sight. This was the worst place for an ambush he could have picked. Too full of shadows and light, crevices and barriers to corner anyone, especially someone as determined as Varien. But he still had the advantage. He had plenty of ammunition, and he was on the higher part of the ledge. And he had Ardeth.

He made a sudden decision to abandon this circular tower. It had served its purpose, and he was more interested in why Varien had started working his way back toward the other side of the ruins.

Climbing down the broken stones, he grabbed Ardeth's bound arms and pulled her to her feet. "Come on," he muttered, yanking her painfully toward the back wall. She winced, dragging her feet until he realized what she was doing and slapped her across the face. "You better cooperate, or I'll shoot you now!"

She glared back her hatred at him. "You can kill me, but you'll never kill Nat. He's too good a shot."

"We'll see about that."

She could not tell where he was going, only that he was pulling and prodding her along the back wall of the ruins, dragging up piles of broken stones, leaping down to other levels, but always working toward the far end of the caves. Occasionally he would stop, gripping her arm as he studied the ravine until he thought he detected signs of movement. Then he was off again, dragging her behind him.

Once they reached the last crumbled structure, Toad spotted the hole in the rear wall and knew at once what it meant. Throwing Ardeth down against a corner wall, he bent to peer inside. He knew it would take precious minutes, but he could not resist stepping into the cave where almost at once he spotted the gold bar lying just close enough to the entrance to catch the light.

"So he found it," he mumbled delightedly. Ardeth, hearing him, scrunched over to the entrance where she could look through. The greedy delight on Toad's face, the way his tongue ran over his bulbous lips, told her they had stumbled onto Nat's Spanish gold, and her heart sank. Unless Nat was able to kill this loathsome man, everything would be lost. The gold, her future, the man she loved. . . .

She pulled against the ropes, trying, as she had for the last hour, to work them loose. But the tightness with which they bit into her flesh prevented her from budging the knots. She started to call out but remembered the violence of Toad's crack across her cheek. Instead, she began easing her way to the

other side of the roofless dwelling, closer to the ravine, hoping he wouldn't notice.

She was almost there before he saw her. Bending
to leave the cave, he bounded across the floor to
grab her up and throw her back against the corner.

"Try that again and you'll regret it," he warned as
he positioned himself against the ruined wall, his
pistol aimed toward the ravine, waiting for Nat to
appear.

Ardeth watched him as the heavy, ominous silence of the ruins settled over everything. Then she
saw him start, his head jerking forward as he raised
the pistol to sight the barrel.

She screamed, "Nat! Look out!"

A barrage of gunshots drowned her voice.

Ebal sat with his back to the rough wall, his arms
around his drawn-up knees, absently cracking his
knuckles. His mind was a turmoil of indecision.
The occasional zing of gunshots across the ruins
only reminded him how dangerous a situation he
had gotten himself into. He wasn't used to having
guns go off around him. The only guns they had
ever used back on the farm were for hunting game.

He wished his brother, Elbe, was here to tell him
what to do. Elbe had always known the best way to
handle difficult situations while all he had to do
was follow directions. But Elbe was too good a
worker, and their father could not spare him to go

looking for their older sister. Of course, that was why he had been given the job in the first place; he was the only brother who could be spared.

In fact, Ebal thought, twisting his hands, his pa had probably been glad to get rid of him for a while, with his blundering, short-sighted ways. Well, he had done good; he had found his sister. His sin was in tagging along with her and Nat on this crazy adventure, just because he wanted to see something of the world and make something of himself. And now, his punishment was this mess he was involved in.

He allowed himself a quick, wistful thought of how proud and impressed his family would be when he showed up carrying a wagonload of gold bars, then came back to struggling with his present dilemma. Ardeth was lost and maybe in danger, and someone was trying to kill Nat. And here he sat, like a coward, afraid to move from behind this protective wall!

He was worse than dirt! Elbe would never hide behind a wall like this, afraid to move for fear of being shot. Elbe would go out there and try to save his sister and help his friend, Nat Varien. Could he really do less?

His head shot up as he heard a woman's scream followed by several shots. He recognized his sister's voice, urgent and frightened. But both the scream and the gunfire came from the far end of the overhang.

Very tentatively he crouched down and began working his way to the other end of the wall.

Beneath the cover of the gunfire, Nat threw his body to one side and rolled over several times, bringing him twenty feet from where he had originally fired. His heart was pounding painfully in his chest. So Ardeth was up there with the man who was trying to kill him. He wanted to shout out to her, to reassure her, to show her he knew the danger she was in. But any sound would only give his position away, and he wasn't ready yet to do that.

Carefully he worked his way along the ravine, crawling on his stomach until he was in position to make a crouching run up through the trees closer to the last crumbling cubicle where the gunman waited. He could not get any closer without being seen, and even then, it left such a large distance to cover that he could not hope to make it before being shot. Then he heard a man's voice ring out. It had been a long time since he heard that voice, but he recognized it at once.

"That's right, Varien. I've got your lady friend here. If you want to see her alive again, you throw down your gun and walk up here nice and easy."

Toad Turnbull! Of course, it would be him. He had known it from the first but had been too half-afraid he was wrong to assume it was so. The hairs on the back of Nat's neck came alive, and a wild joy went coursing through him. At last the confrontation he had been seeking all this time had finally come. An old score would be settled, an old, searing wound finally cauterized.

And then he remembered Ardeth and cursed. It was not enough to go blasting his way up there in hopes of killing Turnbull. He must somehow try to save Ardeth first. But how?

The only way was to cross that open land that lay between his hiding place and the wall where the Toad was waiting . . . and pray that somehow Turnbull's bullets might miss him long enough to let him get there alive.

His hand closed around a rock. That old ploy had worked once, but would Turnbull fall for it again? It was worth a try.

Crouching, he threw the rock as far away from him as he could. It arched in the air silently, then went crashing down on the edge of the stones.

"Ow!" Ebal cried from across the other side and rose to his feet, his hand clutching his head. Nat caught sight of him from the corner of his eyes, lost a vital, startled second, then went racing toward the cubicle as the pistol's loud report rang out several times. The boy's scream merged into Ardeth's higher pitched one, but Nat barely heard it. Diving over the wall, he crashed into Turnbull, driving him backward. They rolled over on the crumbling stones, grasping at flesh, gouging and digging at any surface, strength against strength. Nat felt his hands slide around the thick throat, and he squeezed hard, pounding Turnbull's head on the stones. Then Turnbull got his knee up between their two bodies and with a violent kick knocked Nat over and off him, slamming his back on the ground. His two pistols had flown from his hand when Nat knocked him backward, and now he scrambled to reach for one, stepping back, his breath heaving, pointing the lethal barrel at Nat's body, prone on the ground.

"Get up," he snapped.

Slowly Nat's mind cleared. He saw the ugly face of his adversary bending over him and, behind him, Ardeth's white face against the wall. Slowly he dragged himself up.

"Are you all right?" he asked her.

"Yes. But I think Ebal—"

"Shut up, both of you! Get over there," Toad said, waving the barrel of the pistol toward the entrance to the cave.

"Go ahead," Nat muttered. "Shoot. You've got the advantage."

"First you're gonna show me where the rest of that gold is. Go on. Get inside."

Ardeth cried, "My brother is hurt. At least let me help him."

"Let him die. If he isn't dead already. Go on, Varien. Into the cave."

Nat threw Ardeth a glance full of remorse and chagrin, then hobbled toward the cave entrance. She

434

looked frantically around. When Nat had come crashing over the wall, his pistol and Turnbull's two had all flown in different directions. Toad had already retrieved one and was bending to pick up the other, but Nat's was lying directly across from her, against the far wall. If only Turnbull would not remember it. . . .

Nat entered the cave entrance, followed by Turnbull, who grabbed Ardeth's arm and pulled her in after him. The three of them stood just inside, adjusting their eyes to the darker light. Very carefully, Nat bent to pick up the gold bar.

"This is all we found," he said, and Turnbull laughed.

"I don't believe that. Where's the rest of it?"

"I tell you, the cave is blocked. It'll take days to dig it out. We never got that far."

"Then, maybe you better start now." He waved the pistols at Nat. "Go ahead. Start digging."

With the point of one of the pistols dug into his back, Nat was prodded toward the mound of earth that blocked the cave. "I don't have anything to dig with."

"Use your hands. Get to work, Varien. You're going to dig that gold out for me, and then I'm going to leave your bones here to rot with the rest of this dead place. Not your girlfriend though. I'll take her with me. At least, if she behaves herself, I will."

Turnbull's gross features assembled into a grotesque smile. He was enjoying the power he had over them both. He positioned himself halfway between Nat, digging at the mound of earth, and Ardeth crouched against the rock near the entrance. While Nat dug, struggling to loosen the soil where it was soft enough to move with his hands, Ardeth pushed back against the rock wall of the cave. A sudden pain shot through her arm as she felt the sharp edge of a slight irregularity in the rocks. Her hopes trembled into life as she began rubbing the ropes that bound her arms against the edge, feeling it working at the tightness. Moving carefully so as not to attract Turnbull's attention, she felt them loosen slightly for the first time. Then, opening and closing her hands, she twisted her wrists until she felt the ropes begin to give. Her fingers closed around the bindings to keep them from falling as the blood painfully came coursing back into her hands.

She glanced across the cave at Nat, trying to tell him with her eyes that there was hope. He looked up and saw her, and for an instant, it seemed that silent words passed between them. Then he went back to digging, and she wasn't sure.

Remembering the gun, Ardeth edged toward the cave entrance. Then Nat spoke, distracting Turnbull. "I think I can get through," he said, thrusting his arm into the dirt. With his shoulder against the mound of earth, he bent toward it, reaching deeply inside. "I've got something. . . ."

"What is it," the Toad said, edging toward Nat

but glancing back to make sure Ardeth was still up against the wall of the cave.

"I think . . . it's another gold bar."

"Bring it out . . . and don't pull anything funny!"

Very slowly Nat worked his arm out of the hole, his fingers dragging the end of a second gold bar, heavy and gleaming, though smaller than the first bar had been. Turnbull bent toward him, his eyes greedy. As Nat cleared the bar from the mound of earth, he glimpsed Ardeth near the entrance. Then with a sudden swing of his arm, he threw the bar against Turnbull, striking him in the neck.

The solid weight of the gold knocked Turnbull backward. One of his pistols went off as Nat scrambled for the entrance. Ardeth was there before him, throwing off her ropes to dash through the opening, heaving her body toward the spot where Nat's gun lay and grasping it in her fingers. With a roar, Turnbull tried to scramble to his feet just as Nat went racing out through the cave entrance.

"Get out of here! Run!" Nat shouted as Ardeth threw the pistol at him. Catching it, he turned back to the cave and fired straight into the cluster of dynamite sticks that had been lying to one side near the back of the cave.

There was a huge roar, then a rumbling violence deep in the earth. Rocks and stones went bubbling up, walls sheared and fell. Ardeth was only aware of the tremendous blast as she scrambled wildly down into the ravine, hiding under the shelter of the stunted trees to escape the dust and debris that came raining down.

Terror kept her immobile—terror not for herself but for the fact that Nat had not been able to run away before the blast. Then, as the rumbling stilled and grew more faint, she felt his body flung beside hers. His arms went over her, and he pressed her face close to his, both of them scrunching down against the sweet, pure earth.

As the silence settled over them, Ardeth lifted her head. Her face was covered with the yellow dust of the ruins. Above them, where the structure had been, lay a new huge wall of rubble, completely sealing the cave.

Her breath came in painful gasps. "Oh, Nat . . ."

He pulled her face close to his and kissed her dusty cheek. "It's all right," he said, feeling her trembling in his arms. "It's all over."

Chapter Twenty-three

The wavering light from the kerosene lamp spilled an iridescent yellow pool over the table, leaving the room beyond in semi-darkness. Ardeth sat on the edge of a straight-backed chair, nervously plucking at the dust on her skirt. On the other side of the round table, Nat stood looking through the dirty window at the street outside. "Not much of a town, this Durango, is it?" he said absently.

"No, but it has a doctor. That's all that matters. Oh, Nat, do you think he'll be all right?"

He walked to her chair and laid his hand on her shoulder, gently squeezing it. "He survived the trip up here, didn't he. He's young and healthy. That's all in his favor."

"But he was so sick by the time we reached this place. Twice I was certain we had lost him."

"You Royces are a tough lot." Nat smiled as he stroked her neck. "Look how you managed to take over Medora's life."

Waves of soft pleasure from his gentle stroking

subdued the anxiety she felt. She leaned against his hard body, drawing strength from the feel of him. Although they had only reached Durango that afternoon, already the trip from the cliff ruins was beginning to blur and run together in her mind. She remembered the awful anxiousness of it, especially at first when they had not had the slightest idea in which direction help lay. Then they had come across a small group of Ute families on their way to the reservation. Unlike the other group who had chased them into the canyon, these Indians could not have been more helpful. They gave them food and directions and even treated Ebal's wounds with their primitive herbs. Ardeth felt certain it was their treatment that had kept him alive until they could reach a real doctor. That, and the fact that the bullet had gone cleanly through his chest. If they had been forced to try to remove it, the boy would never have survived.

A door opened, startling her out of her thoughts. Ardeth jumped to her feet, turning to the short, elderly man in his shirt sleeves, who blocked the light from the inner room. "I think you can go in now," the doctor said quietly, "but not for long."

"Is he. . . ?"

"He's as good as can be expected. I think he'll heal up pretty well, assuming infection doesn't set in. Good thing you kept the wound as clean as you did. That was smart."

The doctor had a lined face below a shock of gray hair that bore testament to years of hard practice under difficult conditions. Ardeth had thought she smelled whisky on his breath when they first bore Ebal inside his surgery, but now he appeared so clear-eyed and sober that she decided she had been mistaken. With Nat close behind her, she hurried through the door into the small room where Ebal lay on a cot in a corner with a blanket covering most of his body. Ardeth knelt by the bed, hiding her dismay at how pale and drained he looked. His eyes fluttered open, and he turned his head slightly, trying to smile at her.

"I thought . . . maybe I'd died. . . ."

"No, Ebal. You're not dead, and you're not going to die. You're going to get well. We brought you here to a doctor, and he's going to make you well."

"Where's this place?" Ebal whispered.

"It's called Durango. Just a little one-street town with a few saloons and stores and a smelter not far away. Now, don't try to talk. Just sleep and get well."

But Ebal seemed anxious to communicate with them, even though his breath was labored and his color rose alarmingly with every exertion. "Nat?"

"I'm right here," Nat answered, bending over the boy. "We both got out safely, thanks to you."

A tremulous smile touched his white lips. "Me. . . ?"

"If you hadn't drawn Turnbull's fire when you did, I never would have been able to get up there to him. That was clever of you."

Or stupid, Ardeth wanted to add. But the pleasure on Ebal's wasted face warned her to keep quiet. Then he frowned at her. "The gold?"

She looked questioningly up at Nat, who bent close to Ebal's face. "We didn't find any more gold. But we brought the crucifix back. That's enough."

A look of great distress flickered over Ebal's face. He tried to lean closer to Ardeth. "You . . ."

"What is it, Ebal?" she said, straining to understand his whispery voice.

"You won't leave me?"

"Leave you! Of course, we won't leave you. We'll stay here until you're well again, then we'll all leave together. Isn't that right, Nat?"

Nat gently touched Ebal's good shoulder. "Yes, that's right. We won't leave you."

The faint smile trembled on his lips once more and Ebal sighed. The doctor spoke behind Ardeth: "I think that's enough for now. Rest is his best medicine."

Ardeth fussed for a moment with the covers, then rose to leave the room. Ebal seemed to drift off to sleep before she had moved through the door. Behind her, Nat followed, his jinglebobs singing on the pinewood floor. He stayed a few moments, talking with the doctor about a decent

442

place in town to rent rooms, then followed Ardeth outside, onto the plank walkway that bordered Main Street.

She had sat in the stuffy doctor's office for so long that Ardeth was a little surprised at how clear and cool the night air had grown after their long ride. She had not realized how tired she was until now when she let Nat lead her down the walk and across the street to one of the last houses at the edge of town, where they were able to rent a room, wash off some of the dust and have a meal. It was not much of a house; but it was clean, and the widow who ran it discreetly asked them no questions. The only other boarder was an itinerant lawyer who was very intent on a two-day-old paper he had purchased that afternoon and who was just as discreet as their landlady. The meal was excellent and very filling, and after it was over they walked together out into the hilly fields surrounding the house.

Behind them they could hear faint echoes from the town: the soft tinkle of music from the saloon and the neighing of a horse in the nearby stables. There were tiny dots of buttery light from the windows of houses and the saloon, and far on the other side, a faint bronze glow from the smelting works.

Yet, when they turned their backs on the town to look out toward the great sweep of hills and mesas that sprawled before them, there was an awesome dark silence, almost akin to worship, that stirred something mystical within them. They walked to the brow of the nearest hill and paused to look toward the dark sweeping ranges, their crests bronzed by the patina of the moonlight. Nat's arm went around Ardeth's shoulder, and she leaned against him, her arm around his waist, her eyes lifted in wonder to the heavens, where the stars seemed so thick and brilliant she felt she could almost reach out and pluck them with her fingers.

"It's beautiful, isn't it?" she sighed.

Nat studied her face in the moonlight. "Very beautiful."

She laughed. "I meant the sky, the hills, this country."

"That, too," he said and bent to kiss the tip of her nose. Her arms slipped around his neck. "Nat, did you really mean it when you told Ebal we would wait here until he got well?"

"Of course I did. Why would you think I didn't?"

"Well, I was never sure what you would want to do once you found your cave. And now everything you wanted to do is finished. Turnbull is dead, Garth is dead . . ."

"And whatever lay inside that cave is buried forever. No, I've had enough of vengeance and searching." His arms tightened around her. "I've found what I want, right here, and I'm not going to let it get away again, ever."

The joy of her laughter merged with the singing stars. "Oh, Nat. I do love you. But what shall we do now? Where shall we go?"

He traced a pattern on her cheek. "We could always go back to Nebraska."

"Never! What would be the use? I've learned so much about the world and about myself since I left that farm. I've even learned a lot just in the last few days. I could never go back. I think we should go to California. They say that there are all kinds of opportunities out there for someone willing to work. You would do well; I know you would."

"We wouldn't have much money. At least, not at first."

"That's all right. One of the things I've realized these last few days is that wealth and excitement don't matter half so much as someone you love and believe in. Someone who loves you too. We'll take Ebal with us. Between the three of us, we're bound to make our fortune eventually."

Nat took her face between his hands and kissed her lips. "Come on, my sweet. It's been a long day, and we've got a lovely bed waiting for us. I think we should put it to good use."

She kissed him back and slipped her arm around his waist as they started back toward the town. "All the same," he said, growing serious once more, "I hate the idea of you having to do

445

without while I start over again."

She gave a delighted chuckle. "Don't worry about it. After all, if worse comes to worst, I can always go back on the stage!"

HEART SOARING ROMANCE BY LA REE BRYANT

FORBIDDEN PARADISE   (2744-3, $3.75/$4.9

Jordan St. Clair had come to South America to find her fianc
and break her engagement, but the handsome and arrogant guid
refused to a woman through the steamy and dangerous jungle
Finally, he relented, on one condition: She would do exactly as
said. Beautiful Jordan had never been ruled in her life, yet the
was something about Patrick Castle that set her heart on fire. P
trick ached to possess the body and soul of the tempting vixen,
lead her from the lush, tropical jungle into a FORBIDDEN PA
ADISE of their very own.

ARIZONA VIXEN   (2642-0, $3.75/$4.9

As soon as their eyes met, Sabra Powers knew she had to have t
handsome stranger she saw in the park. But Sterling Hawkins w
a tormented man caught between two worlds: As a halfbreed, h
was a successful businessman with a seething Indian's soul whic
could not rest until he had revenge for his parents' death. Sabr
was willing to risk anything to experience this loner's fiery en
brace and seering kiss. Sterling vowed to capture this ARIZON
VIXEN and make her his own . . . if only for one night!

TEXAS GLORY   (2222-1, $3.75/$4.9

When enchanting Glory Westbrook was banished to a two-yea
finishing school for dallying with Yankee Slade Hunter, sh
thought she'd die of a broken heart; when father announced sh
would marry his business associate who smothered her with ins
lent stares, she thought she'd die of horror and shock.

For two years devastatingly handsome Slade Hunter had bee
denied the embrace of the only woman he had ever loved. H
thought this was the best thing for Glory, yet when he saw he
again after two years, all resolve melted away with one passiona
kiss. She *had* to be his, surrendering her heart and mind to h
powerful arms and strong embrace.

*Available wherever paperbacks are sold, or order direct from th
Publisher. Send cover price plus 50¢ per copy for mailing an
handling to Zebra Books, Dept. 3234, 475 Park Avenue South
New York, N.Y. 10016. Residents of New York, New Jersey an
Pennsylvania must include sales tax. DO NOT SEND CASH.*